THE TIMEPIECE

and the Girl Who Went Astray

O. R. SIMMONDS

APPELLATION
PRESS

First published by Appellation Press 2021

This novel is entirely a work of fiction. The
names, characters and incidents portrayed in it
are the work of the author's imagination. Any
resemblance to actual persons, living or dead,
events or localities is entirely coincidental.

First edition

Editing by Heather Sangster

ISBN: 978-1-8384777-1-4

For my boys Emmett and Elliott

CONTENTS

PROLOGUE

London, present day.

It hadn't taken long for a crowd to gather around the man's body as it lay on the pavement. Its limbs were arranged in an unnaturally splayed position: head pointing awkwardly upwards and a knee bent back on itself so that the foot was almost touching the hip. Despite this, it was otherwise surprisingly intact given the height from which it had fallen. Onlookers snapped stills and took videos with their phones as blood seeped from the dead man's mouth and ears. Modern society seemed to have developed a morbid fascination with tragic events and, for some, documenting and sharing them with others had become the norm. No one offered assistance, even though any efforts would have been futile. The dead man might have pondered this disturbing behaviour had he still had the capacity for thought.

Twenty-three seconds earlier, there had been no sound as the man had fallen from the belfry at the top of Elizabeth Tower.

Three minutes and twelve seconds later, the dead man's assailant had completed his descent from the tower and made his way onto the streets. He pushed through the crowd and knelt beside the body. He checked for a pulse, more as a predilection for thoroughness than with any expectation of finding one. His hand slid down to the man's pockets, perhaps searching for identification. The crowd – which moments before had collectively approved of capturing images of a corpse to be shared among their friends, family and the many social voyeurs of the world – appeared to find this behaviour unacceptable. Their delicate sensibilities offended, they frowned and shuffled, looking at one another to see who might object to the dead man having his pockets searched in this way. They all murmured to one another.

'Is this guy a doctor? I think he's robbing him,' grumbled one.

'What's he think he's doing?' spluttered another.

'Should we call an ambulance?' someone else asked.

All the while the cameras continued to flash and roll.

One camera elicited a familiar sound that the assailant was surprised and perplexed to hear in this setting: the distinctive mechanical shutter of a Polaroid-style camera. Turning to the direction of the sound, there was no doubt from where it came. The young woman holding the camera and fanning the photograph through the air was a flash of neon colours. Her voluminous hair was held up in a rough side ponytail. She wore high-waisted jeans with leg warmers bunched around her calves and a polka-dot jacket with wide shoulders and flouncy sleeves pulled up to her elbows. A silver cassette player was hooked into her waistband, a pair of bright orange headphones slung around her neck. She looked as if she was from a different time period altogether.

Twenty-seven seconds earlier, the man had been surprised by the unexpected turn of events that had led to him being pushed to his death. He was one and a half seconds into his fall by the time he even realised he was falling. He spent the remaining three seconds of his life paralysed by fear. Had he had more time, perhaps a scream would have escaped his lips. The ninety-six-metre height of the fall was roughly one fifth of the distance required to reach terminal velocity, but even so, he had still accelerated to almost one hundred miles an hour by then and his body struck the pavement with a crunch. He died instantly.

Three minutes and forty-two seconds later, the assailant turned his attention back to his frantic search of the body. His fingers passed over a shape inside the dead man's jacket that could have been a wallet, but before he could secure it a police officer pressed his way towards the scene behind him. Still hunched over the body, the assailant's eyes met the officer's. The officer pointed an authoritative finger at him and said, 'Sir, please step away. Nice and slowly now.'

The assailant did as instructed. Still kneeling, he moved backwards so he was sitting on his heels. As a sign of compliance, he raised his arms with his palms facing forwards.

The officer seemed to relax slightly, lowering his hand as he approached. The assailant took his chance and rose quickly, springing upwards from his crouched position, shunting the officer aside and hustling towards the crowd. The woman in the polka-dot jacket was still wafting the Polaroid back and forth when he plucked it from her hand as he passed. He was a slight man but wiry and powerful, and he bulldozed his way through the conglomerate of people, shoving to the ground anyone who stood in his way. As he breached the huddle he broke into a sprint, pursued by the officer he'd locked eyes with and another who'd just arrived at the scene. He ran east across Westminster Bridge, away from Westminster Abbey and Elizabeth Tower.

Fifty-four seconds earlier, the man had argued with his assailant in the belfry. He needed something from him, something that would help him escape this place. He had been trapped here, alone and confused, for weeks. His assailant could help him get back to his normal life if only he would listen. He'd asked this of his assailant, but the request had made him more agitated. The man had approached him passively, pleadingly, but it was a mistake. His assailant saw the approach as an act of aggression and the two of them fought.

Five minutes and six seconds later, the assailant had reached the opposite bank of the Thames. He descended a set of steps to his left, passing the famous aged green-ceramic Southbank Lion statue before doubling back under the bridge, the officers in close pursuit. As he raced through the underpass, the officers momentarily lost sight of him, but there was nowhere else he could run. One officer followed him down the same steps to the left, while the other crossed the street and descended the steps to the right of the bridge, hoping to pen him in from both sides. When the second officer reached the bottom of the steps, she expected to find the man running towards her, with her colleague close behind. Instead, the two officers were alone, regarding each other with confused looks. They spun around to check that the assailant hadn't somehow doubled back or changed direction, but the riverbank and underpass were clear. They looked over the low wall into the flowing river below, but neither had heard a splash and they saw no one in the water.

One minute and thirty-seven seconds earlier, the man had stood high above the rooftops, looking over London's night sky. He'd begun to lose hope that he would ever get home. It was an unseasonably warm evening, but he suddenly felt a chill breeze break against the back of his neck. He turned, and in the dim light of the belfry he could make out a disturbance in the air: a strange spherical ripple. Something like a heat haze, only cold. When he passed his hand through the undulating air around this phenomenon, his fingers became instantly cold. This sphere seemed to have its own microclimate, and goosebumps covered his flesh. Without warning the man's assailant suddenly materialised in front of him as if from nowhere.

Five minutes and fourteen seconds later, under the Westminster Bridge, the dead man's assailant had apparently vanished into thin air.

CHAPTER ONE

May 14th, 1984, 17:13

Finally, he'd found what he was looking for. It felt as if he'd asked every resident, business owner and taxi driver in and around Shoreditch, Spitalfields and Whitechapel about the small shop that Abigayle had described to him over breakfast that morning. That was almost nine hours ago. He'd become convinced that the place didn't exist at all and had just about given up when he stumbled across it almost by accident, foolishly lost as he was.

To say William Wells wasn't from these parts was somewhat of an understatement. To a midwestern boy like him, London was a literal maze of stone and concrete, whose confused layout was established hundreds of years before the place he called home even had a name.

He was an unspectacular-looking specimen for a man in his late twenties. He was average height but scrawny, which gave him the appearance of being taller than he was. He couldn't be described as athletic with such a wiry build, but he had a dancer's grace when he moved, almost gliding across the ground. His chestnut-brown hair swung lazily in front of his deep blue eyes, set evenly in the otherwise plain features of his face.

At the head of a narrow alleyway, he was doubled over, his hands on his knees. He was hot and his clothes were damp with sweat. Arching his back, he hoisted himself upwards as a creaking groan forced its way through his lips. He took a step into the alleyway and almost immediately lost his footing as he felt a blister burst on the heel of his foot. He gasped in pain, then said to no one in particular, 'William Wells, you're an idiot.'

Hobbling forwards gingerly, he continued to admonish himself under his breath, replaying in his head the conversation he'd had that morning.

***

Abigayle's directions had been clear: 'This place is easy to find. All you need to do is catch the number 58 bus – the same one we catch whenever we go to Borough Market – it leaves every twenty minutes.'

'Are you sure you can't call in sick and come with me?' Will said half-heartedly, already knowing her answer.

'I really wish I could, but I've got a lot on my plate at the moment,' Abigayle said as she arranged some paperwork in a well-worn leather holdall. 'Besides, I've been dozens of times before.'

'Yeah, yeah, I know. Everything just seems a whole lot more fun when we go together, that's all.'

'Will, you're very sweet, but are you sure you're not just worried about venturing out into this big city without me to look after you?' she said, glancing over her shoulder with a playful smile.

'Now come on, that's not fair. I do okay on my own,' Will said, raising his hands in mock offence, unable to suppress a smile himself.

'Right, well what about the other week then, when I asked you to take *Trading Places* back to Georgie's Video?'

'I really don't know what you're talking about, Abby,' he said, crossing his arms and studying his fingernails.

'What I'm talking about is you going missing for three hours because you got lost on a walk that should have taken ten minutes. I was worried sick!'

'I got the video back before we had to pay the late fee, didn't I?'

'Yes, but only because I managed to find you. At the other end of Kensington, I might add. I was riding around on my bike in my nightie at nine o'clock at night, scared out of my wits that something bad had happened to you.'

'I don't know if I was gone for *that* long. Like I told you at the time, I was just taking in the sights, familiarising myself with the area.'

Abigayle gave Will a teasing nudge and said, 'Fine, you stick to that story if you like, but I'm giving you directions to this place whether you want them or not. Get a pen and write this down. Number 58 bus.'

'Number 58 bus, got it,' Will replied, smiling at Abigayle, unable to take his eyes off her as she turned and continued to haphazardly shove various items into her undersized bag.

'Get off the bus outside the Happy Shopper,' she went

on. 'Then cut through the park opposite and turn left when you come out the other side. Keep walking until you see Woolworths, and Frying Pan Alley is a little further along the road on the right. The shop is…hey!' Abigayle stopped as she turned to look at Will. 'You're not writing this down!'

'Relax, I've got it. It's all up here.' Will tapped the side of his head. 'You forget, I'm a genuine Iowan boy. I don't need a map or detailed directions. All I need is a name and my natural sense of direction.'

It would come as no surprise, of course, that although Will found himself sitting on the number 58 bus, five minutes into his journey he realised that there was an empty space in his memory where Abigayle's directions should have been. Too late he realised that the only thing he could remember with any degree of accuracy was the delicate features of Abigayle's face. As beautiful as she was in his eyes, it was going to be of little use to him now.

William Wells had found himself so utterly and hopelessly in love, but he couldn't escape the feeling that he wasn't good enough for her. That at any moment reality was going to hit and Abigayle would see him for what he really was: a jobless, moneyless, illegal immigrant college dropout who had been disowned by most members of his family. Those who were still alive, at least. There was also the not so insignificant matter of his family's legal and financial problems that had been unfairly forced upon him.

The pressure to be the man he thought she needed him to be, one at the height of his powers, who was really going places, was stretching him beyond his limits. It had made him too insecure to admit that he was lost, literally and figuratively, at a point in life when what he really needed was direction and purpose. Abigayle was the only thing anchoring him, and the thought of her leaving him terrified him more than he'd care to admit. This fear had ultimately led to him spending most of the day walking in circles, hoping that he could find this damned shop and keep up the charade.

Today, fate or luck, neither of which Will gave much credence to, was on his side. Limping aimlessly in his worn shoes, something had made him look up at a rusted iron sign bolted to a damp, moss-covered wall. It read: _Frying Pan Alley_. Will clicked his fingers when he saw it and said, 'Frying Pan Alley! How the hell did I forget a name like that?'

***

Now that he was standing outside the elusive shop described to him by Abigayle, the sense of relief seemed to be easing the pain in his battered feet. He'd walked what felt like far enough to qualify as a marathon, had spoken to more people than he could count and couldn't for the life of him recall how a man selling his wares from a battered old suitcase had convinced him to buy leather gloves in May, but finally, he'd found it.

The shop was nestled down a narrow alley that, aside from the shop itself, was relatively bare. The walls flanking it on either side were a Frankenstein-like mishmash of bricks, varying in colour and size. The various sections of the walls were in fact parts of different buildings, all of which backed onto the alleyway. All, that is, apart from one small storefront, hidden in plain sight, facing into it. A small cast-iron frying pan hung on a flimsy metal bracket alongside it, presumably a remnant of the alleyway's nomenclature.

The storefront couldn't have been any more than two

metres wide with a squat door leaning up against a crooked window. It looked as though the building was once much larger but had been gradually compressed between the two neighbouring buildings and was now wedged awkwardly between them. The glass was covered in a thick film of dry powdery dirt, making it almost completely opaque and concealing whatever mysteries might be inside.

The carved wooden sign that hung above the entrance was barely legible. The faded red paint and gold lettering read:

MR. DIBBEN'S THRIFT SHOP AND WONDER EMPORIUM

The sign's grey wooden frame had deep grooves between the grain after many years of weathering. The neglect was such that the shop had become almost invisible to passersby, reclaimed by its surroundings.

William Wells had been studying the shop for some time now, his head cocked to the side, with a frown on his face. 'Really, Abby? All this fuss over…this?'

But he'd come this far; and with Abigayle's positive words about the store swirling through his head, he gripped the door handle and turned it. The swollen wood made the door stiff, so much so that Will almost abandoned this odd adventure completely until it eventually gave way and swung inwards after a firm shove from his shoulder. He ducked inside, brushing away the clumped grit that the door had deposited on his drab green cargo jacket, and headed down a short set of creaky stairs. When he reached the bottom, he found a surprisingly large but cluttered interior that belied the compact exterior. The entrance opened into a large space split across three distinct levels. The lowest level came immediately after the door, with a step up in the middle and down once more at the far end. It made the space look as if each part of the building was added at a different time over the years, without any thought for continuity. Each of the three levels looked to have small adjoining rooms running off them. The far end featured a large decorative mahogany counter with a dark figure slumped behind it in a chair, reading a newspaper – the shop owner, presumably.

The inside of the shop hadn't fared much better than the outside: the bare wooden floors had been worn smooth by footfall and the stained floral wallpaper was peeling away from the walls, pulling clumps of brittle plaster with it. The air was musty and close, and Will could see dust motes dancing in the air.

Everything in the shop appeared to be divided by department, but it was all arranged in a haphazard fashion. In one area, armchairs were stacked precariously on top of one another alongside tables and chairs in a similar arrangement. A small side room contained a variety of doors, piled flat like a pack of playing cards. Another had fireplaces and mantelpieces. The room opposite had wooden bird cages hanging across the ceiling, enamel-covered metal signs lining the walls, vintage bicycles covering one half of the floor and shelving with everything from old typewriters to wood-effect transistor radios on the other. There was even a wooden canoe hanging from the ceiling in the shop's main space. Will dared not touch anything, fearing the whole shop might come down on top of him, but one thing was for certain: Abigayle was right. He loved it.

Will had grown up in the small town of Le Clair, Iowa, and from a young age had been fascinated with objects or places with a story to tell. His mother and grandfather had worked as pickers in the area, searching local properties, abandoned farms and factories for hidden treasures to sell for a profit. He had accompanied them often as a kid, and the thing that he found most magical was finding an item with a rich and interesting history behind it. This didn't happen often in his experience, but when it did it was an exhilarating feeling. As he surveyed the walls of this cluttered shop, he couldn't help but imagine the stories that each of these pieces had to tell. However, it was one of the side rooms to the right of the counter that piqued Will's interest the most.

Inside, the walls were almost entirely covered in clocks. Larger clocks were arranged with smaller clocks nestled in between them, almost completely obscuring the grime-crusted wallpaper behind them. There were several grandfather-style clocks in one corner and a wooden display case with a glass top in the centre of the room. It contained dozens of old wrist and pocket watches. The sound of the numerous ticking clocks was incessant but strangely relaxing.

Will approached the display case, studying its contents intently. One of the first things he had learned about Abigayle was that she had a fascination with horology. She loved clocks and watches and often went to markets, antique fairs and car boot sales in search of old, interesting or rare timepieces. As he looked at the selection, it occurred to Will that their one-year anniversary was coming up soon. The idea of her smiling with surprise when he presented her with a rare and unusual watch was intoxicating.

13

As Will inspected the contents of the case for anything that looked old or unique to his relatively well-trained eye, he heard a floorboard creak behind him. He turned quickly to see the man from behind the counter standing uncomfortably close, with no apparent consideration for personal space, studying him intently.

Startled, Will attempted to create space between them but was boxed in by the display case behind and the owner in front. By way of escape, he slid sideways inelegantly. The shop owner smiled briefly as Will did this, then said, 'Oh, I'm sorry, my friend, it wasn't my intention to startle you.' His voice was deep, warm and ever so slightly accented.

Caribbean perhaps, Will thought.

'I don't often get customers this late in the day.'

The shop owner was somewhere in his mid-eighties, which showed in the way he moved and how he held himself. He wore a pristine white shirt with a neat brown tie and a knitted sleeveless pullover, patterned elaborately in natural, earthy colours. He had a full head of dense white curls and a neatly maintained beard and moustache, trimmed short. His white hair contrasted with his smooth dark skin.

'Hey, no, it's fine. Really,' Will said, feeling rather sheepish.

'An American?'

'Yeah, that's right.'

The shop owner shuffled his feet. 'Have you been here before, my friend? My eyesight isn't what it once was, but your voice, it seems familiar to me.'

'I don't think so. This is my first time in this part of the city.'

'Ah, I see. I must be mistaken then. Now, are you looking

for anything in particular?'

'I'm looking for something for my girlfriend. Soon to be ex-girlfriend, actually.'

'Oh?'

'Sorry, no, what I mean is we're engaged, so technically… you know what, it doesn't matter. The point is, she loves horology. Collects watches and clocks, especially old and unusual ones like these. No prices I see,' Will said, pointing to the watches in the case. 'That's not always a good sign and I'm on a pretty tight budget here.'

'Do not worry, I'm sure we can find something suitable. Now, let me just fetch the key for the display case. I won't be a moment.'

The shop owner headed back to his counter and began fumbling around underneath it, searching for the key. As he concluded his search, the phone rang. It was a shrill, high-pitched ring and louder than it needed to be. He answered and glanced at Will, giving him an apologetic smile and poking a finger in the air to signify that he would only be a minute. He greeted the caller warmly, still smiling. Whatever the caller had to say, it caused the shop owner's expression to change to one of dismay almost immediately. He tried to recover the lapse in his friendly persona, flashing Will a forced smile before turning away. With his back to his customer, he hunched forwards, talking quietly and gesturing with his arms. As the conversation progressed, he looked over his shoulder at Will for a long, unblinking moment before turning away again and ending the call.

After the shop owner had gathered himself, he spun around to face Will, doing his best to shrug off the effect the call had had on him with another forced smile. 'Sorry about that, my friend. I'm afraid to say that on second thoughts I don't think you'll find anything suitable here after all. These watches are junk. If your fiancée is a serious collector, that is.'

'Huh. Is that so? They were good enough a second ago,' Will said, his face contorted in his best attempt at indignation.

The owner returned Will's look with a raised eyebrow and a shrug. 'Well, yes, but given that you're on a tight budget, these watches are likely to be too expensive.' He seemed eager to steer Will away from the display case.

'Which is it then? Are they junk, or are they expensive? You know what, don't answer that, I see what's going on here. I would have expected this kind of treatment on Bond Street, but *this* place?' Will held his arms out to the side theatrically, palms facing upwards, turning his body one way, then the other. 'I wouldn't have guessed this was the kind of place that could afford to turn customers away. But you've done a *great* job!' Will felt unexpectedly flustered by this brief exchange and headed for the exit.

As he stepped up into the raised middle section of the store, the shop owner called after him: 'Excuse me, Mr Wells, I think there has been a misunderstanding. I meant only to say that I think I have another timepiece that your fiancée will be very happy with.' Will stopped, lowered his head and let out a sigh. Feeling slightly embarrassed now, he turned back to the owner, who he saw holding a bulky, brass-cased wristwatch bound to a thick leather strap. 'I'm sorry,' Will said. 'It's not like me to snap like that. It's just been a long day.'

'No harm done.'

Will walked back towards the shop owner, who said, 'This is a unique timepiece, but one that has never held much monetary value. I'm confident this will be in your price range.'

Will regarded the old man with scepticism, then turned his attention to the watch, which certainly did look intriguing, and like nothing he'd ever seen before.

'How much are we talking here?' Will asked.

'Yours for £15,' came the reply.

Will checked his wallet and with just enough to cover the bill and bus fare home, he nodded to the owner and stepped back down into the far end of the shop. He followed the shop owner as he limped inelegantly behind the counter. 'Allow me to write you a receipt. Should your fiancée not like it, you will of course be welcome to return it.'

The shop owner had placed the strange watch on the countertop while his slow hands worked the till and fumbled with a pen as he wrote out a receipt. Will picked up the watch for a closer look. The face was unusually large, which it needed to be to accommodate the twenty-four-hour time segments. Towards the centre of the face were three additional rings, each smaller than the last, with segments for what appeared to be days, months and years. The watch also featured six hands instead of three, as he was used to seeing on a watch of this size. The brass case was slightly worn but in otherwise good condition. It had no crown on its side, like a wristwatch, but instead had it on the top, as is common with pocket watches. It also featured an outer bezel that appeared to rotate. The strap had a heavy-duty brass frame that gripped the watch body and was riveted to the brown leather. It was slightly wider than the watch and required two separate buckles to hold it in place.

Will held the timepiece to his ear to check whether the movement was still operational. He reached for the crown to adjust the time when the watch was snatched from his hand by the shop owner, who placed it into a brown paper bag and then deposited it into Will's jacket pocket. The shop owner turned back to his till, picked up a small card from the counter and handed it to Will. 'Your receipt. Please keep this safe. I haven't included the price, so that you may give it to your fiancée along with her gift, should she need to return it.'

'Great, thanks,' Will said, smiling awkwardly.

'I'm afraid the shop is closing, so I must ask you to leave, my friend. Now, if you please,' the shop owner said, gesturing to the door in a hurried manner.

'Right, sure. It's getting late.' Will was slightly disturbed by the elderly shop owner's constantly shifting tenor.

'Goodbye. Enjoy the rest of your day,' the shop owner said.

Will headed towards the exit. As he reached the bottom of the steps that led up to the street, he turned back to the owner, who gave him a curt nod, returned to his seat and was soon absorbed in his newspaper once more.

Will scaled the steps, pulled the door inwards and was temporarily blinded by the low, fading sun. He raised an arm to shield his eyes. When he lowered it again, he was alarmed by two men striding purposefully towards him. The two figures – one tall and thin, the other shorter and solidly built – wore identical tweed jackets with matching flat caps, beige corduroy slacks and shin-high brown leather boots. There was something disturbing about the way they bustled past him and headed into the thrift shop, pushing the door closed behind them. Will could hear the unmistakable sound of bolts sliding home.

He walked a few paces down the narrow alleyway before stopping and glancing back towards the thrift shop.

Something feels off about this.

Returning to the shop, Will tried to peek in through the window but could see nothing through the thick layer of dirt. He ducked down, wiped clean one of the small panes of glass with his jacket sleeve and peered inside. From the higher vantage point of the street, he could only just make out the lower halves of the two men who'd entered the shop. They were now standing in front of the counter. He couldn't quite make out the shop owner as he was obscured by his two visitors, but he could hear the muffled rhythm of a seemingly calm conversation between the three men. The words weren't clear, but it seemed friendly enough.

Will was about ready to leave when he saw the shorter of the two men drop his hand to his side. In his hand was a black handgun with a long, bulbous barrel. The conversation remained calm for a brief period, and it was clear that the owner was unaware that one of the men was holding a gun just out of sight below the counter. Will glanced up and down the narrow alleyway, desperately hoping to find help, but there was none – not a soul in sight.

His attention was pulled back to the three men inside the shop by the single dull popping sound from the silenced handgun. It was strange; the immediate sound was no more than a whisper, but it seemed to reverberate and rattle off into the distance. It sounded more like a car backfiring many streets away than a man being shot.

19

Will moved his face closer to the glass now and saw that the two men had parted just enough for him to see the shop owner. He was slumped backwards in his chair, agony in his face, with both hands pressed against his stomach. His white shirt and knitted top were saturated with blood.

CHAPTER TWO

May 14th, 1984, 18:05

Will was immobile with shock, his fists clenched and trembling. He couldn't avert his wide, unblinking eyes from the scene that was playing out on the other side of the murky glass. For a brief moment impulse took over and his hand closed around the door handle as he prepared to burst through the door to the stricken shop owner's aid. But with no real idea what his next move would have been, it was fortunate that this foolish deed was halted when one gunman, perhaps sensing prying eyes on his back, turned his head in Will's direction. As soon as the man's head began to move, Will ducked out of sight and spun away from the window, pressing his back against the uneven brick wall to his left.

I need to get some help, he thought.

After narrowly avoiding what would have been a fateful

display of heroics, Will came to his senses and fled the shop towards the main road. He emerged from Frying Pan Alley and whipped his head left and right before finding what he was looking for. He quickly peeled off to his right towards a phone box.

The phone box's weathered paint had faded, now more pink than red, and the door was heavy and stiff.

As he heaved the door open, a large car rolled up to the kerb beside him. It was an elegant metallic-brown Rolls-Royce Silver Spirit. It had an elongated bonnet housing a powerful V8 engine, which rumbled away like a caged beast. The front end of the car was boxy and modern-looking. The windows at the rear of the car were darkened and Will could barely make out the figure sitting inside. He traced his eyes towards the driver, who was sitting calmly with one leather-gloved hand at twelve o'clock on the steering wheel. A small patch of hair-covered skin was visible between the glove and the distinctive tweed fabric of his jacket sleeve. His other hand slowly raised up from his lap and adjusted the flat cap on his head. He was dressed in almost identical, oddly old-fashioned clothing as the two gunmen. It was too much to believe that it was a coincidence – he must be with them. This time Will didn't freeze or contemplate his next move and instead ran as if his life depended on it, wincing as each blistered foot pounded against the pavement.

After putting some distance between himself and the tragic scene in the shop, he slowed his pace but kept checking over his shoulder to see if the car or the gunmen had followed. There was no sign of the men, but the car had pulled away from the kerb and followed him as he turned down Commercial Street and was there again as he made his way down Brick Lane. Eventually Will came across another narrow alleyway, far too small for a tank like the Rolls-Royce to follow. As he darted into it, he said a silent thank you to the Victorians, and those before them, for rebuilding London in the aftermath of the Great Fire using the same, impractically narrow streets set out by the Medievals.

***

Will had somehow managed to make his way to Abigayle's flat without further incident, taking his time to ensure he wasn't being followed. The last thing he wanted to do was to lead a group of murderers back to Abigayle. If she thought the Blockbuster incident was bad, he'd never hear the end of this.

He hurried off the bus a few stops away from Holland Park and checked that the coast was still clear before resuming his steady but frantic walking pace, confident that he hadn't seen the brown Rolls-Royce or any tweed jackets since he'd left Liverpool Street.

Looks like I'm in the clear.

Abigayle had a ground-floor flat on Elsham Road, just a few minutes' walk from Holland Park Gate. It was a beautiful part of London, with long, sweeping curved streets and pockets of green parks sprinkled evenly among them. Abigayle's building was at the middle of a row of fifty or so four-storey townhouses. The houses featured elegant white moulded stucco ground floors and pillared porches with steps leading up to each front door. Almost all of the houses were constructed from the famous yellow London stock bricks, which were exposed on the top three floors. One house in the middle of the row, however, stood apart from the others and was instead constructed with bold ebony bricks. Although the house was disliked by many of the local residents for the perceived negative aesthetic impact it had on the street, at that moment, the dark spot in a sea of yellow was a welcome beacon of hope for Will.

The flat itself was modest but spacious enough for the two of them, divided in a simple two-up, two-down configuration. The downstairs featured a large, bright living room at the front and a kitchen diner to the rear, opening into a small courtyard. The stairs led to a narrow landing, with the bathroom and office on one side and the master bedroom on the other.

Will had been staying with Abigayle rent-free for the past ten months. She had refused to accept any contribution from him until he managed to tie down regular work – something that he found incredibly emasculating – and he was certain that living in this area of London couldn't have been cheap.

Money, though, didn't appear to be a problem for Abigayle. She had a well-paying government job, one important enough that she couldn't talk about it. Will respected this and instead imagined her to be some kind of female James Bond. However, the sheer volume of paperwork she seemed to be constantly flooded with countered that idea.

Despite her apparent professional success, she hadn't been born into money. Her stepfather had driven a black cab for thirty years and her mother worked as a dinner lady at a local school. Between them they had scrimped and saved all the money they could to put her through university. She had exceeded all expectations when she was accepted to Cambridge University, where she studied history at Christ's

College. She was the first member of her family to go to university, graduating with first-class honours. She later returned to London, where she undertook a master's degree in European history before securing a job as a historical researcher, eventually moving into her current position.

Will, on the other hand, had dropped out of college when his mother had become unwell and was not even legally permitted to work in London. He'd had to get by on whatever scraps of labouring work he could get his hands on.

By the time he stumbled through the front door of Abigayle's flat, he was panting furiously. Even walking briskly had been taxing on his tender, blistered feet, but he cut himself a little slack given that he was also currently working his way through the early stages of shock.

The front door opened directly into the living room, which was growing dark as the light outside faded. Will breezed into the room, running on autopilot, dropping his keys on the side table before slumping down on the sofa. He sat there motionless for a moment, breathing heavily, rivulets of sweat glistening on his forehead. He was still wearing his jacket and gloves and felt too numb to register his rising body temperature.

He kept playing back the image in his head: the elderly owner slumped back in his chair, his clothes soaked in blood. The questions about what he had witnessed tumbled around in his head.

What were the three of them talking about? And how could that have led to a defenceless man being gunned down in cold blood?

He was sure that it couldn't have been a robbery. No one he'd spoken to earlier that day had even heard of the shop or where it might be, so he couldn't imagine it ever being busy or that the till was bursting with cash. No, something else was going on here.

After the panic of the shooting, it was only now that he had even remembered the watch, which sat heavy in his pocket, causing his jacket to hang low at one side. Will removed one of his thick leather gloves, balling it up in his other pocket. His hand was warm and clammy. He retrieved the paper bag, unwrapped the watch and held it in his trembling hand.

Will stared off into the middle distance, wild thoughts racing through his head. The phone call and the change in the shop owner's manner afterwards had stood out to him at the time and seemed even more significant now. He had been oddly insistent that Will buy this watch right after that phone call. And the timing of his leaving as those men arrived hadn't escaped him either. He blinked just then, his dry eyes watering as he looked down at the watch in his hand.

They couldn't have been looking for this, could they?

The more he thought about it, the more this crazy idea seemed to fit. The shop owner did seem to go out of his way to put him off the rest of his stock. And this watch hadn't even been in the display case, he was sure of that.

Where had it come from? Did the shop owner have it on him the whole time?

Will sat forwards, resting his elbows on his knees, and shook his head. He was overthinking all of this and tried to push the idea from his mind. He clamped his eyes shut tight and was flooded with images of what he'd just witnessed, as well as the inescapable thought that he'd run from it all.

When he opened his eyes, he felt calmer and had a clear idea of what he needed to do next. The room had grown completely dark by now and he reached out blindly to his right, where he knew the telephone to be. He squinted to see the numbers on the inside of the handset. As he turned to his left to switch on a lamp, he heard a key in the door, and he stopped short. For a moment he panicked, sure that the two men from the thrift shop had followed him home and were there to kill him. He sat in silence, every muscle in his body taut as he observed a figure silhouetted by the hallway light step through the door.

He soon relaxed, however, immediately recognising her by the way she moved and her scent as it was carried into the room on the light breeze from outside.

'Will, you home?' she said into the darkness. 'Sorry I'm so late. Crazy day at work.' Will detected something in the way she spoke. She was off somehow, not her usual beaming self. 'Oh, and my mother has a new boyfriend. She told me everything in gory detail. Let me get out of these shoes and I'll tell you the whole sordid story.'

For a second his worries seemed to evaporate, and the panic began to pass. All thoughts of calling the police momentarily left his head and suddenly things didn't seem so bad now that Abigayle was here. She tended to have that effect on people, Will especially.

As she struggled into the room carrying her bags and coat, she kicked the door shut and flicked on a light switch with her elbow. As the lights came on, she saw Will sitting motionless on the sofa and let out a high-pitched scream. After the initial fright, she saw that it was Will and said, 'Fucking hell! Will, why are you sitting here in the dark? You scared the shit out of me!'

Will loved Abigayle's perfectly accented English and

imagined that if the Queen of England ever cursed, this was how it would sound. And if she'd had a hard day at work, you wouldn't know it to look at her. Her olive skin was unblemished and even-coloured, aside from a slight blush in her cheeks. There was no sign of tiredness in her eyes and her shoulder-length auburn hair was glossy and immaculate.

Will stood from the sofa and said, 'Abby, I'm sorry. I've had a bit of a day as well. I didn't mean to frighten you.'

Abigayle chuckled uneasily as she set her bag down and hung up her coat. 'Sitting in the dark like that is the kind of thing dangerous people do in movies. You're not dangerous, are you, Will?' she said, winking at him.

Will forced a smile and stared at her, his mind still in too much of a fog to explain what had happened. Abigayle was headed for the stairs but paused, frowned slightly and walked up to him. 'Hey, everything okay?'

Will swallowed hard and opened his mouth, but no words came out.

'Will, what is it?' she said, placing a hand on his arm, caressing it lightly.

He cleared his throat. 'No, nothing. Nothing. I'm fine, it's just…'

She leaned in and placed a gentle kiss on his cheek, gave him a warm hug and said, 'Sounds like we both could do with a cup of tea.' As she withdrew, she caught sight of what was in his hand. It stopped her in her tracks. 'Holy fuck! Where did you get that?' Abigayle said, breaking Will out of his trance-like state.

'Huh? Where did I get what?'

'That timepiece you're holding!' Before he could respond, Abigayle had taken the watch from his hand and was examining it excitedly. Absentmindedly, Will said, 'I bought it. For you, actually.'

'Will, this is amazing, I've never seen a timepiece like it.'

'Well, surprise, I guess,' Will said, doing his best to hide the worry in his voice.

Abigayle shot him a sideways look and said, 'William Wells, you shouldn't spoil me like this. Especially when you owe me rent for the past ten months.' Abigayle poked her tongue out at him playfully, although he hated when she teased him about money. 'Looks like it needs winding, although this isn't a standard mechanism…' Abigayle's words trailed off as she turned away from him and began to fumble with the inputs on the watch.

'Abby, there's something you need to know about this watch.' Will reached out and touched her arm as she began to turn the outer bevel, spinning it clockwise. At that moment, a peculiar thing happened.

At first, they just felt warmth, like stepping under a hot shower in winter. It spread through their fingers, their hands, up their arms and proliferated through their entire bodies. It was exhilarating. What followed was even more so but was accompanied with the unmistakable tinge of fear. Will could taste a distinctive bitter metallic taste in his mouth as a pulse of invisible energy rippled outwards from the two of them in an ever-growing sphere.

Before their eyes, the living room was transformed. At their feet, the pea-green floral carpet started to strip away, replaced with a smooth oak parquet floor. Their mahogany-effect coffee table vanished too, along with Abigayle's favourite cup, a green tinted sheet of glass with a metal frame appearing in its place. Before long, all the furniture had gone, exchanged with strange and wonderful objects. Finally, the magnolia woodchip wallpaper seemed to peel away, revealing perfectly smooth white walls in its wake. Abigayle and Will were standing in the same room of the same building, and yet everything was different.

They both looked around, wide-eyed, conflicting emotions fighting for prominence: excitement, fear, wonderment, disbelief, intrigue, confusion. The sheet of glass where their coffee table once stood was bare, all apart from a small gloss-black rectangular object. It caught Abigayle's eye and she leaned towards it for closer inspection. Without warning, the black object erupted with light and began making a terrible rattling sound, like a venomous insect about to attack. The sudden flurry of activity startled Abigayle and she fell backwards, throwing her arms behind her.

As she did so, the watch slipped from her grasp, falling towards the hard wooden floor. Will reacted instinctively and with impressively quick reflexes he reached out his still-gloved hand, catching the watch just centimetres from the floor. The moment his hand closed firmly around the watch, the sphere of energy receded inwards, and everything seemed to become cold and dark. Will's eyes refocused and gone were the wooden floors, which had returned to their familiar pea-green floral carpet. The walls were no longer smooth and white but were magnolia-woodchip-textured once more. The glass coffee table and all the other fascinating objects had vanished.

He turned to where Abigayle had been standing before she dropped the watch, but she too had vanished.

CHAPTER THREE

May 14th, 1984, 19:37

Will stood from his crouched position with the mysterious timepiece clasped in his hand. His head pivoted left and right, scanning the room for a sign of Abigayle. He was in utter disbelief, panting with panic.

What the hell just happened?

His skin began to prickle with heat, and he felt his face redden. His heart was beating so loud in his chest that he could feel it pulsing in his ears.

'Abby, quit screwing around. This isn't funny, okay?' He hurried around the room, glancing under the coffee table, behind the sofa and tugging the low-hanging curtains to one side. He sprinted up the stairs, calling out her name over and over, his own voice echoing back at him from each of the empty rooms. But she wasn't there. She was really gone.

He was in a daze, unsure of what was happening or what he should do next.

A sharp odour of burning plastic stung his nose and eyes, bringing his attention back to the watch. He'd been so preoccupied with finding Abigayle that he'd somehow overlooked the burning sensation and the dark smoke curling upwards from his gloved hand. Apparently, the watch had become quite hot and was beginning to burn through the leather. Will used his free hand to take hold of the thick leather strap that the watch was attached to and peeled it from his melted glove. The leather strap seemed to be unaffected by the heat, unlike the molten disaster that was obviously a pair of faux-leather gloves. He stripped the destroyed glove from his hand and pocketed it, returning his attention to the watch.

He then held the strap between his thumb and index finger, regarding the peculiar timepiece as it swung loosely in the air. The heat aside, he felt something else emanating from it that he couldn't quite place. He began to move his hand slowly towards it; the heat was easily perceptible even at arm's length. Something was radiating through the air around it that seemed to draw his hand in. His fingers edged closer and closer, despite the heat, and were almost touching when a creaking sound cut through the silence. His nerves were still frayed, and the sound startled him enough to make him drop the watch and duck out of sight.

Someone was moving on the landing outside the front door. He kept low and listened intently. He waited for a few moments but heard nothing more.

Will remained motionless for no more than a minute when he caught something from the corner of his eye. Smoke was beginning to rise steadily from the pea-green carpet. A small circular burn mark was growing around the watch as it lay face down on the floor.

Still on edge about the sound he'd heard at the door, he kept low and scurried towards the kitchen, returning with a well-used copper frying pan. He delicately lifted the watch from the floor by the leather strap and placed it inside the pan. He lifted the pan to the coffee table and examined the damage to the carpet. There was a brown circular indentation where the long-pile fabric had burnt and melted away.

He looked around the living room with a furrowed brow when the thought occurred to him. The room transformed before Abigayle had gone missing so maybe the room might somehow hold the answer to bringing her back. Perhaps if he pulled up the carpet or stripped the wallpaper from the walls, the room would transform once more, and Abigayle would return as miraculously as she had disappeared. He convinced himself that this bizarre logic would somehow help. If the past few hours had taught him anything, it was to not be limited by what he'd previously thought possible.

Will returned to the kitchen and came back to the living room with a paring knife in his hand. He knelt next to the charred mark on the carpet, where Abigayle had been standing, and jabbed the knife into the floor. With both hands he raked it this way and that, cutting a large one-metre-square section of carpet free. He ripped the section of carpet away, discarding it on the coffee table. This revealed the pink rubbery underlay beneath. It was an unseemly sight: stained with browns, yellows and reds from years of abuse. Will didn't want to think what might have caused the brown and yellow stains, but the large red splattered stain still bore the unmistakable whiff of red wine.

Will's thoughts briefly returned to the day he'd spilt the wine on Abigayle's carpet on only his second visit to her flat. He had felt awful, but Abigayle had been calm and gracious about the whole thing. When she walked back into the room and saw the stain, she put her hands on her hips and shook her head in mock annoyance before smiling warmly at Will and saying, 'My god, you are so cute when you're nervous!'

'You're not angry?' Will said.

'Pfft, I never liked this carpet. Who has a cream carpet anyway? We'll go pick out a new one at the carpet shop in the morning. I'm thinking green.'

A little under a year later, Will was on his hands and knees, destroying another carpet, this time cutting right through the underlay. He pulled a section of it free, revealing the wooden boards below. To his surprise, even the wood had been stained red by the wine.

Unfortunately, the wood looked nothing like the polished parquet floor he had seen a moment ago, before Abigayle had vanished. He knew it was a long shot, but the hopelessness and despair of her absence was raging inside of him. He clenched his fist around the hilt of the blade, lifted it above his head and then thrust it downwards, letting out a guttural cry and jamming the end of the blade into the floor.

He gritted his teeth and breathed deeply to try to regain some of his composure.

I can't do this alone. I need to get help.

He rose and stepped away from the butchered floor and walked back to the sofa, retrieving the telephone. He held it firmly in his hand and pondered who he could call. His family back in the States would have no interest in helping him, even if any of them did have passports, and he was ashamed to admit that there really was no one else in the UK he could call a friend besides Abigayle. So, he did what he knew he should have done to begin with and called Emergency Services.

There was a low thrumming ringtone before the voice of a politely spoken woman came on the line: 'Emergency, which service please?'

'I…I don't know. Police, I guess,' he said.

'What exchange and number are you calling from?'

'What? I don't know. It's my fiancée's flat.'

'Hold the line,' the voice said, unperturbed. 'I'll connect you.'

The line went quiet for a moment. The silence allowed Will to concentrate on his breathing, which he now became aware had quickened to short, sharp bursts. As he tried to contain his growing panic, another voice came over the line. It was a man's voice this time and he immediately sounded jaded and irritable. 'Police, what's your emergency?'

'Hi. Hello, it's my fiancée, she's…'

'Has something happened to your fiancée, sir, is that correct?'

'Yeah, something's happened and I don't know what—'

'Are you still with her, sir? Has she been hurt?'

'What? No, I'm not with her. That's why I'm calling. She's gone,' Will said, his voice laced with growing anxiety.

'Sir, can you confirm that your fiancée is unhurt?'

'No, listen, I don't know if she's hurt. She's gone. Disappeared.'

'Did you do something to your fiancée, sir?'

'What are you…no, I didn't…listen, she's gone and—'

'Do you have any weapons on you or in the house, sir?'

the voice asked, becoming sterner and more suspicious with every passing second.

'Weapons? Why would I...' Will's eyes now shot around the room. The curtains had been partially pulled from the rails when he frantically looked behind them, the sofa and pillows were scattered, a lamp was upturned and laying on the floor. Then there was the carpet, with a large section cut free and a knife jammed into the red-stained floor. All of this could be explained, he knew, but none of it looked good.

The voice came back on the line now, firmer and more impatient: 'Sir, are you still there? I need to send some officers to your address, and I need to know if you present a danger to yourself or others.'

This was a mistake.

How could he have possibly hoped to explain any of this? Abigayle had vanished into thin air and if he was going to find her, the last thing he needed was to get himself locked up. If that happened, sooner or later they'd know that he'd overstayed his welcome in this country and he'd be deported. And if that happened, Abigayle would be lost forever. He processed this information quickly and came to a decision, 'Actually, my mistake, it's fine. I'm sorry I wasted your time,' Will said flatly and then placed the phone back in the receiver.

Will stood upright and tried to shake some of the tiredness from his muscles before grabbing his keys from the side table and heading for the front door. When he was within two paces, there was a loud knock at the door.

He froze for a moment, fearing that this was the gunmen. If he didn't answer, they might just go away. That trick had always worked with Jehovah's Witnesses – so long as you remained silent and didn't move, they would slink away to someone else's door.

Wait a sec, murderers wouldn't knock, would they? And the police couldn't have gotten here that fast.

There was another knock at the door, louder this time. Then a voice: 'Abigayle? Will? I know you're in there. Is everything okay?'

It was Kevin, their upstairs neighbour. Abigayle thought him harmless enough, but he gave Will the creeps. He would often make these kinds of visits to their door, and it was clear to Will that Kevin had developed an unhealthy obsession with Abigayle. The very first time they met, he had said to Will: 'I've known Abigayle for a long time and I've always looked out for her. Guys like you come and go, but not me.'

'Well sure, you live upstairs,' Will said.

Kevin flinched, offended, and said, 'Just understand that this thing between you and her is probably just a temporary thing. Okay?'

The guy was strange, and the slightest excuse would result in him appearing at their door. He dropped off a newspaper for her every morning, even though she despised the *Daily Mail*. One evening there was a blackout and he scuttled down his stairs to check on her, as if she needed Kevin, and only Kevin, to rescue her. On the surface some might have considered him rather sweet, but Will had once spotted him intercepting their post so that he could bring it to the door. He wasn't sure if that was even legal, but he had been wary of him ever since.

Kevin banged on the door again, with a clenched fist this time. 'Will! I saw both of you come home so you're not getting rid of me that easily,' Kevin said with a light snigger.

He did that too. As a member of Neighbourhood Watch, he often sat at his second-floor window just watching the street. Will was sure he only watched for Abigayle, though. 'I just want to make sure that everything is okay. Otherwise, I might have to call the police,' Kevin bellowed in a sarcastic, chortling voice.

Having already drawn suspicion from the police when he called them, the last thing Will needed was Kevin making things even worse, so he moved towards the door and pulled it open a crack. He placed himself in between the edge of the door and the doorframe, preventing Kevin from
seeing inside.

Kevin was a short man, at least a foot shorter than Will, who himself wasn't particularly tall. He looked to be in his late thirties and had a round, puffy face, rotund belly and narrow shoulders. He was wearing a pastel-blue polo shirt, collar turned up, with a thin gold chain around his neck and a large gold watch on his wrist. On his lower half, he was wearing tight-fitting, faded blue jeans and bright white high-tongued trainers. His skin was smooth and unnaturally tanned, matching his unnaturally dark head of hair, which was slicked back, gleaming with hair product. The look was completed with a thick black moustache that covered the whole of his top lip and spanned the length of his mouth. If he had to guess, Will would have said he was modelling himself on a Columbian drug dealer. Kevin was actually from Shropshire.

'Hello, Kevin, what can I do for you?' Will said as pleasantly as he could manage.

'What took so long?' Kevin snapped.

'I was just cleaning something up. I, um…spilled a cup of

coffee. Thanks for your concern, but it's all under control. Bye-bye, Kevin.' Will made a move to close the door, but Kevin jammed his foot inside it.

'I'm just on my way to the Spar. Does Abigayle need anything? Milk, eggs?'

'Thank you, Kevin, but I think we're good,' Will said, moving to block his view into the flat.

'Good? Well, here's the thing, Willy. I heard some really strange noises coming from in here. I heard Abigayle scream.'

'Oh, that? I was just horsing around and made her jump. That's all. Anyway, nice to see you, thanks for the offer—'

'Where is Abigayle? I can't hear her. Doesn't she wonder who's at the door?'

'She's…in the bath,' Will said, unconvincingly.

'Oh, really? Well, your water tank is directly beneath my Corby trouser press in the kitchen and I can hear it when Abby runs a bath. And guess what, Willy? I can't hear anything, so try again.'

'Look, Kevin, now isn't a good time. Like I said, I spilled some coffee and need to clean it up. So, if you'd kindly take your foot out of my door…'

'*Your* door? Did you really just say this was your door? This is Abby's flat. You're just a temporary cheapskate Yank! I'm Neighbourhood Watch, you know,' he said, plucking a small, laminated membership card from his pocket that Will was sure he had made himself. 'And something is going on here and I'm not leaving until I find out what!'

With that Kevin pushed his way into the flat. He surprised Will with how strong he was for such a little guy. Kevin paced through the living room, charging up the stairs, calling

Abigayle's name. Will called up after him: 'Kevin, what the hell do you think you're doing?!'

Kevin hadn't yet seen the state of the floor so Will hurried to cover up his handiwork before he came back down. He knelt and pulled on the paring knife, which was still wedged firmly in the floor. The blade protested but finally came free as Kevin came storming down the stairs.

'Okay, Will, where is she? I saw her come home and she didn't go back out so...' Kevin stopped halfway down the stairs and his words trailed off when he saw Will standing in the living room. His gaze was roving from Will's face, to the large paring knife in his hand, to the torn-up carpet, to the red-stained floor and back to Will's face. He seemed to be on a constant loop as the gears were turning in his head, processing what he was seeing.

Kevin pressed his back up against the wall and slid down the stairs as if he were on an invisible stairlift. 'You know what, Will, I can see you're in the middle of something here. So, I'll just see myself out.'

Will was unsure what to make of Kevin's slightly odder-than-usual behaviour at first. He then traced his neighbour's gaze down to the knife in his hand, to the torn-up carpet and finally to the red-stained floor. Kevin was visibly shaken and when he reached the bottom of the stairs he raced through the front door, pulling it closed behind him before Will had a chance to explain. A series of rapid thudding sounds trailed away as Kevin sprinted up the two flights of stairs to his apartment, followed by the dull sound of a door being opened and slammed shut and various locks and bolts sliding home.

Will closed his eyes, exhaled deeply and said, 'Shit.'

CHAPTER FOUR

May 14th, 1984, 19:42

Will had to move quickly.

A buck gets ten he's upstairs right now calling the police.

He was sure that Kevin was telling them all about the crazy American stranger who had just murdered his downstairs neighbour with a paring knife.

He would also give them his name, and it wouldn't take them long to find out why he was really in London and why he wasn't keen to go back to the US.

Will had almost reached the door before he stopped short, turning back towards the strange watch sitting in the copper frying pan. He approached it cautiously, tapping its metal case with the end of his finger to see if it had cooled down. Thankfully, it had, but it was still warm to the touch, so he slid it inside his charred but functional glove and put both in his jacket pocket.

The watch clearly had dangerous properties, unlike

anything he had ever experienced before. His thoughts turned again to the shop owner. His strange behaviour. The men who had come and shot him. Will was sure that he had known this was no ordinary watch, but why entrust it to him? He was also sure that sooner or later the police were going to catch up with him; and when they did, what could he say to possibly explain any of this? They'd never believe his story. Will didn't even believe it himself. If he was ever going to find Abigayle, he needed answers and there was only one place he could think of that he might find them.

***

It had been almost three hours since the shooting at the thrift shop. To Will's surprise – and relief – it appeared as if nothing had been reported to the police. Frying Pan Alley was quiet and deserted. The sun had set, and this once charming part of London was completely shrouded in darkness, looking more like the kind of place Jack the Ripper might have stalked his prey than a trendy shopping destination. There were a series of cast-iron lamps, wall-mounted and spread evenly along the length of the alley. Only one of them appeared to be working, however. It was inadequate for illuminating the whole of the alleyway and instead it created a single small pool of light a few buildings down from the thrift shop.

Will stood at the far end of the lane with his feet planted firmly and his hands balled into fists. He was trying to summon enough courage to step into the darkness, acutely aware of the gruesome scene that it led to. He couldn't quite make out the shop from where he was standing; all that was visible was the shallow pool of light. He decided to tackle this in stages: the first thing he needed to do was reach the pool of light.

Easy, he thought, *no dead bodies there. No big deal.*

He gritted his teeth and scurried into the lane, almost at a running pace. With his focus on finding Abigayle, the tenderness in his battered feet seemed completely insignificant now. In no time at all he had completed stage one. He had expected the light to be some kind of sanctuary from the oppressive darkness of the rest of the alleyway, but somehow the light proved to be worse. As his eyes adjusted, everything beyond the light had become so completely dark that Will could barely make out anything beyond the dimly lit main streets at either end. The space in between was unexplored wilderness as far as he was concerned. He'd never considered himself as being scared of the dark, but when there really was a chance that monsters were lurking there – monsters in tweed, carrying guns – then it suddenly took on a whole new dimension.

His body was full of nervous energy, so he started shifting his weight from one foot to the other in quick, anxious movements. He could feel the panic rising in his chest, and the temptation to turn back was compelling. The feeling of trepidation he had towards the shop was in stark contrast to the way he was drawn towards it earlier that day.

Will forced himself to slow his breathing, which helped to calm his nervous movements. He reminded himself what he was faced with if he didn't do what needed to be done. A life without Abigayle.

Don't worry, Abby, I'll find you, no matter what.

With newfound resolve, he stepped out of the light and marched purposefully into the darkness.

His eyes took a few moments to readjust to the gloom, but he reached the shop front unscathed. This next stage was going to be harder. This stage, he knew, would definitely involve a dead body. He was dreading it, but he took a deep breath, stepped closer to the window and peered in through the small pane of glass he'd wiped clean hours earlier. Most of the inside of the shop was a dark moonlit shade of blue, but he could just about make out the figure of the shop owner, hunched over his desk at the far end of the room in the light of a flickering banker's lamp. He sidestepped towards the door, turned the handle and gave it a firm shove. The door gave way more easily this time, swinging inwards.

Will took care as he descended the steps and ducked back into the multi-levelled interior of the shop. Earlier today he would have described the place as organised chaos; now, though, it was just chaos. The gunmen, after shooting the owner, had clearly turned the place upside down. They must have been looking for something – Will instinctively slid his hand over his jacket, feeling for the shape of the watch in his pocket. The stacks of tables and chairs had collapsed, the sofas had been slashed open and their foam torn out. The fireplaces had been tipped over and the wooden bird cages had been shattered. Even the wooden canoe had been pulled from the wall and hacked to pieces.

The commotion must have stirred up the dust, which was now even thicker in the air than it had been earlier. The shop interior had once been spread across three distinct levels, but as Will looked across the space, the degree of destruction here had made those levels no longer discernible. He very carefully approached the counter at the back of the room, taking care not to trip over any of the objects strewn across the floor.

Will had only seen a dead body once before; his mother had died two years earlier after a prolonged battle with cancer. He had been at her bedside when she passed, and he didn't relish the idea of being reminded of that moment.

Trying his best to avert his eyes from the lifeless form behind the counter, a faint tapping sound piqued his interest. At first, he thought it was coming from the side room with the clocks covering the walls. They had been ticking away furiously on his last visit, but they all seemed to have fallen silent.

When he rounded the counter, standing to the left of the shop owner's body, he forced himself to take in the scene before him. The shop owner was sitting in his seat with his chest resting at a slight angle on the countertop, his head turned to the right, thankfully looking away from Will. His left arm was hanging down over the near side of the counter. It was at this point that Will found the source of the sound. A slow, regular drip of blood was running down the shop owner's arm, along his fingers, and pitter-pattering in a gleaming red pool on the shop floor. Will held the back of his hand to his mouth, the whiff of iron in the air almost making him gag.

The shop owner's right arm was in a position that struck Will as rather unnatural. It was stretched out to the far side of the counter and his fingertips were sandwiched in the middle of a stack of papers. Will tilted his head to one side and carefully lifted a few sheets of paper from the top of the pile, his hand trembling uncontrollably.

The papers appeared to be sales invoices. Glancing at the dates, it was clear that the shop couldn't have been doing particularly well; there was as little as one sale being made a month. And this seemed to have been going on for years.

How was this place making any money?

The shop owner's hand was resting on one invoice in particular. Blood was smeared across the crisp white paper. Will slid the paper out from under the shop owner's hand, dried blood leaving faint diagonal streaks across it as he pulled it free. He studied it, angling towards the lambent light of the desk lamp. In his shaking hand, he could see that it was the invoice from his visit earlier that day.

Will recoiled.

Why would he have reached out for that specific invoice? Was he trying to implicate me in his murder?

It was an incredible coincidence if not. Whatever the case, it looked as though the old guy had used his last dying breath to bring someone's attention to it.

Will studied the invoice more closely, relaxing when he saw that it listed none of Will's personal details. He remembered that, luckily, he hadn't even given the shop owner his name. 'Wait a sec. He knew my name,' Will said out loud, the sound of his own voice alarming him. He reran his conversation with the shop owner in his head. He was certain that the shop owner had called after him and had used his name. Will hadn't introduced himself, hadn't shown any ID or used a credit card.

How had he known? What was going on here?

As he held the invoice in his hand, his thumb passed over an embossed shape on the paper. There, under his thumb, was an odd circular symbol that had been stamped on the left edge of the page next to a paragraph of printed text. It appeared to be a clockface but with many hands of differing lengths, fanning out from its centre.

The effect gave it as much the appearance of a flower as a clock. The symbol stirred something in the recesses of Will's mind, and he reached into his back pocket, retrieved his wallet and pulled out the sales receipt the shop owner had given him for the watch. Right there, along the top edge, was the same odd symbol.

Will shuffled through the other invoices in the stack but couldn't see the same symbol on any of them. He placed his sales receipt on top of the invoice to better compare the two symbols. As he examined them, he noticed a series of small rectangular holes punched into the receipt. They appeared to be scattered randomly. But perhaps not.

On closer inspection, he could see that the two symbols were not quite the same and he noticed that the symbol on his receipt was rotated ninety degrees clockwise from the one on the invoice. He rotated the receipt until the two matched and lined them up beside each other. As he did so, letters appeared in the rectangular holes, spelling out a garbled message.

Could this be a simple fluke, or could it be something more? Maybe the shop owner's last moments were not intended to implicate Will but rather to send him a message?

Despite the situation Will currently found himself in, he couldn't help but feel a sudden surge of adrenaline – as if he'd taken a step closer to finding some answers that would lead him back to Abigayle.

Will composed himself and repositioned the receipt over the page until both clock symbols were lined up exactly. When he did this, a message appeared. In that instant, he understood: the receipt wasn't a receipt at all, not really; it was a cypher. The message was no longer garbled, but not exactly clear either. He read it out loud: 'Answers found in rhyme, are safely locked in time.'

No more than a second after speaking the message, Will heard a low, mechanical thud that originated from somewhere inside the counter. A second later the intricately decorated large brass till began to rise away from the countertop. When it eventually came to a stop, some fifty centimetres above the counter, it revealed a hidden safe, embedded in the front of the till's base. The safe had a number pad and four flip clock-style digits above it, all set to zero.

CHAPTER FIVE

May 14th, 1984, 20:49

The mechanism that revealed the safe was apparently voice-activated. Will had read an article about IBM's work on Tangora; a machine, the article said, that could understand human spoken word. Will was fascinated by the idea of science fiction becoming fact, but he didn't think that this system was even commercially available yet. He crouched down in front of the safe, bringing his head level with the number pad. He waited expectedly for the safe to swing open. When nothing happened, he uttered the words again: 'Answers found in rhyme, are safely locked in time' – hoping that somehow the coded message would also miraculously enter the correct digits for him. Unfortunately, he wasn't quite that lucky.

By this point, Will was certain that the shop owner knew that the two men in tweed jackets were coming for him – or, more accurately, for the mysterious timepiece now sitting in Will's jacket pocket. They must have been looking for this safe as well. The thought sent a shiver of dread down his spine. What he was less certain of was why the shop owner had chosen to give him the watch at all or why he'd gone to such convoluted lengths to pass him a hidden message. No matter the importance of the message, Will just hoped it would explain what this watch really was and what it had done to Abigayle.

The safe was mounted in a cast-iron frame, painted in glossy racing-green paint, one of many coats over the years judging by the visible layers that framed each one of the safe's imperfections. The metal was substantial and formed an unsuspecting base for the till when recessed against the countertop. Looking below the counter, Will could see that the whole thing was bolted to the floor and made for an incredibly strong construction. Forcing the safe open was out of the question. Will was no safecracker – he struggled to get into a bag of Opal Fruits – so his only option was to find the four-digit code.

The shop was dimly lit, save for the flickering light on the countertop, which made searching the place a challenge. On tiptoes, with his back arched upwards, he leaned across the shop owner's body, taking care to avoid touching him, and turned on a lamp situated behind the counter. He let out a muted scream of fright when the shop owner's face was suddenly illuminated only centimetres away from his own as he pulled the lamp cord. The lamp cast a warm glow across the area around the counter and threw dim green hues on the ceiling through its dark green glass shade. He had wanted to avoid using it for fear it would draw too much attention should someone look into the shop from the street, but he had no choice. In any case, two men had murdered a man and ransacked the whole shop without anyone noticing, so he was fairly sure no one would pay much attention to a dim light.

He began by examining the counter, checking every scrap of paper that might have numbers scrawled on them. Thankfully, the countertop was clear aside from the stack of invoices, so Will was spared the task of looking through sheets of blood-soaked paper. The underside of the counter had numerous drawers, nooks and crannies, most of which were stuffed with books, notepads, ledgers and various loose scraps of paper. Just as much paper covered the floor, thrown there when the attackers had carried out their search.

Will was extremely thorough, searching through anything of interest, and took almost an hour doing so. He was becoming concerned about how long he was spending at the scene and had only found a few scraps that had some potential, but he couldn't help but think he was clutching at straws. It had always been a long shot.

Why would the old guy go to such effort to keep the safe hidden, only to keep the combination written down nearby?

But Will was determined and he pressed on with his search: looking under the counter for numbers carved into the wood and taking out every drawer to check that there was nothing taped to the bottoms of them. The one place he'd been hoping to avoid completely was the only place he had yet to check: the shop owner's pockets. Searching a corpse was an experience he hoped he would never have to repeat, and he had to stop several times to compose himself. The whole encounter gave him chills and was ultimately pointless.

With the combination nowhere in sight, he started to pace back and forth, deep in thought. Abigayle had teased him about his pacing, saying it made him look like a third-rate Columbo. Will conceded to himself that she might have had a point, but he was a big fan of the TV show so didn't find the comparison particularly offensive. Moreover, Will thought that it really did help him think. It got the blood flowing.

After a few minutes, he stopped and pulled the watch out from his pocket, looking for an engraving of some kind. No such luck.

He returned to pacing, holding the watch tightly as its many hands ticked away. The watch had a strong movement, and he could feel the gentle vibration of every second against his palm. At that moment, something clicked in his mind.

The room with all the clocks.

On reflection, it was rather odd that all the clocks had stopped the way they had. The ticking had been almost maddening earlier that day, but every single one was now silent. There must have been two hundred clocks in a room no larger than a pool table.

How had they all stopped? Would the attackers have taken the time to silence every single one during their search?

Will doubted it.

He stepped into the room. The glass display case containing the watches had been smashed open and turned on its side. Splintered wood and shards of glass had scattered across the floor. Some of the clocks had been ripped from the wall and strewn around the room, but the majority seemed to be intact.

The past few hours had passed in a blur and Will had no

idea what time it was. Since the clocks had all stopped and reading the time on the watch in his hand proved far too complex a task in the low light, he turned instead to some of the watches that had fallen out of the display case. He picked up a silver rectangular watch with a metal bangle bracelet strap. He read the time, which, according to the watch, was 7:40. That couldn't be right, Abigayle hadn't returned home from work until just after 7:30 and he had been searching the shop for at least an hour already.

He picked up another from the floor, this time a vintage diver's watch with an orange nylon strap. He checked the time and it too read 7:40. He checked another and another. He checked every watch that he could find and all of them had stopped working. All showing the exact same time.

From his crouched position he scanned the clocks that still clung to the walls around him, and like every other timepiece in the room, they had stopped at precisely 7:40.

An idea struck him just then and he felt a ripple of optimism surge through his body.

Safely locked in time. This was the code for the safe, it must be!

Will returned to the counter and approached the safe. He composed himself and carefully entered seven, four, zero into the number pad.

Nothing happened.

He stared at the numbers and his giddy smile faded with every second of inactivity. After a moment, Will laughed and slapped his forehead. 'It needs four digits! Man, I'm such an idiot.' Though his smile returned, it was quickly replaced with a frown as he pondered how to clear the digits he had already entered. Since there was no delete button on the keypad, he resorted to adding another zero to the end of the combination he had already entered. As he pressed final digit, it was met by a metal thud and a sharp buzzing sound. It was the universal sound of failure.

The code was wrong.

Okay, that wasn't completely unexpected. Don't panic.

Reasoning that the logical thing to do was to add the zero at the beginning rather than the end, he tried again, entering zero, seven, four, zero. His expectation had been higher than ever, but it plummeted when he was greeted once more by the sharp buzz of failure.

All the optimism he'd had a few minutes ago had deserted him. He felt so sure that he'd figured out this part of the puzzle, but now he was overwhelmed by feelings of hopelessness and self-doubt. It then dawned on him that a safe with voice recognition would likely also feature some kind of tamper proofing. He had already entered the incorrect combination twice and he now considered it a certainty that a third strike would be catastrophic.

Stepping back from the safe, he suddenly felt lightheaded and weak at the knees. He steadied himself on the frame of the safe; it was all he could do to stop himself from fainting. He'd been on the go all day and couldn't recall the last time he'd eaten anything.

Maybe he should just hand himself over to the police. Maybe his story wouldn't seem so crazy once they saw the watch and the cyphers and the coded messages. Maybe he should have done that immediately after his encounter with Kevin. He was in no doubt that Kevin would have called the police as soon as he got back to his flat. That would have been about 8 pm., but Will had no clue how much time had passed since then.

Will usually wasn't a watch-wearing kind of guy, something Abigayle never understood. She couldn't leave the house without a watch wrapped around her wrist. On a couple of occasions, she had come rushing back through the front door early in the morning to collect her watch on the rare occasion that she'd forgotten to wear one, something that, ironically, would often make her late for whatever appointment she had been heading to.

Will looked at the watch in his hand. He was unsure if this thing even had the correct time. It took him a moment to decipher the complex arrangement of hands so that he could read it. Thankfully, it did appear to be working and it reported the time to be 21:55. It was unusual to read an analogue watch with twenty-four-hour segments to it – or any timepiece for that matter, having been raised in a country where the time format was only referred to as military time.

Will looked up from the watch, eyes wide with the sudden realisation. 'It's a twenty-four-hour clock!' he said out loud to no one in particular. 'Will, you idiot!'

He turned back towards the safe and entered the four digits: one, nine, four, zero. This time there was a series of metallic thuds and scrapes as metal moved against metal. This was followed by a satisfying, high-pitched bell chime: the universal sound for success.

The safe door swung open, smooth and slow.

CHAPTER SIX

May 14th, 1984, 21:58

The solid metal lining of the safe was far thicker than Will had expected. Despite its relatively large exterior, the internal cavity was no bigger than a shoebox. It was lined with black felt, and the surface seemed to absorb what little light shone into it. It gave it the appearance of a bottomless void, like looking out into space. For a ludicrous moment, Will thought he may have opened a doorway to a parallel dimension. Then again, given the events so far that day, perhaps this wasn't such a farfetched concept.

The safe looked empty and Will felt his heart rate increase and his stomach turn. His eyes soon adjusted, and he could make out the flat rectangular shape of a folder, angled on its end, leaning against the inside of the safe. The dark brown manila folder looked disappointingly insubstantial.

Before removing it, Will stood upright and glanced

around the room, momentarily unsure if he was still alone in the shop. There was no one there, but he couldn't shake the feeling that he was being watched.

He pushed the anxiousness from his mind and reached towards the safe, his outstretched hand trembling. He clenched his hand into a fist, then shook the tension from his fingers. He made another attempt, and when he was within a few centimetres of the folder the silence was broken by the shrill ring of the phone, which hung on the wall behind him. The sudden and deafening sound jolted Will's whole body, causing him to rasp his knuckles on the top of the safe's interior. He groaned in pain and pressed his damaged hand between his thighs.

He let the phone ring out, allowing a little chuckle at himself for being wound so tight. Once more he reached towards the safe, and with his thumb and forefinger he slid the folder out. He took a breath and opened the cardboard cover.

Inside was a laminated ID card and a tissue-thin sheet of paper with a crude pencil-drawn sketch on it. He upturned the folder, hoping something more significant might fall out. This, he knew, wasn't a lot to go on. He had hoped for something concrete after stumbling his way through all the puzzles and coded messages. He took another optimistic look in the safe, but it was definitely empty.

The more interesting of the two items, the ID card, looked to be quite old. The once transparent plastic was scuffed and had yellowed over time, but the beige card inside was still legible. The left side listed a number of the man's personal details, printed in dark red ink. He was 5'10", 135 pounds, right-handed, suffered from severe hay fever, was partially deaf in his left ear, wore reading glasses, had hazel-brown eyes, dark brown hair and was born on Pigeon Island in the Caribbean on 4th May 1927.

The right side had a black-and-white photograph of a young Afro-Caribbean man wearing dark-rimmed glasses and a geometrically patterned knit tank top over a white shirt and a neat tie. Even though he was far younger, it was clear that the man in the picture was the shop owner.

He looked to be thirty or forty years younger than the dead man next to him. Happier too, and not just because death didn't agree with him. The old shop owner whom he'd met earlier that day cut a disillusioned figure, tired with life. The man in the photograph looked positive, content and confident.

According to the ID, the man's name was Frenz Belingi.

The ID also revealed that Frenz Belingi wasn't always a shop owner; his job title was listed as Extra-dimensional Geohistorian.

What the hell is that?

The back of the ID card bore the same strange symbol he had seen on the invoice and receipt: a clockface with numerous hands of varying lengths fanning out from it. This time, however, it wasn't stamped but printed, revealing the finer details of the symbol. Below it, printed in large, bold font, were the words:

THE OFFICE OF TIME DISSEMINATION

Will had never heard of this agency, but it was apparently part of the intergovernmental organisation known as The International Bureau of Weights and Measures, whose crest and title were printed along the base of the card.

If nothing else, he now had a name. Perhaps he could track down this organisation and get some answers there.

Will turned his attention to the drawing. The thin paper had a slight blue tint. The pencil markings were faded but still clear enough to make out. At first glance it looked as if someone had hand-drawn gridlines for a graph, but now that he was looking more closely, it was clear that it was actually a crude drawing of a brick wall. At the top of the wall was a small, barred window.

Will flipped the paper over. Printed on the back was a vintage crest for the Metropolitan Police force. Perhaps this was originally some form of police administration document. Most of the text was too smudged and faded to read but from what little was legible, it appeared to detail the movement of a prisoner from one cell to another. A man matching Frenz Belingi's description had apparently been moved to an adjacent cell after he was suspected of tampering with the integrity of his previous cell in some way.

The bottom of the paper was dated, but Will could only make out the year: 1940. He turned to look at the body of Frenz Belingi and said, 'Wait a sec, the year nineteen forty. The combination one, nine, four, zero. And all the clocks stopped at seven forty. There's a pattern here, but none of it makes any sense. But then, I *am* talking to a dead man.'

He gently folded the piece of paper and patted down his pockets, looking for an appropriate place to safely store it. He cursed himself when his hand passed over the balled-up gloves in his jacket, one of which had the watch wedged inside.

You know what would have been ideal things to wear at a crime scene, Will? Gloves. Too late now.

He instead pulled the watch from its molten sleeve and replaced it with the paper and the ID card. The watch had cooled completely, and now seemed far too important to just carry in his pocket, so he wrapped the thick leather strap around his wrist. The end of the strap split into two strips, which he tightened into their buckles.

He took one last look around the counter, turned off the lights, regarded the shop owner's body for a moment, making a silent motion of gratitude towards him, and then carefully made his way towards the front of the shop. He reached the bottom of the steps, climbed them two at a time and exited into the narrow alleyway.

He was then struck by a nauseating feeling of déjà vu. Just as he'd experienced the last time he left Frenz Belingi's shop, he saw two figures striding decisively towards him. Their arms swung commandingly at their sides and their target seemed clear. They were both silhouetted by the single working lamp behind them, and Will could clearly see one of the men reach for something inside his coat.

CHAPTER SEVEN

May 14th, 1984, 22:09

Any feeling of exhilaration Will had as he began to untangle the web of mystery surrounding the murder of the shop owner, Frenz Belingi, the discovery of this unusual timepiece and the disappearance of Abigayle evaporated the moment the two figures appeared. He stood hopelessly still as the men closed in.

With his heels together, arms firmly down by his sides, he clamped his eyes shut tight as the figure on the right fumbled around in his jacket pocket. Will didn't move, fully expecting the impact of a bullet fired from the silenced pistol, which must have been pointing at him by now. When he'd stepped out of the shop, the men were only a few paces away from him. The elongated barrel of the gun would be close enough to reach out and touch, certainly. He waited another beat, but he didn't feel the stinging impact of a bullet hitting his chest, didn't hear that distinctive popping sound and the distant reverb he had heard earlier.

He'd been standing completely still for well over ten seconds now. The sound of the approaching footsteps on the cobbled lane had stopped eight seconds earlier. His eyes were shut so tightly that the skin around them had turned pale, creasing into a dozen folds. He knew that he must have looked quite a sight at that moment.

Thankfully, the next sound Will heard was not a bullet but a voice. 'Erm, sir, is everything all right? Are you in any kind of pain? Would you like me to phone an ambulance?' said the gravelly, vaguely Cockney-accented voice.

Will slowly opened his eyes and focused on the two men standing in front of him. He sensed that the voice had come from the one on the left. He looked to be in his late fifties or early sixties, with a full head of grey hair and a grey moustache. He was wearing a black blazer with decorated epaulettes and breast pockets with silver buttons over a white shirt and a neat black tie. He was holding a pointed hat under his arm. The man on the right was younger, not much beyond forty, with short mousey-brown hair. He was wearing a long tan raincoat with a notch lapel over a white shirt with a loosely knotted brown and yellow tie and faintly pinstriped brown trousers. He didn't have a hat under his arm; instead, his arm was outstretched towards Will, holding an identity badge, with a silver eight-pointed star, bound in a leather wallet.

No silenced pistol in sight.

'He doesn't need an ambulance, Mapson. He's just not overly fond of the police,' said the man with the ID. He had an even, stern tone. He placed the ID back in his jacket pocket and continued. 'I'm Detective Inspector Moss. This is Sergeant Mapson. We need to ask you some questions.'

The police had caught up with Will sooner than he'd thought. As he mentally adjusted to this new turn of events, the realisation that he was currently in the process of fleeing from a crime scene – for the second time in almost as many hours – slowly dawned on him. He obviously wasn't guilty of the first crime of murder, but he was very much guilty of theft. He was so wrapped up in his pursuit of answers that he hadn't given a thought to the fact that he had broken into a shop – one that he knew had a dead body inside it – and raided its safe.

There was also the not so insignificant matter of his fiancée being missing, a fact that was also likely to have been reported to the police by now. The jig was up.

Will cleared his throat and his voice wavered as he said, 'So, um, you're cops?' He felt the blood rush to his face as soon as he spoke, his tongue swollen as the words toppled out of his mouth.

'We're police officers, yes. And you're an American, is that right?' said Moss.

'Yes, sir, that I am.'

'What brings you to London?'

'My girlfriend lived here. Erm, that is, I mean, she *lives* here. And I live with her. At her flat.' Will really needed to regain some composure, immediately cursing himself for bringing Abigayle up in the conversation.

'Name?' Moss said.

'Who? Me?'

'Yes. What is your name?' Moss said, beginning to grow irritated. Or suspicious, Will couldn't tell which.

'William Wells.'

DI Moss wrote Will's name down in his notepad and without looking up said, 'Okay, Mr Wells, would you care to tell us what you're doing here at this time of night?'

'Here? Walking down this alley?'

'The shop,' said the one called Mapson, pointing towards Frenz Belingi's shop, 'the one we just saw you come out of. A silent alarm was triggered a little while ago. Seems as though someone was trying to open the safe and used the wrong combination.' Inspector Moss shot Mapson a glare so cold a shiver ran along Will's spine. Mapson had clearly offered up a little too much information.

'Mapson, would you mind securing the scene, please?' Moss said.

'Of course. Sorry, Inspector,' Mapson said with hangdog meekness as he shuffled away.

'As Sergeant Mapson explained in all too much detail,' Moss continued, 'I'm afraid that the safe here has an anti-tamper system installed. It's usually used for banks. Overkill for a place like this, if you ask me, but some people value their security. We phoned the shop to check that it wasn't triggered by mistake but there was no answer. So here we are. Our question for you, Mr Wells, is what exactly are you doing here?'

The short spat between the officers had given Will a moment to collect his thoughts and to try to calm down. He looked Moss in the face, then Mapson, who was standing sentry outside the shop, and back to Moss. 'Ah, that. Well, officers, I'm just a customer. I was here earlier today.'

'All right, but what are you doing here now?'

'Right, right. Well, the owner sold me a watch. He told

me that if I wasn't completely satisfied, I could bring it back for a rebate. Or a refund, I guess you guys would say.'

'Did it not occur to you that it was a little late for the shop to be open?'

'Well yeah, but the owner said to come by any time.' Will cursed himself once more. Why couldn't he just avoid mentioning people that were either dead or missing when talking to the police?

'Oh? So, he's here then?' Moss asked.

'Who?'

'The owner. Is the owner in his shop?'

'Um, it's hard to say.'

'What does that mean exactly?'

'Well, the store is unlocked, but it's pretty dark inside. I called out to the owner, but I didn't get an answer. So, I left. That's when I bumped into you guys.'

Moss considered this information for a moment, glancing at Mapson briefly before turning back to address Will. 'If you don't mind my saying so, sir, there's something about your behaviour that strikes me as a little odd. Even for a Yank.' Moss held his hands up in mock apology. 'But it's in my nature to be suspicious. Part of the job, I suppose. So, to satisfy my curiosity, why don't we go have a little look inside and get to the bottom of all this?'

'Don't you guys need a warrant for that or something?'

'No, no need for that. After all, the shop is open for business. Isn't that right, Mr Wells?'

Will gulped audibly. 'You know what, on second thoughts I might just keep the watch after all, so I'll just get out of your hair.'

'Not so fast, sunshine, you're not going anywhere. Come

on, inside. Mapson, don't let the Yank out of your sight.'

Mapson nodded. 'Very good, sir.'

Inspector Moss slid his pen neatly inside his notepad, straightened the elasticated fabric strap precisely and returned the bundle to his jacket pocket. 'After you, Mr Wells,' he said.

Mapson took Will by the upper arm and led him into the shop, with Moss close behind. This was now the third time Will had been into the shop and the fifth time up and down the steps just beyond the entrance. It had all become eerily familiar. He felt as though he knew intimately how each step creaked and their distinctive refrain, each one singing under the weight of the three men as they descended. He was well acquainted with the feel of the bare wooden banister as he ran the tips of his fingers along its smooth surface.

When they reached the bottom, Moss and Mapson both retrieved torches from their belts, switched them on and swept their beams over the scene. Moss looked across the ransacked shop interior, turning back to Will and saying, 'What the hell happened in here?'

'I don't know. Really. It wasn't like this when I was here earlier today. I mean, it was messy but not *this* messy.'

'Strange that you didn't think to mention this when we were outside.'

'I know how this looks, but I had nothing to do with any of it, I swear.'

'Well, we'll see. Won't we?'

'Whoever it was, they certainly did a number on this place,' Mapson added.

'Mapson, you and the Yank wait here. I'm going to go check on the owner,' said Moss. He walked precariously towards the back of the shop.

He soon came across the motionless form of the shop owner, Frenz Belingi, and called out, 'Sir, can you hear me? Is everything okay? We're police officers. Your alarm system sent us an alert earlier and…' His words trailed off as he got close enough to understand that he wasn't talking to a sleeping or drunk man; he was talking to a dead man.

Moss pivoted, shot Will a penetrating look and said, 'Mapson, please place Mr Wells under arrest. I'm calling it in. This is a now murder scene.'

CHAPTER EIGHT

May 14th, 1984, 22:31

At DI Moss's request, Will had been handcuffed by Mapson – who did so almost apologetically – and held in one of the side rooms of the shop until backup arrived to secure the scene.

Within ten minutes of DI Moss making the call, six marked police cars had arrived. Twenty minutes after that a boxy unmarked van from the coroner's office and another from the forensics department rolled through the police barricade and half a dozen men in white suits began collecting evidence.

From across the room, Moss gave Mapson a firm nod, at which point Mapson took Will by the arm and led him through the shop door. Outside, the lane was awash with flashing blue lights from the police cars at either end. Will could see his tall, distorted shadow performing a frenzied dance across the buildings around him as the lights pulsed.

The scene was raucous with the sounds of boots on the cobbled street and hurried voices. Mapson led Will out towards the main street, where they ducked under a strip of blue-and-white tape, which was lifted by a uniformed sentry as they passed.

As he angled his head to step under the tape, Will caught a glimpse of a familiar sight out of the corner of his eye. He turned his head for a closer look as he was taken across the narrow footpath and, sure enough, parked on the other side of the street was a metallic-brown Rolls-Royce. He couldn't tell if the figure was still sitting in the back of the car, but he could see the driver, motionless, with both hands on the wheel. His flat cap was tipped low, the amber streetlights casting a shadow over his eyes. A cigarette hung loosely in his lips. As he took a drag, the glowing tip momentarily illuminated his face and Will could see that the driver's eyes were firmly locked on him.

A large crowd had also gathered at the scene and Will could feel their disapproving eyes on him and could hear murmurs of speculation and disgust. The crowd had taken one look at him in handcuffs and their judgement was instant: guilty. To them he was a thug, a thief or a rapist.

Or a murderer.

By the time Will was lowered into the back of a waiting police car, he was glad to be out of sight. Sergeant Mapson closed the door behind him, skirted around the car and climbed into the driver's seat. When the door slammed shut, the silence inside the car was deafening. Will sat in the back of the police car for a few minutes, with the crowd still fixated and looking in through the glass at him. He felt like an attraction at a zoo or a freak show.

Mapson had been instructed to wait for DI Moss, who apparently had insisted on booking Will in at the station personally. Moss obviously thought that he had his man and wanted to ensure that everything was handled by the book. Mapson sat quietly in the front while they waited.

'Hey, Sergeant?'

'Probably best you don't talk, son,' Mapson said without looking back.

'Look, I had nothing to do with this. I know it looks bad, but that guy was dead when I got there. All I wanted to do was return the watch I bought.'

'Trust me, this isn't going to help you.'

Will leaned forwards and spoke through the wire-mesh partition. 'You seem like a decent enough guy and I know you know I didn't do this.'

'Oh yeah? What makes you think that?'

'I don't know, gut instinct? I'm pretty sure that's how cops solve most crimes back in the States.'

'Is that a fact? Look, son, I don't get paid to think – especially with my gut – and I don't get paid to talk. I get paid to do what I'm told. And right now, that's placing you under arrest and waiting for the inspector.'

'I can prove my story,' Will said.

'I have a duty to report everything you say to me, understand? So, take my advice and stop talking until you've got a solicitor present.'

'I have a receipt,' Will said, ignoring the advice. 'And the owner, I think he made out an invoice. It'll have the date and time and…' Will was cut off when the front passenger door suddenly swung open. Will hadn't noticed Moss striding out of the alleyway, lifting the tape above his head smoothly, without breaking stride, and climbing into the car. He got comfortable in his seat and raised a hand towards Mapson, who started the engine and pulled away. Bystanders leered into the car as they passed through the crowd.

The three of them sat in silence throughout the drive to the police station, Will with his head hanging low. Every bump and pothole caused his head to bob up and down as if he was nodding to some unasked questions.

Well, this is it. It's all over. I'm sorry, Abby, some rescuer I turned out to be.

He'd become so wrapped up in the excitement of decoding Frenz Belingi's mysterious messages that he'd been sloppy and gotten himself arrested. He had failed Abigayle, and he was ashamed of himself for not doing better by her.

***

It was a short drive to the police station, which was an old Gothic-style building, traditional red brick with large white stone blocks at the corners and surrounding the windows. It had a large mansard roof with moss-covered dark green tiles. At the centre of the building was a tall arched entrance that spanned both the ground and first floors. At the base of the arch was a set of finely carved double doors and above them a selection of ornate sculptures either side of the crest of the Metropolitan Police Department. The sight of the ancient crest made Will think of the thin faded-blue paper with the crude drawing in his jacket pocket.

Sergeant Mapson drove the car past the front entrance of the building, down a side road and pulled up to a set of large metal gates flanked by high brick walls. This was the back entrance, away from the prying eyes of the main road.

They were met at the kerb by an additional officer, who opened Will's door and roughly manhandled him out. Moss rose smoothly from the car, spun on his heels and closed the door all in one movement. Mapson stayed in the driver's seat and pulled away, presumably to park the car and to return to his duties.

The rear of the building was a mix of new and old construction. The eastern wing had been extended or repaired at some point in its recent history. The architecture was far more modern than the rest of the building, built with dull grey concrete panels throughout. It contrasted horribly with the original building. Although not as impressive as the grand front entrance, the rear side still had a lavish, wide doorway with moulded Gothic features. Will could also see that it had a basement level, with small square windows just above street level, each with sturdy metal bars fixed in them.

Moss joined the other officer by the kerb. The two of them led Will into the station through the automatic glass doors. Another recent addition. The modern touches continued into the interior, where the decor belied the older exterior. The walls had a smooth plastered surface and were painted with a government-issue beige. The floors were covered with a matching cream linoleum flecked with brown and orange. Cheap and effective.

The reception was a wide space that had wooden seats lined up along one wall to the right. To the left was a brown oak-effect desk with a large open-office area beyond.

The room also had a faint but distinctive chemical smell. Will had smelled it before. It was unmistakably the public sector's approved brand of cheap disinfectant, used in all hospitals, libraries and every other government-funded building he'd visited while in the UK. Likely bought in bulk and definitely applied liberally.

An older, rotund police officer was sitting behind the desk on the left. He had a full head of hair, greying at the sides, and stubby fingers with nails chewed back so short that they were barely visible. Perhaps from boredom. Or a nervous disposition.

He looked towards Will, DI Moss and the other officer as they entered. 'You booking this one in yourself, Howard? This guy must be some kind of celebrity to be worthy of such special attention from you.'

'He's a suspect in the shooting in Spitalfields,' Moss said.

'Caught in the act, was he?'

'Close enough,' Moss offered. 'He was at the scene when we arrived. He's been acting very suspiciously as well, haven't you, Mr Wells?'

'I'm telling you, I didn't do this, but I saw—'

'I think we'll allow the evidence to do the talking if you don't mind,' Moss said. He turned to address the desk sergeant. 'I want Mr Wells processed and placed in holding cell E-1. No funny business. My instructions are to be followed precisely. I don't want to see this guy walk because of some administrative error, understood?'

'Yes, gov,' the desk sergeant said with a firm nod.

'And get Sergeant Mapson to contact the US Embassy. I want to know how long Wells has been in the UK and his current visa status.'

This was what Will was most afraid of. Not a prolonged investigation, not losing his own personal freedom, but of being sent away and never being able to help Abigayle. At least if he was still here, in London, he still had a chance.

Who knows, maybe he could try a jailbreak.

'Will do,' said the desk sergeant, who was seemingly thrilled to have something to do.

'I'm going to head back to the scene,' Moss said. 'No one talks to him until I return.'

With that, DI Moss strode out of the station, the automatic doors sliding closed behind him. To Will the whole episode was reminiscent of saloon doors swinging shut in a western.

He's the sheriff around here, I guess.

The officer stood at Will's side, looked at the desk sergeant after his superior was safely out of earshot and said, 'Who the hell's got his goat? Seems very riled up about this one.'

'I don't know, seems to be as big a pain in the arse with this one as any other case,' replied the desk sergeant. He made a few notes, then spun in his chair, pointing his chin towards the room behind him. 'Bennett?' There was no response. 'Bennett?' he said again, slightly louder this time, but still there was no response. Finally, he bellowed, 'Gary!'

The sound of hurried feet screeching over the linoleum floor preceded Officer Gary, who stepped through the doorway to the side of the sergeant's desk and said, 'Sorry, Sarge, what'd you need?'

'This one needs processing. Put him in E-1.' The desk sergeant then glanced up from his notes. 'DI Moss's orders,' he added with a knowing look. Officer Gary grunted in response, then turned to Will. 'Right then, you're coming with me.'

Will was passed from the officer who had accompanied him into the building to Officer Gary's presumably capable hands. He was pushed through the double doors opposite the entrance and taken into a side room. Officer Gary produced a key, which attached to his belt by a chain, and unlocked Will's handcuffs. Will rubbed his wrists. He'd seen people do that in movies and felt compelled to mimic the action.

Officer Gary then began searching Will, who was asked to raise his arms into a T-position. Gary began patting him down, starting under his arms and moving down towards his hips. When his hands patted Will's jacket pocket, he stopped and took a step back. Will tried not to flinch. Frenz Belingi's sketch was in that pocket. If found, it would prove, at the very least, that he had broken into the safe and stolen its contents.

'Empty your pockets, please, sir,' Officer Gary said.

Will had to think quickly, intentionally reaching into the opposite pocket and pulling out his faux-leather gloves. The palm of the glove had a molten circular scar across it and the toxic plastic smell was thankfully quite faint by this point. Will held it out at arm's length, like it was a contaminated substance, and motioned towards Officer Gary, who took one look at it and said, 'What the bloody hell have you been up to, mate?' He scrunched up his nose in disgust, then retrieved a transparent plastic evidence bag and placed the charred glove inside.

He turned back to Will and was about to continue his search when the sound of a commotion could be heard in the entrance room. Officer Gary opened the door of the processing room and glanced down the hall towards the sounds. He turned back to Will, pointed at him and said, 'You. Don't move.'

CHAPTER NINE

May 15th, 1984, 00:03

Officer Gary hurried out of the room, accidentally knocking the evidence bag with Will's mangled glove inside onto the floor as he passed. He heaved the door, swinging it shut as he rushed into the hallway towards the entrance room. Will saw the evidence bag hit the floor by his feet and thinking quickly he flicked it with the outside of his right foot in the direction of the doorway. This mixture of luck and quick thinking saw the evidence bag skid across the floor, coming to a rest against the doorframe. The door hit the evidence bag with a low thud, preventing it from closing.

Will crept towards the doorway, pulling it open slowly. Some unfathomable impulse made him crouch down, retrieve the long-suffering glove from the evidence bag and place it back in his pocket. He poked his head into the hallway and saw Officer Gary jogging away from him. As the officer pushed open the doors to the reception, the sound of the disturbance in the next room became momentarily clearer. Will only caught a few words from the raised voices, but he was sure that one of them sounded familiar.

Will looked up the other end of the hallway. It was deserted. He skulked out of the room towards the double doors, taking slow and deliberate steps. He could feel his heart rate increasing as he moved down the hallway. With every few steps his head whipped back over his shoulder, his eyes darting frantically side to side. When he reached the doors, he placed his ear against the cold painted surface. The voices became stronger, but not enough for him to make out clearly.

He placed one hand on the sturdy steel door handle and the other flat against the door. Very gently he turned the handle and pushed the door firmly until it began to open. He cracked the door inwards just enough for him to see into the reception room. Moss was no longer there, but the desk sergeant, along with Officer Gary and one other officer, were surrounding a shorter man who was acting erratically. The officers were motioning with their hands for him to calm down. He wasn't being violent, but he was extremely agitated by something, moving from side to side in a misguided effort to get past the officers.

Okay, Abby, I'm going to make a run for it while they're distracted.

The shorter man was speaking quickly and kept repeating variations of 'What have you been doing this whole time since I called you?' and 'A woman's life is in danger!' and 'He could be butchering her as we speak!'

Will couldn't quite make out the man's face behind the officers who were surrounding him. But he knew the voice.

No question. The sudden realisation caused Will to delay for a moment too long.

Gary, who had his back to Will, seemed to detect his presence and he turned and locked eyes with him. He grimaced and began half walking, half running towards him. As Gary approached, a gap opened in the huddle of officers and Will caught a glimpse of the shorter man's face. He already knew the face that the voice belonged to – it was their neighbour, Kevin.

Will took a step away from the doors as Gary pushed through and grabbed him by the back of the neck with one hand. Gary was a big guy, and his hands were like baseball mitts, and almost completely encircled Will's neck. Gary turned Will's head so that the two of them were eye to eye, their faces uncomfortably close.

'Oi! What did I say to you?' Gary said.

'Sorry, I was only…'

Just then, another officer came walking down the hallway, heading towards the reception. Gary summoned the other officer with a nod and said, 'Do me a favour and take this one downstairs.' It was an order, not a question. 'Stick him in E-1 for me while I deal with Miss Marple out there.'

The other officer shrugged and took hold of Will's arm and led him along the hallway. They turned left and then right and right again before heading down a flight of stairs. Will was being passed around between the officers like a toy – it was incredibly demeaning. He felt helpless and in a hopeless situation now that he'd missed his chance to escape.

The stairwell was narrow and steep. The walls were cold and damp. Thick plaster was crumbling away, revealing brittle red brick beneath. As they descended, the light retreated into darkness and the walls appeared to close in even further.

When they reached the bottom of the stairs they emerged into a dark, dank room with lofty ceilings. The room was long and narrow, more like a wide corridor than a room. Along the wall opposite the stairwell was a row of cast-iron bars running its length. Additional sets of bars ran at right angles, dividing the room into seven separate jail cells. Bare copper pipes, deep brown and matted with age, ran across the tops of the walls. A skein of cables and ventilation ducts criss-crossed the ceiling, forming complex patterns. Bulbs hung low on long, braided fabric wires. They provided insufficient light for the room, and the small square barred windows near the ceiling provided little extra illumination from the street beyond. The whole space bore more resemblance to a medieval torture chamber than anything Will had expected from a British jail.

He was taken left from the bottom of the stairs to the cell at the far end of the row. The far wall at the end of the narrow room was constructed from blue-grey concrete blocks. It looked as though it had been closed off recently, perhaps as part of the modern extension that Will had seen when he arrived at the station.

The officer pushed him into the cell and without saying a word closed the heavy metal door, inserted a key into the lock and turned it. There was a high-pitched squeal of protest, metal scraping against metal as the lock slid home. The officer looked at Will with a blank expression before moving off towards the stairs and disappearing out of sight.

His cell had nothing other than a metal-framed bed with a thin mattress along the back wall under one of the small square windows. Will stepped up onto the bed and attempted to peer out through the window two metres above. If not for the fact that the old springs in the bed frame depressed almost to the floor under Will's weight, he might have been able to see out to the street beyond. Instead, he had to pull himself upwards by the metal bars, lifting his feet clear of the mattress, to get an unobscured view.

Outside he could see the car park at the rear of the station. He was surprised to see DI Moss, who was having a one-sided conversation with Sergeant Mapson. He was talking at Mapson rather than with him and in an aggressive manner, waving a finger close to his face to emphasise whatever point he was trying to make. The conversation ended abruptly with Moss climbing into the car parked at the kerb and speeding off. Mapson remained on the pavement, watching Moss's car drive out through the gates at the rear of the car park. He took a moment to compose himself, then walked into the station and out of sight.

Will had never been particularly athletic and before long the muscles in his arms were beginning to burn. He lowered himself down from the window and sank onto the bed.

He heaved a long sigh and took in his new surroundings. The jail cell was quiet aside from the slow dripping of water from one of the many pipes that passed overhead. The sound seemed to scream the events of the day back at him with every harsh, unforgiving drop, and he felt tears of despair welling up in his eyes as he pictured Abigayle's face. He'd failed her, he knew, and he held his head in his hands.

He slumped onto his back and began to dry his tears. His eyes opened slowly, unfocused, meandering around the room, eventually resting on the small square window. He stared at it blankly at first. Then his eyes narrowed and a frown formed as he started to concentrate. When his brain caught up and processed the image he was looking at, he shot bolt upright, wide-eyed in disbelief.

Will rooted around in his jacket pocket and closed his hand around the fragile paper and the rigid ID card. He loathed Kevin, but he had to admit to being rather grateful to the guy for creating such a perfectly timed distraction. His theatrics had prevented Gary from completing his search and likely finding the only thing that might help him find Abigayle.

Will carefully unfolded the paper and pondered the crude sketch. He sprung up from the bed and turned to face the wall in a single, swift movement. Standing with his back pressed against the cold bars of his cell, he compared the drawing with the wall in front of him. There was no doubt that the drawing was a perfect match with the wall he was currently standing in front of.

But what does it mean?

He flipped the page over and began reading the few legible sections of the document. Will could just about make out that the name, address and date of birth of the prisoner were all listed as "Unknown". However, the rest of the description was a perfect match for Frenz Belingi. Apparently, he had spent some time in this very prison; the address at the top of the page confirmed this.

The only other detail that caught Will's eye centred around the prisoner's movement to a different cell. The scrawled handwriting described a prisoner suspected of tampering with his previous cell, E-5. Will looked around for any kind of markings denoting the cell he was currently in.

He looked through the bars, straining his eyes to see the concrete floor outside his cell. Tilting his head to read the upside-down characters, he saw, in white paint, E-1. Will cursed under his breath and pressed his head against the bars, frustrated. As he looked down at the lettering, he was just about able to make out a chipped layer of yellow paint below it. The paint was faint, so Will crouched down to better read it. Squinting in the low light, he could make out the old lettering: E-5.

He turned his attention back to the paper, which stated that the prisoner was moved to the adjacent cell, E-4. Will looked to the cell on his left, but the lettering outside it indicated E-2 in the newer white paint and E-6 in the older yellow paint.

What the hell happened to cell E-4?

Will flipped the paper over to the drawing and studied it more closely. The only discrepancy he could see was in the bars. The bars in his cell were horizontal, cylindrical poles, moulded into the stone, but the drawing showed what looked like flat strips of metal that crossed each other at right angles, like a lattice, secured to the wall with bolts or rivets. The shape and proximity of the window to the ceiling was almost exact in both, however. The only other feature of note in the drawing was one brick, which had been shaded slightly darker so that it subtly stood out from the rest. In the drawing, this one brick sat two across and four rows down from the base of the square window.

Will stood on the bed once more and traced his hand across the wall.

Two bricks across and four bricks down.

His hand stopped on one brick that at first glance

appeared no different to the bricks that surrounded it. However, upon closer inspection, Will could see that the mortar around this brick was a slightly different colour. He prodded the mortar with his finger and a generous chunk crumbled and fell away from the wall. He spun his head around instinctively to check that he wasn't being watched, grateful to see that he wasn't. Returning to the brick, he began scraping, prodding and probing until most of the remaining mortar had fallen away.

The brick was now loose and could be wiggled around in the enlarged cavity in which it sat. Will slid his fingers around it carefully and pulled it free. The displaced air around the brick created a mini dust storm, spraying fine powder directly into Will's nasal passages. His attempt to wave away the onslaught of dust proving futile, he coughed and spluttered and sneezed in quick succession. When the dust eventually cleared, Will could just barely make out the leather spine of a small book lodged in the cavity left by the brick. He pulled the book free. It was small, pocket-sized, but had weight, which hinted at the fine quality of the paper and the binding. He wiped the layer of powdered mortar from the cover to reveal something that he had seen before: the now-familiar many-handed clockface symbol from Frenz Belingi's shop.

CHAPTER TEN

May 15th, 1984, 00:43

Will was balanced precariously on the mattress, which nodded erratically to one side or the other, seemingly whenever he moved. He very gently stepped back down to the ground and sat on the bed, holding the unassuming book in both hands, like a delicate, precious treasure.

He took a deep breath, narrowed his lips and blew the remaining traces of dirt and dust from the book's cover. He traced his forefinger around the perimeter of the clockface symbol and the words below it, all of which were embossed into the leather and finished with glistening metallic red and gold ink.

THE OFFICE OF TIME DISSEMINATION
TIMEKEEPER'S GUIDEBOOK

As he looked at the book, a nagging feeling that had been growing slowly inside him came to the surface.

Why does everything that's happened today feel as if it's part of some elaborate plan? And that Abigayle and I are just pawns?

He didn't believe in coincidence. Fate, maybe, when things fell in his favour, but not coincidence. He'd seen a lot of unbelievable things in the past few hours, but he refused to believe that somehow Frenz Belingi had known that he was going to walk into his shop that day and that the two men with their weapons would follow. That he would then return and open the safe. And on top of that, that he would then be arrested and placed in this very cell. The very cell he needed to be in, in order to find the book he now held in his hand.

Will looked again at the strange watch hoping for answers but found he was still confused by its many symbols, hands and dials, and what power it actually holds.

He was being moved around like a piece on a gameboard. This was almost literally the case since he'd been in police custody: he'd been marched from one place to the next, passed from one officer to another and moved from room to room, until he had ended up here, exactly where he needed to be. He didn't like any of it. But perhaps he didn't need to like it so long as whatever was going on helped bring Abigayle back.

He had his doubts that whatever forces had been pulling the strings also had the same motivations as him, but what choice did he really have? He was locked in a jail cell, faced with a possible murder charge and the disappearance of his fiancée. He performed a quick calculation in his head and it all added up to one thing: press forwards and get answers about what this thing on his wrist really was.

Will shook the brewing existential crisis free from his mind and refocused on the task at hand.

He opened the book. His hands were visibly trembling as he did so. The dry leather of the cover creaked and crackled as it swung open, years of disuse being broken loose. The pages of the book were yellowed and worn but were made from quality paper stock. The ink of a handwritten note inside the front cover was slightly frayed but legible. It read:

Cpt. 1, sec 9, sub - sec 40. Sincerely, N.O.

One, nine, four, zero. Those numbers again. And N.O., who could that be referring to?

Will reread the note three times over, to make sure there wasn't some kind of code hidden in the elegant handwritten text. When he was satisfied he wasn't missing anything, he began flicking through the pages until he reached the correct section of the book.

He arrived on page twenty-seven. At the top of the page, in small text, was the chapter title: "Chapter One – Best Practice and Safe Operation." On the opposite page he found section nine, titled: "Safety Protocols and Input Conventions." Below that, there was a short paragraph of text followed by a line diagram of a watch with a striking resemblance to the one currently wrapped around Will's wrist. The diagram appeared to highlight various features of the watch, each feature numbered and annotated with in-depth descriptions.

Whenever the book referenced the watch, it was always referred to as "the Timepiece" and was typed in bold text.

When he'd reached the end of section nine, sixteen and a

half pages further into the book, a mouthful of air escaped his lips in an exasperated fashion. Barely any of it made any sense to him, and the parts that did didn't seem to offer any further clues to why any of this was happening. All he had learned was how to set the time, which already appeared to be correct anyway.

When he flicked back to the start of the chapter, he saw it. He rolled his eyes and looked up to the ceiling, frustrated with himself that he had missed it the first time. Stamped into the margin next to the opening paragraph of text for section nine was the same circular many-handed clockface symbol.

He quickly fumbled around for his wallet.

Had it been taken from me when I was arrested?

He felt a surge of relief as his hand passed over the square outline of his wallet in his pocket. He fished it out and shuffled through the random cards and bits of paper that seemed to accumulate inside it. After a moment of searching, he located what he was looking for.

Will held the book flat across his knee and placed the cypher from Frenz Belingi's shop over the paragraph of text nearest the symbol. He slid the cypher down the page until the symbol on it and the page aligned. With this done, once again a message was revealed:

Seven Septum MCMXL

He settled down on the mattress and took his time over the message. Fortunately, Will had studied Latin for a semester in college years earlier, so the last part of the message was clear and entirely unsurprising. MCMXL was 1940 in Roman numerals. The first word was also obvious, but the second word had him stumped momentarily. *Septum,* he knew, was Latin for the number seven.

So, it's a date: 7, 7, 1940, or 7th July 1940.

He returned to the book, buzzing with excitement and thumbed through to the contents pages until he found what he was looking for. The latter part of chapter one covered the process of setting the time, day, month and year on the watch. From his studying of the book, he now knew that the outer ring of digits on the watch face was used to set the minutes and hours – the hours were in twenty-four segments. The desired day was set by using the ring inside the outermost ring, and this ranged from one to thirty-one. The ring inside this was for setting the month and ran from one to twelve.

The innermost ring was used for setting years, and this was the most perplexing. While the surrounding rings required aligning the corresponding hand with the desired number, the innermost ring featured a tripled-ended hand, which rotated in unison. Each of the three hands was differently coloured and had tiny letters etched into them. The blue hand featured the letters AD, the red hand had BC and the green hand had a circle. Each hand was slightly misaligned from the next, preventing all three hands from lining up exactly with any one digit of the innermost ring. This ring ranged from zero to nine. According to the instructions, this input worked in a similar way to the dial on a safe. You were to begin by setting your first digit in either AD or BC; this would determine the time period desired. After setting the first digit with either the blue or red hands, the remaining digits for the year would be entered with the green hand in sequence. Each digit in the innermost ring would briefly light up in the colour of the hand used to confirm entry. Once the year had been entered, the final instruction dealt with disabling the failsafe, which required sliding the crown along a small G-shaped track on the side of the Timepiece. Once the crown had reached the tail of the G, the Timepiece was primed, and the crown needed only to be depressed inwards like a button to activate it. As Will held the Timepiece, he could see that the crown was in the failsafe position.

If only the Timepiece was in this position when Abigayle had held the watch.

Will read through the steps three more times and when he was comfortable with the process, he rolled his sleeve back, revealing the Timepiece on his right wrist. It looked even more extraordinary now than when he had first laid eyes on it. The crystal glass of the lens appeared even more crisp and clear, the brass case glistened and sparkled like new, the dials and crown moved smooth and sure. It was as if the Timepiece itself had come to life, glowing with anticipation for the action to come.

He carefully and methodically entered the date, 7th July 1940, into the Timepiece by rotating each dial, which produced a satisfying tick with each numeric alteration, discernible only through the tips of Will's fingers. He took his time, checking every number twice before committing its entry. He placed his thumb and forefinger around the crown and prepared to slide it away from the failsafe position. As he started to slide it over the top curve of the G, he stopped suddenly.

Something wasn't right.

He moved his hand away from the Timepiece and returned to the message in the small book.

Why use septum?

He thought for a moment before the answer came to him from some seldom used corner of his memory.

Of course, it's not a number at all, it's a month!

Will recalled that the word *septum* was not only Latin for the number seven but was also the root from which the word *September* was derived. He recollected how, in the original Roman calendar, there were only ten months and September was the seventh month rather than the ninth. It wasn't until later that January and February were added, bringing the total to twelve as we have today.

So, it's not 7, 7, 1940; it's 7, 9, 1940. 7th September 1940. Assuming they're not using US date formatting at least…

Will carefully made the adjustment to the month input.

He wasn't sure what to expect when he pressed the button. He had hoped that he would press it and reappear in that strange room that he and Abigayle had seen before she disappeared. He hoped he would find her there and could bring her home. Then he would destroy the watch so the two of them could get on with their lives.

He stood up from the bed and slid the *Timekeeper's Guidebook* into his back trouser pocket. He looked at the Timepiece once more, double- and triple-checking his time input, and then placed his index finger over the activation button. He closed his eyes and began to breathe in and out rapidly, as if he was about to dive underwater.

Just as he was about to depress the button, he heard tyres screech past his window and come to a stop close to the entrance of the police station, somewhere above him. He climbed back up onto the bed and levered himself up by the window bars as he had done earlier. Squinting into the dimly lit police car park outside, he could just about make out two men as they climbed out of a car that was idling by the kerb.

One tall, one short. Both wearing tweed jackets and flat caps. Both walking into the police station.

CHAPTER ELEVEN

May 15th, 1984, 01:16

Even in the low lighting outside his cell window, Will could tell instantly that he was looking at the same men who had pushed their way past him as he left Frenz Belingi's shop for the first time the previous day. The taller of the two men began to shift his gaze towards Will, who instinctively dropped down from the window and out of sight.

He came crashing down onto the bed with all his weight. The thin mattress and the old, worn bed frame gave way and Will's feet burst through to the floor. Rusted springs sprung in all directions, deflecting off the walls and in between bars. As he landed, he stumbled backwards, catching the back of his calves on the remains of the bed frame and falling to the ground. The whole event seemed to happen in slow motion, but it cut through the silence in a calamitous cacophony. There was no way that everyone in the building – including the two new arrivals – hadn't heard the commotion.

Shit, shit, shit, shit!

Will quickly picked himself up and dusted himself down. To his right, he could hear a voice echoing down the stairs from above. The voice was aggressive and moving closer. Before long the voice was accompanied by footsteps that grew louder and louder on the stairs. Someone had obviously heard his fall and wasn't too pleased with having to come down into the cells to investigate.

One of the officers, he thought, but it could just as easily be the two gunmen, on their way to finish the job. It was hard to believe that they would walk into a police station and stroll into secure areas just like that. Could they have friends inside the police force? Or maybe the two men were police officers themselves.

Refocusing on the task at hand, he checked his right wrist again and ensured that the Timepiece hadn't been affected by the fall. He rechecked the time he'd entered, and it was exactly as the hidden message had instructed.

He was having trouble coming to terms with what the Timepiece was, not quite willing to accept what all the evidence seemed to be pointing to.

Be serious, Will, it's not a time machine. Because time machines don't exist.

He was pretty certain of that. But then he'd been certain that rooms couldn't transform around him and whisk his wife-to-be away before his very eyes. If this were a time machine and he really was about to travel to 1940, he had no idea what he would find there, but he decided that whatever it was, it couldn't be any worse than being at the noisy end of a gun.

Will gripped hold of the crown and completed the movement, tracing around the G, disabling the safety mechanism. He clamped his eyes shut, took another series of rapid deep breaths and pressed the crown inwards, just like a button. It moved with a satisfying click.

A few seconds passed without incident and Will allowed his eyes to crack open ever so slightly. Then he felt it: the same surge of energy and sensation of warmth that had spread through him when he and Abigayle had first used the Timepiece in her flat. A visible, rippling sphere pulsed out from his wrist and began tracing across the walls, floor and ceiling of his small jail cell. The chipped and peeling green-grey paint on the wall to Will's right appeared to repair itself in front of his eyes, gaining more of the green hue that had been lost over time. It now looked smooth, newly painted. The bars behind and to his left were no longer rusted and bent; they too looked almost like new.

The most striking change occurred directly in front of Will, as the sphere passed over the concrete block wall. It didn't just change in appearance; it disappeared altogether. In its place was another set of bars, identical to those in front and behind him. Beyond the bars, the room stretched outwards, doubling its current length. More rows of bars stacked up, adding another four or five cells.

When Abigayle's flat had transformed, it had all happened so fast and so unexpectedly that Will didn't take any time to fully process it. Thinking back, it all felt like a lucid dream. Now, though, he was able to appreciate the effect. This time it wasn't just the visual change that struck him; all his senses now seemed to be heightened in some way.

September 7th, 1940, 01:18

Once the sphere had expanded off into the distance and out of sight, he found the smell of this new place was strikingly different. A faint whiff of burning timber hung in the air among the gloom and the dust. The room felt colder, and the hairs stood up on the back of his neck and arms. There was a breeze passing through the windows of his cell, which he noticed no longer had glass panes set inside them. The vertical bars were also no longer there; instead, there was a set of wooden shutters constructed with neat latticework over a sturdy wooden frame. They were swinging back and forth as the wind circulated outside. Will reached out and touched the bars in front of him: they were cold and hard and very much real.

This was no illusion.

He looked down at the Timepiece, which was humming and vibrating at an almost imperceptibly high frequency. He moved his hand close to it and already he could feel the warmth emanating from it. So far, the leather strapping was insulating his arm from the heat.

As Will's eyes adjusted to his new surroundings, he looked down at the painted lettering on the floor outside his cell. It now clearly indicated E-5. Looking to his right, across the cell that had miraculously appeared, he could see that it was marked E-4.

He caught some sudden movement out of the corner of his eye. A figure sat up from the bed that was against the wall and below the window to his right. The figure swung its legs over the end of the bed and planted them evenly on the floor, before rising from the bed and beginning to walk over to the bars between the two cells.

The figure stepped into the light, and Will was all at once reassured and shocked to see a familiar face. The man looked younger than the last time he'd seen him. His eyes were bright and full of life. His hair and beard were darker, showing no sign of grey. His teeth were straight and brilliantly white in his smiling mouth. His ebony skin was smooth and unblemished. He looked exactly like the man pictured on the ID card Will had found in the safe.

Will was standing face to face with the shop owner, Frenz Belingi.

CHAPTER TWELVE

September 7th, 1940, 01:19

Will backed away from the bars. The two men both stood for a long moment, just staring at each other, assessing what might happen next. Sizing each other up. Until now, Will had refused to believe what the Timepiece really was, despite all he'd seen. Now that he found himself in the presence of not only a dead man – but a far younger version of one – he could no longer deny it. Crazy as it all seemed.

So, this is a time machine. And now I'm a time traveller. Neat.

Will was still staring at Frenz Belingi when the latter broke the silence. 'You look lost, my friend. What are you doing here?' His smile had disappeared.

'I was about to ask you the same thing,' Will said.

'Do you know who I am?'

'I…I think so, yeah.'

'You aren't supposed to be here. I was told to expect

a woman.'

'Look, buddy, if you were expecting some kind of late-night liaison, then you're shit out of luck, okay?'

Frenz bristled slightly, then said, 'No, my friend, you misunderstand me. Tell me, how did you come to be here, now?'

'It was you. You brought me here with your goddammed cryptic messages!' Will said, adrenaline pumping through his veins.

The man paused and stepped away from the bars, frowning in concentrated thought. His hands were on his hips and he was shaking his head lightly. Eventually he turned back to the bars and said, 'My name is Frenz Belingi.' He spoke with the same smooth manner and light Caribbean accent as his older counterpart had.

'I know,' Will said. 'We've already met. Well, you were much older and—'

'Of course, of course. And you are?'

'William Wells, out of Le Claire, Iowa. Nice to meet you.'

'It is a pleasure to meet you, Mr Wells, despite the circumstances.'

'Yeah, about that. Would you mind explaining what the hell kind of *circumstance* this is?'

'You said that I gave you the Timepiece, correct?'

'Yeah. Well, you sold it to me actually,' Will said.

'Interesting. Something in the plan has obviously altered and you've been sent instead. Have you been told nothing of why you're here?'

'Nothing. I was given the watch, then it made my fiancée disappear. Then all those coded messages led me here.'

A look of pleasant surprise appeared on Frenz's face. 'Do

you mean to say that you found your way here with only those messages to guide you?'

'Well, yeah, so what?' Will said.

'It's impressive. That or I've gotten lax in my old age. Still, this changes nothing.'

'Changes nothing? The woman I love is missing! That's all that matters right now.'

'Be that as it may, I still need your help.'

'I was actually hoping you could help me, not the other way around.'

'You really have no idea of the significance of what you have strapped to your wrist, do you?'

Will glanced at the Timepiece, still shimmering on his arm. 'Well, no. Nobody told me exactly what this thing really is.'

'If you had been told what the Timepiece really was, would you have believed it?'

'No, probably not. Is this really a time machine?'

'Well, time machine is a rather simplistic term, but yes, it is. How did your fiancée disappear, what happened exactly?'

'I don't know. She was holding the Timepiece and it activated somehow. Then this glowing thing on the table made a noise which must have startled her because she dropped it. I caught it, but when I did it must have deactivated. When I turned back to Abigayle, she was gone. You need to help me get her back.'

'Before we do anything, we must get out of here,' Frenz said in a noncommittal voice.

'Are you serious? We're not going anywhere until we get her back!'

'Please, my friend, you need to calm down.' Frenz

regarded Will carefully for a moment. 'You really weren't told anything about this plan, were you?'

'No, I wasn't! All I wanted was to get Abigayle something nice for our anniversary and now she's missing and I'm in jail. In two different time periods, apparently!'

'Okay, any moment now,' Frenz said, looking at his watch.

'What're you…' Will's words trailed off as a low-pitched whine rang out from somewhere outside the prison.

The sound began quiet and distant, then it transformed, becoming higher-pitched and seeming to travel towards them, getting closer and closer. It moved at speed until it was on top of them, right outside the cell window. The sound was deafening when it was close, but as quickly as the sound had risen it fell away. After a brief pause the sequence repeated itself once more, starting distant and low and rumbling closer. It was only the second time Will had heard an air raid siren in person. The first time he'd heard one was in history class in the fifth grade. Will said, 'Is that what I think it is?'

'Yes, I'm afraid so. This is 1940, London. There is a war on, after all.'

'Okay, okay. I see what you're doing. You're just trying to scare me into helping you get out of here. I may be new to this whole time-travel thing, but I've read enough comics and seen enough movies to know how this stuff works. So, nice try, but this building is still standing in 1984, so we're safe in here for another forty-four years.'

'I'm afraid this is no trick. We are both in imminent danger,' Frenz cautioned.

'Look, Mr Belingi, I already told you: this building is still standing in 1984. We're fine.'

'Please call me Frenz. And tell me, Will, was my cell still standing?'

'What?'

'My cell. Was it still there in 1984?'

'Well, no. There was just a wall. But it was taken out for improvements to the building. Right?' The more he spoke, the more Will lost confidence in his own words.

'Wrong. At 01:27 am. a German high-explosive shell will drop from a Nazi warplane and hit this building. The east wing will be completely destroyed.' Frenz glanced at his watch again. 'The time is now 01:21 am. We have six minutes to get out of here.'

'What? Why the hell did you have me come back here only ten minutes before this place is going to explode?'

'I was expecting my rescuer to be aware of the plan and prepared to act quickly.'

'Why even put yourself in a building that's about to get blown up in the first place?' Will said.

'It's all part of the plan,' Frenz said, speaking more quickly now. 'My cell is destroyed and as far as the authorities are concerned, I am dead. I no longer exist. Being an invisible man has its advantages.' The siren continued to wail in the background.

Will looked down at the Timepiece, vibrating on his wrist, then back up to Frenz Belingi. 'We're not going anywhere until I have your word that you'll help me get Abigayle back.'

'William,' Frenz said, moving closer to the bars with his arms outstretched. 'We can talk about this when—'

'No, we talk about this now. Don't think I won't let this building collapse on both of us! If I get us out of this, do I have your word that you'll tell me exactly what this thing is and how we use it to find Abigayle?'

Frenz blinked frantically, shook his head, cleared his throat. 'Very well. You have my word, my friend,' he said with conviction. 'I can see how much this person means to you. If you help *me,* I will do whatever is in my power to help *you.*'

Will held Frenz's gaze for a moment and could see sincerity in his eyes. 'Okay,' Will said. 'Tell me what I need to do.'

'This building wasn't always a prison and these bars weren't always here. So, it's simple, we must transit to one of those times. A time when there are no bars or guards and we can walk out of here unmolested. Any time in the mid-1920s should do it. Then we both return to your original time and begin our search for your fiancée.'

'I like that plan. But let's be quick about it.'

'Agreed. Now that you've activated the Timepiece, it's likely that the Timekeepers will be tracking our location as we speak. It won't take them long to find us.'

Frenz approached the bars and invited Will to move the Timepiece towards him. Frenz began inputting values in preparation for their escape. He flinched when he first touched the Timepiece, which was now searing hot. 'Dammit. It shouldn't be running this hot,' Frenz said. Covering his hand with his sleeve, he resumed his work.

'Wait, who are the Timekeepers?' Will asked.

'They are the people I used to work for. And they aren't the kind of people you would wish to cross paths with. Especially if they find you with the Timepiece on your wrist.'

'These people, they don't tend to wear tweed suits and

flat caps by any chance, do they?'

'That is part of the organisation's dress code, yes. Why?'

'Well, in that case, we can't go back to 1984,' Will said.

'Why do you say that?' Frenz asked, looking up from the Timepiece.

'Well, they walked into the police station right before I turned this thing on. But that was back in 1984, so we'll be safe here and in the 1920s, right?'

Four minutes remaining.

Panic flashed across Frenz's face. He backed away from the bars and scurried to the bed in his cell. He flipped the mattress up on its side, revealing a journal. Randomly sized sheets of paper were jutting out in all directions. The cover of the journal was secured shut with a clasp, which Frenz quickly released. He began flicking through the journal at speed, running his index finger up and down the pages. Occasionally he would pull out a loose sheet of paper and examine both sides of it before discarding it and moving on to other pages.

'What are you looking for?' Will asked. 'I thought you said we needed to get out of here?'.

'That is very true, we do, but not in the way I had originally planned. The Timekeepers have found us sooner than I thought and there's only one stairwell leading to this cellar. We're trapped down here, and they know it. They'll be waiting for us at the top and it'll be like shooting fish in a barrel.'

Two minutes remaining.

'Those guys with the guns? They're here? In 1940?'

'Yes. They followed you here,' Frenz snapped.

'How is that even possible? Isn't this watch one of

a kind?'

'It is. Look, I don't have time to explain now. Give me a moment, please.' He continued to flick through the pages of the journal before finding what he was looking for. 'Here!' Frenz rushed back to the bars between Will's cell and his own. He reached through the bars and grabbed a hold of Will's wrist.

'Hey! What the hell are you doing?'

'We need to go to 1872,' Frenz said. He was busy at work, twisting and turning, sliding and switching settings on the Timepiece. 'Are you ready?' Frenz asked.

'Ready? No, I'm not read—' As Will began his protestations, a shot rang out and a bullet fizzed over both of their heads, cracking against the wall to Will's right. The gunshot had that same strange, dull popping sound Will had heard at Frenz Belingi's shop.

Will turned to his left, where he saw two men emerging from the stairwell, charging towards them with their guns raised. Another bullet pinged off the cell bars. Will ducked and turned back to Frenz, who was still gripping hold of his arm.

The gunmen stopped and the tall one said in calm, perfectly accented English: 'Neither of you move or the next shot will be a touch lower. Understood?'

Ten seconds remaining.

'Will,' Frenz whispered, 'we have to go.'

Will gave a shallow, barely discernible nod. The sound of large engines in the skies overhead and bombs exploding around them shook the floor as Frenz pressed the crown on the side of the Timepiece. Warmth rushed along Will's arm and pulsed outwards in a stream of energy.

CHAPTER THIRTEEN

February 5th, 1872, 01:25

A sphere of energy expanded from the Timepiece until it enveloped the whole room. Will had expected to find the room transformed into something newer and crisper – a chance to see this building not too long after it had been built, in a time before it had become old and run down. As he glanced around the room, however, he found the opposite to be true. The whole space was darker and even more musty and damp than it had been in 1940. A rank smell hung thick in the air. It was the putrid smell of decomposition. Something had died down here recently. Or long ago, depending on your perspective.

Will's feet suddenly felt cold and wet and a chill ran up his spine. He heard the sound of running water, quickly followed by a splash. In front of him the short, plump gunman had stumbled over a floating wooden crate, which hadn't been there a moment ago. Will tumbled over it and fell into the water. The subsequent splash was so large that water struck the ceiling some three metres above.

It was only now that Will looked down to find that he and Frenz were standing in water up to the middle of their shins. That explained the smell; the cellar was flooded. As well as the crate that had surprised one of their assailants, Will could see other things floating in the water. There was perished fruit and vegetables, animal faeces and any number of bloated carcases. All these things were now bobbing up and down in the wake caused by the gunman's disturbance to the otherwise calm waters. Waves rippled out from the origin and reflected back off the walls, colliding with one another in a beautifully precise pattern.

The fallen gunman was being helped to his feet by his lanky companion but appeared to be without a gun. The short one then plunged back down into the water and began rooting around, searching the shallow but opaque green pool for his weapon. His search was hampered further by the lack of light. The windows at the top of the walls were no longer there and the only light appeared to be coming from the two stairwells to their left and right. The stairwell to the right was a new addition – or old, technically speaking. Frenz had known that their only means of escape from the prison room would have been the single stairwell from which the two gunmen had emerged. Even with one of them down and unarmed, they surely wouldn't have been able to pass them and climb the stairs before they had been shot. Now, however, there was an additional stairwell they could use, and they were far closer to it than their assailants. Somehow Frenz had known about that too.

The instant Will had made this realisation, he felt a firm hand grab his forearm. He turned to find Frenz's face close to his before he shouted, 'Run, my friend. Now!'

The two of them ran as fast as they could manage, lifting their feet high above the flood water in long bounds, towards the second set of stairs. While one of the gunmen continued to splash around in the water, the other pivoted towards them and opened fire. Bullets whizzed past and masonry exploded all around them. Miraculously, both Will and Frenz made it to the stairwell unscathed. It was almost identical to the one that Will had descended less than an hour earlier, one hundred and twelve years from now. This dizzying thought alone almost caused him to stumble as he scrambled up the steep and narrow steps, but the two of them reached the top without incident.

Frenz pulled Will to the left and pressed through a set of doors into the open space beyond. They found themselves in a large, still room, startlingly different to the police station interior that Will had seen previously. Underfoot was a dark wooden floor with an intricate basket-weave pattern and dozens of tables and chairs scattered throughout. Most were upturned, many were broken, and splintered pieces of wood were strewn throughout. A centimetre-thick layer of clay-coloured dust covered every surface. The walls were divided evenly by thick, elegantly sculpted wooden pillars. Torn red fabric hung from the walls between them, framing the floor-to-ceiling windows. The windows were partially boarded up from the outside, and thin shafts of light seeped through at a steep angle from the gas-fired streetlamps outside.

Will was in a daze. His head was snapping from side to side and up and down as he attempted to take in the new surroundings. The building he'd entered was so drastically different from the one he was now fleeing from. It was as if he'd become part of some grand illusion. If David Copperfield was waiting for them in the street outside with a full camera crew, he wouldn't have been the slightest bit surprised.

Frenz looked over his shoulder to find Will lagging behind and distracted. He called out, 'William, come on, we have to keep moving.'

'Sorry, I'm coming, I'm coming,' Will said, slightly out of breath. 'What is this place? Is this really the same building?'

'Yes, it is. It's not uncommon to find Georgian and Victorian buildings that have served many different purposes over the years,' Frenz said as they ran through the room. 'Before this one was a police station it was a theatre, then a workhouse, before becoming derelict. It then became an army training barracks before being converted to a police station after world war two.'

'How the hell do you know so much about this building?'

'It's my job to know. Now, enough talking. We need to get outside, but we must be cautious. We mustn't be seen by anyone. People are easily scared by what they don't understand, and we can ill afford to cause a scene. Particularly your appearance. People from this era will not understand what they're seeing.'

'Hey, what are you trying to say?!' Will said, stumbling as they turned a corner and entered a smaller room that Will intuited was the reception area of the police station.

Frenz ignored the question. 'Come, this way. This should lead us to the rear of the property and fewer prying eyes.'

They headed towards a set of tall glass doors. They too

were boarded up, but the glass from the left door had been broken. Shards of glass from the broken pane were piled up neatly to the side of the window.

Frenz approached the damaged door and began kicking at the boards, which had been nailed on from the outside. Will joined him, and they soon had two large boards free. Frenz ducked down and squeezed through the new opening. Will followed close behind, feet first. He was partway through when another shot rang out. The bullet struck one of the unbroken panes of glass in the door above his head and splintered through the wooden board behind it. Will moved to shield his head with his arms, bracing himself as the daggers of glass fell from above, when he felt hands grip around his ankles. Frenz pulled him through the opening, narrowly avoiding the glass as it rained down. Once outside, Will sprung to his feet, rubbing the grit free from his eyes as he and Frenz crossed a small, paved courtyard with a jungle of overgrown plants encircling it – the result of years of neglect. A thick green fog hung low in the ether. Visibility was little more than two or three metres in any direction. Will held his hands out in front of him as he walked, feeling his way.

'I can barely see anything,' Will said, coughing slightly.

'This is London in the eighteen hundreds. The fog killed many, but it may help us escape,' Frenz replied.

'Jesus, I can barely breathe!'

'There are almost six million people living here by now, with coal fires burning in every home,' Frenz added, not breaking stride. 'That's what causes the fog, along with London's geography and climate. When it's like this they call it a pea-soupers, owing to the colour.'

When they reached the far side of the courtyard, they stopped and ducked behind a low brick wall. They lay still for a moment. The distinctive sound of horse hooves and wooden cartwheels clattering over cobbled roads could be heard from the main street on the other side of the building.

'Okay, now what?' Will said.

'Will, I need you to think,' Frenz said, turning to face him in the murkiness of the fog. 'Is there anything, anything at all that appears to be different about this place in your time? In 1984?'

'Different? Everything is different!'

'I need you to think fourth-dimensionally, specifically about the terrain. Are there any new buildings, trees, walls, roads? Anything that might help us, but anything that might harm us also. We don't want to reappear in 1984 in the middle of a busy road. However, were our new friends here to find themselves in that situation, then that could be most welcome.'

'I'm not sure. I don't know this area that well. This was the first time I've been arrested, and I was in the back of a police car when they brought me here. It was also dark out, so...'

'There must be something. Please, I need you to think.'

Frenz peered over the top of the low wall, back towards the building they had just fled. Through the mist he could barely make out one of the gunmen standing in the courtyard some ten metres away. He had his gun drawn and was scanning the area, looking for them. The second gunman, it seemed, had found his weapon and was clambering through the opening in the boarded-up door. His once immaculate tweed suit was now soaked through and dripping wet with foul-smelling, putrid water.

Frenz stooped back behind the wall. 'William, I don't mean to worry you,' he said, 'but they are both right behind us. Both armed. You need to come up with something. This wall won't offer much cover once they start firing.'

'That's it!' Will whispered excitedly.

'What is?'

'The wall! Right there,' Will said, pointing to a grassy verge on the far edge of the courtyard. 'In 1984, this courtyard is smaller. There's a large brick wall and a solid metal gate. It's a security gate so there's a good chance it'll be closed.'

'How certain are you of its position?'

'Pretty certain. As much as I can be, under the circumstances.'

'How far out?' Frenz asked.

'Maybe fifteen yards that way.'

Frenz scanned the area and performed a quick calculation in his head. 'Okay, this is what we're going to do,' he said. 'On the count of three, we're going to make a run for it. I need you to run like never before, my friend. Once we cross that verge, I need you to deactivate the Timepiece. Not before, not during. After, understood? Doing so will immediately return us to your origin time in 1984.'

'Okay, got it. Wait, how do you deactivate the Timepiece? I must have missed that part of the instructions.'

'Turn the crown counterclockwise until you feel a click. Do that now,' Frenz whispered.

Will did as instructed. 'Okay, done.'

'To complete the deactivation, push the crown inwards, just like you did to activate it. Do that once we pass the verge.

Is that clear?'

'Yeah, clear.'

'One other thing. The only way we will both travel back is if we are in physical contact with each other. I suggest we hold hands as we run.'

'You're kidding, right? You really want us to run away from men with guns holding hands?'

'That is an accurate description of what I just said, yes,' Frenz said as he retied the laces on each of his shoes in preparation for the vital sprint to safety. 'We should interlock our fingers, that way we will have a firm hold of each other. It will reduce the chance of us losing contact as we transit.'

Will turned to Frenz with flabbergasted acquiescence and said, 'Okay, fine. Just understand that for me, personally, holding hands is a very intimate thing. I mean, I didn't hold hands with Abigayle for the first time until our third date.'

'Think of her as we run. It will drive you to run faster, I'm sure. Are you ready?'

Will nodded frantically.

'On three. One, two, three!'

The two of them leapt from their crouched position behind the wall and began running away from the building and their attackers.

Fortunately, the two gunmen hadn't been looking in their direction when they rose from their temporary cover. This cost them a few precious seconds of reaction time as their quarry made their move.

By the time the gunmen had raised their weapons and prepared to fire, Frenz and Will had already passed from view into the thick fog and within a few paces they had reached the verge. Frenz shouted, 'Now, Will!' as the gunmen fired their weapons blindly into the gloom. Two bullets sailed through the air, both directed squarely at the centre of Will's back. Frenz could hear the dull impact of the bullets as both he and Will lunged forwards through the air. Their elbows scraped, and their bodies tumbled as both men crashed into the stone floor.

CHAPTER FOURTEEN

May 15th, 1984, 02:06

Frenz let out an anguished sigh as he lay face down on the cold pavement. The rectangular slabs of the footpath beneath him were damp and spotted with discarded chewing gum, each piece pressed flat into the stone. He rolled onto his back and looked at the three-metre-high wall that now stood between them and their pursuers. He turned to his right to find Will still lying face down and motionless beside him. Frenz propped himself up on his elbows and said, 'William, it worked.'

When there was no response, he said, 'William, are you okay?'

Still no response. Frenz reached over and pulled Will onto his back and to his relief Will let out a guttural wheeze of breath. His face was flushed a bright pink colour. Frenz asked again, 'Are you hurt? Can you move?'

Will let out another wheezy breath, looking back at the tall wall that had materialised five or so metres behind where they lay. He then looked at Frenz and in a laboured, croaky voice, said, 'Why did you make us dive through the air like that?'

'What do you mean?'

'Look how far we are from that wall. I mean, it might have looked pretty cool if we were running from an explosion or if we weren't holding hands, but we could've just kept on running and I wouldn't feel like I've cracked a half-dozen ribs. This isn't *The A-Team*, you know.'

'The what?'

'It's that new TV show… look, it doesn't matter. I'm just in quite a lot of pain right now, that's all.' Will took in another wheezing breath and laid his head gently back onto the pavement.

'You're just winded, but you had me worried for a moment there. I thought you had been shot. I heard gunshots, but the bullets must have struck the inside of the wall,' Frenz said. 'We should be going. Can you get up?'

'Yeah, I can get up.'

Frenz helped Will to his feet. As they hurried away from the police station, they could hear the growing sounds of commotion and multiple rushing footsteps coming from behind the wall. There were numerous raised and panicked voices, and moments later an alarm was sounded. The police, for obvious reasons, didn't take too kindly to two gunmen suddenly appearing inside police grounds. Especially when they were armed and firing shots into the police compound wall. It was an unenviable situation to be in, and they would surely be tied up for the foreseeable future at least.

It was now the early hours of the morning, so the streets were mostly deserted. Londoners were notoriously early risers, so it wouldn't be long before the streets would be flooded with commuters. Frenz was eager to interact with as few people as possible, given that he was a visitor in this strange period of time. He suggested that they stay out of sight and find a quiet place to lay low and formulate some kind of plan.

Will didn't know many areas of London better than Holland Park, where he and Abigayle lived, but returning to Abigayle's flat was out of the question. There was a high probability that it was now a police crime scene. With Will now adding fugitive to his growing list of alleged crimes, keeping clear of the authorities was even more of a necessity. And it wouldn't be long before the police discovered that he had mysteriously disappeared from his cell without a trace.

That's one crime I'm actually guilty of at least, he thought.

Despite Will's reticence to go anywhere near Abigayle's flat, Frenz insisted that moving to an area that was familiar would give them a tactical advantage should they encounter more resistance.

***

Reluctantly, Will agreed and cautiously navigated the two miles back to Holland Park on foot. The journey seemed to take an age, with the two men ducking out of sight whenever the sound of an approaching car was heard. Will had decided upon a specific location that he deemed to be safe enough, leading Frenz to Norland Square Garden, one of the dozen or so communal gardens in the area.

Many of the gardens were private and were intended solely for the residents living in the neighbouring houses. The gates to these gardens would be locked and unlocked by the local residents themselves and they were the only people entitled to a key. Even so, Will and Abigayle would often sneak into this particular garden after dark, when they could be sure not to run into any residents. They would share night-time picnics and make love under the stars.

When Will and Frenz reached the garden, they found that it was encircled with high iron fences, painted black and topped with spikes that had worn smooth with age. Running along the majority of the perimeter were tall, perfectly trimmed hedges that, at certain points, engulfed the fences completely. As a result, most areas of the garden provided complete privacy from the houses that surrounded it, perfect for staying clear of prying eyes. Inside the garden, rising above the hedges were a number of tall, pristinely maintained trees.

Will and Frenz approached a section of fence and looked up to examine the challenge ahead of them. Frenz shot Will a dubious look. To their right was one of the many gates that led into the garden. The gate was closed and flanked with two low brick pillars. Thick rectangular metal posts were embedded inside the pillars, supporting the large gate between them.

Will approached the gate, stood next to the brick pillar and pressed his back against it. He bent his knees, interlinked his fingers and lowered his hands between his knees. He looked up at Frenz and said, 'Okay, come on, I'll give you a boost.'

'Are you sure about this, William?'

'Sure, I'm sure. Now come on.'

Frenz glanced around, checking that the coast was clear,

then nodded at Will and bounced on his heels in preparation.

'Ready? One, two, three!'

On the count of three, Frenz began a short run up, then placed his left foot in Will's hands and his own hands on Will's shoulders. Will lifted him high enough so that Frenz could place his right foot on one of the brick pillars. This was, however, the easy part of the manoeuvre. From here, Frenz needed to haul himself up using only his arms, lifting his body high to avoid the blunted spikes at the top of the gate. As he reached the top, he wedged his ankle between two of the metal spikes, grimacing as he forced it free. Lactic acid was building up in the muscles of his arms, but he eventually managed to shift his weight to the other side. With his hands gripping the base of two of the blunt spikes, he lowered himself as far as he could before letting go. He kicked his body away from the gate as he dropped to avoid the rock-strewn ground directly below.

Frenz landed into a roll to break his fall. He got to his feet, then bent over and rested his hands on his knees, panting furiously. Beads of sweat covered his brow, which he wiped away with the back of his hand. He then stood, placed his hands on his hips and arched his back with a groan.

'Oh my, that was a lot tougher than I expected,' Frenz said.

'Yeah, well that wasn't bad for a guy your age.'

Frenz suddenly straightened his back as a thought occurred to him. 'But, William, how will you get over here without a boost? Why didn't we think of that before that whole ordeal? And how on earth will we get back out?'

'Don't worry,' Will said calmly. 'I told you, Abby and I came here all the time. I'm an expert at getting into this place.'

Will took a step back from the gate and strode towards it purposefully, gripping the cool metal with two hands. He pushed firmly, and the rusted metal hinges scraped and squealed. The heavy gate surrendered and swung inwards. Once inside the garden Will spun around, closing the gate behind him. He turned to Frenz, whose face was a picture of anger and confusion.

'William! What the bloody hell?' Frenz said, incredulous.

'What?'

'You knew the gate was open all along?'

'Like I said, Abby and I came here a lot. The main reason being that the lock on this particular gate is seized open.'

'Kindly explain why you would put me through all the effort of climbing. I could have impaled myself on the top or fallen and broken my dammed leg!'

'That was for almost getting me blown up,' Will said, counting his fingers, 'almost getting me shot. For making me dive through the air onto a granite stone pavement for no reason whatsoever. And for giving me this damned thing on my wrist, which somehow caused my fiancée to vanish into thin air.' He smirked and walked deeper into the garden.

Frenz followed and found Will standing at the base of an old, twisted tree. According to the metal plaque pressed into the dirt, the tree had been planted in 1878 and was apparently a rare, protected species. Almost all of the trees in the garden were rare or protected in some way. Scattered around the park on slender wooden poles were numerous red and white plastic signs stating that climbing any of the trees was strictly prohibited. Will had many fond memories from his childhood when his mother would take him, his siblings and their scruffy dog for long walks through the woods. On every one Will had found a decent tree to climb. For this reason, Will found this to be an unnecessary restriction.

Frenz walked past Will and slumped down on a wooden bench beside the ancient tree, its limbs faded and grey with age. The adrenaline had been gradually leaving his system over the past hour and the feeling of exhaustion seemed to hit Frenz suddenly. He leaned forwards, resting his arms on his knees and letting out another heavy sigh.

Will took half a step forwards, positioning himself across from his new friend, and folded his arms expectantly. He prodded his head towards him. 'Okay, Frenz, now that our lives are no longer in immediate danger,' he said, 'it's time for some answers.'

Frenz glanced up at Will lethargically, blinking slowly, and offered only an uncertain look.

Will continued unperturbed, pulling back the sleeve of his jacket to reveal the Timepiece on his wrist. 'For a start, what the hell is this thing? And who the hell are those guys?'

Frenz leaned backwards, resting against the firm wooden slats of the bench. His features softened slightly as he spoke. 'This situation you've gotten yourself into is far more dangerous and complicated than you can possibly imagine. The more you know, the more danger you're in. Are you sure you want to know?'

'You're damn right I do! I did what you asked. I broke you out of jail and now it's your turn to hold up your end of the deal.'

Frenz considered this for a moment. There were so many reasons not to tell Will the truth and under normal circumstances he wouldn't have, but he had given this man his word. He was an old-fashioned sort, and without his word, what kind of man was he? He nodded lightly, then gestured to the Timepiece on Will's wrist and spoke his next words slowly and deliberately. 'I think you already know what that thing is and what it can do, but in simple terms: when the wearer of that watch sets the time – any time – they are able to visit that period of time. We like to say that it's the only watch in the world that really *tells* time,' Frenz said, allowing himself a slight chuckle. 'The instant that it's deactivated, the wearer is returned to their time of origin. Or, to be precise, their time of origin plus whatever time has passed since they left. Are you following so far?'

'I need to sit down.' Will took a few paces forwards and settled down on the bench next to Frenz.

'It's fairly straightforward,' Frenz continued. 'For example, if you left your time of origin at midday, travelled ten years into the past and spent two hours there, you would return to your origin time at 2 p.m. This is something you'll have experienced already, of course.'

Will said, 'To be honest with you, this whole evening has been so insane that I've completely lost track of time. Who the hell made this thing? The government? Aliens? I guess it's not a Rolex or an Omega?'

'Unfortunately, its maker remains unknown. Exactly where it came from is still a subject of much conjecture. We call it, simply, the Timepiece.'

'I read as much in that little book I found in my cell,' Will said, patting his back pocket. He looked down, studying the miraculous life-altering device strapped to his wrist, and then looked up at Frenz. 'You know, that's the second time you've phrased it that way.'

'What?'

'You said *we*. Who's *we*? Those guys that were after us?'

'In part, yes.'

'And who are they?'

'They're very dangerous men. They belong to an organisation that controls the use of the Timepiece. They decide who uses it, when and for what purpose. At least they used to.'

'Is this organisation called The Office of Time Dissemination, by any chance?'

Frenz nodded. 'That is its official name. It is an extremely secretive organisation. As far as anyone is concerned, we're part of The International Bureau of Weights and Measures, responsible for setting the time internationally, defining the precise length of a second, calculating leap-seconds, that sort of thing. At its height it had just under three hundred operatives working worldwide. It has operated for centuries and has remained a secret from all but a select few. Not even people in the highest levels of government are aware of the agency's true purpose. Congratulations, you've just become a member of an extremely exclusive group. Not even the Queen knows about it. At least she didn't where I come from.'

'All things considered, I think I would have preferred to remain ignorant of the whole thing.' Will sighed wearily. 'How could this thing have been kept a secret this whole time? With such a big organisation?'

'Not everyone in the agency actually knew what we really did. Most were able to work without ever really knowing what they were doing or why. That was essential.'

'And what were you guys doing, exactly? A big

organisation like this, it's got to be about money, right? Always is.'

'No, not initially. When the organisation was first founded, it needed a revenue stream, of course, but only to fund some of its more ambitious goals. The solution the founders landed on was to form the world's most unique travel company.'

Will raised a single eyebrow theatrically and said, 'A travel company?'

'The world's most *unique* travel company. Rather than asking their customers *where* they would like to visit, instead they asked *when* they would like to visit. There was no shortage of extraordinary historical events for their clients to witness. If you wanted to witness the American Civil War or the signing of the Declaration of Independence, you could. Perhaps you wanted to see how Harold the second of England really fell at the Battle of Hastings. Or discover the location of Cleopatra's tomb or the fate of the Ark of the Covenant. They offered these experiences to the highest bidder. The operation was incredibly lucrative. Unofficially, we were known as the Time Travel Agency.'

'The Time Travel Agency? Are you kidding?'

Frenz shrugged. 'No, I assure you it's true, but it was a different time then. That name is rarely used anymore. The Office of Time Dissemination was such a successful front and rarely audited by other government agencies.'

'Well, this is just great,' Will said as he stood and spread his arms wide. 'The love of my life is missing, and we've got a gang of, what? Villainous, homicidal travel agents after us?'

'By the time I joined the agency, its members were referred to as "Timekeepers". And I'm afraid this is no laughing matter. These are serious people.'

Frenz stood from the bench and approached Will. He placed a hand on his shoulder and looked him in the eye.

Dawn was quickly approaching; even in the chill air Will could feel the warmth of the sun as it began to break over the roofs and through the trees around them. That, combined with the intensity of Frenz's stare, caused the hairs on the back of Will's neck to stand on end and a shiver to shoot down his spine.

Frenz paused for a moment and then said, 'William, I cannot begin to imagine how crazy all of this must sound, but these people won't stop until they get the Timepiece back. This isn't just about taking away their means of generating revenue. It's the one thing that gives them control over the most powerful force in the universe. Forget gravity, forget light, or dark matter. It's *time* that conquers all and they'll stop at nothing to get their hands on that power.'

'Look, Frenz, I appreciate the history lesson, but how does any of this help us find Abigayle? Right now, that's the only thing that matters to me.'

'If we're going to find her and bring her back, I need you to understand what we're up against. The stakes are too high. Those men will be back, and the next time we might not be so lucky. If they capture or kill me, you'll stand a better chance of success if you know who you're up against.'

'But what about Abigayle?' Will said, turning to face Frenz. 'Wherever she is, or whenever she is, she's alone and probably scared. I can't leave her there any longer than I have to. Let's go get her back. Right now!'

'William, let me be clear. Abigayle is safe where she is. Much safer than we are right now.'

'You don't know that!'

'I know that the only thing that will put her in danger is us going to retrieve her when it's not safe to do so. If we use the Timepiece now, the Timekeepers will know, and they'll find us and kill us. If we take our time, we can make sure that doesn't happen. And don't forget, we have time on our side. When we go to find Abigayle, we can choose to arrive just minutes after you left her, so you see, she'll be alone for no time at all.'

Will nodded thoughtfully and his breathing gradually slowed. 'Okay, okay. What do I need to know? Aside from tourism, what else were these people involved with?'

'When I first joined the agency, it was an amazing place to work. The tourism branch was virtually non-existent. The agency had almost limitless resources and some friends in very high places. We still did the odd leisure trip for those considered important enough, but it was a rare occurrence. Instead, the agency dealt in a more valuable currency than money. It dealt almost exclusively in information. Facts. Real facts, no opinions or theories. Cold, hard, invaluable fact.' Frenz paused, nudging his thick-rimmed glasses further up his nose as he contemplated his next words.

'The main goal was the pursuit of historical enlightenment. History, you must understand, is a series of patterns and structures that helps modern society to navigate the world in which we now live. And we had some of the best minds in the world all under one roof – scientists, historians, scholars – and with the Timepiece we were able to unlock some of the most important discoveries in our history. Both Nikola Tesla and Albert Einstein were members at one time. These great minds would examine the past for answers to questions of the present. We would look at past mistakes and successes so that we might learn from them in the future. We would use this information to further scientific discovery, to help direct and shape government policy and to make the world a better place. Or try to, at least. We have even helped to solve some of the biggest crimes ever committed. You could say we were a kind of historical detective agency.'

'So, I guess you can tell me who really shot JFK?'

'Yes, we helped to catch him, in fact! It really was the lone gunman, Lee Harvey Oswald.'

'What? You're kidding, that whole thing was orchestrated by the CIA!'

'I'm afraid that's just a conspiracy theory.'

'Oh, come on! Dozens of people testified to the Warren Commission that they saw a puff of smoke coming from the grassy knoll. What about that?'

Frenz cleared his throat and scratched the corner of his mouth distractedly. 'Well, that was us. We were there. One of our agents transitioned to the past right on that spot. I don't know if you've ever noticed, but when one transits through time the air at their location ripples. It most closely resembles a heat haze.'

'So, you're saying that that's what all those people saw? One of your guys using the Timepiece?' Will said indignantly.

'I'm afraid so.'

'Why were you there at the time of the shooting?'

'To get to the truth of the incident, of course, and to bring those responsible to justice. How do you think the authorities caught Oswald so quickly? Moments after the shooting, Timekeeper agents were sent back to the scene, twenty minutes before the event. The whole area was searched, and one agent actually witnessed Lee Harvey Oswald taking the shot. He was pictured leaving the book depository, and upon returning to the present, our agents handed his image and personnel file to the police and Secret Service.'

'Well why not just stop the shooting?'

'I'm afraid that history is rather obdurate. It cannot be changed as far as we know. Those who have tried have ended up inadvertently *causing* the very thing they've attempted to prevent.'

Will eyed Frenz with suspicious, narrow eyes. 'Okay, what about Jack the Ripper? No one ever caught him. How do you explain that?'

Frenz shifted his weight on the bench, growing uncomfortable. 'You are talking about a rather dark period of the agency's history.'

'I love history. I studied it in college. It's the whole reason I came to London in the first place.'

'This one is not so easy to explain, but it was a focus of mine personally for many years. We were attempting to catch the Ripper in the act for each of his murders. There was an agent by the name of Crispin Umber. He was a Timekeeper agent, like the ones who are pursuing us right now. He was part of the Operations section of the agency. They went on assignments to the past, they were the ones who actually used the Timepiece. I always sat in an office somewhere with my head in my books, but the Timekeepers were the ones in the field.

'This one agent was eager to volunteer for every assignment, claiming that he had the most extensive knowledge of the period, which I have to say was true. He really knew his late-nineteenth-century London unlike anyone I had ever met. So, he went on the first assignment and he located the site of the Ripper's first kill. And the second, third and the fourth. But every time, he claimed to have just missed catching Whitechapel Jack in the act. After the fourth killing, which I was certain to have pinpointed to within a five-minute time period myself, I became suspicious. It turned out that Crispin Umber wasn't just extremely knowledgeable about nineteenth-century London, he was a Jack the Ripper fanatic. When we travelled back to view the fifth and final murder, I requested that a second team keep Crispin under surveillance…'

'And? What happened?' Will said eagerly.

'An agent from the surveillance team claimed to have followed Crispin Umber, who was seen walking into a building with a woman matching the description of Mary Jane Kelly, the Ripper's final victim. The agent in question, fearing that they would be seen, remained outside the building until Crispin re-emerged. When he did some time later, he was followed down an alleyway, where he was apparently confronted and found covered in blood, attempting to dispose of a number of bloodstained surgical instruments.'

'Wait, are you saying that this Crispin Umber, one of your own agents, *was* Jack the Ripper?'

Frenz nodded slowly and said, 'I'm afraid so. It had us all stumped that the killer seemed to vanish so easily from the scene of each crime and that the killings stopped so suddenly. But all along, it had been one of our own going back there and living out his own twisted fantasies. When he was brought back to the present and his crimes were fully realised, he vanished. I don't know what became of him.'

'Jesus! Well, isn't that kind of thing dangerous? If you guys were going back to the past, couldn't you change something and undo your own existence or something?'

'That was our first instinct, yes, but like I said: the past isn't as easy to change as we first thought. Any notable actions we take in the past have already happened, we just haven't experienced them yet. After the Crispin debacle, we went to greater lengths to ensure we left minimal traces behind. Before any date in the past was cleared for exploration, extensive research would be conducted to ensure we had an acceptable level of certainty for our agent's safety. We would do this for months or even years for certain time periods before use of the Timepiece was given the green light.'

'That's what you did, isn't it? Your ID said you're an Extra-dimensional Geohistorian.'

'Yes, it was my job to research specific days or weeks in the past. Often a specific time if there was sufficient data available. I specialised in geological and environmental changes that might have occurred between the requested destination time and our own time. This was to ensure that we didn't send agents back to the past in an area where the environment posed danger. Appearing in a location where a tree once stood would not be particularly pleasant. We also had teams of people who would exhaustively research everything from period clothing, currency, language and customs to architecture and topography. We did everything we could to mitigate the chances of interference.'

Will rubbed his eyes and ran his hands down his face before dropping them to his sides. 'Frenz, this is all really interesting,' he said, 'but shouldn't we get moving soon?'

'Not just yet. For now, we're out of sight. This is the safest place we can be right now. The sun will be up in an hour or so. When rush hour hits, we can use the crowds to cover our movements. Until then, I should finish your crash-course induction into The Office of Time Dissemination.'

'Okay,' Will said. 'So, causing one of the world's most notorious murder sprees aside, the agency used to be all sweetness and light. Pursuit of knowledge and understanding and all that. What changed?'

'Over the years, the agency became divided. A faction inside the agency felt that the past offered insufficient information to improve the future. They felt that the best way to prepare for the future was to look into the future itself.'

'Well sure, makes sense. If you could see what mistakes are made in the future, you'd know to avoid them, right?'

'It might sound beneficial at first, but it's more complicated than that. Using the Timepiece to travel to the future is dangerous and unpredictable. There's no reliable data. No way of knowing where we could be sending our agents. No one can be sure what the future even looks like. It could be completely alien and like nothing anyone had ever seen before.'

Will's features darkened, something Frenz picked up on immediately.

'William, what is it?'

'I think I know what the future looks like. In our flat, at least.'

'No…'

Will nodded. 'When Abigayle used the Timepiece, what I

saw was unlike anything I've ever seen before. It's only just occurred to me, but when she disappeared, I couldn't shake the thought that everything looked like it was from another world. I think that's where Abigayle is. She's somewhere in the future.'

CHAPTER FIFTEEN

May 15th, 1984, 04:38

DI Moss's service vehicle screeched into the yard to the rear of the police station. The yard was more crowded than usual at this time of the morning, with dozens of additional officers and security staff called in to deal with the commotion that led to a suspect escaping custody. He weaved and swerved the car to avoid people and equipment, the former of which scattered in one way or another as he approached. He stopped abruptly in front of the entrance and parked at a steep angle. The door burst open and Moss exploded from the car through a cloud of tyre smoke and proceeded to scale the steps leading up to the station doors in two large bounds. He pushed in through the doors, knocking an unsuspecting clerk to the floor as he stormed past.

He found his prey in the incident room talking with two oddly dressed men. Mapson's eyes widened dramatically when he saw Moss enter. He appeared to say something to the two men, who quickly made themselves scarce, leaving through a side door. Moss watched the two men depart and then turned his attention to Mapson, who straightened up and prepared for the coming onslaught.

'Mapson! Do you want to tell me what the fuck is going on?'

Mapson squirmed uncomfortably and said, 'I'm afraid it appears that our suspect, William Wells, has managed to escape his holding cell.'

'I'm well aware of that! What I want to know is *how* he escaped?'

'Well, sir, he was securely locked in his holding cell at 01:08. There he remained while we dealt with apparent gunshots heard from the yard. When officers returned to finish processing him, his cell was empty. And still locked, I might add.'

'Is that it? That's your explanation? That the dumb Yank we arrested fleeing the scene of a murder is also some kind of Doug fucking Henning?'

'I'm sorry, sir, but I think Doug Henning was Canadian.'

Moss's mouth curled up into a wicked smile. 'Finally, something you do know. It's just a shame it has sod all to do with actual police work!' Moss's anger at his subordinate was palpable. 'Can you tell me anything that's actually useful? For instance, what was all this shooting about? We're sure it's not connected to Wells?'

'It doesn't appear that way, sir.'

'How does it appear then?'

'It appears that it was nothing more than a car backfiring as it drove past the south wall.'

Moss gritted his teeth as he seemed to physically recoil with rage. He closed his eyes and took a deep breath. When he opened them, he looked at Mapson with more disappointment than disdain.

Mapson unclenched and relaxed slightly before sheepishly asking, 'Anything of interest at the Wells crime scene, sir? Anything that might help us figure out where he's heading?'

Moss fished around in his jacket pocket and pulled out a small, clear plastic bag. A glimmering brass object slid from one side of the bag to the other as he moved it. Moss held up the bag and said, 'It might not help us find him, but it'll help us nail the bastard when we do. He left a shell casing behind. I'd be interested to read the ballistics report on it. I've not seen this calibre of bullet for a long, long time.'

'Great news, sir.'

'It is so long as we find Wells.'

'I've already issued a city-wide alert.'

'Make it national. I want his picture at every port. He's a Yank so I wouldn't be surprised if he's heading home right now. I want it all locked down. Air, rail and sea.'

'As soon as we have his picture, I'll get right on it.'

'Use his mug shot. Jesus, Mapson, this shouldn't be as difficult as you're making it!'

Mapson seemed to physically shrink before he spoke again. 'I know, sir. The problem is that we didn't actually finish processing Mr Wells before he was put in his cell.'

'Say that again, Mapson, just so I can be sure I heard you right.'

'We were short-staffed. And there was an incident with a rowdy member of the public. So, we put Mr Wells in a holding cell while we dealt with it. We didn't think he was going anywhere—'

'Stop talking,' Moss said, closing his eyes once again and rubbing his temples before he turned and began to walk out of the room. With his back to Mapson, he said, 'Get a warrant. Search his apartment and get me a picture. Page me if you hear anything. Anything.'

'Yes, sir.'

Moss ambled out of the room, shaking his head in frustration. He trudged out of the building and down the steps expecting to find his car parked where he left it. Instead he found an eager young officer bouncing towards him. He smiled enthusiastically and said, 'Detective Inspector Moss?'

'Yes.'

'Sir, I had to move your car. This is an exclusion zone right here.'

'You're lucky I'm tired, sunshine,' Moss grumbled. 'Don't you ever move my car again. Understood?'

The young officer turned red in the face. 'Of course, sir. Apologies.'

'Where is it?'

'The car? Yes, sir, I parked it over by the south wall.'

Moss glared at the young officer, concluding the chastising. He snatched his key from his hand and made his way across the yard. The excitement of the apparent shooting seemed to be dying down as officers returned to their duties. Moss found his car parked neatly facing the south wall. He climbed in and shut the door. Staring out through the windscreen lazily, he considered sleeping in his car for an hour or two – it wouldn't be the first time – but he longed for a firm mattress after such a long shift. He leaned forwards and started the engine. He flicked on the headlights and put the car in reverse. As he turned his head to look to the rear of the car, he spotted something embedded in the wall. Something metallic, illuminated and glistening in the headlights.

CHAPTER SIXTEEN

May 15th, 1984, 04:58

Frenz winced as he processed what Will had just told him, doing his best to prevent the increasingly lined features of his face from betraying the disquieting thoughts running through his head. He walked back to the bench, sat down once more and said, 'Her being in the future complicates things but could explain some of what's been going on here.'

'Explain it how?'

'Well, as I said, the future is unpredictable.'

Will nodded. 'Yeah, and?'

'Nothing that has happened in the past couple of hours was part of the plan. You weren't supposed to come back with the Timepiece. The Timekeepers shouldn't have found us so quickly. Something in your future has changed and it's made everything uncertain. Abigayle being in the future could explain it.'

'What about you?'

'What about me?'

'You've travelled to the future too. Isn't that dangerous and uncertain as well?'

'In theory, yes. Although, technically speaking, I'm now part of your present rather than your past. And since you brought me here, our futures are now somehow aligned.'

'I think this is giving me a migraine,' Will said, rubbing his eyes.

'Make no mistake, everything we're doing here is uncharted territory and extremely dangerous. But under the circumstances, it's very much a necessary risk.'

Silence fell between the two men. Will stood motionless, studying his shoes, when a thought occurred to him. He took a step towards Frenz, who, sensing the movement, looked up to meet his enquiring gaze. 'Answer me this: if you guys only ever travelled to the past, how do you know all this stuff about the future?'

Frenz exhaled gently, then said with apprehension, 'Please understand that I can only tell you what I've read in reports, and some of what I'm about to say is based on nothing more than my own theories and observations.'

'Duly noted,' Will said with a hint of sarcasm, not used to talking to someone who spoke so formally.

'Operational reports from the agency's early years are limited. What little we do know is that the Timekeepers conducted experiments with future time travel and, aside from the obvious dangers I mentioned already, they encountered some unexplained… anomalies.'

'You mean anomalies beyond the fact that they were time travelling, right?'

Frenz ignored the comment and continued. 'Agents would bring back small caches of information from the future and compare their findings.'

'What kind of information?'

'The aim was to first establish a baseline before attempting more in-depth assignments, so they would look for things like current stock market reports, various government statistics: crime, birth and death rates. Things of that nature.'

'What was so anomalous about that?'

'There were multiple conflicting reports from different assignments to the same period. This is when it was discovered that the future seemed to be constantly changing. At first they couldn't tell if it was the act of bringing information back from the future that was altering events or if it was something else entirely.'

'What was it?'

'From what I've read in the reports, it was the agents themselves. No one knew what the effects of future time travel might be, so in an attempt to avoid potential psychological trauma, different agents were used on different assignments. However, there was something about the individuals that was causing things to change.'

Frenz removed his glasses and began cleaning the lenses with a handkerchief. As the sun rose above the line of the nearby townhouses, its rays burned through the early morning cloud cover, revealing the orange-blue sky beyond. Long, dark shadows reached out from the roots of the surrounding trees, plants and the bench upon which Frenz was sitting. The dew that had formed atop the encircling fence was rising up, evaporating in the heat of the new day.

As Frenz replaced his glasses, Will said, 'So, if I went to the future, it would be different for me than it would be for you?'

'Correct.'

'Okay, but why?'

'It's theorised that when any person travels into the future – for argument's sake, let's say ten years into the future – they would emerge in a future where they'd been missing for the intervening ten years. It may seem trivial, but removing a single person's interactions in the world for an extended period of time can have a huge effect on future events.'

'You mean like the Butterfly Effect? Small causes having very large effects. I studied a bit of the theory in high school.'

Frenz beamed, pleasantly surprised at his new friend. 'Yes, exactly. For example, tomorrow morning you could bump into a man in the street, making him just a few seconds late into his office building. This minor delay causes him to miss his elevator ride to the floor where he works. This in turn causes him to reach his floor two minutes later than usual, where he has a chance encounter with a young lady whom he would've otherwise missed. The two of them strike up a conversation and agree to go out for dinner. They fall in love and eventually marry and have four children. One of those children goes on to discover a cure for a major disease that saves the lives of thousands, perhaps millions of people. All this because tomorrow you'll bump into a man in the street whom you don't even know. However, if you travel to the future today, you won't be here to bump into this man and that future will never come to pass. You'll arrive in a future where millions of people will have died from the disease that was never cured. This is an extreme example, of course.'

Will shook his head in mock disbelief. 'Wow, I never knew my life was so important!'

Frenz allowed himself to smirk at this.

Will said, 'Is that why they stopped anyone else from travelling to the future?'

'It wasn't the sole reason but it contributed. From some of the reports I was able to get my eyes on, it was suggested that there were many parallel, converging versions of the future. Different timelines crossing into one another. But the main reason for stopping the programme was the danger involved. We lost many good agents in those years.'

Any trace of darkness had almost completely deserted the garden. Though Will was growing more anxious about their being spotted in broad daylight, his interest in Frenz's words won out and he pressed him for more.

'Lost? You mean they died?'

'We can't always be certain what happened to agents lost during time travel. Their files aren't marked as deceased but rather as "astray". Like they were alive somewhere – or somewhen – and might return one day.'

'Did any return?'

'I'm afraid not, but their loss wasn't in vain. Without their sacrifice, we wouldn't know what we do now about the dangers of future time travel. Before long, the Futures Project – as it was called – was abandoned and travel to the future was strictly prohibited. Officially, at least.'

'Only officially?'

Frenz hesitated before proceeding, rubbing his chin, unsure of how much he should reveal to this man who was still relatively unknown to him. Folding his arms across his chest, he continued. 'It was suspected that a faction inside the agency still saw value in the Futures Project. One very senior and influential agent believed he had a way to ensure that the data recovered from future travel would always be reliable. It's thought that they continued to conduct research covertly.'

'How could they ensure the data was reliable?'

'This agent was something of an extremist. His proposal was to send an agent into the future and have them isolated upon their return to limit interactions with others. The agent would then be thoroughly debriefed to ensure all information about the future was gathered. It was never proven, but I suspect that the agent would then be executed. If that agent saw a future that was predicated on them being missing for decades, what better way to ensure that future came to pass than to make sure they stayed missing?'

'Holy shit! Did that really happen?'

'No one knows for sure, but I believe so.'

Will said, 'I guess the agents didn't know they were going on a suicide mission?'

'I wouldn't have thought so, no.'

'Damn, that's heavy.'

'It gets worse. If this rogue faction ever successfully carried out experiments of this kind, there were other things they hadn't considered.'

'Such as?'

'First, if these agents reported on the future that they had witnessed, just passing that knowledge onto others could change the course of history. And second, they had forgotten about the Mimic Watches.'

'What the hell is a Mimic Watch?'

'You recall that physical contact is required for more than one person to travel at a time and we had to hold hands?'

'How could I forget.'

'In the early days, it was common practice for more than one agent to travel, and holding hands isn't exactly the most practical or safe way to do it, as you well know.' Will pulled a face and Frenz continued. 'The agency's horology engineers developed a watch that could replicate the effects of physical contact during time travel. On its own, a Mimic Watch was relatively useless and had no power to alter time. Each one was a slave to the Timepiece, waiting for a signal. But when the Timepiece was activated, each Mimic Watch was able to connect that signal, enabling the wearer to follow the Timepiece to whichever time period it had travelled to.'

'Wait a sec. This is how those two guys were able to follow us through time? They're wearing Mimic Watches?'

'That's the only logical explanation.'

'Why didn't you say something earlier?'

'By the time it became clear how close they were to our location, it was too late to explain.'

'So, what's the problem with the Mimic Watches?'

'When authorised assignments take place,' Frenz said, 'they are done so with huge care. They are meticulously planned and the whole agency is fully briefed and prepared. Safety is of the utmost importance. The problem is that this rogue faction conducted a number of unauthorised assignments, and they did so under the assumption that all Mimic Watches would be deactivated at the time.'

'Well, you know what they say about assumption.'

'I'm afraid I don't. But I do know what I saw. A dear friend of mine, Nestor Ordell, worked in the Engineering

Section of the agency as a horological engineer. We were very close. I would go as far as to say he was my best friend. The two of us had been working late and I visited him in his workshop to ask if he would be attending our weekly stargazing event later that evening. At the time, he was partway through repairing a malfunctioning Mimic Watch. The whole episode is somewhat of a blur, but I do recall Nestor saying that it was locked in its active state.'

'Active state? What's that mean?'

'Mimic Watches are nominally inactive, waiting for a signal from the Timepiece. When a signal is received, an amber light indicates this. Then, when the Timekeeper agent wearing the Mimic Watch is ready, they activate it and follow the Timepiece to the same time period.'

'Right, got it,' Will said, doing his best to take all this in.

'As I was saying, the two of us were talking when he suddenly vanished before my eyes. A few minutes later the Mimic Watch he'd been holding reappeared and dropped down to his workbench. I never saw him again.'

'Jeez, Frenz, I'm sorry. I had no idea.'

Frenz nodded his appreciation.

'Look, I don't mean to sound insensitive to your loss, but how does any of this help Abigayle?'

'I wasn't in that jail by accident, William. I had been sent instructions to be there and to expect a friend of the agency to help me escape. Then you appeared and unless you're a very good liar and have some other agenda, you weren't supposed to be there.'

'We've been over this, and no, I still have no idea what's going on.'

'The fact that you're so closely connected to someone

who has gone astray in the future and that you yourself travelled there with her cannot be unconnected. Somehow Abigayle being sent there is causing uncertainty to bleed back into the present. It's already caused things to change. She's the reason you turned up in my jail cell, after all. So perhaps she's the reason you have the Timepiece, whether she knows it or not. In order to unravel this mess, we need to get the lay of the land from someone in this time period. Someone we can trust.'

'Who?'

'A friend, an old colleague. If she can, she will help us.'

'A friend, huh? You don't strike me as the type.' Will studied his shoes then sighed. 'But you trust her?'

'I trust her with my life. Besides, she used to service and maintain the Timepiece for the agency, and it wouldn't hurt to have her look at it herself. It's been years since it's been used, and it shouldn't be overheating the way it has been.'

'Where does your friend live?'

'In a small village in the south of Ireland called Dingle. At least that's where she used to live.'

'Ireland? We've got to go to Ireland? Can't we just phone her? They even have phones in cars now, can you believe that?'

'In cars? Fascinating,' Frenz said, wide-eyed, then shook the thought from his mind. 'No, we can't risk it. The Timekeepers will be listening. They always had friends in high places, and I wouldn't want to bet on that being any different now, even if they don't have the Timepiece anymore.'

'Can't we just go back in time and stop Abigayle from using the Timepiece in the first place?'

'Putting aside the fact that undoing an event in your own past, which is directly responsible for your being here now, would tear the fabric of the space and time, there is another issue to consider.'

'Of course. The moment we activate the Timepiece, the Timekeepers will know.'

'Very perspicacious, William,' Frenz said in agreement. 'And it won't take them long to track us down.'

He stood from the bench, looked at his watch and began walking back through the garden to the open gate. 'The streets will begin to get busy soon, unless people no longer work in 1984?'

Will turned and began walking alongside Frenz. After a moment, he said, 'Frenz, there's something I've been meaning to ask you.'

'What is it?'

'You keep talking about the Timekeepers as *them* rather than *we*. I thought you worked for them. How is it that the older version of you that I met had the Timepiece and they don't?'

'Isn't it obvious?'

'Not really, no.'

'I stole it from the Timekeepers, of course. Now come on, we must go.'

CHAPTER SEVENTEEN

May 15th, 1984, 07:04

The journey from Norland Square to the small seaside town of Dingle in County Kerry, Ireland, would prove to be a long, sleepless one.

If Will had inherited anything from his father, it was a true, unwavering love of being in an unconscious, sedentary state for extended periods of time. Will tended to only indulge in this pastime at night. His father was rather less regimented in his approach, sleeping through most days as well. Despite his love of a good night's rest and the constant nagging exhaustion in his bones and cloudiness in his head, Will's determination to find Abigayle was the only thing in his thoughts.

After Frenz had marched out of the gardens, he proceeded towards the sound of traffic. He emerged onto Holland Park Avenue, which was the main artery road running east to west through the Royal Borough of Kensington and Chelsea. He was joined by Will, who had half jogged, half walked to catch up with him.

Will attempted to broach the subject of Frenz's theft of the Timepiece from his masters, but Frenz was unequivocal in his insistence that now was not the time. Will was adamant that he would revisit the subject later.

Frenz suggested that they stick to public transport for the entire journey. He was most eager that they keep a low profile. 'Taxis are out of the question,' Frenz said. 'A taxi driver could remember his customers and might talk to the authorities. Passengers on buses and trains are anonymous. Inconspicuous in their movements to the point of being almost invisible. Being invisible at this point in time is to our advantage.'

'Okay fine, but how are we going to pay for all this? I'm completely broke.'

Frenz stopped abruptly and turned to Will. 'The *Timekeeper's Guidebook* I left for you. Do you still have it?'

'Yeah, sure do.' Will twisted his shoulders, reached into his back trouser pocket and pulled out the small, leather-bound book. He held it out towards Frenz, tilting it to one side inquiringly. Frenz made no move towards the book and instead said, 'Check the inside of the back cover. There's a small incision running along the outer edge.'

Will flicked to the back of the book and studied the inside of the cover. Sure enough, there was a small opening running along it, two centimetres in from the outer edge. Will pressed his fingers on the leather-bound exterior of the book and used his thumb to bend the sturdy cover. It was stiff, and he needed to apply considerable force to expose the hidden compartment. His fingers turned white as he peered into the narrow slit that had appeared. He could just about make out several folded pieces of paper inside. He slid his free hand into the opening and retrieved the contents.

Will began unfolding the papers and it soon became apparent that they were in fact banknotes. He made a quick count of the twelve notes, each in £20 denominations. He turned to Frenz and said, 'This'll do it, all right!'

Frenz nodded quietly in response.

Will looked at the notes, his smile quickly turning into a look of confusion. He locked eyes with Frenz. 'Where did you get these? These are legal tender. How could you possibly have these in 1940?'

'All that matters is that we keep moving. We're far too exposed to eavesdroppers for a conversation as sensitive as this. It's probably advisable to limit talk altogether until it's safe to do so.'

Will knew now not to object once Frenz had set his mind to something, and before long they boarded the number 228 bus from Norland Square travelling east towards Euston station. Next, they caught an overground train northwest. On Frenz's insistence, they sat apart throughout their journey. Apparently, a black man and a white man travelling together would be too memorable an occurrence should their fellow passengers ever face questioning from their pursuers. The burning questions racing through Will's mind would have to wait, keeping sleep at bay, despite his exhaustion. They changed trains at Birmingham and then at Chester before arriving at the port in Holyhead, North Wales.

The two men were ravenous by this point, and Frenz reluctantly agreed to stop at a quaint seafront café opposite the ferry terminal. They took a table out front. Will had a full fried breakfast, still not sure why he received such disgusted looks whenever he asked if he could have pancakes and maple syrup with it, and Frenz had porridge with fresh fruit and a pot of tea. They ate outside in the sun, both too exhausted for conversation. When they'd finished, Will rose from the table and went inside to settle the bill. The atmosphere inside the café was stuffy and loud. Two or three families were crammed into the small space, along with their dogs. The only toilet was out of order and the children were screaming about needing to pee, the dogs were barking and the parents were screaming at both for making so much noise. Will had dreamed of one day having children, but now he wasn't so sure.

A TV was mounted high on the wall at the back of the café. Above the din, Will was just able to hear the presenter on the afternoon news: '…police are still investigating the reported prison break in the early hours of this morning. Details are scarce at this time; however, it has been confirmed by an independent source that a manhunt is underway by the Metropolitan Police force, who are working closely with forces nationwide. The fugitive, who was being held in connection with a shooting in north London, is thought to be an American male, and investigators are due to address the media in a press conference scheduled at the end of this programme. In other news…'

Will's blood turned cold. Thick beads of sweat materialised across his forehead. His hands shook as he unfolded a neat £5 note and laid it on the countertop. He forced a smile at the overworked waitress, said, 'Thanks, keep the change,' in his best attempt at an English accent, then walked briskly out of the café. He didn't break stride as he passed Frenz outside. 'Frenz, we need to go. Now.'

Frenz scrambled out of his chair, spilling some tea on his hand. 'What is it?'

'I'm on the news. There's a press conference soon and my face is going to be all over it for a murder I didn't commit.' Will still didn't know how to tell Frenz that it was *his* murder that he was wanted for.

'I'd hoped we would get here before news of your escape had spread. The police move far more quickly in 1984 than they did in my day.'

'What are we going to do? If they're doing a press conference in the next five minutes, then there's no way they don't have my picture.'

'Wait here,' Frenz said.

Frenz entered the ticketing office of the main ferry terminal. There was a palpable military presence both inside and out, which Frenz hadn't expected to see. He waited patiently in line behind a dozen or so people, scanning the area behind the ticketing desk. There was a cork notice board affixed to the far wall. On it Frenz could see various health and safety notices, what looked like a staff rota and a clipboard. A piece of string with a pencil dangling from the other end was attached to the clipboard. Along the left side of the board were a series of mug shots with police force emblems at the top of them. As Frenz moved closer and closer to the front of the queue, the more certain he became that none of them pictured Will. He let out a long sigh of relief.

Once it was his time to be served, he asked for two return tickets to Dublin and paid with cash. While his tickets were being processed, he could hear a machine whirring loudly in a small side office. A rotund man in a brown suit and a stained beige shirt stood from his desk and walked over to the source of the noise. When the sound stopped, the man reached down and tore a single piece of paper free from the reel. He studied it for a moment before walking out of the office towards the notice board. The woman serving Frenz handed him his tickets and wished him a pleasant trip, but Frenz didn't hear her. He was staring far too intently at the board behind her. The large man's greasy head of hair was obscuring the latest addition he'd just pinned up. He seemed to take an age to move away from the board, and an impatient customer behind Frenz began to get riled when Frenz didn't immediately move to let him through. Just as he thought it might come to blows, the large man stepped away and there, just as Frenz feared, was a picture of William Wells smiling back at him with the word *WANTED* printed above.

Frenz left the ticketing office and returned to Will with the news.

'Well, that's it,' Will said. 'We can't go to Ireland. We need to find another way.'

'No, we must go. It's the only way. We're scrambling around in the dark. We need to know what's going on and what we're up against. This is the only person I know whom we can trust.'

'What are we going to do then?'

'I don't know, I'm thinking.'

'Could we sneak on the ferry?'

'We don't have time to plan something like that.'

'Technically we have all the time in the world, right?' Will said, rolling his sleeve back and tapping the face of the Timepiece.

'No. Absolutely not. It's too dangerous. There are also a number of military personnel stationed here for some reason.'

'That'll be because of The Troubles.'

'The Troubles? What's that?' Frenz asked.

'Nothing good. But the soldiers won't be interested in the likes of us.'

'It's still too dangerous.'

'Wait a sec, hear me out. How long did you say it would take for the Timekeepers to find us once it's activated?'

'It depends on a number of factors.'

'Give me a ballpark,' Will said.

'A what?'

'An approximation. A guess.'

'Given our current distance from London, I would say they'd have our location within thirty minutes or so,' Frenz said. 'But even with that, we don't have time to research this location to make sure it's safe to travel.'

'How long ago did they put up my picture?'

'Not long, five minutes perhaps.'

'Then we travel back twenty minutes. We've got our tickets. All we have to do is avoid ourselves, right?'

Frenz raised an eyebrow at Will and began scratching the hair on his chin. 'It's a huge risk.'

'Any more of a risk than doing nothing and getting shot?'

'How are we going to be sure we can travel to a location unseen and that isn't occupied?'

'I know a place,' Will said.

Will marched purposefully away from the ticketing office and back towards the small café, with Frenz following closely behind. Inside, he pressed his way through the cramped interior, which had now emptied itself of the noisy families. The lone waitress was busy tidying up the carnage they'd left behind. 'Be with you in a minute,' she said without looking up.

Frenz had caught up with Will as he approached the disused toilet and spoke in a low voice to avoid being overheard. 'William, that door is locked. I tried the door when we first arrived.'

Will turned to Frenz and with a crazed look in his eyes, said, 'If what you've told me about the Timepiece is true, then we'll have already gone back to the past and unlocked the door from the inside.'

'William, wait…' But before Frenz could offer further objections, Will silently prized open the door of the disused toilet, raising his eyebrows excitedly at Frenz as he did. They squeezed inside together and closed the door behind them.

The room was no larger than a wardrobe. A rank smell hung in the air and something unmentionable floated in the blocked toilet. There was barely room for the two men to stand up without touching the walls or any of the porcelain. They stood face to face, pressed against each other. 'And to think I was uncomfortable holding hands…' Will said.

Frenz ignored him. 'Are you sure about this?'

'Not really,' Will said, before twisting his body slightly and activating the Timepiece.

May 15th, 1984, 16:08
Using the Timepiece to travel across such a short period was a peculiar experience. At first, neither man was sure that it had worked since the toilet's cramped interior appeared not

to have changed, but then it wouldn't have. The only evidence that it had changed wasn't what they saw or what they smelled, but what they could hear: the racket from the feasting families was back. Will manoeuvred awkwardly so that he could unlock the door from the inside, engaging the snib to ensure the door could now be opened by him in the future. He then bumped the door firmly with his shoulder while turning the handle with his free hand. The door inched open and he peeked outside. Thankfully, the café was as chaotic as he expected.

First Will and then Frenz edged out of the restroom. The waitress took no notice of them as she struggled to wrangle the over-stressed parents, screaming children and barking dogs. As they headed towards the back door of the café, Will couldn't help but glance out through the front window. There he saw a sight that made his stomach lurch: he and Frenz sitting at the table outside, eating their breakfast. As he gazed at the scene outside, he felt a firm hand on his shoulder. 'We shouldn't linger,' Frenz said and they continued to sneak unseen out through the rear of the café.

They both hurried towards the boarding gate and through the ticketing office. Frenz scanned the notice board to make sure Will's image wasn't there. They joined the front of the queue so that they would be the first to board. Their tickets were checked by a thoroughly dislikeable security officer. As he studied the tickets, he scrutinised a clipboard with various mug shots attached to it before allowing them through. Once aboard, they hurried towards their private cabin, locked the door and deactivated the Timepiece.

May 15th, 1984, 16:46

Inside the cabin the two men looked at each other and even Frenz couldn't suppress a toothy grin. It was a big risk, but it had worked perfectly.

'How long was that?' Will asked.

'Just over twelve minutes.'

'Are we good?'

Frenz opened the cabin door and studied the hallway. 'I think so.'

At just under one hundred and thirty metres in length, the *Stena Caledonia* ferry was capable of carrying one thousand passengers as well as almost three hundred cars. The size of the vessel and the calm weather promised a smooth journey. Unfortunately for Will, neither prevented him from feeling nauseous during the crossing. He positioned himself in the stern, slouched on a bench with his head between his knees. Frenz, meanwhile, spent the majority of the three-hour voyage sitting in an empty corner of the bar, sipping a glass of rum, quietly absorbed in a book.

As they approached Dublin, Will extracted himself from his seat on the deck and walked unsteadily back into the bar. He took a seat opposite Frenz, who looked up at him. The discomfort was written across his pale green, clammy face. 'You know what?' Will said. 'This is the first time I've ever been on a boat. Apparently, I suffer from severe seasickness.'

'I must say, you are looking rather peaky,' Frenz said, then refocused on his book.

'Please tell me we're almost there.'

'Yes, not far now.'

'So, now that we're alone can you share with me a little more about this friend of yours?'

Frenz grudgingly closed his book, moving his glasses from his nose to the top of his head. 'I suppose so. Her name is Avy Stammers and she joined the agency around the same time as me. She was born in Austria but raised in Germany. She spent her formative years working on her father's sugar beet farm in northern Germany, where she discovered a natural talent for mechanical engineering. She spent most of her free time fixing and maintaining her father's farming equipment, anything from tractor engines to combine harvesters.'

Impressed yet frustrated with Frenz's almost encyclopaedic knowledge of his friend's past, Will nodded but remained silent. Now that he had Frenz talking, he didn't want him to stop.

'When she outgrew the family nest, she joined the Deutsches Heer, as the German Army was once called. She was the first female engineer in the German military at the time. And she was just seventeen – she lied about her age, of course, but that was common at that time. However, the rise of the Nazi Party in the late 1930s meant that she and her family fled to England only a year later. When the war broke out, her talents became obvious to the British government. Being a defector from Germany, she became particularly valuable to the Allied efforts. At some point she caught the attention of the agency, and when the war ended, she was recruited.'

'Wow, she sounds amazing.'

'I assure you, she is. She's a remarkable woman.' Frenz beamed as he thought of his old friend. Will's mood momentarily improved and with a smirk he said, 'Do I detect romantic feelings for this friend, by any chance?'

'No, no. While I confess that I do love her, she is far more like a big sister. My dear friend Nestor and her, on the other hand, well, they did indeed fall in love. The three of us were very good friends for a long time. Thick as thieves, I believe is the saying. When Nestor disappeared, it hit Avy the hardest.'

Frenz pulled his reading glasses back down and resumed reading. Will glanced over the table at the book in Frenz's lap. 'Hey, what are you reading?'

Without looking up from his book and seemingly without stopping reading, he said, '*The Man in the High Castle*. It's a book about parallel worlds and alternative histories. It's riveting. I started reading it before all this and would rather not have to wait the best part of two decades to find out how the story ends.'

'Where did you get it?' Will asked.

'The book shop next to the ticketing office. Please, Will, we'll be docking soon and I'm almost finished.'

Will took the hint and settled back into his seat.

When the boat docked, it became clear that there was a substantially larger military presence here than there had been at Holyhead. Leaving Will aboard, Frenz scouted ahead and found that, fortunately, neither the port security, police or military had received Will's mug shot. From ashore, Frenz signalled the all-clear to a green-faced Will who was peering out of a restroom window.

Will was happy for a delay to their onward journey due to a cancelled bus service and after a two-hour wait had sufficiently recovered before they boarded the first of three buses. The first took them southwest to Limerick. From there they boarded a bus bound for Tralee, changing one final time ahead of their arrival in the town of Dingle.

A little over twenty-two hours had passed since Will and Frenz had left Norland Square garden earlier that morning, and it was approaching dawn by the time they disembarked at the bus stop overlooking the small fishing harbour. The harbour itself was situated in a large bay with flat, calm waters. Dingle was at Will's back, to the north. To the south, east and west were rolling hills covered in lush green. They looked agricultural, divided up into neat squares. The bay opened out to the sea just under two miles to the southeast, where the hills tapered off to sea level. There was a light breeze sweeping in from the south, causing the water surface to ripple and lap gently against the shore. As the sun rose in the east, it broke through the clouds in fine shafts and sparkled on the waves. The whole scene was so exquisitely picturesque that it didn't quite seem real. The fresh scent of sea air shook some of the weariness from Will's head after the long journey. Even the incessant song from the throng of seagulls overhead seemed to lift his spirits.

Man, Abigayle would love this place. I'll bring her here once this is all over.

Eventually the two of them proceeded away from the water, heading inland along Bridge Street, turning right onto Dykegate Street before reaching Main Street. The town was wonderful and beautiful in an entirely different way to the natural beauty of the harbour. It seemed as though the buildings running along Main Street were either public houses or fish-and-chip shops. The pubs seemed to outnumber the chip shops five to one, however. Each establishment was painted a different combination of vibrant colours. The pub on the right was bright yellow with green detailing. The pub opposite had opted for predominantly lime green with red window frames. Further up the street were buildings painted in lavender and burgundy, red and black, cream and blue. Further on still were oranges, purples, teal and pink. As they walked along the street, Will was sure that no colour in the spectrum had been overlooked.

The two of them ducked out of Main Street, turning left onto Orchard Lane. Will followed Frenz as he peeled off to his right through a narrow passageway. They emerged into a small cobblestone courtyard. The square space was closed in by a number of connected but separate dwellings. Opposite the passageway, directly in front of them was a quaint fisherman's cottage, with bright white, lime-washed paint. The ground floor had been converted into a storefront. Running across the top of the large front windows was a sign with the words *DINGLE HOROLOGICAL WORKSHOP* in gold, Times New Roman lettering with a black bevel. Above the sign, perfectly centred with the door below, was a large black and gold clockface. The two ground-floor windows either side of the front door had maroon frames and hand-painted decals on the glass panes. The decals listed the services and clock types available to buy, restore or repair: longcase clocks, carriage clocks, bracket clocks, wall clocks, pocket and wristwatches. Even barometers. The front door was secured by a sturdy metal shutter, which currently down. The two floors above appeared to be residential.

Will and Frenz stood in front of the shop and glanced at each other. 'This it?' Will asked.

'I think so, yes.'

'What time does she open?'

Before Frenz could respond, the two of them caught a glimpse of movement behind one of the first-floor windows, the net curtains still fluttering as they looked up. A moment later the shutter door began to move. Its ascent was slow but steady. As soon as the shutter door slid into its housing, the wooden panel door it had been securing swung inwards.

A woman emerged, elderly but spritely. She had a petite frame, but the way she carried herself indicated surprising strength and athleticism. She had wiry grey hair with darker streaks running through it. She wore it in a tight bun at the top of her head with two wavy strands hanging down, framing her face. She had a surprisingly smooth complexion and were it not for her eyes, which showed wisdom as much as her advancing years, she could have passed for far younger than she was. The fitted, denim dungarees that hung from her shoulders were faded and oil-stained, and the heavy workers' boots on her feet were scuffed and worn.

She looked first at Frenz, then at Will, then back to Frenz. A look that could have been resignation flashed across her face before she smiled warmly and said, in lightly accented English, 'Hello, Frenz. It's been a while. I supposed you'd better come in. Your friend too.'

CHAPTER EIGHTEEN

May 16th, 1984, 06:12

They entered a claustrophobic and cluttered shop interior split between two rooms. Almost every patch of wall and every surface was covered with a watch or clock of some description. The three of them rounded the counter at the rear of the store and entered the workshop area down a small set of steps. The workshop continued the jumbled, disorderly theme from the front of the shop. Here, however, the clocks and watches were all in various states of disrepair and the workbenches were covered in faces, arms, levers, pendulums, cogs, wheels and springs. Will couldn't help but be reminded of the way Frenz's shop had looked two days prior. Avy Stammers seemed to read Will's thoughts as he scrutinised the workshop. Without him saying a word she said, 'As you can see, my workshop is rather chaotic, but believe me, it is organised chaos.'

Will and Frenz remained silent as they followed Avy out of the workshop and up a narrow spiralling staircase to the first-floor kitchen.

By the time Will had joined them, Avy was already at the sink, filling the kettle with water, and Frenz was settling into a seat at the breakfast table in the middle of the kitchen. The kitchen was modest and U-shaped. It had traditional Shaker-style pine cabinets and pale green metro-style tiles over the beige and brown speckled kitchen surface. The floor was uneven – momentarily causing Will's nausea to resurface – and was covered in stained and torn cream linoleum. In the middle of the room was an aluminium-framed table with rounded corners and a ribbed pattern running around the perimeter of the tabletop. It was surrounded by four seats with matching aluminium tube frames and red leatherette fabric with white piping, stretched over well-worn foam padding at the base and back of each seat.

Avy moved this way and that around the kitchen, preparing cups and a plate of rich tea biscuits. The kettle whined and whistled as it came to the boil and Avy deposited the water into a teapot. After allowing it to brew, she poured an equal amount into the three cups she had lined up on the countertop. With surgical precision, Avy turned smoothly and placed one steaming cup of tea in front of Frenz, who was sitting on the left side of the table, his eyes never looking up from his lap, and set another in front of the empty seat opposite him. She looked up at Will as she did this, inviting him to sit. Will did so silently. Avy turned back to the counter, picked up the third cup for herself and placed a plate of neatly arranged biscuits in the middle of the table. The tension in the room was palpable. She took a biscuit for herself, dipped it in her tea and took a bite from the soft half, leaving a half-moon shape behind. She chewed silently, swallowed, then took a step back and leaned against the kitchen counter. An uncomfortable silence hung in the air before she said, 'So, who would like to go first? I'm sure we all have questions.'

Frenz shuffled in his seat and said, 'Avy, we need your help.'

'I gathered as much. Why don't you introduce me to your friend?'

'Of course. This is William Wells. He helped me out of a rather tight spot and has proven himself to be trustworthy. He's not with the agency, he's an outsider, but he knows enough that we can talk freely. He does have troubles of his own. Problems that I have vowed to help him resolve.'

'What kind of troubles?'

'My fiancée, Abigayle, is missing,' Will said.

'If what he tells me is true, she has gone astray,' Frenz added.

'And how exactly did this happen?'

'Will, show her. It's okay.'

Will responded by placing his hand on the breakfast table and pulling the sleeve of his jacket upwards, revealing the Timepiece strapped to his wrist.

Both Frenz and Will spent much of the following hour explaining the events of the past two days. Once Avy was fully up to speed she let out a deep sigh and said, 'Before I commit to helping you, I have some questions of my own.'

'Yes, I'm sure you do,' Frenz said.

'Frenz, I haven't seen *you* for almost twenty years. Tell me, when was the last time you saw *me*?'

'Approximately six days ago, I suppose.'

'I know that I pushed you away after Nestor, but I just needed some time to grieve. Before I could even begin to process what had happened to him, you disappeared on me too. What happened to you, Frenz?'

'I'm truly sorry for that, Avy, but I had no choice. Nestor didn't want you to be involved. He...*we were trying to protect you*.'

'Frenz, what are you talking about?'

Frenz took a breath, then said, 'A few weeks before he disappeared, Nestor came up to my office. He looked pale and unwell; all the blood had drained from his face and he was visibly trembling. I'd never seen him like that before. Avy, you knew him as well as anyone, he was always so optimistic and at ease, so I knew that whatever was going on, it must be serious. He sat down opposite me and told me that he had been visited by someone who wore the Timepiece on their wrist. This person didn't say where they were from, but Nestor was sure they were from the future. This person told him that the agency could no longer be trusted, that Cillian Gander was about to wrestle control of the agency from the others and that we must relieve the Timekeepers of the Timepiece and keep it from them forever.'

Will was literally sitting on the edge of his seat as Frenz spoke. 'Nestor told me that I had to be the one to steal it' Frenz continued. 'He said that he would do what was necessary so that I could get my hands on the Timepiece and escape with it. Nestor then handed me his *Timekeeper's Guidebook*, told me not to open it until I had the Timepiece in my possession and left my office. We didn't speak of it again for weeks. Whenever I broached the subject, he refused to talk about it. He closed himself off to me. After a while I just let it go, and things seemed to return to normal. I thought that perhaps he'd been sick or drunk that day he came into my office and that he was ashamed. That's why I never mentioned it to you, Avy. I thought he would rather you not know how he'd behaved and the things he'd said because, honestly, it sounded crazy.'

'Why didn't he tell me any of this? I could've helped.'

'He wanted to protect you, Avy. We were talking about stealing the Timepiece from the agency, and the less you knew about it the better.'

Will shuffled back into his seat slightly. 'Frenz, you told me that Nestor just disappeared in front of you with no warning. Do you think the person who visited Nestor told him that was going to happen?'

'I'm certain of it. I think Nestor knew what would happen, but I don't think he knew exactly when it would happen until the last few moments. His going astray was key to my being able to steal the Timepiece. And that's why he had *me* do it, because he knew he couldn't.'

'I don't understand,' Will said. 'How did Nestor going astray help you steal the Timepiece?'

Frenz was about to answer when Avy, just now putting the pieces together, responded herself. 'Because in the event of an agent going astray, the Timepiece is removed from the hands of the Operations Section while an investigation is carried out.'

Frenz nodded in agreement. 'Correct. It would have been next to impossible to steal from the Timekeepers themselves, but under an Agent Astray, or AA condition as it was called, the Timepiece is handed over to The Bureau of Game

Theory for analysis. They're more of an administrative wing of the agency and their security is far less substantial. It's also the section where I worked.'

'Let me get this straight,' Avy said. 'Are you telling me that Nestor allowed himself to go astray just so you would have an opportunity to steal the Timepiece?'

Frenz turned to look at Avy and nodded compassionately. 'It seems that way, yes. I'm so sorry, Avy. I didn't truly believe what he was saying until after he disappeared. It was only then that I fully understood, and it was too late to talk him out of it.'

Avy sighed. 'I don't blame you, Frenz. Once Nestor set his mind to something, there was no changing it. The two of you were alike in that way. If there's anyone to blame here, it's Cillian Gander and his damned Futures Project.'

'Yeah, Frenz told me a little about that,' Will said. 'They were using the Timepiece off-book, right?'

Frenz nodded. 'No officially sanctioned assignments were planned for the day Nestor disappeared. They would never schedule a repair to a Mimic Watch if there had been. Especially one malfunctioning the way this one was.'

Avy had a dour look to her and she said, 'I remember. I was scheduled to repair it, but Nestor insisted that he do it. I blamed myself for years for letting him go in my place.'

'Avy, you cannot blame yourself. It's usually safe work. A hundred things needed to happen for Nestor to go astray the way he did. I've never seen a Mimic Watch locked in its active state like that before.'

'Isn't there some kind of warning when the Timepiece is activated?' Will said.

'Yes,' Avy said. 'Mimic Watches have a thin ring of light

that runs around the perimeter of the watch case. It pulses amber for a few seconds when the Timepiece is activated.'

'So, he had some warning. Couldn't Nestor have dropped the watch as soon as he saw it glowing amber?'

'Yes, of course he could have, but he had no intention of stopping what was about to happen,' Frenz said. 'He was determined to go through with his plan no matter what. From the moment I walked into his workshop, I think he knew what was about to happen. When I spoke to him about joining me after work, it was as if he hadn't heard me at all. He just looked me in the eye and said, "Faking your death would be the way I'd do it, Frenz. They won't look for a man if everyone thinks he's already dead. When I'm gone, would you do something for me? Have a burial service for me. It'll give Avy a chance to say goodbye. There's a garden in South Kensington with a series of manmade mounds. I'd like to be buried at the base of one of them. Four feet below the ground should do for an empty casket." He smiled at me just then, that warm, disarming smile of his, glanced at the Mimic Watch he was holding and then he was gone.'

Will looked up at Avy as she stared into her half-empty cup. A single tear materialised from her eye but was intercepted by her hand before it had passed her cheekbone. She looked up, instantly composed herself and said, 'I always wondered why you were so insistent on that service. Especially when you didn't even attend. Why that specific location? It wasn't somewhere we'd ever been before, so it had no significance.'

'I didn't fully understand Nestor's last words at first either, but the man was so brilliant that he'd already planned my escape for me. Well, the basis for an escape plan anyway.

Nestor knew that stealing the Timepiece would be far easier than escaping with it.'

'And how did you do that exactly?' Will asked. 'Because when I showed up and found you mid-escape, you were in jail. It didn't exactly look like it was going to plan.'

'On the contrary, it was all going to plan *until* you showed up. Like Nestor said, you won't pursue a man if you think he's dead. So, I followed those sentiments. And not only would I use my own death to cover my tracks, but Nestor's as well. I arranged an empty casket burial for Nestor. I claimed that we would be burying some of his most prized possessions in place of his body but instead—'

'That was why you weren't at the service,' Avy interjected.

'Yes. Well, technically I *was* there, but obviously nobody knew that I was in the casket, holding the Timepiece in one hand and Nestor's *Timekeeper's Guidebook* in the other. After they buried me, which I have to say is the most terrifying thing I've experienced in my life, I opened the book and by torchlight I read my final instructions and a very specific date. There were also instructions for my would-be rescuer to find.' Frenz glanced at Will as he said this.

'And then we buried you under a manmade mound, just as Nestor suggested,' Avy added.

'Exactly. The casket was buried at the requested depth of four feet, which was approximately one foot above the ground level before the mound was erected. I then set my destination date and time for September fifth, 1940, as instructed. When I activated the Timepiece, I appeared in a field, one foot above the ground. The landing winded me a little, but it was otherwise safe. It was my first time in the field, literally in this case.'

'I don't understand, if you went to the past with the Timepiece, wouldn't the Timekeepers just track you there with it?' Will asked.

'Indeed. By the time Nestor's casket was being lowered into the ground, the alarm would have been signalled that the Timepiece was missing and had just been activated. They wouldn't have had much time to track me because I deactivated the Timepiece less than ten seconds after I arrived in 1940.'

'But I thought you said that deactivating the Timepiece would send you back to your origin timeline.'

'That is also correct, which is why I prepared a dead man's switch for the Timepiece. As I sat on the ground, I held the Timepiece a little over one foot above the ground, attached the dead man's switch and let go of it. The switch did its job: the moment I released it, it automatically deactivated the Timepiece, sending it back to 1967, safely buried in an empty casket at the base of a manmade mound in a Kensington garden and leaving me in 1940. And it hadn't been activated long enough for the Timekeepers to even begin tracking its location. All they would have is a record of a date, but without the Timepiece they had no way of getting there.'

Will said, 'So that's how you had the money that's still legal tender today. You're not from 1940 at all, you're from 1967.'

Frenz nodded, then sipped at his tea.

'But Frenz,' Avy said, 'what did you do to end up in jail?'

'I think it was Nestor's parting gift to me, a practical joke. As it turned out, those manmade mounds were built by the British Army during the Second World War for training purposes. I had let myself go astray in wartime England and

I found myself sitting in the middle of an active army base with no explanation of how I got there. I claimed to be lost, but of course I was immediately handed over to the police, arrested and thrown in jail. Getting myself arrested was always part of the plan, but I hadn't expected it to happen quite like that. Once I was in jail, I planted Nestor's guidebook, then complained to a guard about some loose mortar in the wall but was charged with tampering and attempting escape so they moved me to the adjacent cell. Then all I had to do was wait. A friend was supposed to arrive and get me out of that jail. A jail that would soon be a target of a Nazi bombing run. So even if remaining Timekeepers in 1967 looked in the history books for me, all they'd find was a prisoner matching my description, who died in his cell after the jail he was in partially collapsed due to bomb damage. It was perfect.'

Avy took a sip of her tea, pushed herself away from the countertop and set the cup down on the breakfast table. She pulled out an empty chair, sat down with Will and Frenz on either side of her and looked at them both. 'Frenz, you may never know quite how furious I am with you for keeping me out of this whole thing,' she said. 'Fortunately for you I am even more furious with Nestor. The damned fool. My heart was broken when he disappeared, so I know all too clearly what you're going through, William. If there is anything I can do to reunite you with the woman you love, then I will do it.'

Will smiled coyly and said, 'Avy, thank you, really. I do have one question though.'

'Of course, William,' said Frenz.

'Yes, fire away,' added Avy.

'Who the hell is Cillian Gander?'

CHAPTER NINETEEN

May 4th, 1967, 14:38

Cillian Gander was seated behind a large walnut desk in a green leather high-backed executive chair. He sat silently with his eyes closed and fists clenched, deep in thought.

His office at Central Station, hidden deep below the streets of London, was extravagant in its size and appearance, with a splendid velvet Oriental rug centred over the highly polished wooden floor. The walls had rich teal wainscot panelling encircling the lower third, with white wallpaper with gold gilded vertical stripes above. Behind the desk on either side of the chair sat two large bookcases filled with leather-bound books in weathered shades of blue, red and green. This was one of three such offices inhabited by each of the three Section Heads at The Office of Time Dissemination. Cillian's office was the middle of the three, overlooking the main atrium, where many of the other

Timekeeper agents worked.

Cillian was a gaunt, cadaverous and aggressive-looking man with pale skin riddled with deep lines. For most people, it was difficult to tell whether these folds were the result of ageing or of the frown lines from his continually furrowed brow. Others thought that perhaps he had just been born angry. He had a high hairline with dark grey and relatively sparse hair, which was swept backwards neatly. His eyes were sunk behind thin slits of loose skin and framed with thick dark eyebrows and drooping plump bags of purple-coloured skin.

It had been two days since the mysterious disappearance of Nestor Ordell. When Frenz Belingi made the report of his disappearance, it was met with scepticism and disbelief by some and distress and confusion by others. A Timekeeper agent going astray during an active assignment was rare but did happen. An engineer disappearing from his workshop when no active assignments were even scheduled though, that was highly unusual.

Although all part of the same agency, the three sections operated virtually independently from one another. All of this meant that tensions were at an all-time high at Central Station, and each of its three sections was subtly pointing the finger of blame towards the others. Each had opened detailed investigations to discover how this could have happened.

While no official accusations had been made towards him, Cillian couldn't help but feel vulnerable. His plan to take control of the agency was only just underway and it had already hit an unexpected obstacle. He had taken a huge risk by conducting unauthorised Futures Project assignments, but if his bid for power was going to work, he needed to have an advantage over his opponents. For him, the biggest advantage was information. It was always a powerful weapon and wielding it correctly could be the difference between success and failure. Information about the future was something else entirely. With it he would know what his opponents' next moves were going to be and he could plan and act accordingly. To retrieve this information, he'd sent willing agents months into the future to gather that information. He'd done it before and done it quietly. This time, however, he'd made an awful lot of noise.

He had been sitting in an almost trance-like state for two hours, contemplating his next move, when the silence was broken by the buzzer on his desk. He blinked rapidly for a few moments before turning his head towards the intercom with a look of disdain. He pressed the large black button under the flashing red light and barked, 'What is it?!' He spoke with flawless Queen's English. Each syllable was shaped and carved immaculately. His voice was smooth but with a slightly higher pitch to it than one might have expected.

A timid female voice crackled through the tinny, electronic buzz of the intercom speaker. 'I'm…I'm sorry, Mr Gander, but Agents Tyke and Wigmore are here to see you. They don't have an appointment but claim that you're expecting them.'

'Fine. Send them in.'

'Yes, of course, sir.'

'And Ms Brockett?'

'Yes, sir?'

'Nobody but these two agents are to be admitted for the

remainder of the day. Understood?'

'Yes, sir, understood.'

The intercom cut off with a loud click.

The double doors opposite Cillian's desk swung open as the two men entered. The first to pass through the door was tall and thin. His legs seemed to account for almost two thirds of his overall height. He carried a brown leather case in his hand. The second man was short, with a bulbous stomach hanging over his belt. He had a large round head perched on top of his shoulders. There was no discernible sign of a neck. He pulled the doors closed behind him one at a time and took up position next to his taller counterpart. They wore matching tan green tweed jackets and beige trousers and stood silently in front of Cillian Gander's desk, obediently awaiting orders.

Cillian looked at them and with an irritated tone said, 'Sit.'

The two men did as they were instructed. They looked at each other, unsure who should speak first or indeed *if* they should speak first. They looked at Cillian, who raised his eyebrows at them impatiently. Sensing their superior's growing annoyance, the shorter man, named Wigmore, eventually spoke. He cleared his throat. 'Section Head Gander, we have some news.'

The taller man, Tyke, added, 'Yes, sir. As expected, investigations are underway in all sections of the agency. For appearances' sake, our section has begun its own investigation also.'

'I see, and what about our man? Has he been dealt with and the dossier secured?' Cillian said.

'Well, sir, not exactly,' Wigmore replied.

'Excuse me? You fucking imbeciles! You're only coming

to me with this information now?'

'Our apologies for not coming to you sooner, sir—'

'It's been two days,' Cillian interrupted.

'Well, sir, given that we're under an AA condition, we thought it safer to wait for the dust to settle.'

'What the hell happened?'

'I assure you, sir, that your orders were carried out to the letter just as they have been on previous assignments. We had no problems finding an agent to volunteer. A new recruit, Stephen Robertshaw, only twenty-four years old, enthusiastic, eager to impress, living on his own in the city and not likely to be missed. He was taken to the basement-level complex and placed in room four in the east wing.'

'And he was examined thoroughly?' Cillian asked.

'Yes, sir. The agent in question had a full medical. A dental examination confirmed the absence of any metal fillings. He then showered and was deloused. His fingernails were examined and cleaned thoroughly. As you know, we've encountered some unpredictable behaviour with ferromagnetic materials, so a full-body scan was also performed.

'Finally, he was taken back to room four, where he was placed three feet from the centre of the north wall. Agent Robertshaw was then handed the Timepiece with its destination time already set. He activated it and was gone for no more than twenty seconds. When he returned, he was asked to confirm that contact was made with you, sir, to which he responded in the affirmative. He was then immediately bound, gagged and placed in secure isolation, which is where he remains. Initially, the assignment appeared to be a success.'

'Any resistance?'

'Yes, he struggled and shouted through his gag, but no more than the others.'

'And the dossier?'

'I'm afraid he didn't have one with him, sir. That's why he hasn't yet been processed. We thought that you might like to speak with him to find out why he didn't receive a dossier from your counterpart in the future.'

'It's a risk keeping him here. We can ill afford anyone from outside the Operations Section finding him.'

Tyke sat up in his seat and said, 'He's under guard from agents we can trust, sir.'

'Fine, but I'll want to speak with him as soon as is possible. I have a lot of eyes on me at present, so care must be taken. What's the status of the other sections?'

'Well, sir,' Tyke said, 'it seems that Section Head Doolin was the first to act. Not surprising given that the agency staff member who went astray was from his own Engineering Section. Our sources from within his section didn't indicate that he has any reason to suspect our involvement.'

'Doolin won't be a problem,' Cillian said. 'He's far too invested in his personal financial affairs back in the States to pay much attention to what goes on here anymore. So long as we keep feeding him information garnered from our Futures Project, he'll keep making the money he needs to pay off all the politicians and officials that he needs to, to keep his sons out of jail.'

'Yes, sir. Wigmore and I came to the same conclusion. We think the investigation is just to show that he's doing something. It'll keep the rabble happy until all the excitement dies down.'

'Why do I get the feeling there's more?'

Tyke and Wigmore eyed each other nervously once more before Tyke said, 'While Section Head Doolin has proven relatively toothless, the same can't be said for one of his subordinates.'

'The woman. Avy Stammers,' Cillian said.

'Yes, sir. She's convinced that the Operations Section is responsible. More specifically, she believes that you personally are to blame and she's not being quiet about it.'

'Tell me about her. Is there anything we can do to silence her?'

'Well, we could follow her home one evening. Perhaps she could fall in front of a bus or a train? It's an approach that has worked for us in the past.'

'Not this time. If she's being vocal about her suspicions, then her death will only draw more attention to her and to us. No, we need to deal with her differently. Do we have any other leverage? Partners? Children? Elderly parents, perhaps?'

'Unfortunately not. She has no children, no siblings. Her parents both died shortly after the war. The impression we get from other staff members is that she did have a partner.'

'Did have?'

'It seems that she and our missing man, Nestor Ordell, were... romantically engaged with each other.'

'Well, that explains her tenacity; this is personal for her. In that case we will have to attack her character and discredit her professionally, Wigmore, begin immediately. Everyone has secrets and I want to know hers.'

'Yes, sir.'

'I would like to get the measure of her, so bring her to my

office. While she's here, perhaps you could search her workstation. Go.'

'Yes, sir.'

'Now,' Cillian hissed.

Wigmore started in his seat, stood, gave Cillian a determined nod and waddled out of the room, closing the doors behind him. Cillian watched him leave and then turned his attention to Tyke. 'What about Madame Izri?'

Tyke's eye twitched ever so slightly at this question and he shuffled in his seat uncomfortably. He calmed himself before he spoke. 'Section Head Izri is a little harder to predict, sir. It was a member of her team who witnessed the disappearance of Nestor Ordell first-hand.' Tyke pulled a notepad from his jacket pocket and flicked through the pages until he found what he was looking for. 'His name is Frenz Belingi. He's been at The Bureau of Game Theory for sixteen years. From what I've been told, he's a reliable and able Geohistorian and is well liked by Madame Izri herself.'

'Yes, I know the one. The negro' – Cillian's top lip curled up in disgust as he spoke the word – 'was the only person to witness the disappearance?'

'Yes, we believe so.'

'What was his relationship to this Nestor Ordell person?'

'They were good friends, or so I'm told. Belingi, Stammers and Ordell were apparently a tight group.'

'So, it's personal for him as well. Reporting the disappearance aside, has he vocalised any suspicions towards us?'

'No, not that we've heard. He's certainly not drawing any attention to himself in the way that the Stammers woman has been.'

Cillian leaned back in his chair, staring at the ceiling as if he might find answers there. He then returned his gaze to Agent Tyke. 'Let's see what he does next. Stammers should be our focus for the time being.'

'Yes, sir.'

'One more thing. The malfunctioning Mimic Watch, have you recovered it?'

Tyke reached down to his side, picked up his brown attaché case and placed it on his lap. He carefully rolled the dials for the combination, opened the case and pulled out a black rubber wallet, placing it on the desk in front of him. Cillian picked it up and opened it. He pulled out the Mimic Watch, placed the wallet flat on the desk and laid the watch on top of it. The outer ring of the device pulsed a dim red colour every few seconds.

Cillian ran his hand gently over the surface of the watch, almost tenderly. 'It's still active. So, this is what has caused all of our troubles. How did we miss this?'

'It seems the problem was discovered close to the time we were planning our next Futures Project assignment. We were already underway by the time it was officially entered into record. Given the dangers a Mimic Watch like this could cause, it was sent for repair immediately.'

Their conversation was interrupted when the desk intercom buzzed loudly once more. The voice of Ms Brockett crackled through. 'Mr Gander, sir, apologies for the interruption but Agent Wigmore has returned with Ms Stammers.'

Cillian pressed the intercom button, leaned towards the speaker and said, 'Agent Tyke was just leaving. Please send Ms Stammers in once he has left.'

'Of course, sir.'

Cillian turned back to Tyke and said, 'Keep an eye on Frenz Belingi. Bring him to me the moment he steps out of line.'

'Right away, sir.'

Agent Tyke stood and with long, slow strides reached the double doors in just three steps. He pulled a door open with his right hand and made a theatrical motion with his left, holding it out to one side, beckoning Avy Stammers into the room. She ignored the empty gesture, pulling the other door open instead and walking past Tyke without acknowledging him. Tyke appeared to shrink into himself and retreated from sight.

Avy walked purposefully into the room and stopped in front of Cillian Gander's desk. A thin, satisfied smile spread across Cillian's face. He regarded Avy thoughtfully and then said, 'Please, sit.'

'That won't be necessary, I won't be staying long,' Avy snapped back.

'Is that so?'

'I'm here as a courtesy. I don't work in your section, so you have no authority over me. You know this.'

Cillian smiled again, slightly wider this time. He was impressed with the confidence of this unassuming woman before him. 'My people tell me that you've been making some rather unsavoury accusations about the Operations Section. And about me personally.'

'A good man is gone because someone activated the Timepiece off-book. Your own Operations Section has a responsibility to prevent this kind of thing and it failed. Intentional or not, you are to blame.'

'I find your choice of words interesting.'

'Oh, how so?'

'You talk about responsibility. Was it not your own responsibility to oversee the repair of this particular Mimic Watch yourself, as head of your department?'

Avy didn't rise to this; instead, the features of her face hardened and she directed an arrow-like stare back at Cillian.

'It seems to me,' Cillian continued, 'that if anyone is responsible for a man having gone astray, it's you. Then again, perhaps the blame stretches even further than that. After all, it was Section Head Doolin's decision to appoint a woman as head of your department in the first place. Even after my advice to the contrary.'

Avy had learned to deal with men like Cillian throughout her life and deflected his next attempt to get a rise out of her. 'What is it that you want?'

Cillian leaned forward, placing his elbows on his desk. He could sense victory was within his grasp. She wanted something and a man in his position had a lot to offer. 'I want you to stop your slanderous remarks about this section's involvement in this man's disappearance and get on with your life.'

'And why would I do that?'

'Well, why stop at head of department? Perhaps one day even a woman might be able to become head of the whole Engineering Section? Stranger things have happened.'

Avy smiled. 'You'd really do that for me?'

'Of course. You scratch my back and I scratch yours.' Cillian smiled, this time baring crooked, yellowed teeth. Avy took a step forwards and placed both palms flat on the desk opposite Cillian. Her face was close enough to smell Cillian's stale breath. In a low, seductive voice, she said, 'That really is a sweet offer.'

'I can be ever so nice if I choose to,' Cillian replied.

'Well let me tell you something, Cillian Gander,' Avy said.

'Go on,' Cillian replied. He was enjoying this. Avy willing to do anything, it would seem. But suddenly her face changed, and her tone was icy cold when she next spoke. 'I know it was you. And I will prove it and you will pay for it. No matter how long it takes me, you will pay.'

The smile evaporated from Cillian's face, quickly replaced with an expression contorted with rage. He pushed himself back from his desk, stood and through gritted teeth said, 'You're finished. You have no idea who you're dealing with. This was your chance to come out of this on top and you've wasted it. Leave now and hope you never cross paths with me again.'

Avy stepped back and smiled. 'I told you this would be a short visit. Hopefully your man will have finished searching through my things,' she said with a mocking grin. 'Now, I have a memorial service to attend for a real man who is gone because of you.' With that Avy spun and left the office.

Cillian was still seething after his meeting with Avy Stammers when Agent Wigmore returned to his office, shown in by Ms Brockett. Cillian rose from his desk as he entered and began talking immediately. 'Did you find anything on Ms Stammers?'

'No, I'm afraid not, sir. Her workstation was clean.'

'Blast that woman,' Cillian said. 'While half the agency is at that meaningless empty casket service for Ordell, now might be a good time for us go and speak to Agent Robertshaw.'

'I don't think that's a good idea, sir, there are—'

'Are you questioning me, Agent Wigmore?'

'No, of course not, sir. I'll take you to him right away.'

Cillian picked up the malfunctioning Mimic Watch from his desk and pocketed it. Then he and Wigmore made their way to the derelict sub-basement level of Central Station. They used an old freight elevator with a vintage Otis scissor gate to descend the five floors. Once there they passed through several dimly lit, narrow concrete-walled passageways until they reached one that had two agents standing on either side of a closed door. Wigmore nodded to both agents, who stepped aside. He pulled a key from his pocket, unlocked the large metal door and pushed it open. Wigmore himself stepped aside and let Cillian enter the small room.

Sitting on the floor in one corner was a man with his knees held closely against his chest. His hands and feet were bound tightly with rope, his mouth was taped shut and a white cloth blindfold covered his eyes. Cillian turned and nodded to Wigmore, who closed the cell door. Cillian approached the bound man, knelt down and gently removed the cloth blindfold. Agent Robertshaw blinked frantically as his wild, bloodshot eyes adjusted to the bright light in the room. When he saw Cillian looming over him, he started and shuffled further back into the corner. He tried to talk, uttering something indecipherable through the tape that covered his mouth. Cillian raised his hands and said, 'Could you please hold still and allow me to help? If you begin screaming and acting in a hysterical manner, the gag goes back on, understand?'

Agent Robertshaw calmed down but continued to stare

at Cillian Gander in the same desperate manner. Cillian moved his hand slowly towards him and pulled the tape free in one rapid flick of his wrist. Agent Robertshaw gasped and then began performing a series of movements with his jaw to remove some of the stiffness and tension that had built up over the past two days. He coughed and spat a gob of old dark blood onto the floor. Cillian rose and stepped back. Agent Robertshaw took a moment to compose himself, then said, 'Sorry about that, sir.' He paused to exercise his jaw some more, moving it side to side. 'One of the other agents slugged me when they brought me down here and I've been swallowing quite a lot of blood since then.'

'Don't apologise. It is *me* who should be apologising to *you*. This has all been a terrible misunderstanding, I'm sure.'

'Sir, what's going on? I did everything I was asked. What did I do wrong?'

Cillian slid his hand into his pocket, retrieving the damaged Mimic Watch. Its red ring of light continued to pulse slowly. 'This is what went wrong, Agent Robertshaw. A malfunctioning Mimic Watch. An engineer was repairing it when you activated the Timepiece and now he's gone astray.'

'I'm sorry, sir, I didn't know. How could I—'

'You couldn't have, Agent Robertshaw. You didn't do anything wrong at all. But tell me, when you went into the future, what did you see? Agent Wigmore informs me that you didn't receive a dossier from my future self to bring back with you?'

'No, sir, I didn't. I activated the Timepiece, stood exactly where I was supposed to. When I arrived at my destination time, you were right there, sir, just like they said you would be.'

'And then what happened?'

'Sir, you looked…'

'Go on, it's fine,' Cillian said, 'you're not in any trouble.'

'Well, you looked unsettled, sir. You looked like you hadn't slept or shaved or washed for days. I asked you what was wrong. I asked where the dossier of information was because you had nothing with you.'

'That sounds most unlike me, Agent Robertshaw. Are you certain it was me?'

'It was you, sir, I'm sure.'

Cillian calmly walked back to the door of the cell. He turned to face Agent Robertshaw. Before he could direct more questions to him, his attention was caught by the ring of light on the damaged Mimic Match, which began to flash amber frantically before turning solid green. Cillian Gander looked up and to his surprise the sparse concrete room was no longer so. He was instead surrounded by racks of shelving units filled to the brim with cardboard boxes, each one itself filled with files and stacks of paper. He looked up to the art deco clock hanging on the wall to his right. The top half had a traditional analogue clock and the bottom half had a split-flap display showing the date. It read: September 5th, 1940.

Almost as soon as Cillian adjusted to his new surroundings, the room around him changed once more. The clock and the shelving units had vanished, and he found himself back where he started. An even more agitated Agent Robertshaw sat cowering in the corner of the room. When Cillian looked at him, Agent Robertshaw said, 'Sir! What just happened? What's going on here?'

Cillian ignored his questioning and instead knelt next to

him, grabbing him by the shoulders. 'What did I tell you? My future self, what did I say?'

Agent Robertshaw took a breath and his eyes darted between the floor and Cillian's face. Eventually he said, 'Sir, you told me that the Timepiece had been stolen. Almost two months earlier.'

Cillian stood once more, walked to the door and knocked. Wigmore immediately unlocked it, pulling it open. Agent Robertshaw shouted after him, his desperation evident. 'Sir, you're going to let me out of here, aren't you?'

Cillian stopped, turned back to him and said, 'Yes, I'm done with you. You can go.' As soon as he spoke those words, Cillian pulled a gun from his jacket and fired a bullet through the middle of Agent Robertshaw's forehead. The agent's eyes rolled vacantly upwards and his head lolled back as he slumped into the corner. Cillian placed the gun back in its holster and said, 'Dispose of this.' The two agents who had been guarding the door moved into the room and got to work.

Cillian and Agent Wigmore made their way back to the elevator and ascended five floors. Wigmore pulled the scissor doors open and followed Cillian back to his office. The two of them arrived to find Agent Tyke already there, waiting.

'Agent Tyke, what on earth do you think you're doing in my office?'

Tyke looked rattled and mumbled his words as he spoke. 'I…I, um, sir. Frenz Belingi, sir, I can't find him. No one has seen him for nearly two days.'

'Well what are you doing loitering in my office?' Cillian bellowed. 'Go and find him!'

'But, sir, he's not the only thing missing. The Timepiece, we think he stole it. And a few moments ago, he activated it.'

CHAPTER TWENTY

May 16th, 1984, 08:48

Mapson had been anxious for a positive development in the case and the call he'd been waiting for came in just as he was beginning his morning shift. That's not to say that he'd left the station in the past twenty-four hours; he'd spent the previous night working to undo the mess that his two tweed-clad friends had caused. Detective Inspector Moss was furious and Mapson wasn't altogether sure that he'd bought his story about the car backfiring, but delivering a good lead on the whereabouts of William Wells might help smooth things over with his boss.

He answered the phone on the first ring, his voice gravelly, tired. 'Serious Crimes, Mapson speaking.'

He listened intently to the response, said thank you, then stood from his desk and hurried down to reception. There he was introduced to the subject of the call and the source of his newfound positivity: Mrs Karlita Gesler.

Mrs Gesler was a resident of Norland Square. She'd lived in one of the large townhouses there for almost thirty years. Her husband, who'd died over a decade earlier, was a relatively unsuccessful banker and had inherited the property from his parents. Upon his death, the property had passed into the sole possession of Mrs. Gesler. She'd never done a hard day's work in her life and yet still managed to look down on almost everyone she encountered who had.

She did a deft job of crushing Mapson's spirits in a matter of minutes. He'd led her to his desk, offered her a seat and a warm drink. She was dressed in a fine button-down navy silk dress with large pearls weighing down her earlobes and a matching set around her neck. Her head darted around the office as if the lack of cleanliness might reach out and bite her. She used the newspaper she carried under her arm to brush some debris off the chair before taking a seat. She glanced at Mapson's nameplate on his desk, then said, 'Sergeant Mapson, is it?'

'Yes, madam, it is. Now, would you like to tell me why you've come in to speak to us this morning?'

'This just won't do. I wish to speak to someone with seniority. Whoever is running this operation, I'd like to speak to him.'

'That'll be DI Moss. I'm afraid he's rather busy with the investigation at the moment.'

'Well, I never! Here I am, an important witness, an upstanding member of the community, and they leave me with a lowly *sergeant*. And what about my own safety? I'm offering information on a homicidal maniac. Who's to say I won't be his next target?'

Mapson found her immediately unlikable. He offered his finest faux smile. 'I assure you, madam, that I am an experienced officer. I also report directly to DI Moss. If I could just take your statement—'

'Pfft, very well,' she said, flinging a limp-wristed hand in Mapson's general direction. 'I've seen the man you're looking for. That mass-murdering Yank, William Wells. His face is all over the papers.'

'Mass-murdering?' Mapson said, taking out his notepad and pen.

'Yes! The newspaper' – she waved her copy of the *Daily Mail* in the air – 'says that he's done this kind of thing before. Three other murders in the past two years, they say.'

'Mrs Gesler, I think it's best that we refrain from that kind of unsubstantiated gossip. He's not been convicted of anything yet. He's just wanted in connection with a murder investigation. At the moment, that's all.'

'Nonsense. I knew he was a criminal sort the first time I saw him. And murder isn't all he's involved with. I observed the blighter breaking into our private garden multiple times with his girlfriend. And she's missing now as well. So that's five murders altogether!'

Mapson continued to smile politely. 'Okay, why don't you start by telling me where you saw William Wells and when.'

'Just yesterday morning. I saw him and some other shady-looking character in our private garden – again! It's my duty to know these things. You ruddy police officers don't do a thing about it! I'm the chairwoman of the Norland Conservation Society, you know!'

'Impressive,' Mapson said dryly. 'What time would you say this was?'

'Around 6 a.m.'

'You're sure it was William Wells?'

'Certain of it.'

'And this other man, have you seen him before?' Mapson said, scribbling details frantically into his notepad.

'No, never.'

'Did you see where they went?'

'I most certainly did. As I said, it's not the first time he's done it and I've had enough of it. So, I hurried downstairs and followed them out onto the main road and saw them board a bus. The number 228, I believe it was.'

'This is excellent information, Mrs Gesler. Thank you. Although I must that you avoid any attempts to confront persons who are of interest to the police in future. They could potentially violent criminals.'

Before she could offer a retort, the doors to the Serious Crimes office burst open and in came Detective Inspector Moss. He stormed past Mapson and Mrs Gesler, who was giving the detective an ineffective come-hither glance. Mapson sprung up from his seat, eager to deliver good news for a change. 'Sir, I have a lead on Wells, a solid one!'

Pausing to look at Mapson with mock surprise, Moss said simply, 'Oh?'

'Yes, sir. Mrs Gesler here lives in Norland Square and she saw Wells boarding the number 228 bus at around 6 a.m. yesterday morning.'

'Yesterday morning?'

'Yes, sir,' Mapson said again, barely able to contain his pride.

Moss walked across the room to Mapson, stopping at arm's length. He reached into his jacket pocket and pulled out two pieces of paper with perforated edges and held one in each hand, inches from Mapson's face. 'See these pictures?'

Mapson's shoulders drooped and he nodded slowly, looking at the grainy black-and-white images. One showed William Wells sitting outside a café with another man whose face was obscured. The two of them were deep in conversation. The other showed him passing through security and boarding the ferry to Dublin.

'These,' Moss said, 'were just faxed over. They're from yesterday *afternoon*. Do you recognise anyone?'

'It looks like Mr Wells, sir.'

'Yes, it does, doesn't it? This is him with an unknown male, boarding the Holyhead to Dublin ferry. Now, if you'll excuse me, I need to make a phone call to the chief of the Dublin police.' Moss turned his back on Mapson and continued walking towards his office.

'Yes, sir. Sorry, sir,' Mapson said.

Mrs Gesler, who had been standing over Mapson's shoulder, cleared her throat and said, 'Detective Inspector?'

Moss stopped but didn't turn around. 'What is it?'

'Those images,' Mrs Gesler said, 'they don't make sense.'

'Madam, I really am very busy.'

'It's the timestamps on the pictures,' she said.

'What about them?'

'If they're correct, then we must be looking for two William Wells because the timestamp is almost the same on each image. How can he be in two places at once?'

Moss looked at the images again, then spun around with a kind of crazed grin on his face. 'How indeed?'

CHAPTER TWENTY-ONE

May 17th, 1984, 06:48

Will, Frenz and Avy had continued to speak throughout the day. By the time Avy had finished the account of her experience with Cillian Gander seventeen years prior, they had worked their way through four pots of tea, two packs of rich tea biscuits, a chicken and mushroom pie and a few slices of homemade apple amber. The sun had begun to set, casting near horizontal rays of light through the kitchen.

It was obvious to Will that Frenz and Avy had been close and that Avy had missed her friend over all these years. There were still some things that went unsaid between them. Will had been fighting sleep since they'd arrived in Dingle, so after they'd eaten dinner together, he retired to bed to allow the two of them some time alone. Avy had offered him the sofa in the living room. By this point, Will could have slept anywhere. Before turning in for the night, Will had, with

Frenz's insistence and Avy's reassurance, reluctantly agreed to hand the Timepiece over so that it could be inspected. It was, after all, one of the reasons they had made the journey to see Avy in the first place. He had felt his gut lurch horribly as he peeled the sturdy leather strap from his wrist and handed it over.

With the comforting warmth and weight of the Timepiece – his one true link to Abigayle – stripped from him, he had fallen into an uneasy sleep.

He awoke the following morning to the sound of seagulls. Sunlight was streaming in through the window. Sitting up, he shielded his eyes as his head passed through a bright band of light that shone across the back of the sofa. He arched his back and groaned, clutching at his ribs. They had taken the brunt of the impact when he and Frenz had dived through the air while evading the two Timekeepers and now there was a dull ache when he breathed. That, or the painful longing in his heart to see Abigayle was manifesting itself physically. Either way, he hoped that nothing was broken. He rubbed his eyes, then rose from the sofa and staggered back towards the kitchen as if drunk. Will wasn't a morning person.

He could hear a muffled voice through the frosted glass of the sliding doors that separated the kitchen from the living room. Stopping short of the doors, he felt the anxiety course through him. In the few days since Abigayle's disappearance, Will had become more and more paranoid, wary of the slightest thing out of the ordinary. He pressed his ear against the glass to better hear the voice. It had neither Frenz's Caribbean twang nor Avy's light Austrian drawl.

Is there someone else in the room with them? he suddenly thought, breathing deeply, pushing the pain to the back of his mind.

He stepped sideways and peered in through a narrow gap between the two doors. He could see Avy sitting at the kitchen table in the same seat she'd sat in the night before. The table was covered in all manner of tools, oils and watch parts. She held the Timepiece in her hands, examining it meticulously, polishing any blemishes with a dull blue rag. Will could see Frenz standing behind her with his back turned and both hands placed flat on the kitchen counter.

Will shifted his weight from one foot to the other, the floorboard below him creaking loudly. Avy looked up and Frenz spun around. When Frenz saw the silhouette of Will's frame through the glass, he rolled his eyes, tipped his head to the side and let out an exasperated sigh. 'Oh for heaven's sake, William, why are you sneaking around like that?'

Will slid the glass door to the side, opening the narrow gap until it was wide enough for him to step through. As he walked into the kitchen, he could see the small portable television set on the kitchen countertop next to Frenz. 'Shit, sorry. I heard a voice I didn't recognise. I'm a little on edge.' He gestured to the television. 'I guess it was just the TV.'

'Magnificent, isn't it? The colours are spectacular!' Frenz said.

'Yeah, I guess.'

Will pulled up a chair opposite Avy and sat down. She nodded to him, lifted the tea cosy clear of the teapot and poured him a cup. She slid the cup towards Will, who smiled gratefully. He wrapped his cold hands around the cup to warm them, then said, 'So, what did I miss last night?'

'Oh, nothing important,' Avy said. 'Frenz and I were just catching up. Well, he was, at least.'

'Are we any closer to figuring out a way to get to Abigayle safely? I get that we can go get her seconds after I left if we want to, but I can't sit around doing nothing. I feel guilty just for having slept!'

'You'll be no good to anybody if you're exhausted. You'll need your wits about you for what's to come,' Avy said ominously.

Will nodded, then sipped his tea.

'The good news,' Avy said, 'is that this morning I was able to have a detailed look at the Timepiece. I'm happy to report that it's now fully functioning and safe to use. No more overheating. Obviously, you must still abide by the three laws and remain aware that the Timekeepers are likely still tracking your location.'

'Three laws?' Will asked.

'Does that confused look imply that Frenz didn't care to explain this to you?'

Frenz half turned his head from the television and said, 'Not explicitly, no, but I explained the basics.'

Avy sighed and said, 'As far as I'm concerned, these rules *are* the basics and if he's going to be responsible for holding time itself in his hands, then it's best he knows them. Take another sip and listen up, ready?'

Will swallowed a mouthful and said, 'Okay, shoot.'

'First, never activate the Timepiece while at great height – tall buildings, bridges, aeroplanes and so on. There's no guarantee those things will be there in the time you're travelling to. Second, never activate the Timepiece while travelling at speed. And third, never use the Timepiece to visit the future. There, easy, no?'

Will had locked eyes with Frenz when Avy had recited the

third rule. Avy looked at both of them quizzically and said, 'What is it?'

'Rescuing Abigayle may require that we break one of the three laws,' Frenz said.

'Is that right?' Avy said.

'Frenz and I already talked about the risks of going to the future – it's dangerous, uncertain, ever-changing, yadda, yadda, yadda – but I was holding Abigayle's hand when she activated the Timepiece. So, if I've understood everything correctly, we both went to a version of the future where we had both been missing for the intervening years, right?'

'Yes, that's technically correct, but there's something else,' Avy said with a furrowed brow.

'Avy, what is it?' Frenz asked.

'After the Timepiece was stolen and you disappeared, a huge operation was set in motion to recover both. Resources were pulled from outside the agency: police, military and intelligence services – all with fabricated briefs, of course – and it was strongly suspected that you'd taken the Timepiece, but there was no proof and no one knew how you could've pulled it off.'

'That was the whole idea,' Frenz said.

'Yes, but somehow Cillian Gander knew that the Timepiece was missing before anyone else. I remember everyone being rounded up at the end of Nestor's funeral service and hauled back to Central Station. Cillian stormed into the main atrium and barked orders at everyone in the room, even staff from other divisions. He told everyone that the Timepiece had just been used to travel to a specific date in 1940. At the time, we didn't even know the Timepiece was missing and no one had even looked at Ben's logs. And yet

Cillian already knew for certain that it had been used and even which date.'

'Who is Ben?' Will asked.

'Ben monitors the usage of the Timepiece and logs details of every assignment undertaken. It's supposed to prevent unauthorised usage. Not that that ever stopped Cillian and the Futures Project.'

'How did Cillian know all of this so quickly?' Frenz said.

'The malfunctioning Mimic Watch. When I was speaking to him in his office, he had it on his desk. Then I left to go to the funeral service, and shortly after that you must have made your transit to the past. I think Cillian was holding *that* Mimic Watch and travelled with you.'

'Okay,' Will said, 'so he knew where Frenz travelled to, but he never found him. The escape worked. Why is this a problem for us now?'

'Had either of you been there, you would've seen what losing the Timepiece did to Cillian. If you thought he was bad before…' Avy shook her head, exhaling. 'The agency spent eight years looking for you, Frenz. Eight years without the Timepiece. In that time, they called in all the favours they could, but the coffers still ran dry. Without the Timepiece, the agency no longer had any power, any means to make money or any reason to exist at all. And that's exactly what happened.'

Avy paused to take a sip from her tea before continuing.

'For Cillian Gander, it was never over. He became even more unhinged than before and wouldn't or perhaps couldn't let it go. Ironic really, the way that man thinks – he's stuck in the past but obsessed with the future. He was so sure that you would be tempted to use the Timepiece again, that you wouldn't be able to resist the power it could give you. He was so sure, in fact, that for almost twenty years he has worn and maintained – but never repaired – that Mimic Watch. The malfunctioning watch that started all of this. He was so desperate to be close to that power that he wore the Mimic Watch so that the moment you used the Timepiece, he would know.'

'That's crazy,' Will said. 'What about the three laws? What if Frenz used it while he was on a train or something?'

'You really don't know the kind of man you're up against, William. I still have some old agency friends in London, and from what they tell me Cillian Gander has rarely left his house in the past decade. And when he has, it's always been on foot. He's never been in a car, not ridden a bike. I've even had reports that he spends all of his time on the ground floor of his home just in case the Timepiece is used to visit a time period when the upper floors hadn't yet been constructed.'

'So, this guy never leaves his house. How is he any threat to us now?' Will said.

Frenz pushed himself away from the counter and moved towards Will. 'Don't you see what Avy is saying?'

'That this guy is a fucking nut-job?'

'No – well, yes –but more specifically that if he was wearing that Mimic Watch all day, every day—'

'Then he was probably wearing it when Abigayle and I visited the future!'

'Yes, exactly. Which means that the version of the future that you and Abigayle visited was one where all *three* of you had been missing for the intervening years.'

'Hang on, are you saying that to get Abigayle back, all three of us need to travel to the future? Together?'

'If what Avy says is true, then yes, I'm afraid so.'

'How can we be sure he came along with us?'

'It'll be recorded in the time logs,' Frenz said. 'We'll need access to them.'

'And how do we do that?'

'You'll need to pay Ben a visit,' Avy said.

'Do you know if Ben is still active?' Frenz asked.

Avy nodded. 'I believe so, yes. Ben would've been too important an asset for Cillian to let drop out of service. Besides, if the Timekeepers are still tracking the Timepiece, then they'll be using Ben to do it.'

Will suddenly stood from his chair, which toppled over backwards, and said, 'Okay then, that's it! That's how we find Abigayle! We track down Ben and get the record of when Abigayle travelled, right?'

Frenz turned to Will and shrugged. 'Of course, that's the easy part. The hard part is getting to the information. To do that we'll need to get into Central Station, that's where the logs will be stored. Avy, do you know how we might get in? I take it the trains no longer operate?'

'Trains?' Will asked.

'The Central Station complex is entirely underground,' Frenz said. 'There used to be a secret train route. The agency acquired the King William Street underground station in the early nineteen hundreds to transport agency staff. They ran special services out of King's Cross.'

'I'm afraid there are no trains,' Avy said. 'Not since the early 1970s. Cillian had them sealed.'

'Damn. What about the evacuation tunnels?'

'There's your other problem. Cillian collapsed two of the tunnels after the agency shut down. The only one left is the one that runs from the house of the head of the Operations Section.'

Will bent down and retrieved his toppled chair. He righted it, sat down and slowly placed his hands on the table. 'Avy, humour me for a sec. You're telling us that the only way to find Abigayle is to get access to the operations log.'

'Correct.'

'Which is likely to be inside the old Office of Time Dissemination building?'

'Also correct.'

'And that the only way in is through the house of a crazy old guy – who has already tried to kill us at least once – and who never, ever leaves his house?'

'That is exactly what I'm saying, yes.'

Will's eyes widened, and his jaw became slack, dropping open. Frenz and Avy exchanged confused glances with each other before turning back to Will, who was staring seemingly at nothing at all.

'Will, are you okay?' Frenz said. 'Getting in there won't be easy, but I'm sure we can do it.'

Will blinked, appearing to snap back into the room, 'Huh? No, it's not that.'

'Well, what is it?'

Will slowly raised his hand and pointed towards the television set on the countertop. 'There, look. I'm on TV again.'

CHAPTER TWENTY-TWO

May 17th, 1984, 07:02

Will's photograph was now displayed, full-frame, across the television screen. In the headshot, he looked tired, pale and unshaven.

Why was it that a photo of an unsmiling person immediately made them look guilty of something?

It took a moment for it to register that he, and the thousands of other people watching, were looking at his passport photo. His passport had been in the top draw of a small side table beside the front door of Abigayle's apartment. The police had clearly gained access to the apartment, searched it, found the passport and distributed it to the media.

If they had access to the apartment, then they would have found the red-stained floorboards and the carpet that had been cut to ribbons. They would have found the apartment in a state of disarray, with tattered and torn curtains and upturned tables. They would have also found no sign of Abigayle whatsoever. They would find her suitcase under the bed and all of her clothes and toiletries in the wardrobe and bathroom, untouched. It would be clear that she hadn't left town on a business trip or gone to live with her parents after a nasty row. The scene in the living room, Will's presence at a separate murder scene and the past he was so desperately hoping wouldn't catch up with him painted an unattractive picture of William Gordon Wells of Le Claire, Iowa. They used his middle name in the report as they always seemed to do for murderers and serial killers.

Will's passport photo suddenly reduced in size and moved to the top-left corner of the screen, revealing the newsreader. A headline appeared below his picture:

DOUBLE MURDER SUSPECT ON THE RUN IN IRELAND

The newsreader composed herself, said good morning to her viewers – as if finding out a madman on the loose was the ideal news to begin the day – then smiled politely and proceeded to report on the headline story. 'This morning, a police manhunt continues for a man suspected of at least one murder.' She spoke with a soft, rhythmic Irish lilt. 'William Gordon Wells, an American tourist living in London, was arrested at the scene of a murder in North London on Monday evening. The victim is yet to be formally identified. Wells was remanded in custody but escaped from his cell hours later. The circumstances of the escape are under investigation.'

Will recoiled in his chair, exhaling through pursed lips. The report seemed so thorough and convincing that he even began to question his memories of what had happened. His eyes darted ashamedly between Frenz and Avy, who were both riveted to the TV.

The report continued. 'Shortly after his escape, police began a search at the apartment of Abigayle Ward, where Mr Wells had been staying.' Mercifully, Will's picture disappeared from sight, replaced with a low-angle photograph of the front of Abigayle's apartment. The newsreader continued. 'Ms Ward has been declared a missing person. The police are urging anyone with any information regarding Mr Wells's whereabouts to come forward. Let's join our reporter at the scene.'

The picture cut to a live feed of the exterior of Abigayle's apartment. Police cars lined the street and crime scene tape cordoned off the building's entrance. There was something eerie and surreal about seeing a place that felt so familiar to Will plastered across the television screen. He knew the place well, but in this context it felt as if he was seeing it all for the first time. Will spoke out loud, to no one in particular. 'I just got the weirdest feeling of jamais vu.' His face was emotionless as he spoke, his eyes unblinking.

Frenz gave Will a sideways look. 'I beg your pardon?'

'Jamais vu. It's the opposite of déjà vu. I'm not entirely sure why I know that.'

'And?'

'I've lived in that apartment for the past year, but it looks completely unrecognisable to me now. I can't believe this is happening.'

The weight of Abigayle's absence seemed almost too

much for Will to carry as the reality of the situation flashed across the television screen.

The reporter introduced an eyewitness. As the camera pulled backwards, a short man in a white suit, black shirt and pink tie stepped into frame, joining the reporter.

The reporter said, 'I'm joined now by Kevin Wormwood, the neighbour of the missing woman Abigayle Ward and fugitive William Gordon Wells. First, can you tell us a bit about your relationship with Abigayle Ward and her fiancé, Mr Wells?'

Kevin smirked, impressed with his newfound stardom and the attention he was getting. He adjusted his tie, tilted his head side to side to loosen his neck and said, 'Certainly, John. I've been Abigayle's neighbour for almost thirty-four months now and in that time I've done what I can to look out for her. When I first met Mr Wells, it set off alarm bells for me immediately. There was something in his eyes and the way he moved that didn't sit right with me.'

Kevin's spiel was well rehearsed. No doubt this wasn't the first reporter he'd spoken with and Will imagined how the retelling became more elaborate and dramatic every time.

'You actually confronted Mr Wells in the apartment behind us, is that correct?'

'That's right, John. Unfortunately, my initial feeling towards Mr Wells was confirmed when I entered Abigayle's apartment to find him attempting to cover up what appeared to be her blood on the floor.'

'That sounds frightening,' the reporter added dramatically.

'Well, a normal person might have felt fear, for sure, but I had to set my own personal safety aside. For Abigayle. You see, the two of us shared a special bond, a kind of unspoken love for each other, I suppose. My only regret is that I wasn't able to save her. Perhaps if I'd been there sooner, I could've prevented all of this. I'll never forgive myself, so in many ways I'm a victim now too.'

'Did Mr Wells say or do anything threatening towards you at this time?'

'When I entered the apartment to check that Abigayle was okay, Mr Wells was eager for me to leave. When I refused, he pulled out a large knife and held it to my throat. Fortunately, I've watched all of Bruce Lee's films, so I was able to defend myself and escape.'

The camera zoomed out to show the reporter, who cleared his throat and said, 'Thank you, Kevin. That was eyewitness Kevin Wormwood. To be clear, this is still a missing person investigation until Ms Ward's whereabouts has been confirmed. This case is, however, linked to an ongoing murder investigation taking place in the Whitechapel area of London. Back to you in the studio, Anna.'

The report returned to the newsreader in the studio, who began filling in more details about the two cases before cutting away once more to a police press conference.

The screen blinked furiously as camera flashes were fired and the sounds of a commotion could be heard in the room. Just then a figure came into frame and sat down in the vacant seat. He was introduced as Chief Inspector Voakes, an unexceptional man in his sixties with a head of grey hair to attest to his apparent seniority. He was wearing the same bland suit that seemed to be standard issue in the police force and had a stern look on his face to match.

He hunched forwards into the microphone. 'Ladies and gentlemen, thank you for your patience. Before I start, I'd like to make it clear that there will be no questions during this briefing. I'm going to make a short statement and then return to the important work of solving this case. As has been widely reported, an American man in his late twenties, believed to be one William Gordon Wells, is currently at large. He is wanted in connection with the murder of an elderly shop owner, who is yet to be formally identified, and with the disappearance of his own fiancée, Abigayle Ward. Mr Wells is our prime suspect in both crimes. He was detained by police while fleeing the murder scene late Monday evening and placed into a holding cell at a local police station. Mr Wells subsequently escaped in the early hours of Tuesday morning. An investigation is currently underway to determine the circumstances that precipitated his escape. According to our latest information, Mr Wells is currently at large in the south of Ireland, having boarded a ferry to Dublin yesterday afternoon and travelling south by bus. We also have reason to believe that he's on the run from charges related to fraud in his home country. The suspect's two elder brothers have already been jailed in connection with these offences, and Wells fled the country shortly after they were apprehended. Additional officers have been assigned to the Republic of Ireland and are working closely with local authorities to apprehend this man. He is believed to be armed and potentially extremely dangerous. If seen, please do not attempt to approach this man. We ask that any sightings are reported to the police immediately. Thank you for your time.'

With that, Chief Inspector Voakes rose from his seat and

headed out of the briefing room. As he walked, the frequency of the camera flashes intensified and cries from the gathered journalists built to an unintelligible cacophony. The report then cut back to the studio and the newsreader began elaborating on further details of the case.

Frenz turned away from the television and said, 'Well, Will, this is going to make our journey back to London more difficult.'

'What the hell are we going to do, Frenz? Now the whole country knows who I am!'

Avy leaned forwards, her elbows resting on the table, and said, 'I have an old Lambretta out back. You can take that. It's small but it'll get you where you need to go. I have some helmets and goggles too – that'll help hide your faces.'

'Thank you, Avy,' Frenz said.

The pair locked eyes as though each had more to say but the moment passed, their words unspoken. Avy instead forced a sad smile and turned from Frenz to look at Will. She studied him for a moment. 'Will, I believe their story about Abigayle to be untrue, but is there any truth to the murder of the shop owner?'

Will had been struggling with the knowledge that the man he'd seen gunned down was Frenz, albeit a much older Frenz. He was afraid of the implications of telling Frenz what was going to happen to him when he was the one man who could help bring Abigayle back. He reluctantly decided to keep quiet about it, making a promise to himself to tell Frenz once Abigayle was safe. He looked at Avy and said, 'I never knew the guy. I'm just a patsy. I was there, but it was your pals little and large who did it.'

Avy nodded thoughtfully, then said, 'Tyke and Wigmore?

Yes, I'm not surprised to hear that. What of your brothers and these fraud charges? Is that the real reason you moved to London?'

Will heaved a heavy sigh, dropping his head low in front of him, then looked up sheepishly. 'Parts of what they said are true, but it's not how it sounds.'

Avy leaned back in her chair and folded her arms. 'Well, why don't you tell us about it?'

Frenz said, 'Avy, is this really necessary? We don't have a lot of time here.'

Avy edged forward, a determined look in her eyes. 'I'm not letting this man walk out of here with that thing strapped to his wrist without being sure that he's the right person for the job.'

'Avy, I'll be by his side the entire time if—'

'Even more reason for me to be sure now. If he is who the police say he is, then you'll be in danger too.'

Will stirred, cleared his throat and said, 'Frenz, it's okay. The lie is already out there so let me at least tell you both the truth.'

Frenz said nothing at first, thinking, and then gestured for him to proceed.

'First off, let me deal with what they got right: both of my older brothers *are* currently enjoying the hospitality of the state. They're in for fraud, like the man said, but I had nothing to do with it.'

'Why then, did you flee your home country so soon after they were captured?' Avy asked.

'I can explain that.' Will took a breath as if he was about to unload a heavy weight from his conscience. 'My brothers followed my mom in the family business. They both became pickers like her.'

'Pickers?' Avy asked.

'They go around the country searching through people's houses, barns and sheds looking for stuff. Usually old, valuable stuff. They buy anything that's for sale and then sell it on. My mom always had a great eye for "rusty gold" as she called it. My brothers too, maybe even more so. But my mom was an honest, caring woman. She would sometimes haggle to pay *more* for items just so the people she was buying from got a fair deal. My brothers, on the other hand, were greedy. They'd low-ball people whenever they could, just to make a few extra bucks. After a while though, they got a bad reputation for it. People found out they were taking advantage of their grandparents or their sisters and mothers, and folks just stopped selling to them.

'This all meant that they were both running out of money and they had no other skills to speak of. Picking was all they could do. So, they got into contact with this guy, some wealthy landowner and collector, what was his name? D-something, I think. He had a funny first name, like a military title. His dad was some big-shot millionaire down in Arizona. Anyway, this Mr D was the kind of guy who thought being ruthless and greedy was a good thing. He liked my brothers right away and had them go out and search for a pair of bicycles. Old and super rare. The only two of their kind ever made, my brothers said. Mr D gave my brothers six months to find the bikes. He gave them a couple of leads and paid their way. If they found the bikes, they were due thousands of dollars in return.

'So, my brothers search for months and months and run down all the leads, but they can't find the bikes. What they do find, though, is dozens of similar bikes and hundreds of parts from the same manufacturer. And can you guess what they did?'

Frenz spoke up first. 'They made forgeries.'

Will snapped his fingers. 'Exactly. And my brothers, they know their stuff. Well enough to fool Mr D.'

Avy and Frenz exchanged concerned looks.

'Anyway,' Will continued. 'Whatever my brothers did with those bikes, it was good enough to get them paid. They took the money, and everything seemed great. The story even made the local news. It was a big deal in Iowa, at least.'

Avy asked, 'And you had nothing to do with it or this Mr D character?'

'No! I was in college when all this was going on.'

'So, what happened? How did your brothers end up in jail and you fleeing the country?'

Will took another deep breath. 'My mum got sick while I was in college. The money my brothers had made from the bike scam wasn't going to be enough to pay her medical bills, so I had to drop out. I spent most of what was left of my college savings trying to help her get better, but it was no use. Not long after my mom died a story popped up on the national news about the discovery of two rare bikes in a barn out in northern California. The *real* ones. It didn't take long for the cops to get wind of this since everyone knew how my brothers had made their money. They were arrested pretty quickly after that. I was kind of glad Mom wasn't around to see it,' Will said, the words seeming to wound him as they left his mouth. 'With them locked away in the state pen, it just left me, my dad and my sis.

'It didn't take long for this Mr D guy and his cronies to

come around looking to get their money back. They showed up one day when I was out and pressed my old man. It was my sister who told me about what he did, though. The spineless prick told them that he had no money, but that his youngest son – me – had plenty of savings left and that they should come after me instead. When my sister warned me, she told me to get out of town. To take what was left of my college savings and go. And that's what I did.'

Avy locked eyes with Will for an uncomfortable few seconds, then stood and walked over to a wooden plaque with a series of brass hooks attached to it. Each of the hooks had a set of keys dangling from it. She grabbed a single key with a black rubberised grip and tossed it to Frenz, who caught it clumsily. Avy said, 'You should get going if you hope to cross today.'

Frenz looked to the floor and nodded in response. Will said, 'Thanks, Avy. And I'm sorry about everything.'

Pointing to Frenz, but keeping her gaze locked on Will's face, Avy said, 'William Wells, you look after this man, understood?'

'I'll do my best, ma'am.'

'You two should steer clear of Dublin, they'll be watching the ferries. Head to Ballycotton, it's on the southeast of the island. There's a harbour there with plenty of fishermen and sailors with little love for the English. And not all of them bother with television, and the papers won't have your picture yet. Offer one of them enough money and they'll see you across the channel.'

CHAPTER TWENTY-THREE

May 17th, 1984, 07:25

Avy handed Frenz two scuffed, oil-stained white helmets and two pairs of black-rimmed goggles. She gave him one last look, laid her hand on his forearm then leaned forwards and kissed him gently on the cheek. Reaching into her pocket – a motion that Will eyed warily – she pulled out a large brass key with an unusual cylindrical head and passed it to him. 'I have a feeling you're going to need this when you get there.' Frenz thanked her with a smile. Turning to Will, she said, 'I do hope you are able to find Abigayle.' With a warm smile, she added, 'My mother was always very fond of the name Abigayle, you know?' She then walked to the kitchen and sat down at the table with her back to them.

Frenz led Will down the stairs, through the workshop and out through the back door of the building. The door opened into an alleyway no more than a metre wide, lined on either side with slanted and uneven buildings that looked as if they might topple over any second. The buildings were leaning towards one another to the extent that some of the roofs were almost touching. It gave the alleyway a tunnel-like feel. As Frenz weaved his way to the right, past dustbins and storage boxes, Will asked, 'What do you think she meant by that?'

'By what?'

'The thing Avy said about her mom liking the name Abigayle.'

'Oh, that. Well, her mother liked it enough to give the name to her daughter.'

'What? I don't…'

'The name "Abigayle", as we know it, is in fact derived from the Hebrew name, Avigayil – hence, Avy.'

'No kidding?'

'I kid not. Now, help me with this.'

Frenz was gesturing to a dull green tarpaulin, the topside of which was almost completely covered in bird droppings. The tarpaulin was being held down at ground level by several large, smooth rocks, most likely salvaged from the nearby beach. Frenz and Will moved the rocks and lifted the tarpaulin free. Dried bird faeces cracked and puffed into white clouds of dust. Will unwittingly inhaled some of the dust and gagged, much to Frenz's amusement.

Even though the baby-blue Lambretta had been under the tarp, it had still rusted in the sea air. It was smaller than Will had expected. 'This is it?' he said. 'I thought there'd be a sidecar or something.'

'This will be just fine.'

'How are we going to fit onto that thing?'

Frenz grinned as he tossed Will his helmet and goggles.

'I bet this thing won't even start. How long's it been sitting here?'

Frenz pulled the scooter free from its crusty cocoon, threw one leg over the seat, gripped the handlebars, adjusted the throttle and gave the starter pedal a kick. The engine flashed to life on the first try. Frenz looked up at Will, satisfied, nodded for Will to jump on and said proudly, 'I doubt there's a piece of machinery Avy owns that isn't tuned to perfection.'

Will was grumbling protestations quietly under his breath when at the opposite end of the alley a flash of blue caught his eye. He crouched low and scuttled forwards for a closer look. Hunkered down behind a dustbin, Will could see five or six police cars pulling along Main Street and stopping diagonally along its length, blocking the road. Car doors were flung open and from the lead car Will caught the unmistakable glimpse of DI Moss.

Will rushed back towards the waiting Lambretta before pulling the helmet down over his ears and jumping on the back. 'The police are here. We've got to go.'

Frenz nodded. 'You better hold on.' Before Will could respond, the small bike lurched forwards, forcing him to wrap his arms around Frenz's waist as they weaved down the narrow lane and away from the main road. Will glanced over his shoulder for the first five miles but saw no sign of blue lights in pursuit. Somehow, they had managed to get out of town unseen.

***

Will hadn't enjoyed the bus journey from Dublin to Dingle, but less than ten minutes into the loud, bumpy and petrifying journey riding pillion on the Lambretta, it suddenly didn't seem so bad. The roads leading out of Dingle were treacherous: riddled with potholes and bumps, flanked by sheer drops into rivers and gorges. Some roads barely qualified as roads at all, with loose gravel and mud instead of tarmac. Frenz seemed to be quite enjoying himself in contrast to Will, whose knuckles had turned white as he gripped the slack fabric of Frenz's top.

They headed east out of Dingle, past the sumptuous beauty of Inch Beach and through Midtown. They then angled southeast past Killarney National Park, through Macroom and then onto Cork, where they headed south into the centre of Ballycotton.

The town was small and charming, even compared with Dingle. Aside from the few commercial properties scattered around the harbour, the town predominantly consisted of squat, single-storey residential buildings. The harbour itself had a skewed G-shaped construction, with two narrow jetties sweeping out at either end and an opening at the far side leading to the Irish Sea. It was home to half a dozen large fishing vessels, a handful of smaller boats and at least two craft from the Royal National Lifeboat Institution.

The journey to Ballycotton had taken almost four hours and it was now approaching lunchtime, so Will and Frenz decided to stop by a local pub to refuel and recover from the bone-shaking journey. After climbing off the bike, Will would feel vibrations buzzing through his hands and feet for some time afterwards.

The two of them entered a cramped but charming pub not far from the centre of town. A plaque above the bar claimed that the building had been constructed in the late fifteen hundreds from salvaged oak timbers of the Spanish Armada. Thick beams lined the walls and ceilings and the original cargo mortices and grooves were clear to see. The beams were supported by bare brick walls that were lopsided and irregular. Smoke hung thick in the air. There were just three other patrons tending to their drinks. Even so, the place felt crowded.

They approached the bar and enquired about food, but the bartender offered only crisps and chocolate. They took both, despite their questionable nutritional value and conspicuously smudged use-by dates. While they ate, they asked the bartender – who, as far as Will could tell, were fonts of all local knowledge in small towns like this one – if he might know of a fisherman or boat captain who would be open to undertaking some additional freelance work. The bartender pointed to a man sitting in a darkened corner booth, whom he called 'Beardy John'.

Will and Frenz finished their food and approached the man. He wore stained grey dungarees over a navy and red knitted jumper. His faded blue cap was dotted with numerous fishing hooks sticking through the brim, and his dense grey beard concealed his mouth entirely. He was nursing a small glass half filled with a reddish liquid that could have been a bloody Mary. He was slumped in the booth to one side and appeared to be drunk to the point of being unconscious.

Will settled into the booth opposite the man and said, 'Hi, er, Beardy John, is it?'

There was no response so Will edged forwards and tapped the man gently on the shoulder. Beardy John stirred, coughed, grumbled something, then opened his eyes. Will said, 'Hey, how's it going? You're Beardy John, right?'

Beardy John fixed his eyes on Will and nodded yes.

'We've been reliably informed,' Will said, 'that you might be just the man to help us out.' Will offered his best attempt at an endearing smile, but it fell flat. Beardy John continued to stare at Will, unblinking. Will looked up at Frenz for some support. Frenz, unflustered, reached into his pocket, retrieved some notes and laid them on the table in front of Beardy John, who mumbled something in return but spoke with an accent so thick that they couldn't understand what he'd said. The only indication that his lips were moving at all was the gentle rustling of his facial hair. Neither Frenz nor Will was completely certain their conversation had ended on an agreement until John stood and shook both their hands. He was a giant of a man, a clear foot taller than both Will and Frenz. His hands were large, with ridged fingers that resembled tree trunks. The skin was hard and calloused. John quickly downed the remaining red liquid in his glass and strode out of the pub.

Will looked at Frenz and said, 'Hey, is he going to be okay to operate a boat?' As he spoke, the bartender approached and collected Beardy John's empty glass. 'How many drinks do you think he's had?' Will asked.

Before Frenz could respond, the barman frowned at Will and said, 'What? Beardy John? No, he's teetotal. That was spiced tomato juice he's drinking.'

'But he seems barely conscious,' Will offered.

'He's got twins,' the barman said. 'Girls. Two years old. He's not getting much sleep at the moment, but he'll be fine once he gets some sea air in his lungs.'

Outside, Beardy John climbed onto his bicycle and rolled

down the hill towards the harbour. He didn't seem to pedal at all between the pub and the harbour, and his irregular riding method gave the impression that he relied more on luck than judgement; however, it seemed effective enough. Will got the sense that this wasn't the first time he'd made the commute in this fashion.

Will and Frenz followed on their Lambretta. When they pulled up to the harbourside, the appearance of the two of them on the small scooter drew a warm chuckle from Beardy John, who continued to chuckle all the way along the jetty. He stopped next to a thirty-foot beam trawler called *The Beard of Ballycotton,* then jumped aboard and began making preparations to set sail. It looked as if the old vessel had had a rough life, with multiple layers of flaking paint on the hull and deep grooves in the gunwale where the ropes had worn away the wood over the years.

After pushing the Lambretta up alongside the boat, Frenz paused to contemplate how they might lower the bike onto the main deck. He was eager that they take it with them to avoid the need to find an alternative mode of transportation once they reached England. Will would have been happy to throw the thing in the harbour.

As Frenz was surveying his surroundings, looking for some spare rope or a large plank to use as a ramp, he felt the bike suddenly topple away from him and over the edge of the jetty. He turned his head and reached out an arm, hoping to catch it before it fell, but he was too late. Just as he was about to scream out in frustration, he saw Beardy John cradling the bike in his arms, like it was no heavier than a newborn baby, and gently placing it on the deck. Beardy John looked up and grunted in his throaty, heavily accented English, 'Let's be off then.' Will and Frenz looked at each other, surprised, and climbed aboard.

Beardy John pushed the large boat away from the jetty with relative ease given the size of the vessel, and they began to slowly drift through the harbour and out to sea. As they reached the mouth of the harbour, Will looked back to shore and saw, high on the horizon, flashing blue lights moving along the main road into Ballycotton.

***

Hiring Beardy John had seemed a little too easy, and they found out why midway through the journey. As it turned out, they were crossing one of his regular fishing spots, so the two of them were quickly inducted as free deckhands to help Beardy John make his catch for the day. In total, the crossing would take almost fourteen hours. All they had in the way of food was the chocolate and salty crisps from the pub in Ballycotton. They hadn't thought to bring any water so instead they had to survive on Beardy John's impossibly strong coffee.

Both Will and Frenz spent much of the journey below decks, with Frenz even suffering some of the effects of seasickness. Will had allowed Frenz to take the hammock, which swung and swayed far too much for his liking, while he took the slightly more stable pull-out sofa. Will rolled onto his side and said, 'Hey, you asleep?'

'After that coffee? No, I doubt I shall sleep for a week.'

'Can I ask you something?'

'Of course.'

'Where did the Timepiece come from?'

'Well, that's an interesting question. All I can offer is an interesting story. But a story, nonetheless. The true answer, I'm afraid to say, is a little more elusive. The simple fact is, we don't really know.'

'How is that possible?'

'The earliest record we have of it is from sometime in the mid-eighteen hundreds. The story goes that it was won in a game of cards. An American named Alexander Cobb, a Frenchman named Michel Izri and an Englishman by the name of Warren Wainwright were lifelong friends. They were playing a game together in London, something of an annual event, when they were joined by a fourth player. This player claimed to have no money to enter the game but managed to come to an agreement with the other three to front him some money. So, each man agreed to loan an equal share and they began to play. This mystery player soon found the other three to be no match for him, losing all of the money that had been loaned. The three men felt cheated and demanded they be compensated. Even though each man had seemingly won their money back, under the terms of their agreement, it wasn't his money to lose. The mystery player then laid three unusual timepieces on the table between the three men, offering each as a means of recompense. They were told that what was being offered was worth more than all the money in the world and that they must share this prize and the responsibility that came with it. This mystery figure then apparently disappeared from sight, never to be seen again.'

'Did that really happen?'

'No one knows. There's no written record of the events, only hearsay and word of mouth.'

'You said three timepieces. I thought this thing was one

of a kind?'

'It is. This is why many believe the story to be nothing more than a myth.'

'Why didn't the agency just go back and see for themselves? That's what you were all about, right? Finding out things from the past and learning from our history.'

'We tried, but we found nothing. We were never able to pin down an exact date or location, and after a while we moved on to other mysteries of our past and forgot about it. We had the Timepiece and that was all that mattered.'

The rest of the journey passed by in silence, as both Will and Frenz, weary and in need of sleep, instead suffered through the relentless barrage of an angry sea. By the time they'd reached the shore they were broken men. Beardy John seemed completely unfazed by the whole experience, however. He had docked at the beautiful port town of Boscastle in northern Cornwall, arriving in the early hours of the morning. He weighed and unloaded his catch, taking payment in cash. He unloaded the Lambretta next, shifting it with as little difficulty as he'd stowed it, and then walked to a nearby café with his wallet significantly thicker than it had been the previous morning.

Boscastle looked enchanting at this hour, with the sun creeping up over the horizon and catching the slate rooftops of the houses that lined the small river running through town and out to sea. The tide was high, and the village was quiet aside from the lapping waves beyond the harbour mouth and the distant bellowed laughter ringing out from the café that Beardy John had entered just moments ago. Perhaps he was regaling them with the story of the two foolish men who were ill-suited to life on the open ocean and the money he'd made from them.

Will and Frenz gingerly pushed the Lambretta inland along the gently flowing river Valency until they came across a bed and breakfast. Although Will was eager to get moving, they decided that they ought not to attempt to confront a man like Cillian Gander in their current state. Frenz arranged the booking and paid for a room with the little remaining cash they had. Will, who was still the most wanted man in Britain at this point, slunk into the room unseen for some much-needed rest.

They awoke later that evening refreshed but disorientated, having slept through the day and leaving their room to find the sun now setting. Their clothes were filthy from the ride from Dingle to Ballycotton and from the laboured channel crossing. They slipped into a local charity shop just as it was about to close and bought a change of clothes, dropping their soiled ones in a dustbin outside. With that done, they climbed aboard their trusty scooter, donned their helmets and goggles and set off for Barton Street, London, and the home of Cillian Gander.

The journey north started out much the same as when they left Dingle, with painfully bumpy, unsurfaced roads. However, as they neared London, the surfaces became smoother and more manageable. Eventually, some seven hours, two refuelling stops and three toilet breaks later, they finally had Westminster in sight. They ambled slowly along Millbank. To their right, the river Thames was flowing rapidly past them at a seemingly faster rate. The poor Lambretta was low on fuel by this point and running on fumes. Frenz made a left turn, then a right, following the road around to the right until they reached Barton Street.

They stopped some distance away from a four-storey townhouse built with dark brick. A set of steps led up to a large green front door, black iron fences topped with sharp spikes on either side of it. This was it: the home of Cillian Gander.

Will and Frenz climbed off the Lambretta, which finally spluttered and died. Will pulled the goggles away from his face and onto the top of his helmet, then rubbed his eyes. Frenz joined him on the kerbside, keeping his helmet and goggles on for fear of being spotted. Will looked up and down the street, blinking and frowning. Frenz could see that something was troubling him. 'William, is everything okay?'

Will paused for a moment, gathering himself, and then said, 'I'm not sure.'

'What is it?'

'I don't know…'

'Come on, Will, spit it out.'

'I recognise this place.'

'Recognise it? From where?'

'The house with the green front door. I've been there before.'

CHAPTER TWENTY-FOUR

December 23rd, 1983, 04:51

Although the series of events that had ultimately prompted his decision wasn't part of any kind of plan, it had always been a lifelong ambition of Will's to travel to Europe and specifically to London. The wealth of history surrounding Europeans might be taken for granted by many, but it fascinated Will completely and he would seek out information on the history of the world wherever he could find it.

He loved his country, but there was no escaping the fact that its history only went back so far. He'd once read about a drinkable wine that was almost as old as the US Constitution, and for most Americans the only castle they'd ever seen was made from fibreglass. What he really wanted was to walk the halls of a *real* castle, one made from stone and mortar, one where real kings and queens had lived and died. Places where history had been made and written in the floors and in the walls. There was something intoxicating about the idea of seeing these buildings and relics of the past, each with their own story to tell, first-hand. That he would eventually end up witnessing history in the making was far beyond his wildest dreams.

The first thing Will did upon arrival was to take a tour of Westminster, the Tower of London and Buckingham Palace. He could swear that he saw Prince Charles and Princess Diana walking through the gardens with Prince William in their arms at one point. It was all a dream come true to see these places in the flesh. Unfortunately, that was all the sightseeing Will had been able to afford and he found himself – three months later – out of money and facing a return home.

Returning home was not an attractive proposition, but he'd just about managed to pick up enough side jobs to keep a roof over his head and food in his belly – but no more than that. He'd done everything from manning market stalls, digging footings for driveways, to clearing and repairing gutters. He thought his fortunes had changed when he landed a job at a painting and decorating firm. They paid in cash and didn't seem to be overly concerned with his lack of a work visa. He'd worked there for five weeks when he was given a job painting the entire ground floor of a plush townhouse in Westminster. Will got the impression that none of his colleagues particularly wanted the job, but he needed the money and had volunteered for it. He'd visited the house Monday to Friday for three weeks; each time he was shown in by a person who he assumed was the butler or doorman and never once did he see the owner of the house.

When the work was complete, he was told that no payment would be forthcoming until the master of the house had personally approved the quality of the work.

Under pressure from his employer, he returned to the property the following week to collect payment but found the place apparently deserted. Will had explained the situation to his boss, who didn't seem particularly surprised by, nor sympathetic to, the situation. It was made clear to Will that should he not return with payment by the end of the week, then he shouldn't return at all. So, Will had ventured to the property three times a day for the remainder of the week, every time finding the house seemingly empty. On one occasion Will saw movement at a ground-floor window, but when he rang the bell there was again no answer.

It was the last Friday before Christmas and also his last chance to keep his London adventure alive. If he couldn't get a face to face with the owner and get the money he was owed, then he would lose his job and have no choice but to return to the US with his tail between his legs. The thought was unbearable.

Will had been living in a hostel in Elephant & Castle, as much for the enjoyment he got from writing the address on postcards and letters he sent to his sister as for his interest in investigating the theory behind its name in his spare time. He discovered one theory, or rather urban myth, that the name was a corruption of *La Infanta de Castilla*, after Catherine of Aragon, far more romantic than simply being named after a local inn.

It was the end of the week and his last chance, so he'd been giving some careful thought to his approach and wanted to make sure all bases were covered. He'd never been able to catch the owner leaving the house; perhaps he worked in the city and left very early in the morning and returned late in the evening. Therefore, Will would be there early in the morning and late in the evening also. He made an effort to wake up before sunrise and head over to the address on Barton Street. He even took the step to wear his dirty overalls and to carry some painting supplies with him just in case the owner had been mistaking him for a Jehovah's Witness in all his other attempts throughout the week. He wouldn't be mistaken for anyone else this time.

It would take him around thirty minutes to walk there on foot, so he left just after 4 a.m., confident that his target wouldn't leave the house before 5 a.m. He headed west towards the river, through Lambeth and over Lambeth Bridge. He then turned north along the bank of the river Thames towards Westminster.

He had prepared and rehearsed what he would say to the owner should they finally come face to face. He marched along the bank of the Thames, running things over in his head, thinking through any excuse that the owner might have for not paying, until he was certain that he was ready for any outcome. All he needed was to catch the guy. He headed away from the river, weaving left and then right, admiring the architecture as he walked until he reached the now-familiar Barton Street. Even in the early morning light the entire street was aglow with hundreds, thousands of brilliantly festive Christmas lights and decorations. Large, sparkling banners hung between the buildings, spanning the road below. Christmas stars, stockings, bells, reindeer, snowmen and Santa Claus himself were depicted in one way or another.

Lights twinkled in whites, reds and greens on almost every house apart from one. Even from the end of the street he could see his destination: the house with the green door.

This guy is a regular Scrooge, Will thought.

As he got closer to the house, he could feel his face reddening and the anger increasing at the sense of injustice for his current situation. He tried to calm himself down and to silence the butterflies swirling in the pit of his stomach. He failed miserably and without realising had picked up his pace to the extent that he was now closer to running than walking.

He was no more than ten metres from the house when he saw a figure turn away from the front door and proceed down the steps to the footpath. Will couldn't tell if this person lived there, or was simply another visitor like him, unable to rouse anyone from inside. Whoever this person was, they moved in an elegant, almost balletic way, gliding down the steps as if they weren't there. As the figure reached the bottom and stepped onto the footpath, they turned and came face to face with the on-rushing Will. The figure was startled by his sudden presence and let out a high-pitched yelp as they both narrowly avoided running directly into each other. It was only now that he could see, under the thick cream woollen hat and matching scarf and the sturdy upturned collar of her dark coat, a strikingly beautiful woman. The butterflies in the pit of his stomach fluttered to rise up through his chest.

Will felt guilty immediately for rushing towards the house at such a fast pace and wouldn't have begrudged her thinking he was an attacker of some description. He raised his hands in way of apology and said, 'Gosh, lady, I'm so sorry!'

The temporary look of shock on the woman's face subsided and was replaced with a frown, which quickly turned into a thin, enquiring smile.

Will said, 'Entirely my fault, I'm sorry.'

The woman continued to smile at Will, but there was something like suspicion in her eyes. Will could only smile back dimly. He'd never been a natural when it came to talking to the opposite sex, and found himself even more inept when it came to ones he found quite so exquisite. An awkward silence fell between them, both seemingly unsure what to say next. For a fleeting moment during the silence, Will thought he saw movement in the curtains from the corner of his eye. He began to look towards the house, hopeful that finally someone might be home, but quickly returned his gaze to the woman in front of him when she spoke. In an English accent, which made Will go weak at the knees, she said, 'Okay, so what are you, some kind of magician?' She was looking him up and down, taking in his paint-stained overalls.

Will looked down at his soiled work clothes, confused, and said, 'A what? No, I'm a painter and decorator. It's why I'm here, actually. I painted this place' – he gestured towards the house, jabbing the air with his thumb – 'and the owner never paid me. He's been dodging me for almost a week. If I don't get the money today, I'm out of a job.'

'Is that so?' she said, still smiling.

'Sure, it's so,' Will said, feeling a little uneasy that this woman seemed to find him so amusing. 'Hey, do you know the guy who owns this place? I thought I saw you just come out of the house a second ago.'

She looked coy and said, 'I'm afraid he's not home. Sorry.'

'Dammit. That's it, my boss is going to fire me.'

'I'm terribly sorry to hear that.'

'It's not your fault, but thanks anyway. Sorry again if I startled you.'

'It's fine, no harm done. Well, I should be going. Good luck with your boss. Maybe we'll bump into each other again some time?'

'That'd be swell, but that job and a plane ticket home was all I had left. So, unless you find yourself in Iowa any time soon, I'm afraid this is goodbye. *Forever*,' he added theatrically.

'God, are all Americans so melodramatic?'

An uncontrollable toothy grin shot across Will's face as she spoke. There was something in the warm, jovial tone of her voice that he found terribly disarming. He started to relax; the nerves he'd felt when he first set eyes on her had evaporated. He said, 'Not all of us, no. I know a bunch who'd take issue with the blasphemy, though. And anyway, I wasn't being melodramatic. I really do need this job to pay my rent. If I can't do that, then I've got to go back home. But I don't want to do that. I really do love it here.'

'What do you love about London?'

'Well, everything, I guess. I love the history. I love the sound and smell of the city. And I love the people.' As he spoke those last words, he felt himself suddenly flush with colour. He attempted to rescue the conversation. 'Well, not all of them,' he said, gesturing towards the house with the elusive owner.

'Yes, well, not all us Brits are like that, I assure you,' she said, smiling warmly once more.

Will cleared his throat. 'Look, um, I'm not normally this forward, but it's Christmas, it's really early in the morning and it's cold out, so what the hell.'

'Go on…'

'Would you like to go grab a cup of coffee with me?'

The woman pursed her lips playfully, seeming to hesitate for a moment, then said, 'Yes, I'd like that.'

'Yeah? Great! Maybe this day isn't a total bust after all. I'm Will, by the way…'

'I'm Abigayle. Nice to meet you, Will.'

CHAPTER TWENTY-FIVE

May 19th, 1984, 05:21

At some point during the retelling of his first encounter with Abigayle, Will had slumped down onto the front doorstep of a neighbouring house. He was shaking his head, attempting to make sense of it all. 'Frenz, what does this mean?' he said. 'You think she could be involved in all this?'

'I really don't know, William, but I think we should consider the possibility.'

Will shook his head again, more vigorously now. 'No, there's no way.'

'How long did you say you'd known her for?'

'Long enough!' Will snapped back before lowering his eyes apologetically. In a softer voice, he said, 'The Abigayle I know is the most selfless, caring and warm person I've ever met.'

'I am sorry, and I know this must be difficult, but I need

to be objective about this. Remind me, what was is her profession?'

'She works for some government department,' Will said, picking up a discarded bottle cap and tossing it along the pavement absentmindedly. 'Doing research, I think. She told me that her job required a level of security clearance that meant she couldn't tell me a whole lot about it.'

'Well, if she is involved in all this, then what she's told you fits. And at least it appears that she didn't lie to you. She told you she couldn't tell you more, and that would have been the truth,' Frenz said.

'I just can't see her working for a murderous sociopath like Cillian Gander. Plus, if she's involved, then that would mean she knew what the Timepiece was when she saw it and intentionally went astray – but that's crazy, right?'

'A couple of weeks ago I would have argued it was bordering on insanity for someone involved with the agency to intentionally let themselves go astray, but that's exactly what I saw Nestor do and it's what I myself did. It might still be crazy but it doesn't seem too unbelievable to me now.'

'Jeez, thanks, Frenz. Did anyone ever tell you that sometimes it's polite to spare one's feelings with a white lie?'

'I think we're at a juncture in our journey where honesty is the best policy. But I'll bear your emotional sensitivities in mind whenever I can.'

Will seemed to shrink into an even lower position on the step and clasped his face in his hands, rubbing his eyes once more.

Frenz thought for a moment, then said, 'Did you ever see her inside the house?'

Will spoke a slightly muffled response through his hands.

'I can't be sure. I don't think so, no.'

'I need you to focus, William.'

Will lowered his hands from his face. 'All I saw was her walking down the steps away from the front door. Maybe she was just calling at the house like I was. Maybe it was just a coincidence. I mean, I was there too – for weeks, in fact – and I'm not involved with the Timekeepers in any way.'

'True. Still, it's strange that she was there at that hour. Did you ever see her bring her work home with her? Any paperwork?'

'Look, I didn't ever go snooping around her office and she was professional enough not to leave classified documents laying around the flat.'

'Is there anything that springs to mind about the conversations you'd had? Did she have any hobbies that could be relevant?'

Will thought for a moment when a spark of a memory ignited in his mind. 'Hang on, hang on' – Will clicked his fingers excitedly – 'not long after we first met, we were talking about why I came to London. I told her that I came for the history and that it all fascinated me. She told me that it was a passion of hers as well and that she was lucky enough to be able to study it as part of her work!'

'Very good, William, that is interesting,' Frenz said.

'It must have been on our first date and I hadn't even thought about it since then. She must be a historical researcher, just like—'

'Just like I did for the agency,' Frenz said.

'Shit. You don't think that's what she's been doing all this time? Doing your old job, but for Cillian Gander?'

'It's a possibility, I suppose. But researching what exactly?

Cillian had very little interest in the past when I knew him.'

'That's easy. Cillian knew what year you went to. So maybe Abby was looking for a sign of you from the past.'

'Yes, looking for me. And for the Timepiece.'

'Yeah, that makes sense. Horology was a hobby of hers. More than a just hobby, I guess. That's the whole reason I was looking to buy her a watch in the first place. Now that I think about it, the way she reacted when she saw the Timepiece, I thought she was just excited to see a watch that looked unlike anything she'd ever seen before. But maybe it was the opposite. Maybe she was excited because she knew exactly what it was.'

'That's all plausible. But it still doesn't explain why she would intentionally use it to go astray. In fact, it makes less sense if she knew exactly what you had found. If she was working for Cillian, then why not bring it to him?'

'You're right. Whatever her involvement, she's on our side, Or at least not on Cillian's.'

'I agree. Our enemy's enemy is our friend, as the saying goes.'

Will nodded. 'This changes nothing for me. I know Abigayle can't be working with Cillian. It's got to be something else, so our deal still stands: priority number one is getting her back.'

'Very well,' Frenz said. 'In that case, we need to focus on the present, not the past. Right now, we need to come up with a way to get into that house without being seen. Then we need to find Cillian's private entrance to Central Station.'

'Agreed.'

'Let's hide the bike and try to stay out of sight. Then we'll see if there's a way into the house from the rear or any rooftop access.'

'Right, the last thing we need is to be spotted…'

Will's words trailed off as he caught sight of the large metallic-brown Rolls-Royce Silver Spirit that was easing along the road towards them. It rolled to a stop by the kerbside, loose stones crunching under the wheels that supported its enormous weight. Before either Frenz or Will could move, the driver jumped out of the car, a gun already in his hand. He held it right-handed and pointed it at the two of them. He had it rested flat on the roof of the car, concealing it from the view of passersby.

He was a large man; over six feet tall with broad shoulders, a square, clean-shaven jaw and neat, closely trimmed dark hair. He was wearing a brown tweed jacket over a white shirt and black tie. He spoke with a deep, thrumming voice. 'In. Now.' Will detected a slight accent that could have been French or perhaps Italian.

The footpaths were narrow and there were no alleys or escape routes through the buildings behind them. They were trapped. With no reason to think that the man with the gun wouldn't fire on them if they ran, they surrendered. The passenger door closest to the kerb popped open and a plume of thick white smoke wafted out. Frenz and Will looked at each other solemnly and ducked into the car.

CHAPTER TWENTY-SIX

May 19th, 1984, 05:42

Frenz climbed into the rear of the car first and was still shuffling along the back seat when the driver began to slide in behind the wheel. Will, who only had one foot inside the vehicle, thought for a fleeting moment that he could make a run for it. The driver was a big guy so there was a good chance that he wouldn't be able to shift his weight fast enough to get a shot away before Will was at a safe distance. He still had the Timepiece after all, and Frenz had gone to great lengths to educate him on the Timekeepers for situations just like this. If he ran, he had a slim chance of saving Abigayle by himself.

But Will couldn't seriously consider this option. Given what he now knew about these people, he just couldn't leave Frenz to face the music on his own. This and the fact that, without realising it, Will had become awfully fond of Frenz and already considered him a good friend, despite having only known him for a few days.

Will gulped hard enough for it to be audible, kept his head low and settled into the back seat next to Frenz. The interior was spacious and luxurious and they both sat facing the rear of the car, with a minibar stocked with water and snacks between them and the front-facing seat opposite. Adrenaline was coursing through Will's veins and he found himself trembling because of it. He pulled the door shut behind him and immediately felt the car rumble and pull away. He continued to look down at his feet when a voice said, 'Seatbelts, gentlemen.' Will looked up in the direction of the voice and squinted through a fog of smoke. He coughed and waved a hand, attempting to clear the air.

When the smoke had dissipated sufficiently, he could see their host staring back at them. Sitting calmly and dressed in opulent silks and furs of cream and gold was a woman with white-gold hair, intricately applied makeup and deep blue eyes. She looked to be anywhere from seventy to ninety years old, but the extent of the makeup made it hard to tell at which end of the scale she lay. She smiled back at the two of them, with a gold cigarette holder balanced loosely between two fingers.

Will turned to Frenz and to his surprise he found him sitting equally calmly, with both hands neatly arranged on his lap and a smile on his face. Will frowned and felt that now-familiar wave of confusion overwhelm him once more. He looked back at their host, then to Frenz and said, 'Frenz? Are you doing that "smiling defiantly in the face of danger" thing, or is that a regular smile?'

Frenz didn't respond.

Instead, the voice opposite said, 'I like him, Frenz. He could've run just now. My driver gave him a window and I saw him hesitate for just a second, but he stayed with you. I value loyalty, isn't that right, Frenz?'

Frenz's smile had now disappeared. He looked at Will and said, 'Will, I'd like you to meet my boss. Or should I say, former boss, Madame Izri. She was the Section Head for The Bureau of Game Theory.'

Will turned back to the figure sitting opposite them and began to speak. 'Nice to meet you, Madame Izri, I'm—'

'I know who you are, William Wells,' Madame Izri said. 'You're all over the news, you know. You're lucky I found you before the police did. They can't be trusted. Not all of them, at any rate.'

'Look, I had nothing to do with any of that. I mean, sure, I was at the scene of a murder, but I've never even held a gun, let alone fired one. That might be hard to believe given that I'm an American,' Will said with a smirk, 'but it's the truth.'

'Yes, yes. I know it wasn't you. I was there too, you know?'

Will snapped his fingers as realisation struck. 'Yeah. I knew I'd seen this car somewhere before. I was going to call the police, then I saw your driver wearing that jacket and I thought you were with the other two.'

'I'm sorry that we startled you, William, but calling the police wouldn't have been wise. We have reason to believe that Cillian Gander has at least one officer working for him, probably more.'

'Shit, I bet it's that Inspector Moss. He's had a hard-on for me from the moment he saw me.'

Frenz shuffled in his seat and then leaned forwards. 'You'll have to excuse William's manner of speech, Madame Izri.'

'It's quite all right, Frenz. I find it rather refreshing. What I cannot excuse, however, is one of my subordinates conspiring in the disappearance of fellow agents and theft.'

Frenz retreated back into his seat. 'Madame Izri, I can explain…'

'Yes, I'm sure you can,' she said. 'But save your breath. Avy already sent me a secure telegram about your paying her a little visit. She brought me up to speed and told me what you're planning to do.'

'She did?'

'She did. She told me about your missing woman, Abigayle Ward. You have my sympathy, but your plan is never going to work.'

'I'm not giving up on her,' Will said. 'If getting to Ben is the only way to find her, then it's what I'm going to do, no matter the cost.'

'Why, of course, it's the only move you have left. The problem is that Cillian knows that too. He would've caught you the moment you stepped anywhere near that house. Even if he hadn't and you managed to access his private tunnel network and reach Central Station, you wouldn't have gotten inside.'

Will said, 'What? Why not?'

Frenz closed his eyes and said, 'The vault doors. I'd hoped we could avoid this.'

Madame Izri nodded. 'Yes, the vault doors.'

'Vault doors?' Will asked. 'I thought this place was like an office or something, not a bank.'

'The vault doors were there only as an emergency measure,' said Madame Izri. 'Everything the agency did was extremely sensitive and needed to be protected. Early on, large blast doors were installed in the event of war or a security breach. The doors are large and circular, so it came to be known as the vault. In all my time at the agency, they had only been used once – until Frenz disappeared, that is. After you took the Timepiece, Cillian became paranoid and suspicious of everyone. Even more than usual. He insisted that all agency staff be at their desks by 7 a.m. every day, at which point he'd close the vault, sealing everything and everyone inside. And now, since the Timepiece has resurfaced, he's closed them once more.'

'There's got to be some way to open them,' Will said.

'There is,' Frenz said. 'There were three keys made, one for each Section Head. Two keys are required to open the vault. That's the way things were set up at The Office of Time Dissemination: no one Section Head had the power to do anything on their own. That's one of the things Cillian wanted to change. Avy had Section Head Marshall Doolin's key and she gave it to me before we left Dingle.' Frenz pulled the large brass key with the complex cylindrical head from his pocket and displayed it for Will to see.

Will's eyes widened. He turned to Frenz and said, 'That's it!'

'What is?' Frenz asked, looking at the key with a frown creased across his brow.

'Marshall Doolin! That's the name I was trying to remember back at Avy's place. Marshall Doolin was the name of the guy who my brothers were working for back home. He's the one who was coming after me before I came to London. Do you think it's the same guy?'

Frenz had a strained look on his face as he spoke, 'Marshall Doolin has got to be in his eighties now. It's possible it could be one of his sons. It could also be a coincidence.'

'Marshall Doolin Senior is dead, and I don't believe in coincidences,' Madame Izri cut in, looking troubled.

'I agree that it's a concern, but I believe William when he says that he didn't know who he really was.'

'I couldn't even remember the guy's name,' Will pleaded. 'And I had nothing to do with my brothers' problems. I just got dragged into it.'

'It sounds as if you have a nasty habit of doing that, Mr Wells,' Madame Izri added curtly.

Frenz said, 'If there's anything to this, it's a matter for another day. And it changes little, we still need one more key.' He held the bulky brass key in his hand.

Madame Izri considered this new information carefully, then said, 'Cillian Gander keeps his own key on his person at all times.'

She then paused and began to undo a series of buttons below the neckline of her sparkling gold dress. Will and Frenz glanced at each other uncomfortably. She reached her perfectly manicured fingers inside her dress and pulled out a long gold chain comprised of hundreds of tiny, neat links. At the end of the chain hung a large brass key. Unlike a traditional key with grooves cut into the shaft, Will could see that the head of this key featured a thick outer ring with concentric circles running to the centre of it. It was identical to the one in Frenz's hand. Madame Izri held it up in front of Will and Frenz and said, 'Fortunately for you, I also keep my key close by.'

'Why are you telling us all this when you've taken us both hostage?' Will said.

'I would hardly call it that. I just saved you from certain failure and probable death.'

'You don't know that. We've done pretty well without you so far.'

Madame Izri smiled and turned to Frenz. 'He's sceptical of everyone, just like you, Frenz. If I didn't know any better, I'd have thought you'd been training him for years.'

Frenz said, 'We've both been through a lot. I think it's only natural at this point.'

'Madame Izri,' Will said, 'with all due respect, you didn't answer my question. Why are you telling us all of this? Do you intend to give us your key?'

'Yes, you can have my key.'

Will straightened his back and with eyebrows raised said, 'Wow, really? Great, thanks.'

'Not so fast, handsome. You have to do something for me first.'

Will's posture shrunk to a slouch. 'Of course we do. What is it?'

'I need something from you, William Wells. You can give me something that I haven't had in a long, long time.' She spoke the words slowly and seductively.

Will pressed back into his seat even more, grimacing as his imagination ran through the possibilities of her request. He spoke tentatively. 'My fiancée might be trapped in a parallel dimension, but I'm still in a committed relationship, you know.'

Madame Izri laughed heartily. 'Oh my, you are adorable.

Don't worry, I'm interested in nothing of that sort. I'm a wealthy woman and have no shortage of young men looking to get their name inserted into my will. No, what I want is far more valuable to me.'

'Okay, so what is it?'

'You're the keeper of the Timepiece now. I need you to take me somewhere, one last time. You grant me this request, and the key is yours.'

CHAPTER TWENTY-SEVEN

May 19th, 1984, 06:17

The driver wheeled the car west through Knightsbridge and Kensington, darting through the traffic expertly, before heading south across Hammersmith Bridge. He continued south into Barnes, then eastward down a series of narrow winding roads, which were flanked on either side by wetlands with unchecked plant and tree growth. Ducks drifted through the waters to their left, bees and dragonflies buzzed through the air above wildflowers and all manner of creatures scuttled through the tall grasses and up the thick twisted trees. The environment was in stark contrast to the bustling city they had left behind some six miles back.

Neither Will nor Frenz had spoken a word since Madame Izri had made her request of them. The three of them sat in silence, choosing instead to gaze out at the beautiful landscape.

After half a mile of weaving this way and that, the car came upon a set of high wooden gates. The driver barely slowed as he approached and just as it seemed as though the car was about to crash into them, they swung smoothly inwards. The gates opened to reveal a wide gravel driveway that wound its way towards a large property at the far end. Both sides were lined with large, full hedges, which eventually opened to a magnificent estate with vast green lawns and tall, imposing trees. Beyond the relatively well-tended gardens to the front of the property, overgrown lawns stretched off to the east and west, and to the north the Thames rushed past. Despite its unkempt appearance, the estate was grand and, Will sensed, full of history. A twang of sorrow struck him at that moment as he was reminded of Abigayle's continued absence. This was another place she would have loved to see and explore.

The car came to a stop in front of an expansive stately home, constructed from red brick and sandstone. Though impressive, the building itself appeared to be falling into disrepair. The western side of the house was almost completely covered with ivy, with many windows obscured by it entirely. Walls and fences around the perimeter had crumbled and toppled over. Bricks and mortar from the outer shell of the building had weathered and disintegrated. It was clear that – as wealthy as she appeared to be – Madame Izri was struggling to maintain the upkeep of such a substantial property. It was telling that the most well-tended part of the lands, just beyond the entrance gates, was also the only part visible to outsiders. The estate was large enough to require a full staff of possibly ten or fifteen people, but aside from the driver she seemed to have only one other permanent staff: a slow, hunched woman in a dark, well-worn, long-sleeved dress who emerged from the heavy, crooked oak doors at the front of the property.

The maid approached the passenger door of the car as it came to a stop. She pulled the door open and offered an unenthusiastic smile towards Will, who was sat closest to the door. He hesitated a moment, waiting for Madame Izri to exit the car first, but he was hurried into action when the maid snapped in a coarse Cockney tongue, 'Come on, out! I haven't got all day!'

Will flinched a little, then began to clamber out, saying, 'Okay, okay. Sorry!'

'Hmph, a Yank.' She spat the words out.

'That I am. And what a pleasure it is to meet a ray of sunshine like you, ma'am,' Will exclaimed sarcastically.

The maid glared at Will, one eye twitching angrily as she stood holding the door open for the others.

Madame Izri allowed Frenz to exit the car next. Once standing, he turned and offered his former boss a hand, much to the displeasure of the grumpy maid, who walked off towards the house, grumbling as she went. 'I suppose you'll be wanting tea...'

'Thank you, Frenz,' Madame Izri said, taking his hand, 'ever the gentleman. William, you'll have to excuse Ms Brockett. We don't get too many visitors.'

'It's okay, it's not the first time I've had that reaction. But please, call me Will. Before I came to London, used to be that my mother was the only one who ever called me William, I guess people on this side of the pond are more formal than back home.'

Madame Izri said, 'She is dead? Your mother?' Will

recoiled slightly at the bluntness of the question, something Madame Izri intuited. 'Forgive me, William. I'm a plainspoken old French woman. Getting to the point saves so much time, which is something I've been sorely short of thanks to your companion Frenz here.'

Will softened slightly and said, 'Hey, no, it's okay. And yes, she died. I came to London not long after the funeral. Needed to get away, I guess.'

'I'm sorry to hear that. Is she the reason for your interest in history?'

'How did you…you know what, I don't want to know. But yes, her and my grandfather. They were both pickers. I'm not sure if you guys have that over here in Europe, but they used to travel around looking for things of historical significance. Anything that had a good story behind it. They'd pull stuff out of barns and garages that had been forgotten and they'd give them new life. My mother had a real keen eye for that stuff.'

'Losing a mother is life-altering like few other things. Now, let us get inside.'

The three of them entered the building through a gnarled wooden door that hung crookedly in its frame. The building was in a similar state of disrepair inside as it was out. They were shown upstairs to a large open study with a frayed and worn dark green rug over the timeworn wood floor. The walls were lined with family portraits and painted in luxuriant teal and deep yellows. Will reached out to touch the paint, which had a unique patina, when Madam Izri's hand snapped around his wrist, stopping his fingertips millimetres from the wall.

'I'm so sorry,' Will said, embarrassed. 'It's pretty delicate,

I guess? My mom always told me to look with my eyes and not my hands.'

'These walls are almost two hundred years old and probably delicate,' Madame Izri said, 'but that's not the reason for my concern. It's the paint. To achieve these vibrant colours, they used a pigment that contains high levels of arsenic.'

Will pursed his lips, nodded, then said, 'Okay, looking with my eyes it is then.'

They followed Madame Izri and sat down on elegant but not very comfortable sofas on either side of a low, glass-topped coffee table. Ms Brockett arrived with a tray of tea shortly thereafter, before being dismissed by her employer.

'Ms Brockett, she used to be Cillian Gander's secretary, did she not?' Frenz asked.

'She did, for her sins.'

'Do you trust her?'

'I don't trust anyone,' Madame Izri said forlornly.

Frenz edged forwards, his elbows resting on his knees and worry lines etched deep above his thick-rimmed glasses. 'Madame Izri, what you're asking of us – of Will – you must realise the danger this puts us in. All of us.'

'Oh of course I do, Frenz. I was Section Head for almost twenty years before you pulled your little disappearing act. I know full well the consequences of this request.'

'Then why ask it of us? The moment Will uses the Timepiece, Cillian and his mob of Timekeepers will descend upon this house, take the Timepiece by force and probably kill us in the process.'

Madame Izri dismissed Frenz's pleas and began idly brushing small traces of lint from the arm of the sofa.

'William, did Frenz tell you,' she said, now looking up to meet his gaze, 'that for six generations a member of the Izri family has held the position of Section Head at The Office of Time Dissemination?'

Will's eyes shifted from side to side. He couldn't help but feel a little intimidated by this woman. 'In a manner of speaking. He told me the story about how the Timepiece was first discovered. About the three friends playing a game of cards. And that one of them was named Michel Izri.'

'Yes, he was my great-great-great-grandfather. It saddens me that I will be the last to bear the Izri name at the agency, but thanks to Frenz, the agency is no more. A not altogether bad thing, perhaps.'

'Are you telling me they picked their leaders like the Royal Family? By birthright?'

'Of course. I may be French, but the Izri family – like the Cobbs and the Wainwrights – followed the great British tradition of nepotism.'

'What happened to those other families?' Will asked.

'The same that will eventually happen to me. The last of their family line died with no natural-born heir. When a Section Head reaches a certain age without an heir, they are required to personally select one – usually a trusted, capable subordinate. That person must then be ratified by a vote from all agency members. Though tradition dictated that this was usually a formality.'

'So, the agency was like a constitutional monarchy, one that occasionally flirted with democracy?' Will enquired.

'That is not inaccurate,' Madame Izri replied with a satisfied smile. 'I suppose it is a rather outdated practice, but it is a custom that has been vehemently upheld by the most senior members of the agency for decades. For my family, it was always the first-born lady of the house who inherited the position of Section Head. Men have a tendency to be reckless and to think with their balls rather than their brain. The agency had too much power to be left solely in the hands of men.' She smiled a mischievous smile at Will.

She continued, her features becoming sterner. 'That is, until my father. If you'll allow me to tell you about him, you may better understand what I'm asking of you. Once I've told you my story, you can then decide whether to grant my request or not. Fair?'

'Sure, that's fair,' Will said, glancing at Frenz for his approval. He received a curt nod in response.

'Thank you. My father and mother met when she was only seventeen and he was in his thirties. This was before she had the opportunity to assume her position at the agency, of course. Our family has always had great wealth; though, as you can see, we were not always blessed with beauty.'

Will was about to offer some kind words to the contrary, but Madame Izri held up a hand, cutting him off. 'Please. I know what I am and what I am not. My mother was no different; she was a wonderful woman, but some might call her… homely. My father, on the other hand, was a dashing, tremendously handsome man. He could have had his pick of any woman he desired but he chose my mother. Her mother – my grandmother – was suspicious of his motives and didn't approve of this at all. One wouldn't call my father low-born, but he certainly had no real wealth to speak of and she could see him for what he really was: a gold digger. Despite her parents' disapproval, my mother's infatuation with him resulted in their marriage. I was born a year later.'

Madame Izri paused to take a sip of her tea. Will and Frenz waited patiently for her to continue. 'Over the early years of their marriage, my father managed to win over the rest of the family and appeared to be an honest and caring husband. He even took my mother's family name when they married, something my grandfather approved of immensely. But he had them all fooled; my father was a wicked man.

'My earliest and most enduring memory of him was from when I was three or four. Some nights, when I couldn't sleep, I would creep out of my room and roam the halls. One summer's evening I came across my father. He was standing on the west balcony watching the sunset, or so I thought. Instead, his focus seemed to be on a figure who was moving towards the house through the grounds. My father had a gun with him as he often did – he rather liked to shoot foxes or rabbits or any bird that strayed into our land. He looked at this man in the same way that one might look at a rodent, and I saw him smile before he picked up the gun and without hesitating shot him dead. I saw the body the following morning through my bedroom window as they carried it away. It turned out to be a homeless man who had wandered onto the property. The authorities ruled it to be self-defence and my family's ties to the British government through the agency saw to it that the case went away. Although at this time my father was unaware the agency even existed.'

'Jesus. Did your father ever talk to you about what had happened?' Will asked.

'I never really had much of a relationship with him. When I was young, he always seemed to be out late, and I have no doubt that he was having numerous affairs behind my mother's back. But despite all that, I had a wonderful childhood and my mother was the kindest, most loving mother a child could ever wish for. However, things changed when my grandfather was killed during the First World War. He was a high-ranking officer in the infantry and was killed by a sniper's bullet when a rookie infantryman saluted him. My grandmother was Section Head when this happened. She was distraught and fell into a deep depression, but never shied away from her duties at the agency. A few lugubrious years later though, she too died, such was her grief. My mother was immediately instated as the new Section Head. Of course, she'd been aware of the agency from a young age and had been groomed for this very moment. She, like myself, never attended traditional school. Instead, we had private, home tutoring, usually from former agency staff. When we reached the age of thirteen, we were told of the Timepiece, the agency and our future role in it. We were to speak to no one of what we were taught, including other family members. Such secrecy made for a rather lonely, friendless childhood.

'My father, despite all the goodwill he'd managed to build in the family, was expressly forbidden from finding out about the agency. My mother had to keep her new role from him, but he became instantly suspicious of her increased absence. She'd told him she needed to take over the family business after her mother's death, but he'd convinced himself that she was having an affair. Despite his own infidelity, that was something he couldn't allow. Not because he loved my mother, but the affection of another man would endanger the lifestyle he'd become so accustomed to.

'One evening he confronted my mother and at just six years old, peering through a slit in the door, I watched my father assault my mother with a belt until she would admit where she'd been going to for so many hours. This continued for weeks and the first time she told him the truth about the agency, he thought she was taking him for a fool, and he beat her further. My mother was an immensely powerful woman, but she couldn't escape my father's poisonous hold over her.'

'Madame Izri, I'm sorry, but I have to ask, why? Why didn't she leave him?' Will said. 'She was one of the most powerful people on the planet, wasn't she?'

'It is not an easy question to answer. She kept the abuse from everyone, perhaps through shame, perhaps out of a sense of duty to keep the family together, no matter the cost. But I often wondered if it was love that kept her from fighting back. It sickens me to recall the happier moments between my parents, but my father really could be a charming man when he wanted to be. For my mother and me, growing up with the sole focus on what you are one day destined to become makes for a lonely and loveless existence. I think that she craved the moments when my father would show her love and affection, whether it was real or not. And I think she clung to that feeling, knowing she may never have it again.

'Over time, my father's persistent attacks broke her will and eventually she agreed to take him to the agency and to show him the Timepiece and the power it had. My life would be forever altered from that moment on.'

Madame Izri paused once again, taking another long sip of tea from her cup. She took a moment to compose herself, wiping some of the moisture that had pooled in her eyes as she relived those painful events from her past.

'From the moment that my father discovered the

existence of the agency, he realised that my mother's wealth was not in the money she had but in the power that the Timepiece could give him. I was only six, but I could sense a change in the way he talked and the way he moved about the house. He began playing the part of willing househusband and did something that I'd never experienced in my six years on this earth: he began eating dinner with us as a family. As a child there was no way of me knowing what was really happening.

'He administered the poison to my mother slowly, over seven or eight months, I think. She was eventually forced into constant bed rest, and in the last few months she'd become delirious and experienced hallucinations and spoke of strange visions, often becoming violent. He took advantage of my mother's worsening condition and, despite her obvious mental incompetence, had her sign numerous orders that would see him named her heir at the agency. This wasn't seen as especially odd by anyone since I was too young at the time to take her place, having only just turned seven, and my father was thought to have a good standing in my family. With this, he had succeeded in becoming the first male Section Head in the family since Michel Izri almost two hundred years earlier.

'To make matters worse, my mother's violent behaviour meant that I was unable to spend any time with her at all. I awoke one morning and walked to her room to see if her condition had improved only to find her room empty. I had a sudden rush of excitement: perhaps she was better and had gone for a walk in the grounds. I immediately rushed outside, where I saw a casket being loaded into the undertaker's wagon. I couldn't remember the last time my mother and I had spoken to each other or the last time she'd plaited my hair or pushed me on our garden swing or bathed me. But my mother was gone, and I didn't even get a chance to say goodbye. My father, on the other hand, seemed happier than ever. He was finally free of her and had all her money and her power to himself. He enjoyed playing the part of grieving widower and loved the attention it brought him, but soon enough he began bringing other women home.

'I quickly became a nuisance to him and a reminder of my mother and the things he'd done to get where he was. As a result, he had all the photographs of my mother and I removed from the house. They were either destroyed or put into storage. Whatever the case, I never saw them again. Whenever he had company, I was banished to the study, which is where we sit right now. He didn't know it at the time, but this became my sanctuary, as you can see.' She gestured to the walls all around them.

The room was large and rectangular and aside from the two tall doors at either end and the two windows on the southern wall, on every inch of the walls there hung large paintings. Each one featured the same two people: a man and a small, smiling girl.

Will and Frenz traced their eyes around the room, taking in all thirteen paintings. Will turned back to Madame Izri and said, 'I don't get it. These are all paintings of you and your father, right?'

'Correct.'

'Then how was this any kind of sanctuary?'

'Every single one of these paintings is a pentimento. Do you know what that is?'

'Sure,' Will said. 'They're paintings that have been

altered, right?'

'Very good, William. These paintings used to feature my mother. When my father began sending me here, I would spend all of my time sitting in front of each of these, looking at my mother and me together. She insisted that we have at least two family portraits done every year, one in spring and one in autumn. I would study each of them, sometimes for an hour at a time, remembering our time together. In some I am no more than a babe in arms, but I have a memory attached to most of them. She was my mother and these paintings were all I had left of her. At first, my father didn't know that by sending me here he was doing me an unintentional kindness. But it didn't last. One day he came into this study with whatever woman was auditioning for a slice of his wealth. I was sitting in front of a painting, my mind buried deep in a memory of my mother. He must have spoken to me, but I didn't hear him because the next thing I knew he was grabbing my arm and shouting at me not to ignore him. He felt embarrassed in front of his lover. When she looked up at the painting of him and this unattractive woman, he was mortified and stormed out of the room. The following day I was sent back to France to live with an aunt and uncle. And there I lived for the next ten years. My father had to keep up the pretence that I would replace him upon his death and knew it would draw too much unwanted attention from others in the agency should he have prevented this. So, my tutoring continued and it was there, when I turned thirteen, that I was officially made aware of the Timepiece and the agency. Even though I had overheard my father beat this information from my mother, I was too young and too terrified to really understand it at the time.

'When I turned eighteen, I returned to this house to continue my induction into the agency. I had missed the paintings awfully while I was away, but when I returned, I found them as you see them now. My father, as means of punishment, had my mother painted out of each and every one of them. I was devastated. When I saw him for the first time in ten years, he seemed to have aged by more than my ten-year absence would suggest. His clothing appeared more ragged and frayed and his hair was long and dishevelled. I found out later that he'd been foolish with my mother's wealth, making numerous poor investments. As a result, most of the women who had leeched onto him over the years had lost interest and he'd been drinking excessively for some time. He'd become a pitiful man and even more cold and vile towards me, but I resolved to bury the hatred I had for him until the timing was right.

'Many months passed, and I was at the agency every day, so I began to show an interest in his work. Since he wasn't able to share the existence of the Timepiece with the few women who still bought into his lies, he revelled in being able to speak with me about it. He loved to boast of the power he had, and he did so, extensively. And I listened to him. Without him realising it, he was grooming me to replace him. I feigned admiration for him and his lofty station, and I was able to cultivate something close to respect between us. So much so that on my twenty-first birthday I asked a gift of him. Something that only a man of his stature and power could provide: I asked to see my mother once more.

'At first he refused, but it's surprising how far a little flattery and reverse psychology will go,' she said, narrowing her eyes and smiling a wickedly playful smile at Will and

Frenz. 'One morning I suggested that I should perhaps approach one of the other Section Heads for this gift if he didn't have the authority to procure it, and later that evening he returned home with a Mimic Watch. He had called in a favour and smuggled one out of Central Station. He said that later in the week an assignment was returning some fifteen years into the past and that he would allow me to use the Mimic Watch. He explained that I would need to be far from the house, on the outskirts of the property. I agreed but told him that I was scared and asked if a brave man like himself would accompany me there and await my return. Thrilled to be thought of as brave, he agreed. And so, on the prescribed day we set out and found a spot to the rear of the property, shielded from view of the house. I put the Mimic Watch on my wrist and waited for the signal that the Timepiece had been activated. I moved my hand to my wrist and activated the watch, but as I did so, I grabbed my father by the arm and we both travelled fifteen years into the past. He was furious, but I could see that it was really fear behind his eyes and in his wavering words. Not quite so brave after all. I gave him one last look, right in the eyes to make sure he knew I had done this to him. I released my grip on his hand and deactivated the Mimic Watch.'

CHAPTER TWENTY-EIGHT

May 19th, 1984, 07:18

With neither realising it, both Will and Frenz had gradually edged forwards on their seats as Madame Izri told her story. Their teas were untouched and now cold. Will edged forwards further still, now barely in contact with the firm sofa, and said, 'So you just left him there in the past? Isn't that a little dangerous? Couldn't he have wandered into the house or something?'

A satisfied smirk crept across her face. 'Why of course, I was counting on that.'

'But—'

'The moment I returned from France and laid eyes on my father again after all those years, it triggered a memory I had of him from long ago. I realised that I had seen the old man my father had become once before, charging through the grounds towards our house when I was a child. I also remembered my father as a younger man, standing on the balcony with a rifle in his hand.'

Will flung himself back in his seat with both hands on his head and said, 'Holy shit! He shot *himself*! The homeless guy your father shot *was* your father, only older, right?'

Madame Izri nodded slowly in return.

Frenz looked across at Madame Izri with a newfound level of respect, as well as increased wariness, knowing what she was capable of. He'd heard stories about how intelligent, resourceful – and ruthless – she could be, and now he knew why. He then said, 'You want to use the Timepiece to see your mother again?'

Madame Izri looked over at him, shaking her head. 'No, as much as I would love to, I would never be able to get close enough to her. After my father's apparent disappearance, I took over at the agency as Section Head. I was the youngest there has ever been at only twenty-one. The official story of my father's disappearance is that he stole a Mimic Watch to show off to his latest girlfriend and that the watch was lost with him. He is now listed as one of the many agents who have gone astray. But I kept that Mimic Watch and whenever an assignment was taking place at an appropriate period of time, I would use it to come back here, to this room, where I could see these paintings transformed to their original form. I would sit in front of each, as I had done as a child, and I would remember my mother. It's one of the few things that brought me happiness and is something I've been unable to do for seventeen years thanks to you, Frenz. If you would allow me to see these paintings one last time, then the key is yours.'

Frenz glanced across to Will and said, 'This is your

decision, William. If we do this, we not only endanger our own lives, but we also endanger any chance of bringing Abigayle back.'

Will pondered for a moment, then said, 'If we don't do this, we're done anyway. We need that key.'

Frenz said in a hushed tone, 'We could negotiate. We could offer to do this after we have Abigayle safely returned.'

Will leaned in towards Frenz. 'No, we owe this to her, Frenz. If we fail, she might never get this chance again. It's the right thing to do. It's what Abigayle would do.' He turned to Madame Izri and said, 'We have an agreement, madame. Where to?'

Madame Izri grinned a wide, toothy grin, then said, 'September seventh, 1928. Just after noon, if you please. The light in this room was always at its best at that time.'

'How much time will we have before the Timekeepers track us here, Frenz?' Will asked.

'It's hard to say. Perhaps twenty minutes, maybe less. Then another twenty for them to get here.'

'Okay, well, let's do this. No time like the present. You ready, Madame Izri?'

Madame Izri stood from her seat briskly, completely reinvigorated. She strode purposefully towards the doors at the end of the room, opened them and screamed into the hallway, 'Ms Brockett, you are dismissed. Please take the rest of the day off.' She turned back to Will and said, 'Okay, I'm ready. We were away in France on this day, so the house will be empty, do not worry.'

'I will wait here and keep an eye out for unwelcome visitors,' Frenz said.

Madame Izri nodded and said to Will, 'The furniture has

changed position in this room, so you would be best to stand clear of it, lest you lose a leg. The floor in front of the paintings was always kept clear, so please take a position in front of one of your choice.'

Will did as instructed. He raised his wrist and carefully entered the date, checking it a second and third time. He turned to Frenz and said, 'Back in thirty minutes, okay?'

'Better make it twenty-five. When you return, stand in the same place as you are now, just in case,' Frenz said.

Just as Will prepared to slide the Timepiece's crown around the expertly engineered G-shaped track before activating it, a thought struck him. He snapped his head towards Madame Izri, who was standing too far away for him to hold hands with, as he had done with Frenz up until now. 'Madame Izri, don't you need to…'

Will's words were halted when Madame Izri calmly slid back her sleeve, revealing a pristine Mimic Watch strapped to her wrist.

With Will's question answered before he had asked it, he activated the Timepiece once more. He was beginning to get the hang of time travel and found the idea of seeing the 1920s with his own eyes incredibly thrilling. He had travelled to London for the history of the city, but he never expected to experience history in quite this way.

September 7th, 1928, 12:15

The now-familiar pulse of warmth ran through his body and a sphere rippled outwards, transforming the room. The previously run-down study was now gleaming and clean and full of light. The painting in front of him transformed before his very eyes. In it, a stoic-looking man stood with one arm on the shoulder of a young girl of four or five. They had been standing unusually close to a large tree and the composition had bothered Will. As the ripple of energy expanded outwards, the tall painting was enveloped, and the oddly placed tree disappeared completely from the canvas, revealing a young woman, in a red dress, grinning the same toothy grin Will had seen on Madame Izri's face moments ago. Will had to agree that she wasn't a traditionally attractive woman, but that smile and the happiness that was radiating through the canvas was a more than worthy substitute.

Will looked to his left and saw Madame Izri standing in front of another painting. She reached out a hand, stroking the canvas tenderly. She then fell to her knees. Tears of joy mixed with tears of grief streamed down her face as she looked up at the image of the mother, who had left such a hole in her life. Will allowed her a moment's privacy and walked out of the room, down the polished wooden staircase and out through the now perfectly aligned front door.

He walked across the bright white gravel driveway, which seemed to glow under the midday sun. To his right, something metallic glistened and shot a hot flash of light in his direction. There, parked squarely alongside the west wing of the house, was a large, elegant-looking car. It was a pale yellow Rolls-Royce 1928 Phantom I, Sport Phaeton with a dual cowl and adorned with chrome polished to a mirror shine. It was a convertible with a cream soft-top, which was down, folded neatly and resting above the rear seats. A spare, white-walled wheel was sitting securely on each of the chrome wheel arches, which flowed along the car like a crest of a wave, frozen in time. Will wasn't an expert on cars, but he was sure that this was nearly identical to the one Robert

Redford had driven in *The Great Gatsby*.

Will ran his hand gently along the curves of the car. He checked over his shoulder for onlookers before gripping the door handle. The car was unlocked, and the door swung open silently. He slipped in behind the wheel, sliding over the smooth, white leather interior. He took the large steering wheel in his hand. Looking down, his face was reflected in the varnished wooden dashboard. He barely recognised the person staring back at him. He hadn't shaved or washed for days and hadn't had a decent meal since Avy's house. He slouched back in the seat, which was far more comfortable than the sofas inside, and he closed his eyes, resting them for just a moment.

Will hadn't realised quite how exhausted he was, and he quickly drifted off into a deep sleep. He didn't know how long he'd been asleep when the sudden and violent crash in the distance jolted him awake. He opened his eyes, immediately alert when he heard another loud bang. He looked up into the sky and saw a small turboprop plane flying low overhead. The plane popped and spluttered through the air, but somehow avoided dropping out of the sky. Relieved, he made his way back into the house and up to the study, where he found Madame Izri.

She was a woman transformed. Her skin seemed to have more colour and her eyes were alight. She smiled warmly at Will as he walked back into the room.

She was about to open her mouth to say something when another loud bang rang out. The sound was different this time, however, and much closer. It sounded like a minor explosion followed by a metallic clang. Perhaps the aircraft he'd seen had crashed after all. He ran from the study, down the stairs and burst back out onto the driveway. It was quiet for a spell as he looked in the direction of the main gates that they'd passed through an hour earlier, when yet another explosion broke the silence and rattled through the ground. As the sound echoed and reverberated through the air, he saw the gates swing inwards and two men armed with shotguns striding through. It was Tyke and Wigmore. They began jogging down the driveway towards the house, some one hundred metres away. Behind them, walking at a slow, even pace, was the pale, hunched figure of Cillian Gander.

CHAPTER TWENTY-NINE

September 7th, 1928, 12:47

Unlike his previous encounters with Tyke and Wigmore, Will didn't hesitate; he sprinted back into the house, sending gravel spraying in all directions. He burst through the front door and looked around desperately for something to bar it. It took a moment for him to remember that there was no use barring the door in this time period as it would no longer be blocked once they returned to 1984. Admonishing himself, he then rushed upstairs and into the study. There he found Madame Izri on her feet and waiting for him. 'I assume the disturbance outside is our cue to depart?' she said, unable to mask the bitter disappointment in her voice.

'Yeah, I'm afraid so. Cillian and his goons will be knocking at the door any minute now.'

Madame Izri quickly steeled herself, lifting her head, straightening her back, and said, 'Thank you for this, William,

I will never forget it.'

Without another word they both took up their original places in front of the paintings, where Will deactivated the Timepiece. The two of them instantaneously reappeared in the room they had just left.

May 19th, 1984, 07:55

Frenz had been keeping watch at the front of the house for the moment Will deactivated the Timepiece. The instant he did, the three figures of Tyke, Wigmore and Cillian materialised in front of him without warning. He quickly turned and sprinted across the gravel driveway, spraying stones in his wake just as Will had done moments, or rather decades, earlier. He closed the large wooden doors behind him, bolting them. To the right of the door was a sturdy oak sideboard, which he just about managed to move on his own. He pushed it against the door, wedging it under the large brass door handle, preventing it from turning. He then raced upstairs and burst into the study, where he saw Madame Izri and Will waiting for him.

'What the hell happened?' Frenz bellowed. 'You were supposed to return five minutes ago!'

'I know, I'm sorry, I must have dozed off for a second there,' Will said sheepishly.

'Well, your little nap might get us killed. They're already here,' Frenz said sternly. Will had never seen him so indignant.

'How did they find us so fast? I thought we had at least another ten or fifteen minutes.'

'Someone must have tipped them off. There's no way they would've made it here so quickly if they didn't already know where we were.' At that moment there was another explosion and a loud crash of splintered wood as the front doors gave way.

'Madame Izri, is there another way out of here?' Will asked.

'Yes, the boatyard in the basement. Follow me.'

The three of them hurried through the study, into the west wing of the house. They kept low as they skirted across the landing that overlooked the entrance hall of the property. Frenz and Madame Izri ducked into an adjoining hallway that led away from the front of the house just as a volley of shots rang out from the lower floors. Will crawled low towards the banisters and looked down at the scene below. One of the front doors lay flat on the marble floor, the other hung precariously from the splintered doorframe. The sideboard Frenz had moved to bar the door was split in two as it had taken the brunt of the explosion. On the floor, he could see Madame Izri's driver, who only a few hours earlier had pulled a gun on him. He was lying prone, trying to stem the flow of blood seeping from a sizeable piece of wood shrapnel protruding from his stomach. A thin, frail-looking man in a tweed jacket walked through the open doorway – it was Cillian Gander. Seeing the man this close gave Will the chills. Cillian approached the driver, crouched down and began speaking to him. The driver spat at the ground in response. Cillian stood calmly, slipped his hand into his jacket and in one smooth motion pulled a gun and shot the man in the head. A fine spray of blood and brain matter streaked across the floor. He seemed to take no more trouble in shooting a man dead than wiping sweat from his brow. He replaced the gun in its holster, then began to look up. Will rolled away from the banisters, barely escaping being seen.

Will didn't want to press his luck any further and crawled towards the hallway where Frenz and Madame Izri were waiting. As he crawled, he heard a voice call out, 'Won't the lady of the house greet her guests? And why not send the dear Ms Brockett down as well. Your man here has made an awful mess of the marble.' His voice, while not loud, seemed to carry through the whole house.

Will moved down a long, narrow hallway and rejoined the others as they descended a set of stairs in the west wing. The stairwell was dark, with only fine pockets of light breaking through the vine-covered windows that spanned the full height of the building. When they reached the bottom, Madame Izri pulled a key from her pocket and used it to open a concealed door that had been built into the wood panelling at the base of the staircase. Behind this secret doorway was a bare brick stairwell, with steep stone steps. Will entered the doorway and began navigating the treacherous incline as Frenz offered a hand to Madame Izri. She held her ground; instead of taking Frenz's hand, she bowed her head and lifted the thin gold chain over it. The bulky, odd-shaped vault key swung back and forth. She placed it in Frenz's outstretched hand and said, 'Here. I am a woman of my word.'

'What are you doing?' Frenz pleaded.

'Frenz, I'm too old to run from this. Besides, it's been a while since I gave that wretched Cillian Gander a piece of my mind,' Madame Izri said, grinning defiantly.

Will reappeared at the doorway and from behind Frenz said, 'What's going on? Are we going or what?'

'Madame Izri isn't coming with us.'

'What?! We're not leaving her behind with those guys!'

'It's my choice to make,' Madame Izri said, 'and somebody needs to lock this door behind you.'

'We can't just leave you here!' Will said.

'You can, and you must. Now go.'

Frenz moved towards the doorway, but before more objections could be made, Madame Izri pushed the door closed. From inside the now dark stairwell, Will and Frenz could hear the key turn in the lock and the bolt slide home.

Grudgingly, they both stumbled down the staircase, finding that the bottom opened out into a long, tunnel-like room with a low arched ceiling. At first, the room appeared to be part of some kind of sewer system, with damp red-brick walls coated in moss and algae. The ceiling was dark green and slick, saturated with water dripping from multiple orifices. A harsh vinegary smell hung in the air. The far end of the room was open, with daylight streaming in.

They walked several paces towards the end of the tunnel where the floor dropped and a set of steps descended into a dock large enough only for a single boat. At the base of the steps was a small concrete platform. Beyond that was a shallow stream of water that led out towards the end of the tunnel some twenty-five metres away and into the Thames, which was flowing powerfully past the tunnel opening. A small boat with an outboard motor mounted to its transom rocked gently in the dock.

Will untied the mooring lines while Frenz climbed aboard and got to work on the engine. He set the shift lever to neutral, pulled out the choke, set the throttle arm to the 'start' position and gave the starter rope a firm pull. His first attempt was unsuccessful. Will climbed aboard towards the stern, reached over the side of the boat and began to walk the boat out towards the end of the tunnel with his arms. Meanwhile, Frenz unscrewed the fuel cap and inspected the levels. As he did so, more muffled gunshots rang out from above.

Will and Frenz looked at each other, pain and sorrow etched into their features, their thoughts left unspoken.

Will continued to push the boat silently along the underground canal, now passing the halfway point. He whispered, 'Come on, Frenz, we really don't want to float out of this tunnel without the motor working. We'll be sitting ducks.'

'I know, I know.'

Satisfied that they had sufficient fuel, Frenz replaced the cap. Will continued to push the boat and they were now only metres from emerging from the tunnel and into the open air of the Thames. Frenz made another choke adjustment, then pulled the cable once more. The motor turned over briefly, spluttered some dark smoke from its exhaust, then died. As the boat passed the threshold of the tunnel, emerging from under the house, they both squinted in the sunlight. Will scanned the rear of the Izri home, hoping not to see one of their pursuers overlooking the river. It appeared that luck was with them, for now. Frenz pulled the starter cable once more and the motor spluttered into life. Frenz immediately opened the throttle and the boat pitched upwards. He then turned eastwards towards Westminster and the now unoccupied home of Cillian Gander. As they moved further and further downriver, Will kept his eyes fixed on the windows and balconies until the house drifted completely out of sight.

The small boat hit its top speed at around twelve knots;

as such, Will and Frenz were thankful that they'd appeared to have escaped the Izri estate unseen. Leaving Madame Izri behind was playing on the minds of both men for the entirety of the forty-minute journey upriver.

They disembarked just south of Lambeth Bridge, not wanting to get too close to Westminster while so exposed on the river. Fortunately, the tide was out so they allowed the boat to run aground on the western riverbank before climbing a nearby ladder to street level. They walked north along Millbank with their heads lowered to avoid being spotted, but the streets were busy once more, the masses of people comfortably camouflaging them. Once close to the house, they decided to take a slightly different route, overshooting Great Peter Street and turning west so that they entered Barton Street from the north.

The smell hit them well before they saw the cause of it with their own eyes. As they rounded the corner, both Will and Frenz were stopped in their tracks. The street was lined with police, firefighters and ambulances. The house of Cillian Gander was nowhere to be seen.

It had been burned to the ground and all that remained was a black, smoking shell where the house once stood.

CHAPTER THIRTY

May 19th, 1984, 8:29

DI Moss sat behind his desk, slouching lazily in his chair. He was enduring a frustrating week. Not only had he had to contend with a murder on his patch and the resulting manhunt, but he couldn't shake the feeling that it was all part of some bigger, far-reaching plot.

He'd returned from his unsuccessful visit to Ireland early that morning, convinced that William Wells had somehow managed to evade capture once again and had come back to England. He had no solid proof that Wells had even left Ireland, but his experience and instinct for the truth told him that was the case. Everyone he'd spoken to in the port town of Ballycotton had no love for the English and they were hiding something, he was sure of it.

Part of the reason Wells was proving so hard to catch, Moss had told his unsatisfied superiors, was that he was behaving so unpredictably. Wanted men usually do one of two things: they either lay low and hide or they try to leave the country. In this case, Wells had been remarkably successful in doing the latter; however, for reasons Moss couldn't fathom, the fugitive had then decided to return to England.

There were other characteristics to the movements of William Wells that Moss was so far unable to offer a rational explanation for. Namely, his ability to vanish into thin air and to be in two places at once. He looked on his desk at the two CCTV images of Wells at Holyhead and he had to admit that Mrs Gesler had made an astute observation: the timestamps on each image were within seconds of each other. He'd called the security team at Holyhead personally and they'd assured him that the time codes on their cameras were accurate. He'd had them double- and triple-checked, much to the security team's annoyance, but the same answer had come back.

As punishment for allowing Wells to escape in the first place, Moss had ordered Mapson to personally trawl through the footage of every camera in the station, combing through each frame from the hour before Wells was brought in, to the hour after he was reported missing. While he had serious doubts about Mapson's ability to lead an investigation without his oversight, he was a solid police officer, hardworking and hungry for approval. When he'd reported to Moss the following morning that he'd found no trace of Wells on any of the camera footage, beyond that which showed him entering the station, he took him for his word, confusing as the news was.

To make this case even more complicated, the coroner had still been unable to make a formal identification of the thrift-shop shooting victim. His name wasn't coming up in any database the police had and there appeared to be no family or friends willing to come forward. They couldn't even say for sure that the shop had had any customers to speak of. Other than William Wells, that is.

More troubling was the news Moss had just received concerning the shell casing and bullets recovered from the scene and from the body of the victim. It had been confirmed that they'd all been fired from the same unusual calibre of pistol. What he'd neglected to inform the ballistics lab was that one of the bullets he'd submitted for inspection hadn't been retrieved from the thrift-shop shooting at all. He had substituted one of them for a bullet he'd pried out of the southern wall of the police yard.

That last revelation had Moss more worried than anything else. Whatever had taken place during Wells's escape, it certainly wasn't a car backfiring that had caused the commotion in the station yard. Someone had fired a weapon during the escape. That same someone had fired a weapon that used identical unusual-calibre bullets as the murder weapon in the thrift-shop shooting. For reasons unknown, that fact appeared to have been covered up. Someone in the police department was lying to him about the whole thing.

While DI Moss sat contemplating all of this, Mapson appeared at his door. 'Ah, sir, you're back.'

'Incredible. We'll make a detective out of you yet. What is it?' Moss said.

'We've just had a call. Possible shooting in progress at the Izri residence.'

'Give it to Brooks. I'm too busy with the Wells case.'

'That's just it, sir. We have a witness who claims to have

seen Wells at the scene.'

Without responding, Moss grabbed his coat and hurried out of his office.

CHAPTER THIRTY-ONE

May 19th, 1984, 08:49

Will and Frenz stood for a moment, mesmerised by the swirling dance of the rising smoke and the trickle of water that was running from the base of the house and pooling onto the street. Frenz shook his head in disbelief, a chortle escaping his lips at the absurdity of it all.

'I don't know the guy,' Will said, 'but in some ways you've got to admire his commitment.'

'Cillian Gander isn't just committed, he's obsessed to the point of madness.'

'You sure this isn't an accident?'

'No, this was very deliberate. He will have known that we'd try to access the Central Station building and he knows that the only way in is through here.'

'Well, we can't stay here,' Will said. 'This place is crawling with cops and in case it had escaped your attention, I'm currently a fugitive from the law.'

'Agreed, let's move.'

Frenz began to walk away from the scene when Will reached out and grabbed his arm, stopping him in his tracks. Frenz turned back, surprised. Will said, 'Frenz, where are you going?'

'Doing as you suggested and getting out of here. This is no time to fool around.'

'Frenz, come now, you of all people must know that our perception of *here* is all relative,' Will said, grinning in a way that Frenz found a little unsettling.

'I don't like the way you're looking at me. What is it?'

'The thing that was going to be difficult about this whole plan was getting into Cillian's house unobserved, right?'

'Yes, and?'

'Well, what don't you see anymore when you look at his house?'

'Nothing, it's all gone. Will, can you please get to the point before somebody spots you?'

'No walls, no windows, no front door. We can walk right into the place.'

'What good will that do? The entrance tunnels would likely have been in the basement and that will be under a tonne of rubble by now.'

Will's expression seemed to grow even more manic. 'Precisely, *now* it's under rubble.'

When realisation struck Frenz, he immediately began to shake his index finger in Will's direction in objection and said, 'Oh no. Absolutely not!'

'Why the hell not?' Will asked, throwing his hands wide, exasperated.

'Why? Because the Timekeepers will find us, and they'll kill us, of course! On top of that, even if we go into the past and get into the house, we won't know what we're going to be faced with when we get there.'

'What if we did know what we would face? What if I knew an exact date and time when this house would be empty?'

'How could you possibly know that?'

'The day I met Abigayle for the first time. She'd called at the house before me and there was no one there. All we have to do is travel back, I don't know, ten minutes before Abigayle knocked on the door. That should do it, right?'

'It's still too risky. What if Cillian was home and just refused to answer the door? Or worse, that Abigayle had lied to you about him not being home?'

'I don't know a man alive that would refuse to open a door when Abigayle is on the other side of it. And I know Abigayle, and I know she wasn't lying to me. Look, it's as certain as we're ever going to be. Besides, what other option do we have? If we run now, what's next?'

Frenz began to offer further objection, but before any words were uttered, he realised that Will was right: they were all out of options. His shoulders slumped slightly, he nodded glumly and said, 'Okay, fine, we'll do it your way. But how do we get in there? This whole street is still crawling with police and firefighters.'

Will said, 'Exactly, it's chaos. The fire might be out, but there are people all over the place. We'll follow your advice and use the crowds as cover. It's worked for us so far.'

Behind them, a number of firefighters were pulling back from the scene and attending to their equipment. Hoses and tools were being gathered and stowed in fire engines. Soot-covered helmets, jackets, trousers and gas masks were being removed and piled against the wall of a house opposite. Police were attending to their paperwork and talking on their radios.

'Quick, follow me,' Will said. Before Frenz could respond, Will had turned and headed confidently towards the scene once more. He approached the front door of the house opposite, with the firefighters' uniforms and equipment piled along one wall. A firefighter moved to block Will's passage, but Will cut him off, claiming to live in the house. Will walked assertively to the front door and began fumbling around in his pocket as if he was trying to find his front door key. Satisfied that Will was just a local resident innocently returning home, and clearly fatigued from a long shift, the firefighter walked away and continued with his duties. As soon as he was out of sight, Will grabbed a helmet, trousers and jacket and thrust them into Frenz's arms in a crumpled ball. Frenz looked around anxiously, more certain than ever that they would be spotted. As fast as Frenz had ever seen him move, Will had turned and picked up another full uniform for himself and ushered Frenz into the narrow passageway between two houses. Once safely out of sight, the two of them began wriggling into the sweaty gear.

Will stepped into the inflexible, tough but baggy trousers, pulled them up around his waist and slid his arms through the elastic braces one by one. They hung heavily on his shoulders as he proceeded to put on the jacket, which was equally rigid and heavy. After securing all the zips, buttons and buckles, he placed the yellow helmet on his head and tucked the strap under his chin. When he was done, he looked at Frenz, who was still working on his jacket. Will picked up Frenz's helmet, dropped it onto his head and then wiped his hand across a thick patch of soot on his own jacket before smearing it across Frenz's face. Frenz flinched at first before acknowledging Will's intentions. He was quick to return the favour, appearing to quite enjoy covering Will's face with the black powder.

Now suitably disguised, Will approached the neck of the alleyway and checked that the coast was clear before emerging and striding assuredly forwards once more. Frenz followed Will, doing his best to look as if the two of them belonged. They rounded the side of a parked fire engine and carefully navigated the tangled, snaking hoses weaving across the road. The two of them crossed the street, stepped up onto the footpath and up the steps to where the front door of Cillian's house used to be. Will took a breath and stepped unmolested through what was left of the front door, with crumbling black bricks stacked precariously on either side of it.

Once inside the house, things got a little trickier. Piles of rubble covered most of the ground floor and large wooden beams lay at crooked angles, propping up the few internal walls that remained.

Will turned to Frenz. 'Okay, Frenz, you're the expert, where's the safest place to do this?'

Frenz glanced around, then pointed to a room to the right. 'Through there, into the study. We'll be out of sight from the street and I can see a patch of floor that looks to be intact, but for the record, I don't like this one bit.'

'Noted. Let's go.'

They stepped carefully over the blackened obstacles in their way. Residual smoke, which was still quite thick even though the fire was long extinguished, caught in Will's throat. They made it safely into the study, surrounded by charred remains of furniture, books and even a bathtub, which had presumably fallen from one of the floors above. Frenz glanced around once more to check that no one was approaching, then looked at Will and nodded. The two of them quickly discarded their borrowed gear. Will then rolled up his sleeve and began turning the dials on the Timepiece quickly and deliberately until he'd entered a time and date that he knew by heart.

Will glanced at Frenz one more time, almost expecting him to change his mind, but instead he found a stern, determined face staring back at him. Will took Frenz's hand and activated the Timepiece.

CHAPTER THIRTY-TWO

December 23rd, 1983, 04:41

Will had almost got used to the overdose of visual stimuli that came with seeing the world around you melt and meld into something new. In this case, the effect was magnified as the charred ruins were replaced in such contrast by the bright, gleaming interior he now found himself in. But the thing that struck him most in this instance was the smell: gone was the near suffocating stench of burning wood, stone and metal, replaced instead with the far more welcoming aromas of pine, leather and tobacco smoke.

Both Will and Frenz remained still for a moment, listening intently for sounds of activity in the house. The place was deathly silent. Frenz quietly scanned all of the downstairs rooms before he was satisfied that the house was indeed empty.

The study was a place of ostentatious splendour. Cream

silk curtains hung from decorative, gilded rails. The ceiling was moulded with intricate plastered patterns. The walls were smooth, painted by Will's own hands in rich green paint. The wide wooden planks of the floor were gleaming with a fresh coat of varnish. A high-backed reading chair sat to the right of a fireplace and a tobacco pipe rested on a small side table nearby. The bookcases on either side of the window were covered in neatly arranged, leather-bound volumes. It was a place that Will had spent many hours and the kind of place that he fantasised about one day owning himself as he painted its walls.

Will approached a wood-panelled wall, placed his palm flat against it and pressed firmly. A large panel popped open, revealing a hidden bathroom. Will entered the room and washed the soot from his face and relieved himself in the toilet. When he was finished, he left the room and said, 'Sorry, I couldn't resist. When I was working here, they wouldn't let me use the bathroom in the house. I had to walk a half-mile down the road and use the public restroom.'

After washing the soot from his own face, Frenz said, 'Right, let's get to work.'

'Where do we start? Basement is through there.' Will pointed back towards the entrance hall.

'If it's here, it has to be down there somewhere. Let's go.'

Will led Frenz back towards the front door of the house. The entrance hall was also brightly lit, with a wide grand staircase to one side. The floor was finished with elegant black and white tiles, which had been cleaned to a brilliant mirror finish. Will opened a door under the main staircase and said, 'Here it is.'

'Allow me to begin the search,' Frenz said. 'I have a clear

idea of what I'm looking for. You should stay up here and keep a lookout just in case we get company.'

'Yeah, sure. Good idea.'

Frenz ducked through the low basement door and disappeared from sight.

Will could hear his footfall on the creaking steps fade off to near silence as he descended. He returned to the study and made himself comfortable in the tan leather reading chair, propping his tired feet up on the matching and well-used footstool. He glanced around the room, trying to imagine what it must be like to be Cillian Gander. He scanned Cillian's vast collection of books, wondering how many had ever been read. He looked at the reading lamp, which had a decorative ring at the end of a silver chain. It was such a graceful thing to simply offer a little light to the room. His eyes then fell upon the tobacco pipe that lay on its side atop the antique side table beneath the lamp. He picked up the pipe and rolled it between his fingers. It was a beautiful piece: the bowl and shank had been carved from a single piece of briarwood and polished to a high shine. The base of the bowl had an intricate carving of the many-handed clockface adopted by The Office of Time Dissemination. A gold ring had then been embedded into the wood between the shank and the mouthpiece. The mouthpiece itself appeared to be made from amber.

As Will studied the pipe, he paused when he thought he heard a faint sound coming from the entrance hall. He froze and concentrated his ears. His eyes darted around the study as if it may somehow aid his hearing.

There it was again.

Will could hear a faint clinking of metal on metal. He

tiptoed hurriedly towards the study door, dropping the pipe delicately on the side table as he passed.

He reached the study doorway and peered out into the entrance hall towards the front door. He heard the sound once more, louder and more defined. The gentle metallic sound was followed by a solid clunk. The door handle then began to turn, and the door groaned open.

A figure stepped through the door and Will pivoted backwards through the study doorway to avoid being spotted. He pressed his back against the wall and tried to control his breathing. He could hear a staccato click-clack of heeled shoes on the tiled floor approaching ever closer. They grew louder and seemed almost upon him.

Will closed his eyes and braced himself.

Suddenly, he could feel the floor below him shudder and the high-pitched clatter diminished to the lower-pitched thud of shoes on wooden floor.

He opened his eyes as the figure walked past him and into the study. The figure turned to the right and stopped in front of the desk, picked up a paper knife and began working the blade into one of the closed drawers in the desk.

As the figure attempted to break into the drawer, their head turned slightly; without warning, a jolt of electricity surged along Will's spine. He opened his mouth and attempted to speak her name, but his voice failed him. The rasped sound that arose from his mouth instead only startled her, and she let out a high-pitched scream followed by a series of profanities.

Hearing Abigayle's voice again made Will go weak at the knees. Even the tirade of obscenities pouring out of her mouth did nothing to dampen the joy he felt at seeing her again.

As she laid eyes on the would-be intruder, she pointed the paper knife in his direction and said, 'Who the bloody hell are you? What do you want?'

The realisation that she didn't recognise him jolted Will from his gooey-eyed stupor. It had barely been a week since Will had last seen her, but it was as if years had passed in that time. Looking at her now, it felt as if he was seeing her for the first time all over again. Abigayle, he realised, really was seeing *him* for the first time and her first impression of him wasn't going well. She was pointing a knife at him and seemed ready to use it.

When Will didn't respond to her initial questioning, she spoke again, 'Excuse me, sir? If you come any closer, I will cut that pretty little face of yours, so I suggest you leave immediately!'

Will couldn't help but smile. It was a side of her that he'd never seen before: afraid but fierce, like a cornered animal. 'You really think I have a pretty face?'

His retort caught her off guard. She took half a step back, frowned with slight irritation – something Will *had* seen a hundred times before – and said, 'I beg your pardon?'

'I said, do you really think I have a pretty face? Because I'd always thought I had a disproportionately large nose. I get that from my father's side of the family.'

Abigayle's stance softened slightly, then she said, 'No, don't say that, you have a quite lovely…' She suddenly caught herself, shook her head before continuing. 'Now wait just a minute! Why on earth are we talking about your nose? You're trespassing! Tell me what you're doing here at once or I shall be forced to call the police.'

'Right, right. I can explain. I think. Um…'

'Come on, out with it,' she said, taking a step forward with the knife still raised towards Will.

'Okay, okay. I'm the painter.'

'The painter?'

'Yeah. The walls. I painted this room, as a matter of fact.'

Abigayle tilted her head to one side, processing this information. 'Let's just assume I believe you, but that doesn't explain why you're inside this house.'

'Well, see, the guy who owns this place, he didn't pay me for the job, and he's been ducking me for over a week. So, I thought I'd sneak in and confront him when he comes home and ask for an explanation face to face.'

'There are so many reasons why that's a bad idea, not to mention the fact that it's illegal. And a little sinister. Perhaps I *should* call the police.'

'Yes, I agree. Terrible idea. Which is why I'd changed my mind. I was just going to scrub his toilet with his toothbrush and then be on my way, honest.'

This brought the tiniest smile to Abigayle's face, which she did her best to hide. 'That's utterly vile! You were really going to do that?'

Will had picked up on the smile and the change of tone in her voice. He grinned back a shock of white teeth and said, 'Yeah, sure I was. My mother always told me to treat well those who have access to your toothbrush.'

Abigayle's smile grew wider. 'Well, I'm afraid I simply can't allow you to do that, sir. It wouldn't be proper.'

'Yeah, you're probably right. Say, talking of proper, you mind telling me what you're doing here?'

'This is my employer's home.' Will's stomach lurched and

twisted at the news, something he'd hoped wasn't true. She continued. 'I have a key. I'm permitted to be here. Not that that's any of your business.'

Will motioned towards the desk. 'The drawer. You were trying to jimmy it open with that knife in your hand.'

Abigayle blushed, her cheeks suddenly awash with colour. 'What? No, I think you're mistaken. I was just, um…'

Will raised his hands defensively. 'Hey, look, no need to explain. It doesn't sound like either of us are here with completely honest intentions, am I right?'

Abigayle said nothing and could only manage a shrug.

Will said, 'How about this: we both leave, one by one, and forget that any of this ever happened?'

Abigayle nodded reluctantly. 'Yes, fine. Let's never talk about this again. To anyone. Agreed?'

'Agreed.'

'We should probably go now,' she said.

'Yeah, as unforgettable as this encounter has been, I think it's time we go our separate ways. You go out the front, I'll head out the back, the way I came in.'

'Yes, okay. Well, it was nice meeting you.'

'Yeah, it was. Maybe we'll bump into each other again soon.'

Abigayle smiled at Will, walked back into the entrance hall and opened the door. She gave him one last look, then waved and closed the door behind her.

Will strode towards the door as it closed, rested his head against it and slid his hands along the coarse grain of the wood. He could feel Abigayle's presence on the other side of the door as she slid the lock home. He was gripped with dread at the thought that the first time Abigayle spoke to him might be the last time he spoke to her.

Will shuffled to his left and pulled back the lace curtain to the side of the door and looked out onto the street. He saw Abigayle reach the bottom of the steps before being startled by a familiar-looking man in dirty paint overalls. The two of them spoke hurriedly to each other. Will's entire body shook when he saw himself, unintentionally disturbing the curtains in the process. He then saw his other self turn his head in his direction as the curtains moved. Will had an odd memory of this moment and so anticipated this and managed to duck out of sight just before making eye contact with the younger version of himself.

CHAPTER THIRTY-THREE

December 23rd, 1983, 04:55

Will was hunched over with his right shoulder pressed against the front door when he felt fingers close around his arm. He let out an unnatural squeal of fright, jumping a clear foot in the air, then turned to see Frenz standing close by, his hand outstretched and a look of bewilderment on his face. 'Frenz! What are you trying to do, give me a heart attack or something?'

Frenz took a step back and held his hands out to the side, palms forward in apology. 'I'm sorry. Are you okay? You seem rather on edge.'

'I'm just not used to breaking and entering, okay? I'm a little out of my comfort zone here, you know.'

Frenz said, 'Nonsense, we've broken nothing, but I do believe that we shall need to break out.'

'What do you mean, break out?'

'Come with me, I think I've found it.'

Frenz led Will back through the entrance hall, through the basement door and down the steep cobweb-infested steps into the basement. The two of them skirted along a narrow red-brick passageway with a low ceiling. As they walked, they passed a series of smaller rooms with small, open archways leading into them. One was being used as a wine cellar while another seemed to contain years' and years' worth of dried and tinned food. Another appeared to contain weapons crates, high explosives and chemicals all covered with terrifying looking warning labels. The only room with a door was almost completely empty, save for a single chair that sat in the middle of the room. It had leather straps hanging from the front legs and armrests. It was bolted to the concrete floor, which was mottled with brown-red stains. Neither Will nor Frenz could bear to think of what horrors might have occurred in there.

At the very end of the dimly lit passageway, Frenz darted left and down another set of concrete steps. The room they emerged into was far wider than the other rooms and at least four times longer. The floor was also lower and therefore had a higher ceiling. The floor itself was clean and fashioned from smooth, polished concrete.

The far wall seemed to stretch far enough to be well beyond the footprint of the property above ground. The centre of the room was dominated by a series of heavy-duty metal storage units. The frames of these units appeared to be constructed from thick square bars of solid steel. There were eight units in total, each one with a slightly different configuration. Some were entirely comprised of closed storage compartments, with doors and drawers made from heavy steel sheets, the corners folded and riveted fast. Others were completely open shelves, stacked with large books, ledgers and files. Others still were a combination of the two, but all were tall, wide and substantial.

Below the storage units and embedded in the concrete floor were rows of metal tracks. These too were extremely robust and resembled those used for trams or cable cars. There were four separate tracks that ran lengthways towards the far wall. At the base of each storage unit were sturdy metal wheels with durable plastic treads. Each wheel sat snuggly inside the tracks, and with a little effort the storage units could be slid from side to side to gain access to each. Attached to each of the wheels was a bulky square block that appeared to act as a dampener to prevent the storage units from gathering too much momentum and derailing. They were tuned to perfection: not so restrictive that sliding the units by hand was a chore, but restrictive enough that once on the move the units didn't pick up speed. Instead, they glided to a gentle stop once released. It really was an ingenious bit of engineering that both Will and Frenz had to admire.

After spending a few moments pushing the units back and forth, Will said, 'These things are cool and everything, but how do these files help us, exactly? Is there a file in here somewhere with some secret blueprints or something?'

'No, no. Nothing like that.'

'Oh, thank god! There must be ten thousand pieces of paper here.'

'It's not the paper that I'm interested in. Take a look at this wall. Do you notice anything odd about it?'

Will walked over to the far side of the room where Frenz

was standing. He examined the wall from top to bottom. It was constructed with red bricks like the rest. 'I don't get it. It's a wall, same as…'

Will didn't finish the sentence, as something about the construction caught his eye. He walked to the corner of the room and examined where the two walls met, starting at the bottom and tracing his way up to the ceiling. On closer inspection he could see that although the colour of the bricks didn't appear to vary a great deal, the size did. Will looked over his shoulder to Frenz and said, 'The bricks on the far wall are smaller than all the other walls. They're offset from one another.' Will looked up to the top of the wall and pointed out the disparity. 'The rows of bricks on this wall are pretty well aligned with the other wall at the bottom, but the farther up the wall you go, the bigger the disparity.'

'Perhaps this far wall is newer and was therefore constructed with smaller bricks,' Frenz said.

Will clicked his fingers. 'The metric system. The UK switched to metric in 1965. They must have made bricks a different size after that.'

'Yes, of course. I remember the furore around the introduction of the metric system. Although many places weren't properly incorporating it even by 1967. Whenever this wall was built, I'd wager that it was after that.'

'Sure it was. And look' – Will pointed to the base of the wall – 'the tracks run right through the wall. It was built on top of them.'

'My thoughts exactly. That's why I brought you down here in the first place. I'd noticed that the tracks run under the wall, although I have to confess that I hadn't noticed the misaligned bricks. You know, you're beginning to get rather good at this,' Frenz said with a proud grin.

'That's the nicest thing you've ever said to me.'

'Don't let it go to your head, we've still got to figure out a way to bring this wall down and fast. We've already had the Timepiece activated for far too long. They'll be here soon.'

Both Will and Frenz began frantically searching the basement room. Frenz got lucky first. In the far corner of the room, he came across a rusted metal toolbox with chipped metallic-blue paint. Inside he found a large hammer with a wooden handle and a heavy metal head. He marched back over to the wall, calling out for Will to join him. He then angled his arm high above his head with the mallet in hand and swung a wide arc, smashing the metal head against the brick wall. The force with which the mallet struck the wall made an almighty crunch and sent debris flying in all directions.

Unfortunately for Frenz, however, the debris was mostly in the form of fractured wood. The wooden handle had become brittle over the years and had virtually disintegrated in Frenz's hand. Frenz had let out a yelp of pain as the mallet had met the wall. He reeled backwards, clutching his wrist.

'Are you okay?'

'Yes, I'm fine. It's just a sprain. My dignity, on the other hand…what a foolhardy thing to attempt.'

'Well, I've got to say, Frenz, that was a little bit optimistic if you ask me.'

'What else is there? That was the largest tool in the box aside from some screwdrivers.'

'Screwdrivers! Frenz, that's perfect.'

'William, we don't have time to chisel our way through this wall.'

'That's not what I had in mind. Where did you find the tools?'

Frenz pointed to the other side of the room and Will hurried over, returning with a variety of rusty screwdrivers. He set them down on the floor and began to examine each one. He looked at the first, scrutinised the type and size, grunted in dissatisfaction, then discarded it. He looked at the next one with the same result. He picked up the third, dismissing it even quicker than the previous two. This went on for a further thirty seconds until finally, at the second to last screwdriver, he found what he was looking for. He then slid the tool into his back pocket.

Will stood, kicked the discarded tools to one side and then proceeded to push all the storage units one by one towards the entrance of the room and away from the far wall. Frenz stood by and watched as he repositioned the final storage unit, sliding it home so that all eight were neatly pressed together. Will knelt down, pulling the large screwdriver from his back pocket, and began getting to work on the bulky metal blocks attached to the wheel of the storage unit. Realising what he had in mind, Frenz moved to assist him. By the time Frenz had reached the unit, Will had already removed one dampening block from its wheel. Frenz held back the large metal unit while Will began working on the second of the four dampeners. Once Will had released the second, he pressed all his weight against the unit before passing the large screwdriver to Frenz. With Will now holding the storage unit back, Frenz removed the third and fourth dampening blocks.

'What about the blocks on the other side of the unit?' Frenz asked.

'Let's leave them. Each unit has eight perfectly tuned dampeners to slow this thing down, so it should move pretty fast with only four. Besides, it'll help stop the unit from toppling over as we push it if we leave the dampeners on the back.'

'Truly excellent lateral thinking, William.'

'Well, let's find out. You ready?'

Frenz nodded and moved to the end of the storage unit. Will moved to the opposite end and said, 'On three. One two, three!'

Together the two men began pushing the large, heavy storage unit. There was only ten or so metres between it and the wall, where the tracks terminated abruptly. They both pushed with all their might. The unit moved painfully slowly at first, the remaining dampeners still doing their job. Now that a gap had opened up between the storage unit that they were pushing and the adjacent one, Will and Frenz moved quickly from pushing at either end of the unit to pushing from behind. They both kicked their feet off the units behind them, becoming almost horizontal as the gap opened up. This move seemed to help immeasurably as the speed the unit was moving increased. They had almost reached the halfway point, the unit now barely six metres from the wall, but it was still moving far too slow. Fortunately, the remaining dampeners completely failed and with only four metres to go before impact, both men were approaching a full sprint. By the final two metres, the unit had picked up so much speed that neither Will nor Frenz found themselves pushing it anymore; its momentum had increased to the point that they could no longer keep up.

Barely a second later it happened. The unit smashed into

the wall with a deafening clang. Metal thundered against stone and the heavy papers that were once neatly organised on the unit spilled into the air followed by a cloud of thick red and grey dust. Within a few moments, the entire room had been engulfed in a powdery haze. Will and Frenz covered their mouths and shielded their eyes. Will approached the wall, sweeping his hand back and forth in an attempt to clear the air. As he neared the twisted, mangled remains of the storage unit, the dust began to settle.

Although the wall had obviously taken some damage, he could see no clear way through it, and he feared it was still intact. He was soon joined by Frenz, with whom he exchanged a concerned look. Frenz grunted defiantly and, fighting through the pain in his injured wrist, grabbed hold of one of the boxes of ledgers, which was sitting at an odd angle on one of the shelves, and pulled it loose, letting it crash to the floor. It was followed by a torrent of brick fragments. The wave of red rock flowed out towards Frenz, almost swamping his feet before he was pulled away by Will. The red rocks brought with them another cloud of dust, which thankfully settled faster than the last.

Will approached the wall, then crouched and peered into the dark, dusty hole beyond the storage unit. He turned to Frenz and said, 'We did it! We're through!'

'Well, what are we waiting for? Let's go!'

With that, Will began climbing on all fours through one of the shelves of the storage unit. Frenz meanwhile suddenly turned and ran back towards the remaining seven storage units, saying, 'One moment, I saw a torch back here.'

Will looked back as he crawled through the wall and said, 'Okay, but be quick. The rest of this wall might come down any second now.'

Frenz returned to the crumbled wall just as Will emerged on the other side. Will hauled himself to his feet and turned to see Frenz clambering through the opening with a brightly illuminated, metal-bodied torch in his hand. As Frenz was almost through, he reached out a hand to Will to help him to his feet, but before Frenz could feel Will's hand close around his own, he felt another slender but strong hand close firmly around his ankle and begin pulling him back through the wall.

CHAPTER THIRTY-FOUR

December 23rd, 1983, 05:07

'And where do you think you're going, my old friend?' the somewhat high-pitched voice said through the jagged opening in the wall. Through the gloom, Will could see the grinning face of Agent Tyke behind Frenz. He was an even more frightful sight with that disturbing smile on his face. His thin skin creased dozens of times over his bony cheeks, while his crooked yellowed teeth seemed far too large for his mouth. He was laying on his front across one of the metal shelves of the mangled unit on the other side of the collapsed wall. His long, outstretched arm reached through the opening in the wall and his leather-gloved hand was clamped like a vice around Frenz's ankle.

Will tightened his grip on Frenz's hand before he was dragged back through the wall and an unusual human tug of war ensued. He pulled at Frenz's arm with both hands, but despite Tyke's disadvantageous position, he was somehow able to match Will for strength. Frenz began kicking at Tyke's hand with his free foot, but even the heaviest of blows appeared to make little difference, with Tyke grinning wider still, saying, 'Go on, Frenz, that's the spirit! It's always better when they put up a bit of a fight.'

Frenz locked eyes with Will and with his free hand pulled both vault keys from his pocket. He held them out to him and said, 'Take them and go!'

Will looked at the keys, then back to Frenz. 'What? No way!'

'Will, you must. I'll hold them back as long as I can. Now go!'

Still gripping Frenz's ankle firmly, Tyke turned his head and shouted back into the file storage room, 'Wigmore! Down here, I've got 'em down here!'

Frenz looked into Will's eyes once more, pleadingly saying, 'Let go of my hand and go find Abigayle. Don't worry about me!'

Resigned to the situation, Will released his left hand from Frenz's arm and reached out for the vault keys before hesitating. A flash of inspiration suddenly struck him, and he was no longer focused on the vault keys but instead the pulsing Timepiece peering out of the upturned sleeve of his right wrist. While still holding on to Frenz with his right hand, he pulled with all his strength, gaining just enough distance to edge Frenz's foot clear of the opening. With Frenz safely clear of the collapsed wall, Will immediately deactivated the Timepiece.

May 19th, 1984, 09:17

The Timepiece whirred and Will and Frenz lurched backwards, away from the wall, the tug of war suddenly over. They landed in a heap together, Will groaning awkwardly as he broke Frenz's fall. The two of them heaved themselves to their feet and dusted themselves off. The room had fallen suddenly darker, save for the flickering light from the torch that lay on the floor pointing back towards the collapsed wall. Only the wall was no longer collapsed. Gone were the piles of red brick and the unstable wall. Instead, in their place, was a sturdy, neatly constructed grey breeze-block wall. Muffled screams of anguish could be heard from behind it. The sound was blood-curdling and would stay with Will forever. He moved nervously towards the wall to retrieve Frenz's torch. As he picked it up and its light played across the floor and over Frenz's feet, Will let out a gasp and said, 'Holy shit!'

Frenz spun, shielding his eyes from the light, and said, 'What is it?'

Will pointed towards Frenz's ankle. 'Look!'

He aimed the torch at his feet and there, still in its vice-like grip, was the severed hand of Agent Tyke holding on to Frenz's ankle.

Unflustered, Frenz calmly crouched and one by one bent back each of the fingers. The screams of agony were still ringing through the wall. Upon releasing the last digit, the hand fell limply to the floor. Frenz looked back to Will and said, 'There. Now, shall we continue?'

'How can you be so calm? That's a severed hand! I did that! I cut off a man's hand!'

'You did. And it's a valuable lesson for you as well. Those are just the kind of dangers that come with using the Timepiece.'

'Are you serious? You're using this as some kind of teaching moment for me.'

'You are the Timekeeper now, but you're inexperienced. Dangerously so. I would say this is a good lesson to learn and is one you'll not easily forget.'

'Damn straight I won't forget it! That guy may have been a bad guy. He may have tried to kill us more than once, granted, but he just had his hand, Mimic Watch and all, removed from his body because of me.'

'Mimic Watch?' Frenz quickly turned back to the hand and picked it up, holding it out in front of the torch light. Congealed blood oozed from the base of the wrist, where the forearm should have been.

Will gagged. 'Oh God, I think I'm going to puke.'

'Please don't vomit, just hold the torch steady.' Frenz proceeded to carefully remove the Mimic Watch from the wrist of the severed hand, tossing the watch to Will and discarding the hand. 'Okay, now we can go. No more holding hands when we use the Timepiece. You can give this to Abigayle when you see her.'

'Yeah, sure. Thanks.'

Frenz walked past Will, taking the torch back from him. He led the two of them away from the newly constructed wall down a spooky, dimly lit tunnel that stretched off into the distance for what looked like eternity. The tunnel had walls that curved at the ceiling. As the light from the torch flickered over them, Will could see that they were covered in white metro-style tiles with dark grey grout. Many of the tiles had fallen, the broken remains littering the floor along the corners. He couldn't make out exactly what type of material was beneath their feet. It was damp and slippery in places but generally firm enough.

As they walked hurriedly along the tunnel, a breeze of unknown origin cooled their faces. The walls shuddered as distant trains trundled through tunnels overhead. Fine debris fell from the ceiling, sending dust swirling through the air. Will said, 'Wait a sec, are we in the subway?'

'In a way, I suppose. This is part of an abandoned underground network.'

'Is this part of the old King William Street underground station you told me about?'

'No, that's further east, near the Tower of London. That was used for regular agency staff. These are just unused passenger transit tunnels. There are hundreds of tunnels like this running under the capital. Stations too. They're called "ghost stations", and most of them ended up in the hands of the agency after they closed to the public. The agency purchased properties that lay above these tunnels so that directors and high-ranking agency staff could move to and from the headquarters building unobserved.'

'They're safe though, right?'

'I'm sure they are, but from the sounds of it Cillian Gander has had virtually all of them sealed or collapsed, so who knows.'

'Well, that's comforting,' Will said as a chill shuddered up his spine.

The two of them continued on through the dark tunnel for half a mile when the darkness began to recede. Passing through a bulky iron archway secured to the walls with hugely oversized bolts, they found themselves in a comparatively well-lit vestibule. Looking around for the source of the light, Will saw thin shafts of dancing blue-green pouring in from cylindrical openings in the ceiling.

'Where is that light coming from? And why is it moving like that?' Will asked.

'We're under the Thames.'

'The Time Travel Agency is under the Thames?'

'I wish you wouldn't call it that. But yes, part of it is. Come along, we're almost there.'

Less than a minute later they emerged from the underwater tunnel into a larger octagonal room with four passageways converging from different directions. Three of the passageways were blocked with rubble and had apparently caved in years before.

Frenz gestured to the collapsed tunnels. 'Cillian's handiwork, no doubt.'

To their right, between the tunnel they had just emerged from and one of the collapsed ones, was an immense circular door. It was huge, spanning some ten metres from floor to ceiling, and appeared to be cast steel. The steel hadn't rusted but had faded, with dull white and green streaks running from top to bottom as the damp from above had seeped through the ceiling. To the left and right of the giant door were colossal hinges, each the size of a telephone box.

Frenz approached the door, with Will tailing behind. He fished around in his trouser pocket and retrieved both keys. He handed Madame Izri's vault key to Will and kept the one given to him by Avy. Frenz traced his hands over the door, eventually locating the two keyholes after clearing away some kind of disgusting fungal growth that had blocked them from view. He motioned for Will to move to the right-hand keyhole. He nodded cautiously before moving into position. They both inserted the circular-shaped keys and on the count of three turned them anticlockwise.

A loud metallic clunk could be heard as the keys rotated the internal lock mechanism. With that done, Frenz took hold of a large circular bar in the centre of the door and turned it clockwise a full three rotations before he heard another clunk.

'Would you mind helping me with this?' Frenz said.

Will walked over eagerly, took hold of a thick horizontal bar on the right side of the door and began pulling the vault door outwards. Each half of the large circular door began to move, with Frenz pulling the left half and Will working the right. The hinges were stiff with inaction and protested valiantly before giving in and opening fully to reveal the long-lost Central Station of The Office of Time Dissemination.

CHAPTER THIRTY-FIVE

May 19th, 1984, 10:32

Will was doubled over, his hands on his knees, still panting from the effort of opening the stubborn door. Frenz, who was apparently far fitter than Will despite being almost a decade older, continued to move forwards. Will eventually joined him, stepping through the doorway and into a vast rectangular chamber. The room was four stories high, with a large, reinforced glass skylight at its peak. With the Thames at low tide, light danced through the shallow waters, illuminating the room from above.

'Hey, Frenz, are you sure this place can't be seen through the water when the tide is low?'

'No. The Thames is so filthy you can't see a thing at this depth. They've been pumping raw sewage into it for years. Let's hope they never clean it up, though.'

'What if there's a drought or something?'

'That hasn't happened for decades. The last I'm aware of was in 1858, the year of the Great Stink. Fortunately, the river was so full of waste that those windows were covered with a thick layer of it.'

'That sounds awful. I'll be sure to steer clear of that year if I can help it.'

The lower level of the main atrium was filled with disorganised desks covered in disused typewriters, stacks of crumpled paper and a thick layer of grey-brown dust. Toppled chairs were scattered across the floor. On either side were doors and corridors leading deeper into the facility. To Will's right, a plain ceramic sign with the words *Operations Section* written on it in black embossed lettering hung above a set of dark-stained wooden doors. To the left were a further two corridors, each with similar signs: the closest read *Engineering Section*; the furthest read *The Bureau of Game Theory*, the section where Frenz had worked. The three floors above had raised wooden gangways beyond which were more doors and corridors. It was clear that this was a substantial complex and would have been a hub of activity when it was fully staffed and operational.

Frenz stood for a moment, gazing around the room in disbelief. Will could only imagine what it must be like to see the place that he and so many friends and colleagues had worked now reduced to ruin.

'You okay?'

Frenz startled slightly. 'Oh yes, I'm fine. It's just so strange seeing it like this. Barely a week ago this place was bright and clean and full of activity' – Frenz shrugged – 'a week for me, at least.'

'Look, I gotta ask: was this all a waste of time

coming here?'

'Why do you say that?'

'Well, those doors back there have been closed for a long time. And just look at this place. If this Ben guy is here, what are the chances that he's still alive?'

Frenz shot Will an amused look. 'Whatever gave you the idea that Ben was a man?'

'Wait, what? You, Avy and Madame Izri talked as if...'

Frenz cackled heartily, barely able to contain it. Will was glad to see the warmer side to his otherwise cool demeanour, even at his own expense. 'Oh my, I haven't laughed that hard in years.'

Will looked sheepish and his cheeks were flushed with red. 'I take it that Ben isn't a woman either then?'

Frenz chuckled a little more. 'No, no. Ben isn't a person at all. Ben is right over there at the far end of the atrium. Follow me.'

The two of them weaved their way through the discarded desks and fallen chairs and came to a halt at the far end of the chamber in front of four immense rectangular metal pillars. They spanned the full height from floor to ceiling and likely beyond. Each pillar was lined with bolts and rivets and painted with dozens of layers of glossy black paint. The pillars were interconnected with metal wire grates on the back and sides, forming an open-fronted cage. Half a dozen wooden steps led up to the base of the pillars, and towards the back wall several flights of metal stairs ran between each metal pillar, stopping just below the ceiling.

Inside the cage was an impressive-looking piece of mechanical engineering. Centred between the four large pillars was a smaller, but still extraordinary, cylindrical pillar made from solid brass. Like the other pillars, it also spanned the full room height but seemed to pass up through a round opening built into the ceiling. Unlike the four surrounding pillars, however, it was spinning almost imperceivably slowly. Constructed around the base of this central column was something that at first appeared to be a brass-framed computer terminal of some description, although it lacked a screen. Instead, rows upon rows of dials and gauges covered its top half, with a series of button inputs below. To the right of the control panel was a tall glass window with stacks of brown paper, each no larger than a business card, behind it. At the bottom of this strange glass window was a thin slit with a small brass box protruding from it. Behind this complex facade, an array of iron cogs, gears, pistons and pulleys were visible. The contraption was like a cross between Charles Babbage's Difference Engine and a mechanical clock.

Will took in the giant machine and said, 'Oh you've got to be kidding me. *This* is Ben?'

'Yes, this is Ben,' Frenz pronounced. 'Ben here constantly monitors and records all usage of the Timepiece.'

'Hold on a sec. Where exactly are we right now?' Will pointed to the glass skylight in the ceiling between them and the vault door. 'If that's the Thames flowing above us' – he then turned to point at the machine – 'and this thing is called Ben then…'

'We must be below Westminster,' Frenz said. 'That is correct. And this here is the base of the Elizabeth Tower. More fondly known as Big Ben.'

'But…'

'Yes, yes, I know. When the bell at the top of the tower

became known as Big Ben, we started to refer to this monstrosity ironically as "Little Ben". After a while he became just Ben.'

Frenz smiled and exhaled through his nostrils, still quietly amused by Will's misunderstanding of the whole situation once again. He then approached the large machine and began pressing, sliding and twisting a dizzying array of buttons, levers and dials. He did this naturally, his hands seemingly moving independently of his mind, talking freely as he did so. 'This machine hasn't been operated manually for some time. Nikola Tesla upgraded the transmission range of Ben in the late eighteen hundreds so that it could be accessed remotely. That's likely how Cillian has been able to track the Timepiece without actually coming down here. We'll have to make do with cards and ink, the old-fashioned way.'

The large machine began to slowly come to life as cogs and pistons woke from their long slumber.

'What exactly does Elizabeth Tower have to do with the Timepiece?'

Frenz continued to frantically work various levers and dials as he spoke. 'In order to properly track the Timepiece and for the Mimic Watches to function, the agency needed an antenna, and a large one at that. They used their contacts in government to have the tower built in the mid-eighteen hundreds after a fire, which, between you and me, may or may not have been an accident. However, an antenna alone wasn't going to be powerful enough for the agency's needs, so the bell was installed. But you see, it isn't just a bell; it's an inverted receiver and relay dish, pointed towards the earth rather than the sky.'

'If it was right there in front of us this whole time, why

didn't we just go to Big Ben and come in through the roof? That's what the stairs are for, right?'

'There is access to the ground floor of the tower yes, but only from inside. Those stairs lead to an emergency exit and that's also our escape route. Just as soon as we have what we came for.'

'Well, you'd better be quick. Cillian Gander and his two cronies will be on us any second now.'

'Almost there, one last step. Will, you still have my ID card? The one you found in my safe?'

Will began rooting around in his pockets until he found his wallet. He began looking through, pulling cards and loose bits of paper free until he found what he was looking for. 'Yeah, I got it!'

Frenz then pulled an identical, albeit slightly less faded card from his own pocket, held it up and said, 'This machine requires two ID cards to be inserted to output data. Let's hope it doesn't object to two identical cards.'

'Here's hoping,' Will said.

'Ready?'

Will nodded his head yes. 'Ready.'

Both of them inserted their cards, perfectly synchronised. The moment the cards slid home, the machine fell quiet, all aside from a low humming sound emanating from within. Will looked at Frenz, who could only shrug helplessly and said, 'I don't understand. It should have worked.'

'Shit. Now what?'

Just at that moment a shot rang out, reverberating loudly through the large chamber. The bullet's meaty impact with flesh was followed by a fine spray of blood and then a thud as Frenz Belingi collapsed in a heap on the floor.

CHAPTER THIRTY-SIX

May 19th, 1984, 11:02

The bullet had torn clean through Frenz's leg just below the knee. His body's pain receptors hadn't quite relayed the message to his brain by the time he attempted to put weight on his wounded leg. As further shots rang out, he took a step to his side to find cover. Immediately his leg collapsed under him and he was momentarily bewildered to see the floor rushing towards him. His pain receptors soon did their job as agonising pain rippled up his leg. The feeling was worsened as he tumbled backwards down the wooden steps and clattered onto the stone floor at the bottom. The impact winded him and he let out a guttural rasp of breath. His attention soon returned to his leg, which felt hot, wet and numb all at once. He didn't initially feel pain in the wound itself; the worst of it came as sharp daggers shot up through his knee and into his thigh. He gritted his teeth, fighting back against the natural urge to scream out.

Will called out Frenz's name and moved to the aid of his fallen companion when an unsettling voice bellowed out from across the room. The voice stopped him in his tracks before he'd even reached the top of the steps. 'Don't you dare take another step!' it said. Will looked up in the direction of the command and realised with a sickening feeling of inevitability who has spoken it. At the far side of the room, calmly weaving his way through the desks and upturned chairs, was Cillian Gander. He had a smoking gun in his hand. The light refracting through the Thames above swept across his face as he walked. As he closed in, the sharp creases in his skin became even more apparent. Will found something chilling about the way he moved; he seemed to drift through the tangle of wood and paper as if he were a ghost floating above the floor.

The low hum from deep inside the machine to Will's left continued, appearing to build in intensity as Cillian approached.

He was already halfway across the atrium, accompanied by his corpulent henchman, Agent Wigmore, who was gracelessly waddling in tow. Just then there was a commotion at the far end of the room as the maimed Agent Tyke stumbled into view, clumsily kicking a metal wastepaper bin across the floor. He attempted to steady himself on a desk, sending papers flying in the process. He was doubled over with pain as he walked further into the room, cradling his severed left arm in a blood-soaked rag. The man looked pale and not long for this world. The sight of what Will had done to the man, murderer or not, sent a sickening feeling through his stomach.

Gesturing to the frail Agent Tyke, Cillian said, 'Well, well, well, Mr Wells, we meet at last. And you have been a busy boy. Just look at the harm you've done to my man Tyke over there. How marvellously malevolent of you.' Pointing towards the stricken Frenz with his gun, he continued. 'My former colleagues used to paint me as something of a monster, but compared to you I really do seem rather reserved in my methods. Wouldn't you agree, Mr Belingi?'

'Hey, it wasn't me who cut his hand off, it was your damn wall,' Will said in a steady voice, which surprised even himself.

'You know, I did always wonder what had caused my filing unit to collapse my wall in the way it had. It is such a thrill to discover something new about your past, is it not?'

'Look, old man, I'm not the one who executes innocent men and women. I'm not the one with the torture chamber in my basement.'

Cillian Gander rolled his eyes and held his arms outwards in an exaggerated manner. 'This is always the problem with you Yanks, so melodramatic.' Just like flipping a switch, his tone changed. The mock jovial manner evaporated, replaced with a stony, cold stare, and he raised the gun. 'Now, please stop your prevaricating. Give me the Timepiece and I shall show you a kindness by making your death a quick one.'

Will's options were limited so he did what he could to buy some time. He started with a frank act of defiance, by saying, simply, 'No.'

'No? What do you mean, *no*?'

'No, I'm giving you nothing,' Will said once more.

'Don't be absurd, I have a gun. Give me the Timepiece now and I will shoot you in the head, quick and painless.

Refuse and I will begin shooting little pieces off you one by one.'

'If you start shooting me, then you could hit the Timepiece. Then you'll leave with nothing.'

This possibility gave Cillian pause. He lowered the gun a fraction and whipped his head to the side, with his chin almost touching his right shoulder. Without looking directly at him, he said, 'Wigmore. Go over there and bring Mr Belingi to me.'

'With pleasure, sir,' Wigmore said, grinning menacingly.

Wigmore shuffled over, breathing laboriously through his mouth, something he seemed to do in perpetuity.

Meanwhile, the hum from the machine to Will's left became more regular, more rhythmic.

At the back of the room, Agent Tyke had settled into a chair and was awkwardly hunched against a desk, motionless. His hair was slick with sweat, his skin clammy and deathly pale.

By the time Wigmore reached him, Frenz had succeeded in using his belt as a tourniquet for his leg. He was drowsy and clearly in quite some pain but unlike Tyke was still conscious. Frenz resisted Wigmore's manhandling as best he could, but from his position on the floor and with only one functioning leg and a badly sprained wrist, he was no match for a man the size of Wigmore. He was dragged across the room towards Cillian, leaving a striped trail of blood, the edges of which quickly thickened as they absorbed the dust on the floor. Wigmore propped Frenz up on a desk to Cillian's right, something for which Frenz was actually quite thankful. He swung his leg into an elevated position, which relieved the pressure building in his thigh.

Cillian turned to Frenz and said, 'Frenz Belingi. It is so peculiar to see you after all these years looking no different than the last time I saw you.'

Frenz spoke through gritted teeth. 'No such feelings for me, I'm afraid to say. You look just as old as you ever did.'

Cillian grinned a hideous smile. 'You know, I've been searching for you for a long, long time. Everyone else in the agency gave up so quickly, thinking you dead, but not me. I knew you were still out there somewhere. We'd tracked you to the 1940s.' Cillian paused a moment and reached into his inside jacket pocket, pulling out a small brown card identical to the ones stacked behind the tall glass window of the humming machine at the back of the room. 'I've had this card for almost thirty years. This is where you went, isn't it?' Cillian turned the front face of the card to Frenz and he saw, printed in faded red ink, the date and time:

04:21, 5TH SEPTEMBER 1940

Cillian continued, 'And do you know what we found?'

'I'm sure you're going to tell me,' Frenz said.

'We found nothing but a record of a man – matching your description – who was arrested after he inexplicably found himself in the middle of a military training complex. The report offered no explanation as to how this man managed to infiltrate the facility. He was dealt with and thrown in jail. However – and here is where it gets very interesting – only two days later, that jail was struck by a Luftwaffe bomb, destroying the cell where this man was held.'

'It sounds like a tragic end for the man, whoever he was,' Frenz said.

320

'Oh, but things get even more interesting than that. A brilliant researcher of mine investigated this incident even further. A diary was uncovered, only in the past year or two, written by a prison guard who had worked at the jail. He recorded a vivid memory of the incident. He talked about the voices that haunted him for the rest of his days after that night. The voices he heard coming from the cell just before the bombs hit. He claimed that he could hear not one but two different voices. He also claimed that one of those voices was quite distinctive. His colleagues told him he was imagining it because, as far as everyone else was concerned, they hadn't arrested an American man.' Cillian then snapped his head around to lock his piercing deep-set eyes on Will.

'Is there a point to all this?' Will said.

'My point is that you seem to be a bad omen for our dear Frenz Belingi here.'

'Oh yeah, how'd you figure that?'

'I've been looking for him for years and now you've delivered him to me twice in just under a week.'

Will frowned in confusion. 'Twice?'

'When we followed you to that ghastly shop, we had no idea that you would lead us to Frenz, but you did.'

'You followed me? Why?'

Cillian turned to Frenz and said, 'I must admit that the first time I found you, my men acted somewhat hastily in killing you, slow and painful as they made it.'

A look of shock and confusion swept across Frenz's face, while a sickly grin crept across Cillian's. Cillian turned back to Will and said, 'Wait, you didn't tell him, did you? Oh, this is so delightfully macabre.' Cillian returned his focus to Frenz and said, 'That's right, Frenz. Tyke and Wigmore here shot you and let you bleed out. And despite the slow agony you must have felt before your death, you protected young Will here. Meanwhile, your friend Will watched them do it. And he did nothing. He didn't even call the police. Did you know that?'

Frenz glanced up at Will, who could only lower his head shamefully.

'And now he can stand by and watch you die once again.' Cillian raised the gun in his right hand and pressed it to Frenz's temple. A bullet slid into the chamber after a series of metallic clicks. Will shouted out, 'Wait! Wait, you win. Okay?'

'Will, what are you doing?' Frenz said.

'Time's up, Frenz,' Will said.

The low, steady hum from the machine that had been increasing in intensity for the past few minutes had reached a crescendo. The stack of brown cards behind the tall glass window shuffled slightly. An ear-splittingly shrill bell rang out, cutting through the otherwise quiet room.

The sound momentarily startled the normally cool and collected Cillian Gander, giving Frenz the chance he needed. He arched his left arm sluggishly through the air and batted Cillian's gun from his grasp. It skittered across the floor, some ten metres away. In the same movement, Frenz's arm completed its arc, wrapping around the neck of the dumbfounded Agent Wigmore, who was standing in front of him with his back turned. Frenz clasped his right hand tightly around his left wrist, squeezing his forearm into the flabby, fleshy skin surrounding Wigmore's windpipe.

Frenz then screamed, 'Will! The stairs. Run!'

CHAPTER THIRTY-SEVEN

May 19th, 1984, 11:09

The gun had spun through the air in an arced trajectory, hitting the floor and sliding under a toppled bookcase and out of sight. As Will watched the gun as it left Cillian's hand, he shifted his weight from his heels to his toes, preparing to move. The gun lay closer to Cillian than to him, but for a moment he thought he could get to it first. For a man of such advanced years, Cillian had shown himself to be surprisingly mobile and nimble. This gave Will pause and his thoughts quickly turned to running as Frenz had instructed. As he looked at Frenz, the guilt he felt for fleeing his shop when all this started came racing to the surface once more. How could he now, in good conscience, do the same thing again?

Cillian, he could see, was also hesitating. He had his feet set in a wide stance, planted flat. His head was turned towards his flailing employee Wigmore, whose face had become red and was slowly darkening to a shade of purple with Frenz's arm around his neck. The loyal servant was clawing frantically at Frenz's forearm, desperately trying to relieve the pressure on his airways. Wigmore momentarily released one arm and reached an outstretched hand towards his employer, pleadingly. His eyes were bulging from his sockets, veined and bloodshot. His lips moved but only a faint wheeze escaped them. He might have been trying to say 'Please', or perhaps 'Help', but whichever the case, Cillian's mind was made up. Fear gripped Wigmore more acutely when he understood his employer's true nature.

Cillian spun away from Wigmore and scurried in the opposite direction towards the gun. Before Will was able to reconcile the situation in his own mind, Frenz shouted out to him once more, 'Go! Now!' This time there was more desperation in his voice as he struggled with Agent Wigmore. Will looked Frenz in the eyes and saw resolve there and he gave what seemed to be a nod of forgiveness or at least understanding. Will reluctantly turned and broke into a sprint, grabbing the small card that had been ejected from the large machine before heading for the metal staircase at the back of the underground chamber.

Will pumped his legs as hard as they would go, taking two or sometimes three steps at a time. As he neared the top, his legs were burning and he stumbled up the final few steps. He had almost made it to the top by the time Cillian had recovered his weapon. At the top of the staircase Will encountered a white-painted metal hatch embedded in the arched brick ceiling. It had a hefty circular locking mechanism in its centre. The whole assembly resembled a rotating dog lever that you might find on a submarine door, and it occurred to him that – given they were in fact under the Thames – the comparison was particularly fitting.

To reach the hatch Will scaled a smaller set of black metal steps that were bolted to the sand-coloured brickwork of the far wall. Once at the top, he turned around and pressed his back against the cold bricks for leverage. As he reached up and grasped the circular lever in his hands, a shot suddenly rang out from below. The bullet hit the metal hatch and Will felt vibrations surge through his arms as the bullet ricocheted off it. Before Will was able to duck for cover, another shot rang out: this time the bullet hit a section of the metal staircase below, diverting the bullet up past the side of Will's head, grazing the base of his skull. The pain was instantaneous and brought about a deafening high-pitched ringing in his ears. His vision then seemed to blur erratically, as if his head was being shaken violently from side to side.

Will took cover, lying flat against the solid metal floor at the top of the metal staircase with his head in his hands. The ringing slowly subsided and his rattled vision stabilised. He wasn't sure whether to think it a stroke of luck that he hadn't been killed or simply unlucky that of all the places for the bullet to ricochet, it was towards his head. The pain was intense, but Will knew he couldn't linger so he forced himself back to his feet. He held the wound, which was just below his ear, and felt blood slowly trickling through his fingers. He listened out for more sounds of gunfire but instead heard the metallic thudding of feet on the steps below. Cillian was climbing the stairs and would be upon him soon.

This was Will's only window of opportunity. He could feel the impact of Cillian's feet on the steps below vibrating up through the whole structure. He expected the pace to slow and for the old man to weaken as he climbed, but this was not the case. If anything, his pace seemed to quicken.

Cillian was now directly beneath him several flights below and had no clear shot. Will climbed the small set of steps and pressed his back into the wall once more. He held the circular wheel and attempted to turn it anticlockwise, giving it all he had. His right hand was slick with blood and he found it hard to grip; his hand slipped, leaving streaks of red on the faded white paint of the wheel. The footsteps seemed louder, closer and more rapid now. Time was running out.

He could see movement below him through the narrow gaps in the steps. Cillian was perhaps three flights of stairs away from his quarry now. Will had to get the hatch open now or it was all over for him and for Abigayle. Just the thought of her seemed to give him strength and renewed determination. He had to think fast and reached into his jacket pocket to pull out his one remaining faux-leather glove. He wasn't quite sure why he was still carrying the thing around, but at that moment he was thankful for it. He quickly slipped the glove over his bloodied hand and now, with the grip he needed, gritted his teeth, pushed with his left arm and pulled with his right. The handle rotated ever so slightly at first and then layers of paint, dirt and grime around the base cracked and fell away. With the seal broken, the wheel was moving more freely. Will started spinning the wheel as fast as he felt possible, all the while the footsteps below grew ever closer. Below him he could see Cillian's white hair flashing past the gaps in the steps. He was closer than ever now.

Only one more flight away from his quarry.

The wheel spun and spun before Will felt some resistance. He gave the wheel one final push and felt a metallic clunk as the internal mechanism engaged and released the lock. Will then stood from his crouched position at the top of the small set of steps and pushed the heavy metal door upwards. It creaked and resisted, and more old paint cracked and flaked away around the seam of the door. In front of him Will could now see the back of Cillian's head as he ascended the final few steps. At that moment he let out a roar of effort and gave one final push upwards, his arms, back and legs all working in unison. The pulsing in his veins seemed to make the pain in his head more acute and he felt as if he might pass out. The door angled upwards and tipped away from him, resting against a wall above. Cillian rounded the metal banister at the top of the stairs and began to turn towards Will, his gun outstretched. Will reached above him into the new opening and hauled himself upwards. Another whizzed past, narrowly missing Will's leg, instead bedding into the wall, sending chunks of powdered brick soaring into the air. Will lifted his legs clear of the opening as another shot rang out, creating another cloud of dust below him.

He emerged into a narrow space no larger than a small car. Before properly surveying this new space, he reached over the opening and grabbed the metal hatch. Cillian's face was a picture of pure rage as he came into view below, just as Will slammed the hatch shut. The look in Cillian's eyes was a truly unsettling sight and gave him chills. He looked around the room and saw that the walls were low and constructed from large, grey, rough stone blocks. At the base of the walls were various building supplies, from buckets, used paintbrushes, bags of concrete and plaster to ladders. At the far side of the room there was a narrow set of stone steps and a low wooden door. Will grabbed a heavy sack of concrete and pulled it over to the hatch. He couldn't lock the hatch from this side, but hopefully the weight of the sack would do the trick.

With that done he rushed over to the ancient wooden door. Painted a dark reddish-brown, it was reinforced by black metal framework. Will tried the handle, but it was locked fast. The door may have been old but was certainly still as sturdy as ever. He looked around frantically and could see no other option but to climb the stairs.

The steps spiralled upwards in a clockwise direction. They were narrow, and the stone walls closed in tight on either side. He began to climb, and after a dozen steps the walls opened out and were replaced with metal banisters. Leaning over the waist-high banister and looking up, Will could see almost all the way to the top. It seemed to go on forever and darkened before he could see the summit. It was only at this moment that Will realised where he was. The base of Elizabeth Tower.

Looking around at the scattered building supplies, he remembered that the clock tower had been closed to the public and was undergoing renovations. The walls of the stairwell were being redecorated, something that unearthed a period in Will's past that he'd rather not be reminded of.

The works were only partly finished; the lower levels had new smooth plaster on the walls. They also had a fresh coat of magnolia paint with a deep red accent running along the bottom of the walls. The walls of the upper floors – the area Will was currently ascending into – had the old, cracked plaster, along with more building supplies spread haphazardly on the stairs.

Will had hoped to find alternate means of escape further

up the tower, perhaps one that might lead him to the scaffolding that encased the entire structure. From there he might be able to climb down, although he didn't savour the prospect. He had climbed close to a hundred of the more than three hundred steps of the tower when he realised he was now too high for that to be a realistic possibility. He stopped and looked down over the edge of the banister and decided to attempt to force the old door at the base of the tower again. Maybe there were tools down there he could use to break the door open. He began to descend, cursing himself for so hastily abandoning his efforts on the door. As he hurried down the steps, he heard a distant creaking sound from below, followed by the sound of metal dashing against stone.

The hatch had just been forced open.

CHAPTER THIRTY-EIGHT

May 19th, 1984, 11:14

Will didn't know how he'd managed it, but Cillian had somehow forced the hatch open. Continuing with his descent was now out of the question. Instead, he turned and began climbing the steps once more. The spiralled stairs seemed to go on forever, and after a hundred or so steps a voice echoed up from below: 'It's over, Mr Wells. There's nowhere left to go!' Cillian's voice sounded weaker and laboured. He was trying to disguise it, but it was clear he was taking long gulps of breath between sentences.

Human after all then.

Will said nothing in response and continued to climb when a volley of gunshots rang out, narrowly missing their target. At least one bullet must have struck a can of paint somewhere above because thick red paint began trickling over the steps, dripping past Will. Having already felt the sting of one of Cillian's bullets, he pressed his back against the outer wall of the stairwell for the remainder of the climb to reduce the chance of being struck by another. It slowed his progress but was safer at least.

Cillian spoke once more. 'Is that your blood... I can see dripping its way down here? If you're not already dead, why not... make this easy on yourself, Mr. Wells. Give up now... and I'll spare our mutual friend, Miss Abigayle Ward.'

Hearing her name leave Cillian's lips hit Will harder than any bullet he could have fired his way. Will did his best to keep his voice even. 'What are you talking about?'

'Oh, what a shame... not dead after all. Soon, though, I assure you of that.'

'You're just trying to get into my head and it's not going to work.'

'Mr Wells, surely you've figured this all out by now?'

'You're lying.' Will threw back his response unconvincingly.

'Come now, you know it's true. She's my brilliant... historical researcher whom I spoke so highly of. Who do you think uncovered Frenz's elaborate escape plan? And who do you think found Frenz's little shop?'

'She would never work for a man like you!'

'Really? Tell me, who was it that suggested... that you visit that particular area of London last week? Who mentioned that particular... alleyway you just happened to come across that day?'

Will couldn't face the idea that Abigayle had worked for a man like Cillian Gander. Could he have been so naive as to not see it all this time? Could the woman he loved really be responsible for sending those men to kill Frenz? After all,

Cillian had said at least one thing that was truthful: it *was* Abigayle who had suggested he visit that specific area of London. If the rest of what he said was true, then surely she would have known that he would find Frenz's shop and that he would return with the Timepiece. And it was this part of Cillian's story that didn't quite hold up: if Abigayle already knew what the Timepiece was before Will came home with it that day, then why would she do something so reckless as to activate it and allow herself to go astray? He couldn't explain why she'd done what she had, but he refused to believe that Abigayle was working with a monster like Cillian Gander. Whatever the case, he resolved to ask Abigayle himself when he found her. He pushed Cillian's taunts out of his mind and continued to climb.

Several minutes later Will had finally reached the top of the tower, emerging into a bright open space with a ceiling some ten metres above his head. On his right stood one of the four breathtakingly large clockfaces, glowing white, illuminated by the hazy morning sun. Viewed from the inside and from this proximity, he couldn't fail to be impressed with the grandiose example of craftsmanship before him.

He skirted the length of the first clockface and passed through a narrow, arched doorway in the corner of the tower. This doorway led into an identical space with another identical and equally impressive clockface. He passed through two more similar spaces before heading up another short set of steps that led into the room housing the great clock, ticking away once every other second. Although he couldn't linger, Will couldn't help but steal a glance at the giant pendulum that rocked back and forth on the far wall, complete with its famous pennies stacked on top. The clockkeeper would add or remove pennies to help keep the pendulum swinging in time. If the clock was becoming too slow, more pennies were added; too fast and pennies were removed. Even though Will's whole notion of time was forever changed, he was still struck by the charming simplicity of these pennies that kept all of London running on time.

Turning away from the grand clock, he hurried through another narrow door on the opposite side of the room, which led up yet more steps. As he climbed, he suddenly felt a chill in the air. The reason for this became clear as he stepped out into the belfry; the imposingly large chamber at the top of Elizabeth Tower that housed the great bell, Big Ben. The bell itself was suspended from the tall, vaulted ceiling. The whole structure was supported by a series of hefty arched girders, each of which had dozens of sizeable bolts running along its edges. The outer walls of the belfry were open to the elements via seven elaborate, Gothic tracery windows. Each wall was also lined with a sturdy chest-high metal railing. Will could feel strong gusts of chill wind rushing into the space and swirling around him. Beyond the open windows he could see the large metal poles of the scaffolding that currently surrounded the tower. Resting on them, scaffold boards lay level with the top of the chest-high metal railings. Giant tarpaulins were bound to the outside of the metal structure, rippling and stretching under the strong winds like sails on a grand ship.

Will had hoped that he could use the scaffolding as a means of escape but hadn't intended to attempt it at such altitude. He wasn't exactly afraid of heights, so long as he felt relatively safe, but had a very real fear of falling when he didn't. He surveyed the room, looking for the easiest route out onto the scaffolding. On the other side of the belfry there seemed to be a works access ramp. Will hurried around the outside of the room, along the walkways surrounding the great bell. Now on the opposite side of the room from the entrance, he scaled the paint-stained wooden ramp. Once he reached the top, he found himself standing level with the giant bell. As he prepared to head out through the window, he heard footsteps coming towards the belfry entrance. He looked back through the window and braced himself to step out from the safety of the sturdy stone tower and onto what he considered to be a rickety metal frame with uneven and loosely stacked planks of wood. As soon as he passed the threshold, he made the mistake of looking down, catching a glance of the ground below through one of the disturbingly large gaps between scaffold boards. Will paused for a moment, briefly considering the prospect of talking Cillian Gander down and leaving via the stairs instead, but that approach was made untenable as more gunshots rang out from the other side of the belfry.

Cillian had stepped into the room and without saying a word had fired another volley of bullets in Will's direction. At least one bullet had pinged off the side of the giant bell, causing it to ring violently. The sound was deafening and sure to attract some attention. The other bullets shattered into the stone window frame where Will was standing.

The time for thinking and contemplation was over, so Will ducked out onto the scaffolding, stumbling and falling to the floor. He gasped audibly as he crashed into the wooden boards. The whole structure seemed to shake and sway. The wind also appeared to have increased in strength, whistling in his ears, and was even more chaotic and unpredictable than it had been inside the tower.

Will picked himself up and carefully stepped away from the access window towards the corner of the tower to his right. He had to keep low to avoid giving Cillian a clean shot through one of the many open windows. As he walked, he couldn't help but look down at the giant clockfaces below him. There was something wildly unique about seeing Elizabeth Tower from this vantage point; not many people would ever see the intricate detail of its outer walls quite like this. There was also something masochistic about the regularity to which Will found himself glancing down through the gaps between the scaffold boards to study the walls of the tower, but he couldn't seem to help himself. Although the gap wasn't wide enough for him to fall through, it did send a chill to the pit of his stomach and an involuntary tightening of his sphincter every time.

His legs had turned to jelly as he stepped across the scaffolding, the adrenaline leaving his system and his heart rate increasing. The winds were continually buffeting him as he moved, and he stumbled more than once before reaching the corner of the tower. He stood fully upright and placed both hands flat against a large, cool cornerstone. Positioning himself with half of his body around the corner, he moved his face close to the stone so that his nose almost touched it. With one eye peering around the corner, he studied the access window, waiting for some sign of Cillian Gander emerging from it. Will had waited there for what felt like an eternity and still there was no sign of him.

What is he waiting for?

Will now had a choice to make. On the one hand, he was

more than willing to just bide his time and wait for Cillian to make a move. On the other, there was little chance that the ringing of the bell moments earlier hadn't attracted the attention of the authorities. If they turned up, he would surely be arrested again and if Cillian really did have people loyal to him inside the police force, he would be done for.

There was a brief break in the weather and the wind died down ever so slightly. The rustling of the tarpaulins surrounding the tower quietened. At that precise moment, Will heard the faint sound of footsteps across the wooden boards behind him. He turned his head to see Cillian Gander slowly walking towards him with his gun raised.

'You might not want to believe it, Mr Wells, but Abigayle really does work for me,' Cillian said. 'She lied to you and isn't worth you giving your life to save.'

Startled, Will pushed himself away from the tower wall and steadied himself before he said, 'Yeah? And so what if she does? That doesn't make her a bad person. She could've been working against you, for all you know.'

'Who knows, perhaps she was. Perhaps she was the woman you think her to be. Perhaps that's why she allowed herself to go astray. Perhaps she did that for you, Mr Wells.'

'What are you talking about?'

'You know, it seems to me that you're the cause of all this mess. Although I suppose I owe you some thanks for returning the Timepiece to its rightful owner.'

'Good luck with that. I'll throw it from this tower before I give it to you.'

'You do realise that this isn't the first time we've met, don't you, Mr Wells? I've seen the future. I've seen how this plays out.'

Cillian had continued to take careful steps towards Will as he spoke. The gun was still levelled at Will's chest. He was calm and self-assured as he walked, as if the movements of the boards below his feet, the billowing wind and the towering height were just trivial details.

'You're crazy! The first time I saw you, you were putting a bullet in the head of a defenceless man.'

'The first time you saw me, yes; but I saw you many years ago. I was much younger, I confess, but it was at the top of this very tower.'

'I've never even been here before! And no matter how young you were, I'd never forget your face.'

'Don't you see? This is the power of the Futures Project. Did Frenz teach you nothing?'

Will cautiously edged backwards a step and said, 'Frenz taught me plenty. I think it's you who needs to learn some lessons from Frenz. This isn't playing out the way you saw it.'

When Cillian was almost within touching distance, he made a rare miscalculation with his footing and staggered to the side. He used the arm with which he held the gun to steady himself against the tower wall. Will took this moment to dart around the corner, heading back towards the access window. He sprinted towards the window five or six metres away. As he raised a hand towards the window to pull himself inside, the window was turned into a cloud of smoke and dust. Cillian had found his feet quicker than Will had expected and fired more warning shots, blocking Will's way.

'What a shame,' Cillian said. 'That was your moment, Mr Wells. Unfortunately, you failed to make the most of it.'

'I swear, if you take another step forward, I'll throw the

Timepiece over the edge.'

'Nice try, but I know how this ends. I have seen the future. The details may have changed, but I've seen how this scenario plays out. I've seen how your mind works and the decisions a man like you makes in situations like this. I know how to read the future unlike any man alive. That's what the others could never understand or accept. That's the power of my Futures Project. Even if the details change, human nature doesn't. Once I have what is rightfully mine, it will reach its full potential and the world will be a better place for it.'

'You're wrong.'

'For many years I thought I could be, I confess. The first time I visited the future was purely accidental, but that's where we first confronted each other. Right here at the top of this tower. Although the situation was reversed. You wanted the Timepiece from me. But you were looking at me the same way you're looking at me now. You were hysterical, desperate for it, Frightened like a child. Back then I didn't know who you were or why you were there, and although decades had passed, I would never forget your face. Then about a week ago I saw my dear Abigayle having lunch with the boyfriend she talked about so much.' Cillian continued to walk slowly forwards, closing the distance between them. 'And to my surprise it was you. All these years later.'

Will allowed Cillian to talk. His ego seemed to be one of his only weaknesses.

While he spoke, Will moved his hands behind his back apparently without Cillian noticing.

'I confronted Abigayle about you. She didn't believe me, of course, but I had kept something from the first time we met: a picture of you. A picture of your lifeless corpse as it lay on the pavement just down there.' Cillian pointed down to the road below with his free hand. 'I showed it to her and the look of shock on her face told me she knew it was true.'

'You're crazier than Frenz made out, you know that?'

'That card you stole from my machine, I'm willing to bet that the date on that card is the same date as I travelled to all those years ago. And the same date I told Abigayle about.'

'So, you're a magician now, are you?'

Cillian chuckled, growing ever more confident and entirely pleased with himself. 'Why yes, I suppose I am in a way! The card that you're holding so protectively behind your back has the date 18th December 2016 written on it, does it not?'

Will smiled and shook his head before saying, 'Wow, that's pretty good.'

Cillian beamed. If it were possible, his head might have increased in size. He said, 'Impressed, I see? Now, please, this is your last chance to give me the Timepiece before I shoot you. I really would rather avoid creating too much of a mess.'

'Give me one reason why I would do something like that?'

'Because of the deal I'm offering you,' Cillian said coolly. 'Once I have the Timepiece, we'll go inside this tower and I'll send you into the future to find your beloved Abigayle. Then you'll see for yourself what I have seen and so many others doubted in me. My past and your future. You have my word.'

'She's all I care about. Let me be with her again, and this is yours,' Will said.

Will now moved his hands from behind his back, holding them in front of him. He then used his left hand to pull up his sleeve, revealing the Timepiece. Cillian's body seemed to visibly loosen as The Timepiece came into view, dropping both arms to his sides. Cillian's eyes lit up and a crazed look spread across his haunting features.

'I'm glad you see it that way, I really am. Now that you know Abigayle did what she did to save you, you have no need of that thing.' Cillian held out his free hand towards Will, staring wildly at the Timepiece.

'Before I do, you should know that there was one thing you were wrong about. The card I took from your machine – well, I dropped it climbing through the hatch so I never knew what date was written on it. Too late now, I guess.' Will took the Timepiece in his hand, feigning an attempt to remove it from his wrist. 'Now that you just told me.'

'What…' Cillian blinked frenetically, breaking himself from his momentary trance.

'Frenz was right about the future being uncertain,' Will said. 'And Avy was right about that Mimic Watch you always wear.'

Cillian whipped his head down to the Mimic Watch on his wrist, with its blinking amber light, and then snapped his head back up to Will. Too late, panic suddenly gripped him at the realisation of his grave miscalculation.

In one quick movement, Will bent his knees and propelled himself sideways towards the access window. With his hand on the Timepiece and 07:55 a.m. on the 18th December 2016 safely entered, he activated it the moment his feet left the unstable wooden boards of the scaffold tower.

Energy rippled through his body, more pronounced than before, and he savoured the distinctive bitter metallic taste in his mouth that he had experienced a week earlier with Abigayle. This was something that he now knew must be a characteristic only of future time travel. He didn't notice it as he sailed through the air, but an energised sphere emanated outward from the Timepiece. As it did, the old tower remained structurally the same but became gradually cleaner and brighter. The metal shell and tarpaulin covering it peeled away, like a gigantic gift being unwrapped, until it had disappeared completely.

CHAPTER THIRTY-NINE

December 18th, 2016, 07:55

Will rolled through the air and came tumbling to the ground, crashing into the metal barriers – thankfully on the inside of the belfry.

Outside the belfry, Cillian Gander was too late in his attempts to remove Nestor Ordell's malfunctioning Mimic Watch from his wrist. As the floor vanished beneath his feet, he fully appreciated – with terrifying clarity – the first law of the Timekeepers.

There had been no sound as Cillian fell from the belfry at the top of Elizabeth Tower. He had been surprised by the unexpected turn of events that had led to him falling to his death.

The reality was that his fortunes were drastically reversed from the future he'd seen and been so certain would come to pass.

As Will lay winded on the cold stone at the top of Elizabeth Tower, he heard a distant soft thump from many floors below.

Then there was silence.

He hauled himself to his feet, dusted himself off and looked out through the access window. Some sixty metres below, in the fledgling light, he could just about make out the twisted body of Cillian Gander splayed motionless on the roof tiles of the neighbouring Palace of Westminster. This was the second person whom he'd subjected to serious injury – or, in this case at least, death – in the past twenty-four hours.

The thought was disorientating and Frenz's warning never to use the Timepiece while at great height was ringing in his ears.

He stepped back from the window and lowered his head in a kind of involuntary gesture of respect for the dead man. He was troubled and conflicted by the growing feeling of relief he now felt as a result of Cillian's death.

Maybe Cillian was right. Maybe I am a monster after all.

Staring at his feet, only now noticing how stained and scuffed beyond repair his previously immaculate royal-blue Converse high-tops had got, another one of Frenz's warnings suddenly struck him. He had broken the most golden of golden rules: he had just travelled to the future. For the second time.

He looked up from his sorry-looking shoes and gazed out across the once familiar London skyline.

Looking south, the rooftops of Westminster Abbey were relatively unchanged, but when he hurried to his left and looked out towards the east, Will was left wide-eyed and open-mouthed. It was not yet daylight but even silhouetted against the faintest slither of the rising sun the difference was stark. Across the river Thames and Westminster Bridge, Will's attention was immediately caught by the sight of a giant white wheel that had been constructed on the riverbank. Even though there was no one there to hear it, he couldn't help but ask out loud, 'Is that a giant Ferris wheel?' Looking directly at it, he was at a loss for what else it could possibly be.

So, they turn London into a fairground in the future?

Looking further to his left and to the northeast, the skyline was entirely dominated by towering glass structures, most prominent of which was a colossal arrow-like building that seemed to be the tallest building in the city. To the east was a cluster of high-rise buildings, with one that looked as if it might be egg-shaped.

Aside from the new additions to the skyline, the other thing that had Will transfixed was how bright everything was, even with so little sunlight. He was used to amber streetlights, which in truth offered no visibility at all compared to the brilliant white lights he could now see illuminating the snaking roads below. In addition to the lights from the buildings and streetlamps, the giant wheel had a ring of blinking blue lights running around it. Each lamp along the riverbank was connected by an incredibly luminous string of light running between them. Below him, the trees in the gardens of Westminster Abbey – and almost every other tree he could see for that matter – were also spectacularly aglow. He was suddenly reminded that it was Christmas time in London and his heart was warmed to see that his favourite holiday was still celebrated in the future.

As enamoured as he was with the cacophony of new sights to see in twenty-first-century London, Will knew that this wasn't the reason he was here. He also kept recalling Frenz's warnings about how fragile and uncertain the future really was. Everything he was seeing now could be undone the moment he and Abigayle returned to the past.

Will stepped away from the window to begin his search for Abigayle when an aggressive and obnoxious voice rang out from behind him. A lump instantaneously forced its way into his throat, and he could feel his skin prickling and turning red.

They must have found Cillian's body.

'Oi, mate. What the hell do you think you're doin'?'

Will slowly turned to face the direction of the voice. To his immense relief, instead of a police officer or a man in a tweed jacket, he saw a man in beige overalls and a long-sleeved grey fleece jumper standing at the corner of the belfry. He was a short but muscular man with thick arms and a neck as wide as his head. His hair was trimmed short on the sides and became gradually longer on the top, where it was brushed to one side and slick with some kind of oily hair product.

Is this guy a time traveller too? What's with the '50s hairstyle?

Will did his best to play the innocent, lost American tourist. 'Oh, hey. Sorry. Um, am I too early for the tour?'

'The tour? Mate, what are you on about? There are no tours. The tower closed two weeks ago for renovations. If you want a tour, go on YouTube.'

'What's a U-tube? Isn't that a thing you find on a toilet?'

The man frowned, becoming impatient. 'Fuck me, mate, people stopped making jokes like that ten years ago and they weren't funny then.' The man paused and tilted his head to one side. 'Are you feeling all right, mate?'

'Yeah, great. I'm totally fine, why?'

The man moved his hands to his hips and prodded his wide chin forwards like a pigeon. 'Your head is bleeding.'

Will had momentarily forgotten about the bullet graze on his skull and he let out a snorted chuckle at the idea that he could've forgotten about something as serious as that. His thoughts had been so focused on escaping Cillian and getting to Abigayle that his mind had somehow dulled or at least diverted his attention from the pain. The wound was still tender, and he was reacquainted with the stinging pain, which shot through his head when he touched it. He felt the dried blood on the back of his neck gingerly with his fingertips and began to wipe it away with his sleeve.

'Oh yeah,' Will said. 'I guess I must've banged my head on one of these metal girders or something.'

'How did you even get up here?'

'I, um, I don't know. I got lost, I guess.'

'I seriously doubt that mate. I've a right mind to call the police.'

'No, no. No need for that. Can you just show me the exit and I'll be on my way? No harm done. Right, mate?'

The man rolled his eyes at Will's attempt at a British accent. 'This way, come on.'

Will was led back down the tower and out onto the street. No more words were shared as they descended, but Will could hear the man mumbling profanities under his breath the entire way. Apparently, Americans were no more well liked in 2016 than they were in 1984.

He was ushered out of Elizabeth Tower, attracting more

disapproving glances from the man's colleagues, and pushed out onto the street. Now out of the relative safety of the tower, he glanced around nervously, expecting to see distant blue lights flashing or policemen throwing up barricades across Westminster Bridge to contain the scene of a murder.

Was it really murder? Will pondered.

It wasn't like he pushed him off the scaffolding. And it was Cillian who had the gun. And it was Will who had been shot.

Self-defence at worst, he told himself, to help soothe the growing disquiet he felt.

Strolling slowly down the bustling and busy footpath, he scanned the faces around him, expecting his ejection from the tower to have attracted attention, or for the sight of a man falling from the belfry to have registered in some way. To his surprise, no one could appear less interested. People were walking to and fro across the bridge on their way to work, presumably so absorbed in their own lives that anything else was insignificant by comparison.

How could no one have noticed a man fall to his death at one of the world's most famous landmarks?

The answer soon became apparent as he watched the people walking past. Almost every person he saw appeared to be completely mesmerised by a bright white light that shone up from their hands, illuminating their faces. Like moths to a flame. Some had the device affixed to their hands and were silently obedient to it. Some were talking to the device as heartily as they would to another human being. He even saw one person who had a similar device attached to a large pole and they were grinning at it inanely. The common theme in all of this was that these people were completely oblivious to what was going on around them. For a brief moment, Will was sure all of these people were under some kind of technological mind control.

Will stopped a sweet-looking elderly woman, one of the few who seemed to be alert to the world around her, and said, 'Excuse me, ma'am, can I ask you something?'

'Oh, well, yes I suppose so,' the woman said, a little guarded.

'What's with the glowing lights in everyone's hands?'

'What? The phones? Always on their damned phones, these kids.'

'*These* are mobile phones? Wow!'

'Where are you from, young man?'

'You wouldn't believe me if I told you, lady. Thanks.'

Will walked on, feeling a little more at ease. And completely invisible.

He felt safe from being discovered, for now at least, and turned his attention to finding Abigayle. He might not have long before they did find Cillian's body and he wanted to be out of here before that happened.

She's here somewhere, she has to be.

He headed west away from the Westminster Bridge towards Abigayle's house in Holland Park. That was the last place he'd seen her and therefore the most logical place to start. He pressed his way through the crowds of people rushing this way and that. He bumped shoulders with one woman, who, much to his surprise, looked up from the device in her hand to throw a torrent of abuse at him.

Will was no more than ten metres from the base of Elizabeth Tower when his heart stopped in his chest.

CHAPTER FORTY

May 19th, 1984, 11:58

Detective Inspector Moss was sure he was getting closer to finally recapturing William Wells, but he also felt further than ever from understanding the facts of the case.

After arriving at the home of Madame Izri earlier that morning, Moss had encountered a chaotic scene. The owner of the house was nowhere to be found. It was suspected that Madame Izri had been kidnapped and further investigations were underway.

The front gates to the property were face down on the driveway. Black scorch marks were visible on the stone columns on either side. The working theory at this point was that a breaching charge had been used to disintegrate the substantial metal hinges. This detail alone didn't seem to fit with everything he knew about the prime suspect, William Wells.

Inside the house a man was found dead from multiple shrapnel wounds to his torso, as the result of another blast at the front doors to the house, and a close-range bullet to the head. It appeared that the killer had begun to clean up the scene, but the job hadn't been completed. The body had been moved and the blood had only been partially wiped away.

They were interrupted, Moss surmised.

If this murder was committed by the same person or persons involved with the thrift-shop shooting, then they were getting sloppy. Moss was positive that the two scenes were connected and had personally recovered three shell casings from the gravel driveway. Each one was of the same calibre as the one he'd recovered from the thrift-shop murder scene.

Despite the chaos, Moss did have one solid lead. Mapson had surprised him once more by discovering a concealed door leading to a basement-level dock. The dock had been empty, and a boat registered to Madame Izri had just been located several miles downriver, close to an equally suspicious house fire. The boat had been abandoned but contained two primary sets of fingerprints.

The boat wasn't the only place that fingerprints had been recovered, with multiple sets being found at the home of Madame Izri as well.

Back at the station house, Mapson had spent the past ten minutes on the phone with the fingerprint lab and had been furiously taking notes. Without saying goodbye, he dropped the receiver in its cradle and approached Moss excitedly.

Moss saw him coming. 'Okay, what have you got for me, Mapson?'

Mapson cleared his throat and flipped back to the front

of his black leather-bound notepad. 'Sir, there were positive matches on four of the seven clean sets of fingerprints found at the Izri scene. They're still working on the three unidentified sets – no hits so far – but one of them likely belongs to Madame Izri. Of the four sets that returned matches, one set belonged to the victim, identified as Felix Tuchel. Tuchel, we now know, had worked as personal security and driver to Madame Izri for the past eleven years. Another set belonged to the housekeeper, Ms Brockett. She was the person who alerted us to the disturbance at the house and also to the sighting of William Wells. She has been taken in for further questioning.'

'Good. What else?'

'The third set is the clincher. They also match those found at the thrift-shop murder scene, inside the abandoned boat, as well as at Abigayle Ward's apartment. They belong to William Wells,' Mapson said, thoroughly enjoying himself.

Although Wells hadn't been formally processed at the police station, Interpol had, thankfully, provided his fingerprints after the substantial political pressure generated by the case landing in the international news spotlight.

'And what about the fourth set, who do they belong to?' Moss asked.

Mapson hesitated a moment, then said, 'The final set of prints was recovered from both the Izri residence crime scene and the abandoned boat. And, well…'

'Spit it out, Mapson. What is it?'

'Well, sir, the lab said that you'd asked that all prints recovered be cross-referenced with everything connected to the case.'

'I did. And?'

'They found a match. This set was a ninety-nine-point-eight per cent match for prints found at the thrift-shop murder scene. They belong to someone who we have so far been unable to formally identify,' Mapson said.

'Who?'

'The elderly man. The victim of the shooting.'

CHAPTER FORTY-ONE

December 18th, 2016, 08:17

Though not a literal occurrence, Will always sensed that his heart skipped a beat whenever he saw her. Having faced the possibility that he may never see her again, the feeling was amplified a hundred-fold at that moment and his heart seemed to stop beating for a long second. Seeing her again was so overwhelming that he also forgot to breathe. When he regained his faculties, warmth rushed through his body on that chilly London morning and all seemed right with the world once again.

He'd never been the most observant man in the world, but he could spot her face in a crowd of thousands. And could hear her voice over all others. Even more so when she spoke his name, just as she was doing now.

Will had stopped dead in his tracks, not quite believing his eyes. Right there, rushing towards him through the crowds, shouting his name, was Abigayle. She looked panicked and he could hear the fear in her voice as she moved ever closer towards him. She was looking up to the top of Elizabeth Tower, wide-eyed. He could see the whites of her eyes and her clouded breath in the freezing air as she called his name.

She was now no more than two metres away from him and closing. Still she looked up at the tower, oblivious to his presence. Will was so overcome with joy that it didn't occur to him to call out to her, content to let her move ever closer. When she was in touching distance, he reached his arms out towards her tentatively, as if she might not be real and would pass right through him, as if he'd finally lost it and the whole thing was a hallucination.

When he felt her body beneath his hands as they rested on her shoulders, his eyes began to well up. Abigayle was startled and let out the same high-pitched yelp she'd made the first time they'd met – or, rather, the first time he'd met her as he now knew.

When she fixed her eyes on Will, it took her a moment to comprehend who she was looking at. When the realisation finally swept over her, tears streamed down her cheeks. Her lips were trembling as she attempted and failed to say Will's name once more. The two of them smiled at each other, then began to laugh with uncontrolled ecstasy.

In that moment she was somehow more beautiful than he'd remembered, and they embraced for what could have been an eternity. The river of people on the streets flowed around them like water rolling over a stubborn, immoveable rock.

Holding each other with their eyes shut tight, they could

have been anywhere, at any time. It didn't matter a jot to either of them.

Eventually Will whispered in her ear, 'I can't believe it. All this time I was looking for *you*, and it was you who found me.'

Abigayle broke their embrace slightly, pulling her head away from his shoulder so that she could look him in the eyes. She placed a cold hand on Will's cheek. She always had cold hands, but they were even more so now in the winter morning chill. She was still wearing clothes for a mild May day in 1984 and found herself unsuitably dressed for a winter's morning, no matter the year.

Will took his jacket off and threw it over her shoulders, holding her tight again. He could feel her shivering in his arms, though more from the adrenaline than the cold.

'Oh Will, you're alive! I was so worried about you.'

'Worried about *me*?! You're the one who up and vanished into thin air!'

'I'm so sorry. This is all my fault.'

'None of that matters now, okay?' Will said. 'All that matters is that we found each other.'

She smiled at him again as a tear rolled over her perfect red cheek. He'd never seen her so vulnerable.

'I know, I know,' Abigayle said. 'But I owe you an explanation.'

'Yeah well, that can wait. We need to get back to where we belong,' Will said, pulling up his sleeve and gently tapping the glowing, humming Timepiece strapped to his wrist.

'How…?'

'It's a long story,' Will said.

'I suppose it's a little late to ask if you know what that

thing really is?'

'You could say that, yeah.'

'If we're going to go back, we need to do it somewhere safe. I can't think of anywhere safer than back home, can you?'

'Yeah, makes sense. Let's go.'

'And we should hurry,' Abigayle said. 'There will be people who are looking for the Timepiece. I can't explain now, but as long as it's active, they'll be able to find us.'

'I know all about those guys. Don't worry, I don't think they'll be bothering us anymore.'

'Wait a sec, how long have I been gone? I've only been here for an hour or two.'

'It's hard to say. All the days have blurred together, but I think it's been five or six days since you disappeared.'

Abigayle stepped back, slipping her hands into Will's, and looked at his soiled, tattered and bloodstained clothes. 'Oh my god Will, are you okay? Is that your blood?'

Will followed her gaze. 'Erm, could be, I guess.'

'What the hell happened to you?'

'Let's talk about it later. Or earlier, I guess. When we get back.'

The two of them walked in contented silence, arm in arm, westward through St James's Park and past Buckingham Palace. The rising sun warmed their backs and steam rose as it melted the early morning frost from the leafless trees that flanked them as they strolled along Constitution Hill. They then angled slightly northwest through Hyde Park and Kensington Palace Gardens until they reached Holland Park.

After a quick bus journey they disembarked and turned onto Elsham Road. Will looked around the eerily familiar surroundings and felt compelled to break the silence by saying, 'Isn't it odd how so much of this future seems to have changed and yet so much looks just like it used to?'

Abigayle smiled at this. 'Yes, I know what you mean. I guess this isn't exactly what either of us thought the future would look like.'

'Yeah, I mean, where are all the flying cars? This is nothing like *Blade Runner*. The cars look like spaceships, I guess, but as far as I can tell, they're still driving on asphalt and have wheels wrapped in rubber tyres. And they're still running on gas. I thought they'd all be nuclear-powered by now for sure.'

'London was always a busy place, but it feels so much more crowded here now,' Abigayle added.

'You know, I was worried that when I finally got to the future, I'd stand out and people would see that I wasn't meant to be here. But it looks like '80s fashion is still in fashion and nobody has even looked in my direction. It's weird. I'm not sure I like this place so much.'

'Well, you're going to like it even less when you find out who the next US president is going to be.'

'It can't be any crazier than having a former B-movie actor in the White House.'

Abigayle rolled her lips together playfully and said, 'Can't it?'

The two of them stopped outside Abigayle's apartment building. To Will's astonishment, gone were the distinctive ebony bricks. Instead, the building had been painted an uninspiring pastel yellow. It still stood out from the sand-coloured brick of the neighbouring houses but seemed to have lost some of its charm.

Abigayle could see his disappointment. 'I know. You hate pastel colours. At least we can make sure *this* never happens.'

The two of them climbed the steps and approached the door, which was left ajar. Sensing Will's trepidation at the open door, Abigayle said, 'I couldn't find a key when I left the house earlier, so I left it open, just in case I needed to get back in.'

'Does anybody live here?'

'Yeah, I think so, but they haven't been collecting their post, there's a pile of letters behind the door. Whoever lives here, they've been gone for a few days. Probably away for Christmas.'

Will stopped at the top of the steps and said, 'People still use paper to send information? I was sure everything would be computerised by now.'

The two of them stepped in through the door and closed it behind them.

The living room was just as it had appeared when Abigayle had activated the Timepiece five days earlier. It had smooth white walls, solid oak floors and minimalist metal-and-glass furnishings. And now that he thought about it, no Christmas tree in sight. Will walked into the room and sat down on an uncomfortable white leather sofa. He looked up at Abigayle, who frowned slightly, and said, 'Before we go back, there's something I need to know.'

Abigayle stepped into the room and sat down on a matching white leather armless armchair opposite Will. She said, 'Okay, what is it?'

'Cillian Gander. How do you know him?'

Abigayle lowered her head and rested her elbows on her knees. Hands clasped together loosely, she fidgeted with a ring on her index finger, something Will knew she did when she was nervous. Then she nodded, looked him in the eyes and said, 'I work for him. Or used to, at least.'

The words hung in the air like a foul smell. Will sat back into the sofa, cupping his hands on his lap. It wasn't what he wanted to hear, but it didn't come as a complete surprise. Eventually he said, 'How could you, Abigayle? Didn't you know what kind of man he was?'

'Yes, I did, but I can explain.'

'You knew he was a murderer. You knew he was obsessed with this thing on my wrist and that he was willing to do anything it took to get it back. And yet you still worked for him?'

Abigayle shifted forwards on her chair, attempting to close the space that now existed between them. 'Will, you have to believe me, it was all part of the plan.'

'What plan?'

'My plan. And Frenz's. You met Frenz. He gave you the Timepiece, didn't he?'

'Yes, I know Frenz. How is it that you know him?'

'You know that I've always loved horology, because of Dad, right? One day he took me to Frenz's shop, and I fell in love with the place. Turns out Frenz and my father had been good friends for years, but he'd never really mentioned his name to the rest of the family. He said he was an incredibly private man. After that, the two of us grew close and I kept coming back again and again. I spent many afternoons in that place, especially after my dad died. And the shop was always empty, it was like he hardly ever had customers, so most of the time it was just the two of us. Talking and examining his collection of timepieces.'

Will interjected and asked, 'When was this?'

'This would have been six or seven years ago, before we'd met. Like I said, I spent a lot of time there over the years, but one day I went to the shop and it was closed. It was never closed. As I stood there wondering what to do, Frenz leaned out of a first-floor window and told me he would be down shortly. He took me to Norland Square Garden and showed me the broken lock on one of the gates.'

'*That's* how you found out about that?' Will said.

'Yes, although I'm not sure how he knew about it because he didn't live nearby.' Will averted his gaze and said nothing. Abigayle continued, 'Anyway, we walked through the garden and sat down on that bench under the big willow tree. He told me that he was putting his life in my hands with what he was about to say. He told me that he was a time traveller. He told me about the Timepiece and The Office of Time Dissemination.'

'The Time Travel Agency, you mean?' Will offered.

'He never liked that name,' she said, smiling. 'He told me about Cillian Gander and Avy Stammers and the disappearance of Nestor Ordell. He told me how he stole the Timepiece back in '67 and had escaped to 1940 with it. The whole story.'

'And you believed him?'

'Of course I didn't! I thought my good friend was losing his mind. I feel awful thinking about it now, but I was so freaked that I didn't go back to the shop for a while after that. Then one day I received a package through the door with a strange clock icon on the front. It was a book called the *Timekeeper's Guidebook*. It looked authentic enough and had all this detailed information about the Timepiece, exactly as Frenz had told me. There was also a photograph of Frenz with Avy and Nestor from the '60s. It was clearly him, but there was no way he'd have looked that young in the '60s given his age now. I was still sceptical, but I went back to the shop. After a long time, Frenz convinced me that it was real and one day he showed it to me, along with his ID card from the agency.'

Will shifted forwards in his seat, mirroring Abigayle by resting his elbows on his knees. He said, 'Okay, then what happened? How did you wind up working for Cillian Gander?'

'Frenz told me the outline of the plan, about the escape, but he wouldn't tell me the details. He said I'd be safer if I didn't know everything. Instead, he said he would leave instructions for me and that when the time came, an old friend he had in the police force would give me the access I needed to the jail.'

'I know how that part goes, believe me. Something tells me this friend would have given you a better welcome than the one I got,' Will said.

Abigayle continued. 'The biggest danger in the whole plan was using the Timepiece. He was sure that even though the agency had seemingly disbanded years earlier, that a man named Cillian Gander would never stop looking. Frenz told me about Ben, which tracks the Timepiece's location and destination whenever it's used.'

'Yeah, I've seen it, and it's not just a guy, you know, it's a huge machine!' Will added defensively.

'Right,' Abigayle said, a frown twitching on her brows momentarily. 'Well, anyway, the plan was to infiltrate Cillian's operation and shut it down so that they could no longer monitor the Timepiece. The problem was, we didn't have much information on Cillian, so I started doing some digging. With Frenz's help I managed to track him down. He apparently ran a consultancy company in the city – an obvious front – and had some openings for researchers. Frenz didn't like the idea, but I volunteered to apply for the job. Frenz coached me on all the things to say and what Cillian would be looking for in a candidate and it worked. I got the job as a historical researcher.'

Will shuffled to the end of his seat. His hands were almost touching Abigayle's. Slowly her story was causing all of Will's uncertainty about her to dissipate and he felt guilty for ever doubting her. 'And that's why you were at his house the day we met?'

Abigayle appeared momentarily caught off guard by this. 'Well, yes. I'd not even met the man personally, but I was often asked to stop by his house, mostly to retrieve documents that were stored on the upper floors, somewhere he apparently never went. Every time I was alone in his house, I would search for a key that I needed to get access to Ben. You interrupted me that one time. I know we both promised never to talk about it again, but you never did fully explain what you were doing in his house that day yourself, you know.'

'It's a long story for another day. Let's just say that the first time you met *me* wasn't necessarily the first time I met *you*.'

Abigayle sat upright, tilted her head to the side ever so slightly and with a furrowed brow began to say, 'I don't…but that doesn't make any…'

'Believe me, this whole thing makes my head hurt just as

much. I'm still trying to convince myself this isn't all some horrible dream, so let's move on, okay?'

Abigayle nodded yes, then continued. 'Once I got the job and we both knew what we had to do, Frenz and I decided to break all communications with each other until it was time to make our move. It wasn't safe to be seen together. For either of us. And they could never know where he was, that he was so close by. The plan was for me to send someone I trusted to him instead. Someone who knew nothing about him or the Timepiece. That person would pass him a coded message without even realising it, and that person would bring one back to me that only I would be able to understand. Depending on the message, it would either be that we should abort or that Ben had been disabled and we were ready to begin phase two.'

'And you sent me to do what, exactly?' Will said curtly.

'I never intended for him to give you the damn Timepiece if that's what you mean! That was never an option we discussed. You were meant to send an abort code to him. You'd mention that a friend had recommended the shop to you and that would be it.'

'So, what happened the day you sent me to him?' Will pressed.

Abigayle edged closer to Will once more. The feeling that he was pulling away from her caused her voice to shift slightly; there was an edge of desperation to it as she proceeded. 'The day before you went to see Frenz, I had met Cillian Gander for the very first time. I'd been working for him for almost two years and had never even seen him until that day. I was called back to his house, but this time someone was home, two men I'd never seen before. One tall, the other short.'

Will nodded knowingly. 'That'll be Tyke and Wigmore. We've crossed paths once or twice.'

'Whoever they are, they gave me the creeps. They took me into the basement, into this small room, and strapped me into a chair bolted to the floor. I was terrified.'

Will's jaw clenched and his hands bunched into fists at hearing this information.

Abigayle resumed her story. 'For a while there, I really thought they were going to kill me. They sat me down and left me there for hours. Eventually Cillian Gander walked into the room, seemed to size me up and then thanked me for my time and let me go. Even though he didn't really say anything to me, I knew that something was seriously wrong, so the following morning I told you about Frenz's shop so that you'd take the message to him that we needed to abort.'

'Okay, but what changed? Frenz gave me the Timepiece so somehow your message didn't get through,' Will said.

'Well, that's just it, it did get through. I called Frenz while you were in the store.'

'That was you on the phone?'

'Yes. He told me he had a customer, an American. I couldn't believe it. It was just pure luck that you were still there, I thought you'd have been and gone hours earlier. I told him your name and that he should be certain it was you.'

Will slapped his knee with an open palm, then said, 'So *that's* how he knew my name! But why call at all, I thought it was too dangerous?'

'I didn't have much choice; it was highly likely that the Timekeepers had been watching you and that they likely followed you to his shop. I told Frenz I was sorry and that he needed to get out of there and take the Timepiece with him before it was too late.'

'Well, I wish he'd listened because he sold it to *me* instead.'

'I didn't tell him to do that, you must believe me. I would've never put you in that kind of danger,' Abigayle said, taking Will's hand in hers.

'I guess he thought it was safer with you than it was with him,' Will offered.

'Maybe. Maybe he was just tired of running.'

'What made you think the Timekeepers were watching me?'

Abigayle dropped her hands from Will's, and she began to play with the ring on her index finger again. 'Cillian called me into his office at work just before I left for the day, around the time you were no doubt lost while looking for the shop I gave you *clear* directions to.' Will rubbed the back of his neck guiltily.

Abigayle rolled her eyes at this and said, 'When I sat down, he threw an envelope at me. It contained dozens of pictures of the two of us having lunch earlier that week. He then told me that he knew who you were, that he'd seen you before and that he thought you were working with Frenz and had helped him to steal the Timepiece. He said that years ago, at the beginning of his Futures Project, he'd gone into the future and that you were there. He said that the two of you fought and that he had killed you by throwing you from the top of Elizabeth Tower. He said that he hadn't seen you since that day. That is, until he saw me having lunch with you. I didn't believe him, but he showed me… a picture. A Polaroid of you and…' She reached into her pocket and retrieved the small square photograph. It was soiled and faded, but the image was unmistakable. She handed it to Will, who studied it uneasily. 'It was just like he said. You were dead. Then he showed me a newspaper clipping from 18th December 2016. The day he said that he'd killed you.'

'So that's what Cillian was rambling on about in the tower? The guy was talking on and on about knowing the future, that he knew how everything was going to play out. But I guess he was wrong. So, he tells you all this and then he lets you go, just like that?'

Abigayle shifted uncomfortably in her seat. 'Yes, he just thanked me for my cooperation and let me go.' She shook her head as she studied her restless hands.

'And that's when you called Frenz,' Will said, piecing her story together.

She looked up, brightening slightly. 'Yes, and then I came straight home. You have no idea how relieved I was to see you. I had no idea that you had the Timepiece with you until you showed it to me.'

'But why did you use it? You must have known how dangerous it was to travel to the future.'

Abigayle nodded slowly and offered a sad sort of smile. 'I didn't think I had time to do anything else. I was sure the Timekeepers were going to kick the door down at any minute. I knew the plan was always to go to the past to free Frenz, but I couldn't face the idea of doing that and losing you. And there was something about that picture that Cillian showed me.' She looked into Will's eyes as moisture pooled around the edges of her own.

'What?'

'You looked the same. Exactly the same as you do right now. The same age, same haircut, even the same shoes and jacket, which meant that your death could have happened at any moment. The moment I saw the Timepiece in your hands, and I thought of that photo, I did the only thing I thought that would save you. Frenz always told me that it's almost impossible to change the past, but that the future was uncertain and *always* changing, so I figured that I'd have a go at changing it myself. I went to the future to try to save you. But I see now that it was just stupid.'

'It wasn't stupid, Abby,' Will said, taking her hand this time.

'Of course it was! I didn't save *you*. All I did was put myself in a position where I was the one who needed saving.'

'Doing what you did stopped me from becoming a smudge on the sidewalk—'

'Pavement,' Abigayle added with a smirk.

'Whatever. And, okay, activating a time machine to save your boyfriend from the future might not be the smartest thing you've ever done, but it sure is the bravest.'

'Thank you, Will,' Abigayle said, her cheeks flushing crimson. 'After I activated it, it began to overheat. At first, I thought it might be normal, but it got so hot so quickly that I had to loosen my grip on it slightly. Then that damned thing on the table – which I'm now pretty certain is a phone – lit up and made that awful rattling sound and the Timepiece just slipped from my hand. I watched it as it fell and the moment it hit the floor it just disappeared. And you disappeared along with it.'

'It came as a bit of a shock to me as well, if I'm being totally honest,' Will said. 'I didn't even know what the Timepiece was. Turns out I'm pretty good with puzzles, though. So, I rescued Frenz myself. Then we visited Avy

Stammers, who repaired the Timepiece to stop it from overheating. The rest I'll get into later. The big problem was that after the Timepiece hit the floor, whatever date you entered got wiped, so I had no idea *when* you'd gone to. But Frenz, he helped me find you.'

'I'm impressed, Mr. Wells Maybe Frenz giving you the Timepiece was more calculated than I first thought,' Abigayle said, grinning at him. 'Where is Frenz now, anyway? Was he with you?'

Will cupped both of her hands in his, looked her in the eye once more and said, 'Abby, I don't know how to tell you this. I'm so sorry, but the Frenz you knew is dead. They shot him. I saw them do it.'

It was as if Will had just dosed her with a sedative. Abigayle's eyes snapped shut, and she wavered in her seat, collapsing back into it. When she opened her eyes again, they pleaded with Will to say it wasn't true. She held back the tears and spoke in a low, pained voice. 'Oh Will, no. It's all my fault.'

Abigayle rested her head on Will's shoulder, and he placed a hand on the back of her head. 'You didn't kill him, Abby. It was them. And Frenz knew the risks and he did it anyway. There's no way on earth that he would've blamed you for any of this. Okay?'

Abigayle looked up at Will with renewed strength, nodding vigorously. 'Thank you, Will. At least you freed Frenz like we planned. At least the younger Frenz is safe.'

Will leaned backwards slightly, placed his hand on the Timepiece and said, 'Well, I didn't exactly complete all of the plan. I freed him, sure. But he still needs my help.'

Will and Abigayle stood up from their seats. Will reached

into his pocket and placed Agent Tyke's Mimic Watch on her wrist, then said, 'You ready?'

Abigayle nodded, smiling nervously. 'Ready.'

CHAPTER FORTY-TWO

May 19th, 1984, 13:13

In a flash of light, warmth and pulsating energy, the room around them transformed from the sterile futurist one back to the home they knew and loved. Though it was now in an extreme state of disarray, with strips of police tape strewn on the floor. Five days since she had first gone astray, Abigayle had been returned to her rightful place in time.

Will let out a huge sigh of relief and closed his eyes for a long moment. When he opened them, he said, 'Abby, I need to go.'

She nodded reluctantly. 'Okay, but you're taking me with you. If Frenz needs help, I'm not standing by and doing nothing.'

Will knew that it was wasted energy trying to change her mind once it was made up. She was like Frenz in that way. He simply nodded yes and took her hand in his. Touching her again still felt unreal after everything that had happened and it sent electricity coursing over his skin.

As the two of them turned to leave, there was a loud rasping knock at the door, causing them to tighten their grip with fright. They looked at each other and Will whispered, 'Dammit. That's probably the police. I forgot to mention that I'm the major suspect in Frenz's murder. And yours.'

'What?!' Abigayle said in hushed astonishment, only now noticing how much her apartment resembled a crime scene.

'You should probably stay out of sight. Here, take the Timepiece. If they arrest me, you'll need you to go to Westminster and find Frenz.'

'What?! Will, this is crazy!'

'Welcome to my life for the past five days.'

Will walked tentatively towards the front door. He grasped the handle, closed his eyes and inhaled deeply. Exhaling, he opened them and turned the handle, pulling the door inwards.

To his surprise, instead of being greeted by a group of London's finest, he instead found Kevin standing in front of him. He had an unbearably smug look on his face and a brick-sized mobile telephone pressed against his ear. Will looked at the phone and smirked at the absurd size of it compared to what he'd seen in the future.

Will was about to speak when Kevin cut him off, saying, 'I thought I heard something, *William. Gordon. Wells.*' Kevin spoke his name as if it made him physically revolted to do so. He then said, 'The police may have given up searching your apartment, but not me. They're on the line listening in, by the way. Do you think I'm really that stupid that I wouldn't hear when you came crawling back?'

Will attempted to explain. 'Kevin, you don't understand—'

'Oh, I understand perfectly well. You won't get away with what you did to my Abigayle. You were never good enough for her. The two of us would have been together if it wasn't…'

While Kevin was speaking, Abigayle had moved up to the door to stand at Will's side. She pulled the door open further to reveal herself to the dumbfounded Kevin.

The look on his face was the perfect combination of confusion and total and utter embarrassment. It contrasted with the uncharacteristic look of rage on Abigayle's face.

Just as Kevin was about to speak, Abigayle stepped past Will and planted a firm, close-fisted punch square on the end of Kevin's nose. He stumbled backwards and landed in a heap at the bottom of the stairs.

Abigayle turned to Will, smiled a small, satisfied smile and said, 'You have no idea how long I've wanted to do that! Now let's go.'

Abigayle handed Will the Timepiece and the two of them hurried through the front door, stepping over the stricken Kevin. Abigayle flagged down a taxi and they quickly traversed the now-familiar route between Holland Park and Westminster.

Elizabeth Tower soon came into view in the distance, standing high above the nearby trees and rooftops that surrounded it. As they neared Westminster Abbey, Will could make out the faint flashing of blue lights dancing rhythmically across the building frontages. A sick feeling began to well up in his stomach.

We're too late.

They approached more cautiously now. Will was wary that he was still very much a wanted man.

Once they reached Westminster Bridge, they could see that a large crowd had gathered at the base of the tower. They both slipped into the throng of onlookers and slowly worked their way through.

They eventually made their way to the front of the crowd just as firefighters and medical services could be seen carrying a stretcher from the base of Elizabeth Tower.

No, they've found the agency's Central Station.

Will clambered further forwards for a closer look before the police encircled the spectators, urging them backwards. The body on the stretcher, which was covered by a thick white sheet, could only be one of the three people who were left behind in the underground chamber. As the stretcher was lifted into the back of a waiting ambulance, Will's spirits were dashed. The proportions didn't match that of the tall, lanky Agent Tyke nor the short rotund Agent Wigmore. It could only be that of his dear friend, Frenz Belingi.

Were it not for the press of the people who surrounded him, he would've collapsed to the ground as he felt his legs go weak beneath him. As it was, he was held upright, almost floating in a sea of bodies. Abigayle managed to catch up with him and took his hand. She pulled him clear of the crowds and said, 'Will, what is it?'

'The body on that stretcher. It's got to be him. It's got to be Frenz. I'm too late.'

'That's impossible, Will. I still remember Frenz. I remember him as an old man, so he can't be dead.'

As he was coming out of his daze of despair, he felt a firm hand land on his shoulder from behind. The hand was strong and pulled him backwards, spinning him around. To his surprise and relief, Will found himself standing face to face with Frenz Belingi once more.

Frenz had a neutral, unreadable look on his face. He said, 'Abigayle, did you find her?'

Will nodded yes, stepped aside and said, 'Frenz Belingi, please meet Abigayle Ward.'

Frenz looked over Will's shoulder at Abigayle's smiling face. Tears were rolling down her cheeks and she said, 'Hello. It's a pleasure to meet you.'

'It's a pleasure to finally meet you too,' Frenz said, smiling a thin toothless smile, which gradually became a broad toothy grin and finally Frenz chuckled heartily at his friend. 'William Wells,' Frenz said, 'my friend. It's over. It's okay to smile now.'

'I thought you were dead. They just carried a body out from the tower. I was sure they'd discovered Central Station.'

Frenz grinned back and said, 'Do you really think I would allow that to happen?'

'But you were shot. I left you down there with that brute Wigmore.'

'That overweight fool? I struggled with him for a moment, yes. He almost got the better of me, I'll admit, but then I saw his Mimic Watch flashing with an amber light. So, I used one of the moves I learned from you and activated it for him.'

'Whoa, what happened?'

'Well, let's just say that in some version of the future that we may never see, there is a desk down in that chamber with a fat man's head sitting on top of it.' Frenz flinched. 'If you don't mind, I'd really rather not think about that incident ever again.'

Will agreed. 'Jeez, I felt bad about the severed hand!'

'Severed heads and hands,' Abigayle said. 'What the hell have you guys been up to? This is what happens when there's not a woman around to keep you guys in check.'

'You really don't want to know. Here,' Frenz said, handing Wigmore's Mimic Watch to Will. 'He has no further use for this, but something tells me that you may well do.'

'What's that supposed to…wait a sec,' Will said, 'if that wasn't you or either of the other two, who did they just put in the back of the ambulance?'

'It's Cillian. They found him on the roof. He was in a particularly horrid state. Remind me never to get on your bad side.'

Will looked up to the sky for a moment, then said, 'Well, when the police finally catch up to me, at least they can put me away for a murder I'm actually responsible for.'

'Oh, I wouldn't worry about the police,' Frenz said.

'And why's that?'

'Well, after I patched myself up, I headed up the tower – not easy when you've been shot in the leg – and about halfway up I saw a body from one of the windows. At first, I wasn't sure if it was you or Cillian, so I made my way out onto the roof. When I saw it was Cillian, I took the liberty of placing Agent Wigmore's gun on his person.'

'The gun he used to' – Will paused briefly – 'the one he used to shoot you.'

Frenz nodded. 'It's okay, William. I knew that the man you saw them kill was a future version of me. And I could see you struggling with it and how to tell me.'

'I'm sorry, Frenz, I should have told you from the very

start. But I wasn't sure how you'd react.'

'I'm at peace with it. But what I cannot accept is the wrong man going to jail over my own death. So, when I found Cillian's body, I also might have left some of my blood on his clothes. I hear that the police have recently made a breakthrough in the field of DNA testing.'

'Frenz, thank you. For everything.'

'It's been a pleasure, William Wells. It's not every day that you get to solve your own murder.'

Will and Abigayle placed their hands under Frenz's arms and helped him limp away from the crowd. Will glanced down to see Frenz's bloodied leg with his belt tightly bound above his knee as a makeshift tourniquet. 'How's the leg?'

'It hurts like all hell, but I'll survive.'

'Yes, but you'll have a limp for the rest of your life,' Abigayle said. 'I've seen it.'

'She's right. Come on, we need to get you to a doctor,' Will said.

'No, too many questions that I cannot answer. Just get me to the police station, then you can send me back to where I need to be.'

Will stopped walking, turned to Frenz and said, 'Send you back?'

Frenz nodded. 'Back to 1940, where you found me. That was always the plan. My cell was destroyed, remember? They will think I'm dead, and I've already got my new identity lined up. Then I can get this leg looked at. They'll just put it down to an injury from the bombings.'

'Frenz, are you sure about this? If you go back…'

'There's no changing that now. If my death in this time means the Timepiece is safe from the likes of Cillian Gander, it'll have been worth it.'

The walk was slow, but the three of them eventually found themselves standing outside the tall red-brick walls of the police station where Will had been held five days earlier. They skirted down the side of the building, along a narrow, quiet road to the rear of the station. Frenz leaned against the wall and said, 'Okay, Will, this area should be safe. I've reviewed the history, we won't be seen.'

'Are you sure about this?'

'Yes, quite sure. It has been a pleasure, my friend.'

'I'm never going to forget you, Frenz. You know that, right?'

'I don't imagine that I could forget about you, but I'll do my very best,' Frenz said with a mischievous smile.

'Abby, you should stay here. Keep a lookout and keep this area clear for my return. This exact spot, okay?'

Abigayle nodded at Will, then looked at the young Frenz Belingi. She paused a beat, then strode towards him and wrapped her arms around his shoulders. Through the tears she said, 'I know you don't know me yet. But you will. Thank you for everything, Frenz.'

She stepped away from him, wiped her cheeks and nodded at Will to begin. Will looked at Abigayle and said, 'I'll be right back.' He smiled at her and began entering the date, 7th September 1940. As he did so, Frenz said, 'The bombing should have finished by 2 a.m., so that time would be best.' Will nodded, made the adjustments, took his friend by the hand one last time and activated the Timepiece.

September 7th, 1940, 02:00

Instantly the tall police station wall disappeared, replaced with a partially collapsed one. Behind them was a wood-panelled fence, damp and rotten at the bottom and grey from weathering. It was night time, but the sound was deafening. Further southwards, rescue efforts were underway in the aftermath of the bombing. Fortunately, the street where they stood was completely deserted. It was lit only by the faint moonlight angling down from above. Not a single light could be seen in the streets nor from inside the surrounding buildings.

'You sure you're going to be okay?' Will said.

'I'll be fine. I always had such fondness for the past. And I'm sure I have something to offer to the war effort.'

'What should I do with this?' Will gestured to the Timepiece, pulsing on his wrist.

Frenz shrugged and said, 'You are the Timekeeper now, William. It's up to you. You and Abigayle will do right by it, but the agency always had three Section Heads for a reason, so if you find a third person you can trust as much as you trust each other, maybe you can form a new agency. Better than the one before.'

'How am I going to find someone I can trust with all this? Who's even going to believe it?'

Frenz smiled. 'You might find someone sooner than you think. See you in about forty years. Take care of yourself, and Abigayle. Goodbye, William Wells.'

Frenz offered his hand to Will, who, instead of shaking it, took a step towards him and threw his arms around his friend. The move caught Frenz by surprise and he tentatively returned the gesture. Will parted from their embrace, took one last look at his friend Frenz Belingi and deactivated the Timepiece.

CHAPTER FORTY-THREE

May 19th, 1984, 21:47

What had started as a straightforward robbery-murder case quickly spiralled into something far more complex, with arson, kidnapping, a jailbreak, an international manhunt and multiple homicides. Despite all this, the case now appeared to be coming to a close.

Hours earlier a body had been pulled from the roof of the Palace of Westminster. It had been identified as the owner of the house that had recently been the subject of an arson attack. Two pistols had been recovered close by. Both weapons had been fired recently and matched the unusual calibre of the shell casings that Detective Inspector Moss had been finding all over London. He fully expected the ballistics to come back confirming that one or both of these guns were the murder weapons used in the recent spate of shootings.

He was reluctant to admit it, but it seemed as though

William Wells wasn't their man after all. Even so, Moss still wanted to find him. And there was still the small matter of two missing women: Madame Izri and William Wells's fiancée, Abigayle Ward.

Added to that were the baffling movements of Wells himself and a string of other strange happenings around the case. Moss had wracked his brain for explanations to how Wells could have existed in two places at the same time and had come to one possibility, no matter how improbable it might sound. This was not a conclusion that he could share with his superiors, however. They seemed content to have caught the killer and were eager to chalk it up as a win and take the plaudits from the public and the press.

Moss was a keenly meticulous man, so, as he did most nights when he was working a case, he headed back to the station to go over the case files for the hundredth time. The front of the station was crowded with a gaggle of journalists and photographers keen for a scoop on the story, something he'd rather avoid getting in the middle of. That was for his bosses to deal with, they'd be in their element out there. Instead, he parked his car and took the scenic route around the side of the station on foot, heading towards the rear entrance, where he could enter unmolested.

As he turned the corner, he could see the figure of a woman leaning against the station wall, alone in the darkness. He approached cautiously, not wanting to alarm her. He'd made it a dozen or so steps along the road when she saw him. She pushed herself away from the wall and looked in his direction, but held her ground. For a moment he considered turning back and finding another way around, worried that she might be a reporter, but there was something about her that he recognised. He continued to walk ever closer, stopping three or four metres away. Even in the dimly lit street he could see who it was. To his surprise, he found himself staring at none other than missing woman number one, Abigayle Ward.

He continued to move closer to categorically confirm that it was her, but he stopped when she said, 'Okay, that's close enough. Not another step.'

Moss attempted to calm her down by saying, 'It's okay, miss, I'm a police officer.'

'A police officer, you expect me to believe that? What are you really doing here?'

'I'm telling the truth, miss. Now, if I'm not mistaken, you're Abigayle Ward, is that right?'

She frowned slightly, then said, 'So what if I am, what's it to you?'

'Well, miss,' Moss said, 'I really am a police officer, and my colleagues and I have been looking for you. And your fiancé, Mr Wells. He's in an awful lot of trouble, miss.'

'Well, whatever it is…' Abigayle's words were cut off as William Wells abruptly reappeared between her and the dumbfounded Detective Inspector Moss.

Will glanced towards Abigayle and smiled affectionately. Abigayle, with a look of shock on her face, pointed at something behind him. Will turned and saw Moss standing there, eyes wide with disbelief.

Will held up his hands and said, 'Okay, officer, I can explain. This isn't what you think.'

'You really think he's a police officer? Don't you know who that is?' Abigayle said, her voice wavering.

'Well, yeah,' Will said, 'this is the cop who's been chasing me this whole time.'

'No, it's not,' Abigayle said.

'If he's not a cop, then who is he?'

Abigayle took a step towards Will, linking her arm through his. With her free hand she pointed towards Moss, who had remained uncharacteristically silent, too stunned to talk, and she said, 'I've seen him before, in a photograph, standing with Frenz and Avy. That man right there is Nestor Ordell.'

-THE END-

ACKNOWLEDGMENTS

This book simply wouldn't have been possible without all the encouragement, hard work and patience from friends, family and a not insubstantial number of total strangers.

First and foremost, I'd like to thank my wife Rhiannon for reading every draft of this book and for her thorough and invaluable notes on each one. That very first draft was an unrefined mess that I wouldn't wish upon anyone and I feel like there ought to be an 'Apologies' section to atone for that!

A big thank you is also due to Ollie Trimble-Rodriguez for all the honest feedback, advice, breakfasts and help with the book launch. It's tough enough to self-publish a book as it is, and I can't imagine how much tougher it would have been without him.

The book you are about to read would have been a very different beast (and with more unintentionally humorous typos) were it not for the great work done by my fabulous editor Heather Sangster and I really can't thank her enough.

I know it's already dedicated to them, but I absolutely must thank my boys Emmett and Elliott for being the book's biggest fans (even if some scenes needed to be edited on the fly for their young ears). If they end up being the only two to enjoy it, I'm just fine with that.

I also want to thank my brother Jack for letting me take up near-permanent residence at The Dabbling Duck cafe in Shere where he is head chef. A huge chunk of this book was written at that round table in the corner where the only distraction was the irresistible food he'd serve up.

Of course, I would also like to thank all other family and friends who have played a part in making this book what it is, but I'd really rather keep this to a single page! Besides, they all know who they are.

Last and by no means least, I'd like to say a final, massive thank you to all of my Kickstarter backers, reserving extra special thanks to both Stephen Robertshaw and Karlita Gesler for their unbelievable support.

KICKSTARTER BACKERS

Alex Crouzen
Alice Ryland
Amy Simmonds
Andy Davenport
Benn Simmonds
Bet Davies
Brian Welsko
Brian A Morton
Bryan, Joy, Alamea,
Kai, & Millie Hill
CJ Kenny
Calista Wielgos
Callista Welsh-Marshall
Ceredig Davies
Chrissey Harrison
Cory Padilla
Dan McDonald
Daniel "The Bear" Ashwell
Dave Holets
Darren Pankhurst
Donna Pankhurst
Deborah Tucker
Dom Garner
Dre Lotthammer
Edward Beale
Elia F.
Emma Nash
Eron Wyngarde
Francesco Tehrani
Geneviève Hannes
Greg Levick
Greg Smith
Keith 'Hurley' Frampton
Jack Simmonds

Jane Exton
Jenna H
Kai Enna Aedan Holmes
Karlita Gesler
Kerstin Bodenstedt
Lenne Wheeler
Livey Mumpower
Martin Lingonblad
Matthew Bennett
Micha Schlieper
Michael Burnham
Michael J Howe
Nathan Law
Dr. Nicholas R. Watkins
Owen Davies
Patrick Veale
Peter Martinez
Peter McQuillan
Rachael Treagus
Rajiv Kumar
Robert Kickbush
Roger Sinasohn
Rosalie Lo
Sherry Mock
Simon Reveley
Solomon St. John
Stephen Robertshaw
Steve Prior
SwordFirey
Vicki Hsu
William McGill
William Stocks
Wilma Jandoc Win
Zach Sallese
Zachary Williams

ABOUT THE AUTHOR

O.R. Simmonds is a Writer, Director and Artist working in the Games Industry and author of *The Timepiece and the Girl Who Went Astray*.

Before working in the games industry, he spent nearly a decade dreaming up deep, detailed worlds with weaving narratives only for them to be 'value engineered' by clients. It was during this time that he decided he no longer wanted to be a frustrated writer and to try to be an actual writer instead.

He ran a successful Kickstarter campaign to help fund the publication of this very book. His second book, *Very Much Mistaken Perry*, is currently being edited and slated for release sometime in 2022.

Ollie lives in Surrey, UK with his wife and two young boys. His eldest son is named after *Back to the Future*'s Doc Emmett Brown and his youngest's middle name is Adventure (yes, really). It's not all that surprising that his debut novel is a time travel adventure then.

www.orsimmonds.com

Made in the USA
Coppell, TX
28 January 2022